STARGATE
ATLĄNTIS ™

SECRETS

Book five of the LEGACY series

JO GRAHAM & MELISSA SCOTT

FANDEMONIUM BOOKS

An original publication of Fandemonium Ltd, produced under license from MGM Consumer Products.

Fandemonium Books
United Kingdom
Visit our website: www.stargatenovels.com

STARGATE
ATLANTIS™

MGM

Print ISBN: 978-1-905586-59-2   Ebook ISBN: 978-1-80070-004-8

For our nieces and nephews

Eric and Thomas Keller
Elizabeth Scott

and

Sara and Glenn Thompson

Her lips were red, her looks were free,
Her locks were yellow as gold:
Her skin was as white as leprosy,
The Nightmare Life-in-Death was she,
Who thicks man's blood with cold...
The sun's rim dips; the stars rush out:
At one stride comes the dark.
— *Samuel Coleridge*

CHAPTER ONE

Lifepod

RONON struggled to consciousness, aware at first only of the overwhelming need to run. He caught his breath with a gasp, fought to keep from flailing in the darkness. His limbs were free — that was good, meant he wasn't trussed for feeding, wasn't pinned waiting for some Wraith to insert another tracker. He shifted cautiously, feeling a body against his own. Two bodies, one with a spill of long hair — Jennifer, he thought, with renewed fear, and McKay. Faint lights were coming on, as though his movements had triggered them, glowing pinpoints that outlined Wraith controls, and in the dim light he recoiled from the Wraith who lay tangled beneath them. Not a Wraith, not really — it had McKay's face, McKay's sharp nose and thinning hair, but Ronon's skin still crawled at its touch. He pressed himself back against the walls of the lifepod, trying to get himself under control.

OK, yes, they were in a lifepod, a Wraith lifepod, because they'd been cut off from the others and there was no other way off the hiveship: the plan had been to steal aboard Death's hive, rescue McKay, or kidnap him, depending on whether or not he was cooperative, but Jennifer had collapsed before they could rejoin Sheppard's group or contact the Hammond.

He shifted awkwardly, trying to fit himself into space designed for a single Wraith, worked himself free of McKay until he could reach Jennifer and drag her into a less crumpled position. The convulsions had stopped — if he didn't know better, he'd think she was asleep. But then nobody slept through something like this. He touched her cheek, brushing loosened strands of hair back from eyes and mouth, but she didn't stir. He could feel her breath on his hand, felt for a neck pulse anyway. Her skin was cool, her heartbeat steady. Whatever had happened, she wasn't in any immediate danger, or at least not from whatever had caused her to collapse.

The situation, however, was another matter. He settled her as safely as he could into the protective niche, wormed his way around McKay's unconscious body to study the controls. Unfortunately, nothing looked familiar. A few lines of data trickled down the small central screen. To the left of that, he saw a button with a symbol he did recognize: tracker. He swallowed old, irrational fear, his back twitching where the scars no longer were, and kept his hands well away from the console. The button wasn't lit, so presumably it wasn't working: they were safe from that, at least. He took a deep breath and scanned the symbols again. All right, that one — the glowing blue shape like a child's image of lightning — that one, he was pretty sure was visuals, and he pressed it before he could change his mind. The falling data stopped abruptly, was replaced by an image of a starscape. It was rotating slowly around a point that seemed to be a hive-ship, drifting disabled. Or not disabled: a hyperspace window opened, and the ship vanished through it.

Ronon blinked. Not exactly a good thing, unless the *Hammond* was still lurking somewhere nearby, and he didn't really see any signs of that. There was a schematic in the corner of the screen and, if he was reading it right, there was a planet nearby, along with an awful lot of debris…

McKay chose that moment to stir, and Ronon jumped, reaching for his gun. He had it out and the barrel against McKay's skull before McKay opened his eyes and bared sharp Wraith teeth at him.

"Get that away from me," he said. "What the hell did you do to me?"

His voice was so much the old McKay that Ronon blinked, though he didn't lower the gun. "Stunned you," he said. "And drugged you."

"What? Why would you do that?" McKay's glare deepened.

"And wasn't that redundant?"

"Because the last time we tried to rescue you, you tried to kill us," Ronon said.

"I sent you a message," McKay snapped. "I've been waiting for ages — and why is Jennifer here?" His face sharpened. "And what's wrong with her?"

"She's out cold," Ronon said. "I don't know why. And she's here to get you back in one piece."

"By drugging me?"

"The IOA wanted to shoot you."

"Oh, that's very helpful," McKay said. "Where are we?"

"In a lifepod."

"What?"

"We blew up the hive," Ronon said. "That was part of the plan. Only we couldn't get back to the jumper because Jennifer passed out. So I put us all in a lifepod."

"You blew up the hive," McKay said. "What about the ZPM?"

"The one you stole?" Ronon glared. "When you led a bunch of Wraith into Atlantis?"

McKay had the grace to look abashed, but rallied quickly. "And you couldn't get it back? We need that!"

"I don't know," Ronon said. "That was Sheppard's job. I was supposed to be capturing you."

"They couldn't have destroyed it," McKay said. "I mean, how hard could it be to unhook it?"

He sounded less certain than his words, and Ronon shook his head. "McKay." McKay turned on him with a Wraith's speed, and it took all his willpower not to press the firing stud. "Do you know how to work this thing?"

"Of course," McKay said. He wriggled around until he was facing the controls, peered thoughtfully at them for a long moment, then touched a button. The viewer disappeared, and was replaced by another cascade of data. McKay reached under the screen and folded out a small keyboard, typed something.

"Well, that's not good," he said.

"What?"

"We've got about seventeen hours of air left, with three of us on board. And I'm not picking up any ships in the area, Wraith or human."

That wasn't good, Ronon thought. "What about the planet?"

"That's not good either," McKay said. "In fact... Oh, no. No, no, that's definitely not good." He typed frantically for a moment, but got only a few pained beeps from the console. "We're caught in the planet's gravity well, and we don't have enough power to break free."

"These things are designed for reentry, aren't they?" Ronon asked. "They must be."

"Yes, of course they are." McKay punched more keys. "And it looks as though the planet — yes, it's perfectly habitable and it has a Stargate. No signs of people, though, no settlements, no wreckage. It was either abandoned or Culled a long time ago."

The hairs on Ronon's neck stood up, hearing this Wraith who was McKay talk so casually about Cullings.

"I should be able to get the guidance computer on line," McKay said. His hands were busy as he talked, bringing new systems into play, eliciting soft noises from the console. "Yes, there. And track for the Stargate. We've got inertial dampeners, and thrusters, we should be able to make reentry."

"Couldn't we just signal the *Hammond*?" Ronon asked.

"We have seventeen hours of air," McKay said. "And it won't be very nice air toward the end. No, we need to get this thing down onto the planet, and then we can worry about signaling the *Hammond*. In fact, if we land it right, we could dial Atlantis and go home."

Which presented another problem, Ronon thought. Could he trust McKay? Yeah, it sounded like him, he sounded normal, as far as that went, but he was still clearly Wraith. Could they risk going straight to Atlantis? He shook his head. First things first. He couldn't land the lifepod himself, but McKay seemed to think he could. Let McKay get them down safe, where he could take a good look at Jennifer, and then they could worry about getting to Atlantis.

"I wish Sheppard was here," he said.

Rodney studied the tracking display, touched keys to study the course the autopilot had laid for them. It was a good thing there was an autopilot, because he wasn't exactly checked out in Wraith lifepods, or any other kind of Wraith craft, and while he could handle a puddle jumper, flying still wasn't one of his major talents. The system was homing in on the planet's Stargate, which was good, but the engines seemed to be having trouble following the autopilot's instructions. Already there were datapoints blinking white amid the gold, warning him that they'd missed course corrections. Probably because the lifepod was overloaded; it was designed to carry a single Wraith, not three humans. He frowned at the screen, toggled to the power supply and back to the navigation screen, trying to decide whether or not to intervene.

Something cold and hard jabbed the base of his neck: Ronon's blaster. In the same moment, Ronon said, "What's wrong, McKay?"

"Would you put that thing away?" Rodney toggled back to the power supply. OK, they had some room to maneuver if he had to go to manual control, but not much. Not much at all.

"No." Ronon's voice was cold. "Tell me what's going wrong."

"Besides being stuck in a Wraith lifepod?"

"With a Wraith?" Ronon said. "Yeah. Besides that."

"I'm not—" Rodney began, but of course he was. And that was something he couldn't afford to think about, not right now. "You want to know what's wrong? Fine. The autopilot is having trouble getting us onto a proper course for reentry, probably because this lifepod isn't meant to carry this much mass. I mean, presumably there's some margin for overload, but we've clearly exceeded that. And that means our course is starting to shallow out, which means we'll hit the atmosphere and bounce off it — like skipping a stone on a pond, if you ever did anything that benign. And then we just drift off into a random orbit — well, not really random, but cometary, a nice long orbit that gives us plenty of time to suffocate, so that if anyone ever bothers to look for us—"

"McKay," Ronon said. "Shut up."

Rodney blinked. All right, maybe that had been a little over the top. Unfortunately, though, the physics of the situation wasn't improving.

"Can you fly this thing?" Ronon asked.

"You don't fly a lifepod," Rodney said. "They're meant to land on autopilot—"

"McKay!"

There was something perversely comforting about that shout of exasperation. Rodney said, "Maybe. Just—give me a minute."

The pressure of the blaster against his neck eased slightly, and he bent forward to study the screen. The thrusters fired again and the numbers shifted, but the key data continued to flash white. The programmed course was still too shallow. He touched keys, toggling to the screen that showed the power cells for the thrusters. It took him a minute to work out the system—not a direct burn of fuel, that would create too much of a risk of explosion in a hard landing, but a pressurized fluid that worked much the same way—and he closed his eyes for a moment, working out the numbers.

"McKay," Ronon said again, his voice urgent.

Rodney opened his eyes to see the screen flashing white. A whistling alarm began to sound, but he slapped it to silence.

"What's going on?" Ronon asked.

"We've slipped out of the safe corridor for reentry," Rodney said. "I'm taking control." He touched keys as he spoke, switching off the autopilot. The screen faded to a normal display, though half a dozen readings still flashed white. The calculation wasn't complicated, just a simple matter of force applied along the lifepod's long axis. He switched screens again, entered the parameters, and set his hand on the thruster controls. The lifepod's computer counted down the seconds; at zero he pressed down hard on the plate. He felt the rumble as the fluid was vented, saw Ronon look uneasily at the walls around them. The second countdown was running, timing the maneuver; it reached zero, and he released the key. The images on the screen swam and reformed: they were back in the corridor, and he reengaged the autopilot.

"OK," he said. "OK, that's got it. We're back in the corridor."

"How long till we land?" Ronon asked.

Rodney glanced at the screen, the numbers rearranging themselves in his mind. "Forty — no, thirty-seven minutes to atmosphere. Then — well, it depends."

"Depends on what?"

"On the exact angle of reentry, on the ability of the autopilot field generators and the internal dampeners to compensate for the increased mass, and — you know what?" Rodney glared up at the Satedan. "Why don't we figure out a safe way to ride out that reentry instead of wasting time on pointless calculations?"

Improbably, Ronon's mouth twitched into a grin. "You don't know."

"Of course I —" Rodney stopped. "No. I don't. So we might as well get Jennifer someplace safe. Unless she's waking up?"

"No," Ronon said. He shifted awkwardly, trying to find a way to brace himself that didn't brush up against any of the controls twining the lifepod's walls.

Jennifer was slumped in the niche that was intended for the lifepod's single occupant, her eyes closed, a few strands of hair falling across her face. Rodney reached out to brush them away, ignoring the twitch of muscles as Ronon controlled the impulse to stop him.

"What's wrong with her?" Rodney asked.

"I don't know," Ronon said. He shifted his weight again, crowding Rodney back, and lifted Jennifer's slack body, settling her more solidly into the niche. The padding shifted under her, cradling her body — protecting it, Rodney hoped. "I told you, she just collapsed."

For a moment, Rodney wished he'd paid more attention in the mandatory SGC field rescue classes, particularly to the sections on bizarre and unlikely first aid situations. For all he knew, this could be something really simple, something that could be fixed with a slap on the back or an injection of Vitamin B — But, no, he wouldn't be that lucky.

"McKay," Ronon said. "The screen's flashing again."

Rodney turned, putting Jennifer out of his mind. The numbers were flickering white, the course line rising again even as the autopilot tried to compensate. "Oh, no." He touched keys, the numbers shifting in his head, set up another course correction. The thrusters rumbled, releasing fluid, and then cut out. "No, no, no, that's not —"

"McKay," Ronon said again.

Rodney stared at the screen. "OK, this is not good. That wasn't enough — we're still too shallow, and we're not going to make it into the atmosphere. And that was the last of the propellant, unless…" He was touching keys as he spoke, releasing a tiny bit of fluid from the opposite thrusters. "If I can turn us, I can use the forward thrusters — as long as I leave enough to get us back into the optimum angle for reentry, or the whole thing's going to just burn up —"

The numbers shifted in his screen, proof that the lifepod was turning, even though the inertial dampeners kept him from feeling the motion. The bow thrusters spoke — a different rumble, shivering through the lifepod's hull — and he cut them off as soon as he thought they'd reached the corridor. He waited then, counting precious seconds, while the computers checked and confirmed that they were back inside the corridor. Not far, not as far as he would have liked, and he hesitated. One last release? A literal second, just to be sure? No, the screen was starting to flash again, warning that they were out of position. All he could do was let the autopilot right them, angle them against the atmosphere, and hope for the best.

"OK," he said. "OK, that's it. That's all I can do."

An alarm began to sound, a slow, steady pulse.

"Maybe you should do something more," Ronon said.

Rodney bared teeth at him, and Ronon lifted his blaster.

"There is nothing more," Rodney said. "Right now, we're good, and if that changes, well, it's too late for me to fix it. Even Sheppard can't fly something that isn't meant to be flown." That wasn't strictly true, but he waved it away. "We're in the atmosphere, that's what the alarm is for. We're just along for the ride now."

Ronon took a breath, tipped his blaster up and away. "OK," he said. He pressed himself back into the niche next to Jennifer. The padding shifted slightly, trying to accommodate his bulk. "Brace yourself."

Like that's going to help if we've missed the corridor, Rodney thought. All the padding in the world isn't going to do one bit of good if the angle's bad and we burn up before we've slowed enough for the gravitics to compensate — He wedged himself into the niche on Jennifer's other side, the padding stiff and unyielding now.

"Keep your hand where I can see it," Ronon said.

"What?"

"Your — hand. The feeding hand." Ronon gestured with his blaster. "Keep it away from her."

"I can't believe you're saying this," Rodney said, but he lifted his feeding hand, held it out. "If I break my arm, I'm going to hold you responsible."

"Fine." Ronon's teeth were clenched.

"And it's not like I can't control myself," Rodney said. The alarm was louder now, drowning his words. Out of the corner of his eye, he could see the screen flashing white data, the hull temperature flaring, the autopilot flickering, the gravitics pegged at maximum. "I mean, this is Jennifer we're talking about — my girlfriend, though I don't think that's really a very dignified word? Except I can't think of anything more appropriate under the circumstances. Anyway, popular fiction notwithstanding, I really don't see anything particularly appealing about feeding on somebody you care about —"

Ronon's face was set in a pained grimace, his body braced

against the edge of the niche. Jennifer lay between them, still and silent, peaceful as if she slept. They were coming down, the alarm pulsing, indicators going from gold to white, systems failing under the strain. And then they hit and tumbled, the inertial dampeners flickering in and out, flinging them against the sides of the pod. Ronon braced himself against the edges of the niche, held himself in position by main force, pinning Jennifer beneath him. Rodney grabbed for the nearest handholds, head and hands and hip banging hard against objects that seemed too hard and sharp to belong in a lifepod. Then the movement stopped, the alarms cutting out, and there was nothing but silence.

CHAPTER TWO

Down

THE CESSATION of sound was almost painful. Rodney untangled himself from the control panel, wincing. His wrist hurt, and his hip and knee, sharp pains already fading as he moved, his body healing itself. Something to be grateful for, he knew, but his feeding hand throbbed a warning. He clenched his fingers over the hand-mouth and turned his attention to the central console. Behind him he could hear Ronon moving, struggling to his feet, but he ignored him, concentrating on the flickering display. It had been damaged in the landing, and he hoped it was just the screen. He reached for the keyboard, jerked back as something failed, spitting sparks and then a more definite flame. He slapped at it with his off hand, beat them down, and squinted at the failing display. They'd landed well, not too far from the Stargate — well, far was a relative term, he thought, converting Wraith units to kilometers, but it was a distance they could reasonably expect to walk. Fifty kilometers was something they could manage, and he wasn't going to think about what would happen if Jennifer didn't regain consciousness —

The display steadied under his touch, instructions spilling down the screen. He followed them, touching keys to transfer data to a portable device, deactivating the claws that held the hatch closed. There was a heavy click and a hiss, and a crack appeared in the hitherto seamless hull.

"Nice, McKay," Ronon said.

Rodney ignored him, watching the screen, the power fading even as he typed. "No, no, don't — crap."

The display was dead, the last of the lifepod's power spent transferring the systems' data into the handheld device. Rodney pulled it from its dock, slipped it into his pocket.

Ronon pushed past him, braced himself against the frame of the hull, used feet and shoulders to shove the hatch fully open. Air rushed in, sweet with something that made Rodney brace himself, expecting to sneeze, and Ronon tipped his head back.

"OK," he said. "This looks — safe enough."

Rodney turned toward him and Ronon recoiled, the blaster coming up.

"Would you stop that?" Rodney asked. "Hello? Rodney McKay? Remember me?"

"You're also a Wraith," Ronon said, but after a moment he slipped his blaster into its holster. "And if you make one wrong move, toward me or Jennifer, I will kill you."

Rodney opened his mouth to protest, but his own memories stopped him. He had fed — through intermediaries, yes, Dust and then Ember feeding him like a child, but it was still feeding. People had died because of him. He shoved that thought away, too, and fixed Ronon with what he hoped was his most sincere gaze. "It's me," he said, softly. "Ronon, I —" He shook his head, unable to find the words, and, anyway, there wasn't likely to be much of anything that would convince Ronon. "Let's get Jennifer out of here, and see what we've got."

"We'll check out the area first," Ronon said, and dropped the half meter from the hatch to the yielding ground.

Rodney glanced back at Jennifer, still held safely in the niche, and Ronon glared at him from the open hatch. "Come on, McKay."

Rodney sighed, and scrambled out of the lifepod. They had landed among trees, and the air was filled with the scent of broken branches. That was the sweetness that he had smelled, almost like maple sugar, and for an instant he was overcome by a sense of deja vu. These trees could have been Canadian, the heavy conifers of the northwestern provinces: it would be fall there, golden leaves showing among the dark green of the pines. Madison would be starting school, and Jeannie would be finishing up that year's hats and mittens, readying them all for the winter to come.

He glanced down, seeing his own hands green and misshapen, the heavy vein twining around his feeding hand. There would be no going back, not if he stayed like this — and he would not. Carson would find a way. Carson and Jennifer would find a way to reverse the process, and to that end, they needed to find the best way to the Stargate. He fumbled for the device in his pocket, keyed it on and let the screen fill with data. Fifty kilometers from the Stargate — really, not bad under the circumstances — and in a direction that the device called eight points north of northeast.

"Ronon!"

"Yeah?" The big man turned back to face him, the blaster loose in his hand.

"I've got a fix on the Stargate." Rodney pointed into the trees. "That way. Fifty kilometers."

There was a pause while Ronon converted that into some unit of his own. "OK. What else does that thing do?"

"What?"

"Lifesigns?" Ronon asked. "Humans, Wraith, large carnivores?"

"Oh." Rodney touched the controls, found the local sensors. "Nothing in the immediate vicinity. And the scan from orbit didn't show any signs of human habitation. Or Wraith landing sites."

Ronon nodded thoughtfully. "And I don't see any indication of big animals. Just little ones. I think it's safe to set up camp and see what we can do for Jennifer."

"You're sure you don't know what happened to her?"

"I told you what happened," Ronon said. "I don't know why."

Rodney made a face, and turned back to the lifepod.

"McKay." Ronon fixed him with a look. "I'll carry Jennifer. You see what's in there that we can use."

Rodney bit back his first response, and stood aside as Ronon climbed back into the pod. He reappeared a moment later, Jennifer cradled in his arms. Her hair had come down from its severe ponytail, fell in a curve across her cheek. Her head was tucked against Ronon's chest, as though she slept, and her arms were folded at her waist. Rodney looked away as Ronon jumped lightly down — Jennifer never moved — and pulled himself back into the cooling pod.

There were no emergency rations, of course, or a first aid kit: a stranded Wraith would either heal himself and feed, or die. He rummaged in the storage compartments beneath and beside the niche, found a set of empty clips that should have held a stunner. The Old One will hear about that, he thought, and only then remembered he was no longer Quicksilver.

In the next compartment, though, he found a folded shelter, an all-purpose carrier that was probably watertight, and a thick metal rod that could be extended to form a walking stick, with prongs that folded out to make a trident, and a narrow shovel-like blade concealed in the opposite end. He refolded it, and climbed back out of the pod.

Ronon had laid Jennifer down in the shade of one of the sweet-smelling pines, propping her back against the smooth bark, and was busy gathering stones to surround the bare circle he'd made in the grass. He straightened at Rodney's approach, and Rodney held up the shelter.

"It's a tent," he said. "Well, sort of. See, there are pockets in the corner—"

"I know how it works," Ronon said. "We need wood. For a fire. And something to carry water in."

"I've got that," Rodney said, and flourished the carrier.

"Good." Ronon reached for his knife, began sawing at a nearby sapling.

"You want me to find water?" Rodney asked. "I mean, I kind of failed completely at the whole Boy Scout thing."

"You can hear it," Ronon said. "There's a stream, that way."

Rodney tilted his head to listen. Sure enough, once he paid attention, he could hear the sound of water running over stones. "How do you know it's safe?" Ronon gave him a look, and he lifted his hands in surrender. "OK, OK, but don't blame me if you get some Pegasus Galaxy version of giardia."

He made his way into the trees, over ground carpeted in years of fallen needles. They were springy underfoot, and gave off a fainter sweetness; something fluttered past, vivid blue against the green, a large insect, or a tiny bird. It was all very quiet, except for the sound of the water.

Ronon was not going to leave him alone with Jennifer. That was obvious, and not entirely unexpected, and it hurt more than he would have believed. For God's sake, I'm Rodney McKay. I'm the man you've been looking for, at least I assume you've been looking for me, for the last three months. And now that you've found me, you're going to treat me like a Wraith?

He reached the edge of the stream, the water loud over a bed of fist-sized pebbles. He flipped the carrier to its spherical form, and knelt on the bank, the skirts of his coat spreading around him. He dipped the carrier into the water, and his distorted reflection looked back at him: white hair, too short for beauty, Quicksilver's despair; yellow eyes and pale green skin and the long sensor pits outside each nostril. Ronon of all people wouldn't be able to see past that. Probably nobody would, except maybe Jennifer and Carson. They understood what had been done to him, they'd have an answer. His feeding hand throbbed again, the first pangs of serious hunger, and he flattened it against his coat. They would be back to the Stargate in a day or two or three, and everything would be all right.

By the time he made it back to the clearing, Ronon had put up the Wraith shelter, twisting and staking the multi-pocketed fabric to make a three-sided lean-to, and started a small fire in the ring of stones. He had collected grass and leaves for a cushion, too, and Jennifer lay curled on her side, still apparently asleep. He looked up sharply at Rodney's approach, one hand starting toward his blaster, but then controlled himself.

"I got water," Rodney said. "And the stream looked clear enough, though of course that's not something you can tell by looking."

There was a sound from the shelter, the familiar snort and whuffle that Jennifer made on waking. Rodney caught his breath, shocked by the relief that flooded through him, and Ronon slid toward her.

"Jennifer?" he said. "Easy."

Jennifer's eyes opened, gaze vague and unfocussed, and then sharpening as she came fully to herself. "What — where?" She sat up, shaking her head, and Rodney cringed as she met his eyes. He saw her face change, shock, fear, and last of all recognition. "Rodney?"

"It's me," he said. He wanted desperately to take her hand, but he knew Ronon would stop him. "It's really me."

"Rodney," she said, relief and acceptance in her voice, and started to push herself to her knees.

"Easy," Ronon said again, and she fell back, shaking her head.

"OK, that's — weird, but I think I'm OK. But we got Rodney back, right? That's the main thing."

Ronon gave a sideways smile, and sat back on his heels.

Rodney said, "It's a start. And, believe me, I'm grateful! But we have crash-landed — well, lifepod-landed, which isn't exactly the same thing — on an uninhabited planet, so we're not, and I say this with a painful awareness of the pun, out of the woods just yet."

Jennifer looked at Ronon. "Really?"

"You know McKay," Ronon began. He paused. "Yeah, pretty much."

Jennifer leaned back against the nearest tree, watching as Ronon tended the fire and Rodney — yes, Rodney, despite the green skin and claws and the feeding hand he was trying to keep out of sight — grumbled and complained. Her head wasn't spinning any more, and there was none of the weird tunnel vision she had experienced on the hive ship. She pressed her fingers against her neck, her pulse steady to the touch; her skin was dry and cool, no hint of fever and none of the cold sweat of nausea. In fact, she felt entirely normal.

"What happened?" she asked, and Ronon sat back on his heels.

"Don't ask me," Rodney said. "Chewbacca there knocked me out before whatever it was happened to you."

"You passed out," Ronon said. "I don't know why."

Jennifer shook her head, trying to remember. OK, the last thing she was sure of was being on the hive, following Ronon down the dark organic corridors, her head swimming, stomach roiling. Nerves, she'd thought at first, and then she hadn't known what it was. Ronon had waved her back, broken through into the labs — and then she remembered Rodney, sprawled on the floor. She'd injected him with the sedative, that had been the plan, and then — She shook her head again. After that, nothing, until she woke here, feeling only as though she'd slept badly.

"OK," she said. "Yes. I remember the hive. And feeling bad."

"How are you feeling now?" Rodney asked. He was sitting on the opposite side of the fire, his hands resting on his knees. She could see the heavy claws, the thick vein that wound around the forefinger of his left hand, and knew without having to see it that the palm was crossed by the handmouth, his fingers curved to hide the fleshy ridges of the feeding organ. She shuddered in spite of herself, and hoped he hadn't seen.

"All right, I think," she said. She paused, assessing. "Everything feels normal."

"So why'd you pass out?" Ronon asked.

"I don't —" Jennifer stopped, considering. OK, what was behind her reaction? She'd been in good health before they started; the only thing that was at all out of the ordinary was the retrovirus, but she had taken that days before, and it had had no effect. Or had it? She had calculated that any effects would show themselves within thirty-six hours of the injection, but if she'd been wrong... She said, slowly, "It might have been the retrovirus. It didn't do that before, but — this was a different formulation."

Ronon scowled. He hadn't liked the idea in the first place, and he looked as though he was having a hard time not telling her so.

Rodney said, "What retrovirus? Why are you testing things on yourself, anyway?"

"Because I couldn't ethically test it on anybody else," Jennifer snapped.

"It's one of Todd's bright ideas," Ronon said.

"Not entirely," Jennifer said. She looked at Rodney, green-skinned, white-haired, his slit pupils narrowed to a thread against even the filtered sunlight of the clearing. If she hadn't known him before, she would not have recognized him as anything but Wraith, hunched there in his black coat like a crow on a branch. "We, Carson and I, have been working on a treatment that would counteract the effects of Wraith feeding — that would allow a human to survive being fed on. As Ronon said, Todd has also been working on the same idea, and, well, we ended up pooling our knowledge."

"You and Todd," Rodney said slowly. To Jennifer's surprise, he began to laugh. "Of course he did! It must be at least a quintuple cross by now! No wonder Ember was scared to death the whole time."

"Ember?" Ronon said.

"One of Guide's — Todd's — clevermen." Rodney paused, as though he'd just realized he was translating Wraith terms. "Scientists. In fact, it wouldn't surprise me if he was involved in developing it, it's his kind of project." He shook his head. "But that isn't really relevant. So you tried this retrovirus yourself?"

Jennifer felt herself flush. "Yes. Look, after I let Todd feed on me the first time, I couldn't let anybody else do it."

"You let Todd feed on you?" Rodney's voice scaled up, and Ronon gave a sympathetic grunt.

"You've missed a lot of fun, McKay."

"Yes, I let him feed on me," Jennifer said. "Somebody had to test it, and I trusted that he would revive me if the virus didn't work. Which it didn't, the first time, and he did."

"You let Todd feed on you," Rodney said again, more quietly, this time. "And restore you. Did you have any idea of the risk you were running?"

"Yes, as a matter of fact, I did." Jennifer glared back at him. "And I still do. And you may be grateful for it in the long run."

Rodney winced at that, and Jennifer bit her lip. That wasn't something she'd meant to say, at least not yet. She didn't really want to know if Rodney had fed, though he must have done, to stay alive this long.

Ronon said, "So you think you passed out because of the retrovirus?"

Jennifer took a breath. "Yes. At least, that seems the most likely cause. There's nothing else that was different."

"Does that mean it worked?" Ronon's expression was unreadable.

"I don't know." Jennifer couldn't look at Rodney, looked at her hands instead. "I won't know until we can test it."

"Well, I'm not going to test it," Rodney said. "That's not going to happen."

"Damn right it's not," Ronon said.

"Rodney." Jennifer laced her fingers together. She couldn't come right out and say it, couldn't ask him when he'd last fed — couldn't bear to think about it, Rodney with teeth bared, his claws, his handmouth fixed on someone's chest. "Look, I'm going to need to examine you, to find out what they did to make you change."

"If I'd known you were coming," Rodney said, "I'd've stolen a dose of the drug they were giving me. At least, I assume that's what it was, something to keep me — I don't know, wraithified. But, no, you had to stun me first."

"That's because you tried to kill us the last time," Ronon said.

Jennifer closed her eyes for a moment. "I can probably get an idea of what they were doing from a blood sample, but not here. Though it's actually good news that this process requires a booster, that means it ought to just wear off, more or less." Except that all their simulations showed that it didn't wear off entirely, that Rodney would be stuck halfway, partly Wraith and partly human, just like Michael. She shoved that thought aside. "So. Do we have a plan for getting back to Atlantis?"

"Yeah." Ronon pushed himself to his feet, began collecting more scraps of fallen wood. "McKay says we're about fifty kilometers from the Stargate, and the terrain's not much different

than here. I figure we can walk that in two days, three at the most."
He squinted at the sky. "I'm guessing it'll be dark in a few hours,
so there's no point in getting started today. I say we get a good
night's sleep here, and start for the gate first thing in the morning."

"OK." Jennifer reached into her pockets, began taking stock of
what she found. There was no sign of her P90, she realized, and
guessed it had been left on the hive. Basic first aid kit, a case with
a second dose of Wraith-level tranquilizer — they weren't likely to
need that unless something went drastically wrong — three, no,
four power bars, plus a multi-tool. She checked the last pocket.
Two more power bars and a crinkly mylar emergency blanket
still in its wrapper. A twist of string, and three spare elastics for
her hair.

"You've been taking lessons from Teyla," Ronon said, with
approval. He dropped another load of wood beside the fire.

"It seemed like a good idea," Jennifer began, and made herself
stop. "Thank you."

"If you don't mind sharing," Ronon said, "that'll get us through
tonight and still leave some to spare. I'll set snares overnight.
From the tracks, there's plenty of small game."

"Couldn't we just, I don't know, find fruits and berries?"
Jennifer asked.

"Sometimes they pick up weird trace minerals," Ronon said.
"It's not so bad with animals." He pointed to one of the elastics.
"Can I use that?"

"Sure, go ahead." Jennifer watched as he twisted it around a
thin, flexible stick — making a snare, she guessed.

"We'll need to split the watches, you and I," he said, and Rodney
lifted his head.

"Hello? What about me?"

"You're what we're watching," Ronon said. "If you weren't you,
I'd tie you up overnight. Or stun you."

Rodney opened his mouth to protest, closed it again, a look
almost of misery flickering across his face, before he bared teeth
in a snarl that did nothing to reassure anyone. "Fine. Be that way."

Jennifer closed her eyes again. Somehow she'd imagined that when they finally found Rodney it would just be a matter of getting him into the infirmary, that it was just a medical problem, the kind of thing that, while admittedly difficult, she knew how to handle. She had no idea what to do about Ronon, about Rodney as a Wraith, about Rodney and Ronon together or anything else that involved interpersonal relations. They were all professionals, she told herself. More than that, they were a team. Rodney and Ronon were teammates, they were friends, and somehow that would be enough to get them to the Stargate. Surely.

CHAPTER THREE

Queen's Return

THE RAIN was streaking down in sheets, soaking Sam in the short distance from the *Hammond*'s ramp to the door. There were no transfers this time to Atlantis's infirmary, which was a good thing. No one was critical, just bumps and bruises and a few second degree burns. That was a thing she'd look forward to reporting when she uploaded for the databurst to the SGC.

The transport chamber doors opened on Atlantis's control room level, and Sam stepped out, almost plowing into Richard Woolsey. "Excuse me," she said. "I was on my way up."

"I was on my way down to see you," Woolsey said, and that was almost unheard of. The person in charge in Atlantis waited on the starship captains to come to them. It was a protocol Elizabeth Weir had established in her first days working with Caldwell, a protocol she'd been careful to keep when she was in charge. Atlantis did not answer to the starship captains. The chain of command was made absolutely clear.

Woolsey shifted from one foot to another, stepping back to let her actually get out of the transport chamber. "Is Colonel Sheppard with you?"

"No." Sam wondered if she looked as perplexed as she sounded. "He's not back?"

"No." Woolsey's face was drawn. "We haven't heard a word from any of the team. Nothing." His voice sharpened. "I thought they were to return with you."

Sam shook her head. "That was the original plan, but we had trouble getting in close enough to beam them out. I had a radio message from Sheppard that indicated they had been beamed aboard Todd's hive ship. I thought they'd be back by now."

"No," Woolsey said. "We don't know anything."

Sam blew out a breath. If Todd were holding them prisoner they'd be getting demands any time now. But that was less likely, given that Teyla was still masquerading as his queen. "It's possible that the hive ship also took some battle damage," she said. "That may be more of a priority than getting to a gate and reporting in."

A twitch of Woolsey's eyebrows showed what he thought of Sheppard's enthusiasm for immediately reaching a gate and reporting in. "Did they recover Dr. McKay?"

"I don't know," Sam said. "There was a lot of interference on the radio. Sheppard said they were aboard Todd's ship, but I don't know if they had McKay with them or not." She shook her head. "If not, he's dead. Queen Death's hive ship exploded. There would have been no survivors." Surely they had him. Sheppard wouldn't have beamed out without him. And if not… It was better than orders to kill him. Better than Sheppard having to fulfill those orders, if he had died at the *Hammond*'s guns rather than Sheppard's hand. "I expect they have him," she said. "I'm not certain. The communications were very spotty."

Woolsey nodded, looking somewhat comforted.

He was worried, Sam thought. He was worried about his people. The Woolsey she'd known wouldn't have been. When had that happened and what had changed him?

"I'm sure they will report soon," he said.

"Yes," Sam agreed.

Dr. Kusanagi had approached, standing well back to not be rude but close enough to indicate she had something to say, and now Sam turned to her. "Doctor?"

"The SGC has dialed in again and sent through supplies. I thought you would be pleased to know that it includes material for the *Hammond*."

"Absolutely," Sam said, "What have we got?" With a nod for Woolsey, who headed back into his office, she went down the main stairs with Kusanagi. The floor of the gateroom was filled with boxes and pallets, a couple of hundred boxes sent through the Stargate containing everything from kitchen supplies to vital medicines. One big pallet looked like it was stacked with seven or eight hundred pounds of metal plating. It also had a big red ribbon around it.

"I think these are for you," Kusanagi said, smiling. "They're 640 hull plating."

"I expect they are." Sam couldn't help but grin. There was a tag attached to the big red bow, Jack's handwriting. Happy Birthday.

"I did not know it is your birthday, Colonel Carter," Dr. Kusanagi said. "Many happy returns."

"It isn't my birthday," Sam said, as Kusanagi tilted her head and looked confused. It was Jack's. Happy Birthday. Carter is still in one piece. Again. She supposed that made a pretty fair present.

Thorn looked about the audience chamber with grudging satisfaction from his place behind Waterlight. All was as it should be. Four drones guarded the doors with pikes in hand, while blades and clevermen in their numbers assembled within. If their numbers were less than Queen Death might assemble, or their colors more muted and less ostentatious, still they made a brave show. A martial show, to his eyes. Even those who stood closest their queen were dressed in plain leathers, their ornament limited to richly embroidered borders, hair clasps of silver and steel.

A blade knelt at her feet, dark green finework at his sleeves a compliment to her dress, his eyes raised. Not pallax, not yet, though that one aspired to be. His adoration was as evident as his ambition.

Her consort ignored him. Guide's back was straight, the proud lines of his face belied his age. He wore unrelieved black, so secure in his place that he might scorn ornamentation, standing directly to her left to place himself across her heart should the need arise, off hand dagger at the ready.

Between them in tableau, Steelflower. Night dark hair fell from a fillet of iron set with moonstones, her beautiful face cast down as she listened to the blade at her feet. She wore no elaborate dress to reveal her charms. It was not necessary. Every man knew what she was, and rather than modest she seemed determined. The severe lines of tight bodice and flowing emerald overcoat spoke of stern control, of the economies of a warrior queen who loves weapons better than jewels.

And forward where the first courtiers should be, where other ambassadors should stand... Thorn let out an inadvertent hiss.

Steelflower's eyes fell upon him just as he felt Waterlight wince.

"These too are ambassadors," Steelflower said aloud, "in so much as you are. And we do not disdain any who come under our peace." She nodded with her chin to the young woman who stood in front, red gold hair as tightly bound as Steelflower's over her black coat. "This is She Who is Wreathed in Plants of Victory, kinswoman to She Who Carries Many Things, who comes before me on behalf of that greatest queen of the Lanteans. And he you have met before, the Consort of Atlantis, who is also called Guide." Her eyes fell on the third human, a little man who stood beside the Consort. "And a cleverman of Atlantis, He Who Is Son of a Famous Ruler."

John Sheppard looked straight back at him. This one Thorn had seen before indeed. He had been their prisoner, and he had groveled at Steelflower's feet as abjectly as any.

Whatever Thorn might have said was forestalled by Waterlight. "You treat with the humans of Atlantis?"

"I hear out any who come to me in peace," Steelflower said, rising from her carved chair. "Is it not true that She Who Carries Many Things is a great queen, an adversary worthy of our interest? It is she who reduced the Asurans to nothing when they had spoiled many hunting grounds and left many hives queenless. If she sends her own consort and kinswoman to treat with me, should I not hear them?"

There was no murmur of dissent within the hall, Thorn felt with surprise. Even Waterlight was more curious than afraid.

And yet Steelflower answered him, though it seemed she spoke to all assembled. "Why not speak of what we all know?

We must feed. A galaxy without humans would be to us a barren desert, and we should surely perish. What else awaits us at Queen Death's hands? If she spoils the hunting grounds that sustain us all, how shall we live? Or is it that she will bite us to the bone thus, leaving all hives at her mercy? If she controls the only foodstuffs, who then shall gainsay her anything?" Steelflower's eyes swept over the crowd. "That is not as it should be, not as the First Mothers taught us. To each her blades and clevermen, to each her children in the chrysalis. We do not answer to one alone. Each queen shall take her own course, and any man who disagrees is free to follow another queen who better suits him." Her eyes rested upon Thorn's. "Is this not so, He Who Was Honored by Firebeauty?"

"It is," Thorn said, and he felt the appreciation deeply, that she did not name him failed consort, but rather reminded those assembled that Firebeauty had chosen him not only to guard her, but to be Father to her daughter. No greater honor and trust could have been given him.

Her eyes turned from him to Waterlight, and she came down from her dais and took both Waterlight's hands in hers as though they were near kin. "Be welcome in my zenana, dear sister. I have greatly desired to speak with you."

"And I with you," Waterlight said in a clear, strong voice. She was girl still, not woman, but she was queen. "I bring you alliance and name you sister. We shall stand together!" Her words rang through every part of the room, and more than one blade turned with his heart in his eyes, caught by her precocious courage. Thorn's chest swelled with pride. Young she was, in her gown of white, her face still with the soft roundness of childhood, her tight bodice emphasizing the shape of budding breasts, but her resolution marked strength of will. She would be a worthy queen in her time. If he could but guard her so long. If he could but guard her until she grew up.

"I will stand with you proudly," Steelflower said, hand in hand, though it seemed to Thorn that for a moment her eyes flickered

over Waterlight's head to meet those of the Consort of Atlantis.
"I give you my word, my sister."

The audience was over. Through the twining corridors
that led to the Queen's Chambers Steelflower retired, her
Consort at her side, her hand lightly on his wrist. Behind,
the Lanteans' ambassador walked with her entourage, honored thus with a private audience with the queen. They had
nearly reached the doors when Steelflower swayed, and it
was Guide and the Consort of Atlantis who caught her, one
beneath each elbow.

"Are you ok?" Sheppard whispered.

"She is faint," Guide said. "Here and now." He triggered the
door to open before them, made as though to lift his queen in
his arms to carry her.

"I am all right," Steelflower said, waving away his hands. "Let
me be." They went inside and after the doors closed she sunk
down on a padded bench, her hands clenching against the tufted
fabric as though to keep the world from swimming.

"What's the matter?" Laura Cadman asked, coming around
Radek Zelenka, whose face was a study in concern.

"I am only a little dizzy," Teyla said, but her hands did not
unclench.

"She hasn't had any solid food in nearly a month," Sheppard
said, going down on one knee beside the bench so that he could
see her face. "Cadman, get one of those protein shakes out."

"I am fine," Teyla said.

Guide's brow furrowed. "She must feed?"

"She can't live on nothing but nutrition drinks," Sheppard
snapped. "They're not meant for this. They're ok for a few meals
or even a few weeks, but she has to eat real food. She can't just
go on like this. She's been doing it too long as it is." He stood
up, not so tall as Guide, but nearly. "She needs to go home. She
needs to get off the meds and eat actual meals and sleep normal
hours. She can't keep doing this."

Guide nodded slowly. "It is reasonable that eventually she must feed as a human."

"She can't with the dental work in her mouth. And these meds are messing up her blood pressure. We need to put an end to this."

"I can't yet," Teyla said. "I must meet with Bitterroot first. She will come soon, and I must be here."

"Todd can do it for you," Sheppard said, handing her the can that Cadman had opened.

"He cannot." Teyla took the can carefully, angling the sipping hole against her lips. "It must be queen to queen." She looked up at Guide. "Is that not true?"

"Yes," he said, but his voice was concerned. "Still, if you must feed, then you must."

Sheppard shook his head. "Look, Teyla. You said you had to do this meeting. Now you've done it. We need to find the nearest gate and go." He glanced at Todd. "Unless we're his prisoners."

"We are his allies." She tilted her head up to Todd's, and perhaps she said something else that could only be heard mind to mind. "Are we not?"

"You are," Todd said. "But there is truth in what Sheppard says. You must not become ill. That will avail no one."

"We need to get back to Atlantis," Sheppard said. "It's been a full day since the fight. By now Carter will be back in Atlantis with Ronon and Keller and Rodney, and we need to find out what happened. Teyla," he looked at her, his eyes serious. "It's time. We need to go."

She nodded slowly. "I know. I have carried this on too long. But I must meet with Bitterroot first. What if we go to the nearest gate and you and Radek and Captain Cadman go back to Atlantis without me? I will meet with Bitterroot, and then I will join you in a day or so."

"Leave you with Todd." His voice was flat.

"John," she said quietly.

"I know." Sheppard let out a long breath. "Ok. We'll head back, and you'll be a day behind us." He looked at Todd. "No more."

"I would no more endanger her health than you, Sheppard," Guide said.

"I doubt that."

"There is no need to." Guide gave him a mirthless, betoothed smile. "I know that you will kill me if any harm comes to her."

Steelflower watched the Lanteans disappearing through the Stargate, and her eyes were hooded. They betrayed nothing, and not for the first nor probably the last time did Guide wish she were Steelflower in truth.

Yes, my Guide? She turned her face to him as surely as if he had spoken her name.

It is nothing, he said, but of course she did not believe him. Her mind slid easily over his, stealing the thought that was uppermost.

If she were Steelflower in truth… If the retrovirus that Queen Death's clevermen had created for the scientist McKay would work on her as well…

I should find out eventually, she said. *And I should kill you.*

I expect Sheppard would do it first, he said, his mental voice a humorless bark of laughter.

Perhaps. She did not look at him, only turned at his side away from the Stargate, her hand on his wrist as they returned to their shuttle. They boarded in silence, took off into the planet's gathering night. He could not take her silence for anything good, and Guide wondered if he had made a fatal mistake. A threat, backed by his desire…

You would not be happy with the results, Guide, she said quietly, and there was no anger in her voice. *I would not be Steelflower. A queen with no memories would not be me.* She lifted her beautiful chin, her eyes meeting his. *You need a queen who can rule, a queen with Osprey's memories. Amnesiac and fragile, who must be kept ill enough that she does not question the medicines you give her… Such a queen would avail you nothing. She would be an empty figurehead, not the leader of an alliance.*

And where would I get such a one? he asked, and could not keep the regret from his mind. *All who might have served are dead.*

That I cannot tell you, she replied, and her mind was filled with regret too.

CHAPTER FOUR

Traveling

THE WOODS were growing thicker, the trees smaller but more closely spaced, forcing them closer to the banks of the stream. At least it was running steadily in the right direction, and the going was easier along its edges. They were making good progress, Ronon thought, had covered close to 6 faerings since morning — that would be, what, 17 or 18 of the Lanteans' kilometers. Jennifer was holding up well. If anything, she'd been getting stronger, didn't seem at all bothered by whatever had made her pass out on the hive ship. He was beginning to think maybe it was just a reaction to the retrovirus after all, something that had happened once, and would not repeat. Rodney, on the other hand... He glanced over his shoulder to see McKay leaning heavily on a thin metal rod, sharp teeth bared in a silent snarl. Rodney saw him looking and straightened, glaring, but Ronon wasn't fooled. They had a serious problem on their hands.

He squinted at the sky, trying to gauge the sun's position among the branches. Definitely past the zenith, declining toward sunset, but he'd hoped to get a little further while the light lasted.

"If you were thinking of going easy on me," Rodney said, "I want you to know that I'm fine. Well, as fine as I'm going to be, hiking through an alien forest just waiting for something to trigger my allergies, but, as these things go, generally all right."

If he didn't look back, Ronon thought, it was unmistakably Rodney. Take a look, though, and it was a Wraith, a hungry Wraith, too close behind. The skin between his shoulder blades crawled at the idea.

"Maybe we ought to take a break?" Jennifer looked from one to the other. "You know, take a drink, maybe split a power bar?"

Ronon nodded reluctantly. Rest now, and maybe McKay could

make it another faering before they camped for the night. "OK."

He swung the improvised pack off his shoulder, offered Jennifer the container of water. She fumbled with the unfamiliar fastening for a moment, then drank deeply and handed it back. Ronon drank, too, and out of the corner of his eye saw Rodney settle onto the ground at the edge of the stream. He trailed his feeding hand in the cold water, his face tight and expressionless, and Jennifer took a breath.

"Rodney."

"Yes?" McKay didn't look at her.

"Rodney, I have to ask. When was the last time you fed?"

Rodney flinched, and Ronon looked away, unable to bear the picture that formed in his mind: Rodney in the feeding cells of a hive, choosing from among the bound humans that filled the niches, Rodney with his hand buried in a stranger's flesh, drawing the life from their body in a single terrible rush of pain.

"It's been a while," Rodney said. He wouldn't look at them, as though that made it easier. "Not since I — remembered who I was. Which makes it several weeks, at least, maybe as many as five." He paused. "Too long. So if you're going to shoot me, make it somewhere non-lethal, please. I'm not sure how well I'd regenerate."

Ronon grinned at that, but Jennifer just nodded.

"So you can regenerate?" she asked. "We weren't sure how — complete — the transformation had been."

"Complete," Rodney said. He paused. "At least — well, I can, could regenerate small things, cuts, bruises, minor burns. I didn't get shot or anything like that."

"Let me see your arm," Jennifer said. Rodney hesitated, and she frowned. "Come on, Rodney, I'm going to have to examine you sometime."

"I'd prefer it were in slightly more sterile surroundings," Rodney said. "The chance of some weird alien infection seems way too high."

He broke off, flushing, and Jennifer grinned in spite of herself. "That's one thing you don't have to worry about right now.

Take your coat off."

Rodney shrugged himself out of the supple leather, and Jennifer knelt beside him, her long hands moving deftly over his neck and shoulders. Ronon reached back, rested his hand on his blaster for reassurance. This was Rodney; there was no reason to think he'd snap, snap and spring, his feeding hand flashing up and out to fasten on Jennifer's throat — The image was too clear, clear and true and shocking, and Ronon shook his head, trying to drive it away.

Jennifer was still talking as she worked. "— no bruising at the injection site, which I would have expected since I wasn't, well, very careful about it? We were kind of in a hurry. So I'd say you still have some ability to heal yourself. Otherwise —" She had taken the notebook and pencil from the first aid kid, was jotting down information as she spoke. "Otherwise, I think you're in pretty good shape. From what we've been able to figure out about the Wraith, anyway."

She pushed herself to her feet, and Rodney looked up at her. "Which is how much?" he demanded.

"Enough," Jennifer said. Her eyes flickered, but she plowed on anyway. "Enough to manage getting you back to yourself. You said there was a maintenance drug?"

"Yes."

"When did you have your last dose of that?"

Rodney shrugged the coat back over his shoulders. "The morning of the attack. So that means I've missed one, almost two doses now."

"OK." Jennifer stared at the notebook, her hands still, and Ronon cleared his throat.

"You should eat. If you're going to. And then we need to keep moving."

"Right." Jennifer's voice was just a little off, and she turned hastily away to rummage in the makeshift pack. "Do you want half?"

"Yeah," Ronon said. It wouldn't do much for his hunger, but it would do until they made camp — there was a pair of coneys in the pack that he would cook then, solid protein to sustain them. Jennifer unwrapped the bar, broke it scrupulously into two sections. Ronon took his share, and she turned away, wandering a little way up the stream as she ate. Ronon watched her go, made himself finish the sweet sticky rectangle.

"Ronon," Rodney said. He spoke softly, too quietly to be heard more than a foot away. "I wouldn't — you know I wouldn't do anything to hurt her."

In spite of knowing better, the image came flooding back, Jennifer withering under a Wraith's hands, and Ronon suppressed the desire to reach for his blaster. "Damn right you won't," he said, and stooped to collect the pack. "Come on, let's get moving."

They stopped at sunset in a small clearing beside the stream. Ronon set up the shelter and cleaned the coneys while the others collected wood for the fire, then spitted the coneys and set them to cook above the flames. The pinewood burned fierce and hot, sending up puffs of sparks when a particularly resinous branch caught, and the air smelled of burnt sugar and the roasting meat. Jennifer sat cross-legged by the fire, frowning over her notebook, pausing now and then to scribble something. Behind her, Rodney moved restlessly along the edge of the circle of firelight, still gathering wood as though that would take his mind off things. In the gathering dark, his shape was too familiar, white hair and black coat, and Ronon felt his shoulders twitch again. Wraith had circled outside his fires before.

"Hey, McKay."

Rodney turned, too fast, and Ronon shuddered. "That's enough wood for now. Come and sit down."

"Yes, fine," Rodney said, and stooped to pick up another branch.

Jennifer looked up, the firelight gleaming on her hair. "Ronon. Is there any way we could make, I don't know, broth of some kind? Boil some of the meat?"

Ronon considered for a moment, running over his mental inventory. "Not unless — hey, McKay."

"What now?" Rodney dropped his armload of wood on the pile they'd already gathered, dropped down on the far side of the fire. They were sitting at the three points of a triangle, Ronon realized, equidistant around the fire, each as far from the others as they could get.

"Is that carrier thing fireproof?"

"What?" Rodney frowned. "No. No, definitely not."

Ronon looked at Jennifer. "Then, no."

"What?" Rodney asked again, and it was Jennifer who answered.

"I was hoping I could maybe boil up some broth for you. If you — if the drug is wearing off, that might help get your digestion working again."

Not much chance of that, Ronon thought, but said nothing. He turned the spitted coneys again, and fed another branch into the fire, watching the sparks flare.

"I could stand to eat a little something," Rodney said, almost wistfully. "I mean, actual food — this smells really good."

Jennifer hesitated. "It probably couldn't hurt," she said.

When the coneys were done, Ronon pulled them off the fire, set them on broad leaves he'd collected earlier and cut them into manageable portions with Jennifer's multi-tool. He had a feeling she'd be more willing to eat if it looked more or less like a normal portion. After a moment's hesitation, she took the tool herself, carved off a sliver of the meat for Rodney.

"You can have some of mine, too," Ronon said, but she shook her head.

"You need more food than I do. And he's not getting much, anyway."

She was right, and Ronon settled back, methodically stripping the meat from the bones. It was tough and savorless, tasting more of smoke than anything. If he'd been on Sateda, he would have had salt, carried in a jar no bigger than his thumb: common issue in the army, common property for anyone who traveled wild. This tasted like a Runner's meat. He killed that thought, made himself keep eating.

Across the fire, Rodney nibbled gingerly at the sliver of coney breast. There was an odd look on his face, as though he were remembering something and wasn't sure if it were good.

"How do you feel?" Jennifer asked, after a moment, and he looked up with a quick smile.

"Better, I think. I think it's helping."

"Do you want some more?" Jennifer was carving as she spoke, and Rodney nodded.

"Thanks."

Ronon watched him eat, caught in the wavering firelight, a shape in black hunched over a strip of meat. It was not a reassuring sight, even though Wraith do not eat, and he looked away.

"More?" Jennifer asked, and Rodney shook his head.

"No — well, yes, but I think it would be smarter to wait and see."

"I'll take first watch," Ronon said, gruffly, and Jennifer nodded.

"Yes," she said, and looked at Rodney. "Good night, then."

Rodney looked back at her across the fire, his face tired and thin, the firelight giving him a passing hint of human color. "Good night," he said, and for an instant his voice wavered.

Ronon woke in the cool light of dawn to the sound of someone being comprehensively sick on the far side of the dying fire. He rolled over, expecting it to be Jennifer, but she was sitting upright in the shelter's mouth, her face unreadable. Beyond the fire, Rodney straightened, wiping his mouth on the back of his hand.

"I should know better," he said, weakly, and Jennifer pushed herself to her feet.

"Let me take a look at you."

"I'm fine," Rodney said. "It's just — you know how I am with strange foods, and alien animals cooked over an open fire kind of fit that description."

Jennifer ignored him, came around the fire to inspect the mess. Rodney backed away.

"Oh, god, that was bad enough when Newton had a hairball! Don't tell me you're going to — oh, that's disgusting!"

"You said you felt better after you ate," Jennifer said. Her voice was remote.

"I did!" Rodney paused. "I did."

"Don't lie to me!" Jennifer glared at him. "None of this has been digested. At all."

"I did feel better," Rodney said. "Until I didn't."

Ronon rolled his eyes, crawled out of the shelter. It wasn't that he had expected Rodney to be better, to be less a Wraith — but, he admitted, he had allowed himself to hope. And they were still a long way from the Stargate. Reluctantly, he picked up the Wraith device that someone — Jennifer, he told himself firmly — had left within reach, and checked the nacreous screen. It showed that they had covered a little more than half the distance to the Stargate, but he couldn't find that as encouraging as it should be. Not with Rodney still doubled over, one hand pressed against his stomach.

"I'm fine," Rodney said, to Jennifer, and was promptly sick again.

They got a later start than they had the previous day, and Ronon resigned himself to at least another day's travel. He'd hoped that maybe, if Rodney was stronger, if everything had gone right, that they might reach the Stargate in one long day's march. At least he'd managed to snare another coney for this night's meal, and, if he couldn't catch another on the march, there were always roots and berries. He recognized several edible species, or at least their close analogues, and the meat had agreed with him and Jennifer well enough that it was unlikely there was anything actually poisonous in the vegetation.

What he didn't like was the way the ground was changing. The trees were thinning out, the grass growing taller, coarser, and the stream they had been following seemed wider. The current was stronger, too, the sound of the water louder, and he wasn't surprised when they came out from under the last of the trees to find themselves on the edge of a cliff. The stream plunged over the edge, and ten meters below, rainbows glimmered in the cloud of spray.

"Oh, that's just lovely," Rodney said, and sat down hard underneath the closest tree.

Ronon leaned forward, mindful of the loose stones and crumbling soil, and peered down into the canyon. A river had carved it, still ran down its center, shallow but fast, its bed strewn with boulders. It had been higher in the past, Ronon thought, judging from the debris scattered along the banks, but it was fast enough that it would be a struggle to cross. More to the point, the cliff face was close to vertical, and the rock looked loose and friable. He could — maybe — climb down, but he doubted he could get either Rodney or Jennifer down without rope. And rope they didn't have. Nor were there vines or anything else that looked like a likely alternative.

He straightened, looking along the length of the cliff. Downstream, it seemed to rise higher, but once you crossed the waterfall, it looked as though the slope might ease. If he followed it further, there might be a place they could get down without a climb. And get back up the other side. Except — He looked over his shoulder at Rodney slumped beneath the tree. Rodney didn't have the strength to waste casting up and down the cliff for a safe crossing.

Jennifer forced a smile. Her hair was coming loose from its severe tail, wisps clinging to her skin, and he couldn't help thinking again how pretty she was. "I'm guessing this is a problem," she said, and he nodded.

"Yeah." Beautiful and fragile and indomitable, he thought, and as hard to read as the Earth people always were.

"I don't think I can get down there," she said, and leaned cautiously over the edge. "Not without rope."

"Which we don't have," Rodney said. "Nor, may I point out, do we have anything to make a rope with."

Jennifer grimaced at that, as though at a memory.

Ronon said, "Rodney's right." He glanced at the sky — after noon already, which meant he'd need to find a way down fairly quickly. The river below them looked relatively shallow, no more than waist deep at the deepest points, but the current was fast, and it wasn't something he wanted to try to cross in failing light. No, he'd have to find a crossing, and to do that, he'd need to leave the others here. Jennifer with Rodney. Jennifer with a Wraith — no, Jennifer with Rodney in a Wraith's body. That was the only safe way to think of it, the only way he could bear to leave them. He drew his blaster before he could change his mind, held it out to Jennifer. "It's set on stun," he said. "I'm going to look for a place to cross. Shoot him if — if there's any trouble."

"Oh, for —" Rodney broke off, looking pinched and miserable.

"There won't be," Jennifer said, but she took the blaster. "Thank you."

"If there is," Ronon began, and stopped, knowing it was pointless. "Don't hesitate," he said at last, and turned away.

Rodney rested his head against the bole of the tree, and closed his eyes so that he didn't have to look at Jennifer turning Ronon's blaster over and over in her hands. Somehow this was not what he'd expected from a rescue. First of all, he'd assumed they'd pull it off neatly, and that he'd be back on Atlantis, safe in the infirmary while Jennifer and Carson figured out how to reverse the transformation. Though, given the way missions usually turned out, that was probably too much to expect. He'd lost track of how many plans had gone wildly wrong, starting the first day they walked through the gate. So being stranded on a strange planet three days from the Stargate was probably just more of the same. And he'd expected that the whole team would be there, John and Teyla, and probably a couple of squads of Marines — they'd brought in the heavy guns when Teyla was missing, after all. And, most of all, most painfully of all, for some reason he'd thought that if Jennifer had come to his rescue that somehow it might end up like the movies, Jennifer in his arms promising everything would be all right. He could almost smell the faint clean scent of her hair pressed against his lips, her skin giving way under his claws as he fed —

He jerked upright, appalled by the thought, by the pulsing hunger, closed his feeding hand painfully tight over the hand-mouth. Jennifer gave him a wary glance.

"How are you feeling?"

"Tired," Rodney answered. It was true enough, though not the whole truth. He felt — lost, alien in this body, caught up in instincts he still didn't completely understand. It wasn't that he couldn't control himself, of course he could; it was more that the lines were blurring, Rodney McKay and Quicksilver, Atlantis's cleverman and Death's scientist. Jennifer was still looking at him, and he made himself smile, hoping it was more than a baring of teeth. "Lightheaded. Which, you know, really isn't that surprising—"

"How long can a Wraith go without feeding?" Jennifer asked. Her voice was still remote, too controlled, and suddenly Rodney wanted nothing more than to smash that calm, to drive her into his arms.

"I have no idea. They made me think I was one of them, just the way we did with Michael, which, by the way, was an even more stunningly bad idea than we thought it was at the time, so they weren't exactly telling me things that I was supposed to already know. It all depends, whether you were well fed to start with, whether you have to heal, or if you're exerting yourself — maybe even your genetic heritage. There's no single factor! It's all completely individual."

"And you last fed — a month ago, you said?"

Rodney stopped, his anger too hard to sustain. "About then, yes. Look, Jennifer — I didn't feed myself." That seemed important, something she needed to believe. "They fed me, first Dust, and then Ember — they were the clevermen who took care of me, who — managed — me. I mean, I know it's — people are still dead, but —"

He stopped, unable to go on, and Jennifer gave him a wincing smile. "Oh, Rodney. I'm so sorry."

That was something, though he would have liked the touch of

her hand. "I'm all right," he said. "I can make it to the Stargate."

"You know," Jennifer said. "Um, I've been thinking."

"That's not a good thing," Rodney said. "Thinking, on a mission — that's usually a bad sign."

She smiled, but abstractedly, and worked Ronon's blaster into the front of her jacket. The butt protruded at an awkward angle, but it left her with both hands free. "Carson and I have been doing a lot of work toward getting you back to normal. We've made good progress, and in the process, we've learned a lot more about Wraith physiology. And about how Wraith feed, what actually happens —" She fiddled with the zipper of the jacket, holding the blaster more securely. "That's part of how we developed the retrovirus, you know? Well, that, and working with Todd. He was working on something like it already." She took a deep breath. "My point is, I think this version of the retrovirus works. It worked in simulation, and I think it will work now, so I think it's time —"

"Oh, no," Rodney said. "Absolutely not. No, no, no, that's a terrible idea —"

"The transformation is — in all our simulations, it's a strenuous process," Jennifer said. "It puts an enormous strain on the system. And you're hungry already."

"Hungry," Rodney said. "Not starving." He hoped it was true.

"You — we may need to test the virus," Jennifer said. Her voice was perfectly steady. "We need to get you back to Atlantis in as good shape as possible."

"No," Rodney said again. "Jennifer —" He stopped, shaking his head. "OK, hypothetically, I see your point. And, maybe, once we're back in Atlantis, if there are no other options, then, OK, yes, we could maybe have to revisit this. But not now. Not here. If anything goes wrong —"

"You are changing," Jennifer said softly. "You may need to feed while you still can."

"Ronon says we're only one more day from the Stargate," Rodney said. "One more day." He held up his feeding hand, felt the mouth throb with his heartbeat, with the pulse of his hunger. "I'm still — I haven't changed that much. Not enough to matter." The words were bitter on his tongue.

Her mouth thinned, but she nodded reluctantly. "OK," she said. "One more day."

CHAPTER FIVE

Proving Ground

"WHAT do you mean, you don't know where they are?" Sheppard's hands were balled into fists at his sides, and behind him Radek Zelenka was frowning deeply. Cadman just looked uncomfortable.

"I thought you had them!" Sam said incredulously. "You radioed from the hive ship. I thought you said that you had them."

"I said I didn't have them!" Sheppard replied. "I thought you had them. The plan was that you were supposed to beam them out!"

"I couldn't get in range," Sam said. "I was trying to, and I thought you said that you were on the hive ship with Ronon and Keller and Teyla." She looked around the gateroom. "And where is Teyla anyway?"

"With Todd," John said. "She needed to finish up some stuff. She'll be back tomorrow. What about Rodney?"

Sam took a deep breath. "I don't know. The hive ship blew. That's all I know. Our shields were down completely and we had to get out ahead of the shockwave. We barely got our 302s on board in time." Rodney was probably dead. But that had been the math all along — less and less likely he'd survive this. But Ronon and Dr. Keller… "If we'd stayed…"

Sheppard's face was grim. "If you'd stayed with no shields you'd have lost the ship and all aboard."

He knew the math too. The whole crew of the *Hammond*, a hundred and eight lives against three, Ronon, Keller, and Rodney. And yet. It was always easier from the other side, Sam thought, one of the team at risk rather than the ones who had to write them off. But she'd been written off again and again, and she was still here.

"They might have gotten out of there somehow," Sam said. "There were Wraith ships all over the place. If they'd stolen a ship…" She'd done it that way once with a Death Glider. Of course, they'd nearly run out of air in a decaying high Earth orbit before they were picked up.

Sheppard's face looked gray. "Ronon's good," he said. "He'd do something. We've got to get back and search the debris field."

"As soon as the *Hammond* has shields again, we'll do that," Sam said. She made her voice hard. "But I can't jump into a Wraith held system with no shields. Right now we're working around the clock on the repairs."

Sheppard swallowed. For a moment Sam thought he was going to protest, but he didn't. "I know," he said, and from Sheppard that was a concession of almost unimaginable trust. He knew she'd do her best.

And she would. "I'll go see how the repairs are coming," she said. "And put the priority on the shields. We may be able to get underway in a few hours." She looked at Zelenka. "Dr. Zelenka, are you able to assist?"

"Absolutely," Zelenka said, handing his weapon and tac vest off to Cadman. "I will help."

"I'll go tell Woolsey," Sheppard said, and strode off toward Woolsey's office. Cadman hovered uncertainly in his wake.

"You can stand down," Sam said to Cadman. "Go clean up and report to me for debriefing in two hours. I want to hear what happened, but it can wait until you've had a few minutes and I've checked on the repairs."

"Yes, ma'am," Cadman said, looking relieved.

Sam glanced down at Radek. "Let's go fix the *Hammond*." He cocked an eyebrow at her. "Again."

"Somehow it never stays fixed."

Laura Cadman, clean and smelling like Satsuma shower gel rather than hive ship, found Colonel Carter upside down in the crawl space on deck E. "You asked me to report in two hours, ma'am," she said to her colonel's rear end. Carter was lying over a strut working on something beneath it, occasionally bumping heads with Dr. Kusanagi, who was also upside down on the other side of the hole.

"Cadman?" Carter righted herself, shoving her bangs back from her eyes and looking at her watch. "Two hours already?"

"I can come back, ma'am," Laura said, though she hoped she didn't have to. She'd really like a good night's sleep in her own bed, but if Carter was busy she'd have to stay up and come back when it was convenient for her. Captains waited on colonels, not the other way around.

"No, it's fine." Carter got up. "Miko, are you good for a few minutes? I need to talk to Cadman."

"Of course," the upside down Dr. Kusanagi replied. "I will have this rewired before you return and then I will move on to section twelve."

"Ok." Carter dusted off her hands on the legs of her flight suit. "Let's go have a chat." She gave Laura a disconcertingly perky smile, the kind that made Laura wonder what bad news was supposed to follow it. "We can talk in my quarters."

Worse, Laura thought. A private conversation that wouldn't be overheard by anybody. She'd done ok on the hive ship, she thought. Well, except for not rescuing Dr. McKay who was probably dead, and managing to lose Ronon and Dr. Keller in the process. Yes, it had been Colonel Sheppard's mission, but if she'd done something brilliant maybe they wouldn't have gotten separated. Or maybe it was about the bears. She hadn't meant to drop the ceiling on Dr. Robinson! That was definitely her fault. Though what was she was supposed to have done with no ammunition left and a pile of polar bears charging her, besides use a grenade? Trip them? Somebody better at this would have thought of something.

Oh God, with the gate working two ways she'd be lucky if she wasn't on her way home tonight! She'd probably be back in Colorado Springs before breakfast. Washed out.

"Think we're going to wash out?" The other Marine was tall

and lanky, black hair barbered so ruthlessly he was almost bald, Lt. Aidan Ford, age twenty three, one year out of Georgia Tech. She was one year out of Florida State.

Two Marines, two Air Force. That was how it worked. Four lieutenants who had been given a shot at a program so top secret they hadn't even known what it was about when they'd reported to Colorado Springs. She'd been sitting with Ford on the plane, and they'd traded snacks and speculations. Peterson Air Force Base? Why did they need two Marines? NORAD?

"Maybe it's some kind of ceremonial duty," Ford hypothesized. "Like the White House guards or something."

"In Colorado Springs?" Laura looked out the window at the endless Great Plains. "Maybe they need some Marines for Air Force Academy kids to beat on." They were kids, of course, twenty-one, not twenty-three. It made all the difference in the world.

Ford shrugged. "Maybe it's good. Ever consider that?"

And it was. It was better than they'd ever dreamed.

They were going to other planets. They were going to other planets now, without a space ship, to battle real aliens that wanted to conquer Earth. They were going places they could never talk about, seeing things that maybe no human being had ever seen. If they didn't wash out of training.

"Sixty-five percent of you do," Colonel O'Neill said. He had steel gray hair and deeply graven lines on his face though he couldn't have been fifty yet, a ramrod straight bearing even in slightly oversized battle dress and a unit baseball cap with the SGC patch embroidered on it. Laura coveted that cap. Those were special perks, special unit designations for the ones who had made it. "Sixty-five percent of you walk out of here and go back to your normal lives," O'Neill said. "And let me tell you that you don't get any points for being the best and the brightest here. I've seen a lot of smart kids."

Standing at attention next to her in the second row of trainees, Ford frowned. He looked really worried. "Guess I don't have anything to worry about, " Cadman whispered. "Nobody said I was smart."

Ford's mouth twisted in a suppressed smile.

"You have something to say, Lt. Cadman?" O'Neill barked.

"No, sir!" Back straight, eyes front, nice and loud.

O'Neill shook his head. "Don't shout, Lieutenant. I'm standing right here." He went down the row. "And you may wish you'd washed out. Because if you do, your chances of being alive in two years are a lot greater. So if any of you want to voluntarily withdraw at this point, there will be no mark on your record."

Ford's brows twitched. As if, Laura thought. You're going to tell me everything I ever read about is real and think I'm going to walk away?

Afterwards, in the hummer on the way out to the first proving ground, Ford drew her and the two Air Force guys who they were assigned with into a huddle. "We've got to stick together," Ford said. "That's the key. Teamwork. They didn't assign us in four man units randomly. They think we've got complimentary skills. So we need to put our stuff on the table and work it out. What do you do, Cadman?"

"I blow things up," she said.

They spent the next three days screwing up a variety of scenarios. There was a hostage rescue in which they were supposed to save this guy named Quinn from aliens, only Ford shot him instead.

"Lieutenant Ford," O'Neill said with scathing sarcasm, "Your peerless brilliance has just resulted in the death of the man you came to save. Any questions?"

"No, sir!" Ford replied, eyes front.

"And stop shouting."

There was an ambush scenario in which the Jaffa, Teal'c, wiped the floor with all of them except Laura, who blew herself up. Accidentally.

"Cadman, that thing has a timer for a reason!" O'Neill barked. "You're dead. And so is the rest of your team. Once you set the timer, you have to actually leave." He walked off shaking his head.

Sitting on the ground outside together, Laura took a swig from her water bottle. "We're doomed," she said.

Ford looked at her sideways. "So you were assigned to be the pessimist in our group?"

"I'm just saying that we haven't won a single scenario," she began. A line of hummers was pulling into the proving ground, O'Neill walking toward them. In a second everything changed, a swift exchange of gunfire that left bodies on the ground, Laura crawling through the dust and scant cover, Ford at her side.

"Foothold situation," O'Neill gasped, one hand to the oozing blood at his side. "The SGC has been infiltrated by the Goa'uld. Get the hell out of here."

"No," Laura said, fumbling for a dressing. "We can't do that, sir. With all due respect."

It was just her and Ford in the end, dragging O'Neill back to the base so that he could show them how to rig the self destructs that would prevent the Goa'uld from bringing through an army, just her and Ford when they had to leave him unconscious while they went to blow the dialing computers to prevent the gate being used, while they set the charges that would kill the Goa'uld who had taken over the base, including its host, Major Carter. And just incidentally themselves.

Sorry, Nana. Sorry, Pops, Laura thought, crouching in the control room. She wished they would at least know what she'd done, but she supposed it never worked that way. Her eyes met Ford's.

"Do it," he said, and she pressed the firing button.

Nothing happened. And for a long moment her only thought was disappointment.

"Well done, Lieutenants," a voice said over the loudspeaker.

In a moment General Hammond came down the stairs from the conference room above, Major Carter with him grinning broadly. O'Neill followed, his uniform still soaked with stage blood.

"It was a test," Ford said flatly.

"Welcome to the SGC," Hammond said, and shook each of their hands. "Well done."

They'd done eight months of training, some of it in the field on alien worlds, and then Laura had gotten a plum slot on SG-12.

Ford had gotten the Atlantis expedition. She'd cried when he'd been listed MIA a year later. And six days later she'd been told she was going to Atlantis on Daedalus *to take his place.*

Laura followed Carter through the corridors of the Hammond, waited while she opened her door. Please don't let me wash out, she thought fervently. Not now!

Carter's quarters were spartan, her narrow bed neatly made with squared corners, a big framed picture of the *Hammond* bolted to the wall above it. She sat down in the only chair by the desk. "Tell me what happened on the hive ship," she said.

Laura took a deep breath. "We got pinned down. Dr. Zelenka hotwired one of the blast doors, which cut off the Wraith attacking us but also cut us off from Ronon and Dr. Keller. Colonel Sheppard told Ronon to go get Dr. McKay while we retrieved the ZPM…"

It was a long story, all the way through their precipitous departure and Todd's hive ship, all the way through the part where a Wraith diplomatic delegation had been told she was Carter's heir.

"That wasn't my idea, ma'am," she said swiftly. "That was Teyla, and so I followed along."

"Always the best thing to do with Teyla on the subject of anything Wraith." Carter looked vaguely amused, which was probably a good thing. Less like washing her out. "Cadman, have you ever wondered why I'm so hard on you?"

"No, ma'am." One proper answer to that.

"Because you have tremendous potential," Carter said quietly. "You think fast and you're brave and practical, but you don't lack imagination. I think you could go a long way. I want to give you the opportunity to test yourself and to have a variety of experiences. That's what will give you the confidence you need to stand in any company." The colonel looked at her keenly. "You're not a kid from Florida State. Right now, today, you're the best of the best. I'm not saying you need to be arrogant. But you've done two years in Atlantis and three with the SGC before and after that deployment. You're head and shoulders above half of the people here. It's time to put yourself out there. It's time to start making the calls and thinking of solutions rather than waiting for orders. It's time to believe in yourself the way others believe in you."

"Thank you, ma'am." Laura found herself inexplicably blinking. "I don't…" She stopped, squaring her shoulders. Carter was looking up at her from the chair, not nearly as scary as she'd seemed before, forty something and a little worn. Somehow that made it easier to blurt out the thing she was thinking. "I've never been very smart."

Carter was an academy graduate. At Laura's age she'd already had a PhD in astrophysics. There was no comparison.

"There are different kinds of smart," Carter said. "And not all of them come out of a book. Sometimes the most important ones don't come out of a book." She put her elbow on the desk, glancing at the pictures on the wall behind it and back to Laura. "The most important thing is teamwork. None of us have all the skills. Nobody is able to handle everything alone. We don't have Superman."

"And Superman has the Justice League," Laura said, and then felt like slapping herself.

Carter broke into a smile. "He does. Because it's all about complimentary skills. You're not a scientist. And you don't have to be. You don't have to be an anthropologist or an engineer or a physicist. You just have to be the best of what you are. Take the opportunities you're given and shine." She shook her head. "Believe me, Cadman. You're not short on anything. Colonel Sheppard would steal you back in a heartbeat. But I'm not letting him. I get you back as soon as Lorne is up and around!"

"Yes, ma'am," Laura said, which was about all she could manage.

"You're doing fine. You just need to develop the confidence to push when you need to." Carter stood up. "Now go get some rest. Stand down for twelve hours, if the universe will give us that much time."

Major Lorne limped into the control room, maneuvering around the consoles fairly skillfully on his crutches. Sheppard was just coming out of Woolsey's office, still in the dirty uniform he'd presumably worn on the last mission, two days beard on his chin. Asking "How did it go?" would be rubbing salt in the wound. Obviously they didn't have McKay, and everybody had already heard that Ronon and Keller were MIA. Well, maybe not everybody, but he'd already talked to Cadman, on her way out to the *Hammond* to report after getting a hot shower.

Lorne drew himself up, doing his best to look professional. "Sir, if I might have a word with you?"

Sheppard stopped. "Sure," he said, frowning.

Lorne bet he wanted to hit the showers too, so he made it brief. "Dr. Beckett says he'll take the cast off my leg this afternoon. I thought…"

Sheppard shook his head. "You know it's not going to work like that, right? He's going to put braces and things on it, and you'll have weeks of physical therapy. There's no way you're going straight back on full duty."

"Yes, sir, but…"

Sheppard clapped him on the shoulder. "It's a few more weeks," he said. "Light duty for a few more weeks. You don't want to screw that leg up permanently. Right now Cadman's covering for you on the team, and as soon as Beckett says you're ready, I'll give her back to Carter. But you know that's not going to be today."

"I know," Lorne said. And he did know. But he'd hoped anyhow.

CHAPTER SIX
Hunger

RONON made his way back along the cliff's edge at a trot, one eye on the declining sun. It was already brushing the tops of the trees, but if he hurried, there should be enough time to get McKay and Jennifer to the gap he'd found. And down, and across, and up again… But they could do it. He could do it. They wouldn't be able to get very far once they'd crossed the river, not in the waning daylight, and it would be a long march the next day — probably too long, reasonably calculated, to reach the Stargate, but it was better than he had feared.

McKay was still sitting under the tree where Ronon had left him, but Jennifer had made her way to the stream, was filling the water container. That was a good idea — she'd come a long way since he'd first met her, and he couldn't help an approving nod.

"Keller! McKay! I've found a way down."

Jennifer looked up quickly, and Ronon saw the relief in her face.

"That's wonderful," Rodney said, sourly, and hauled himself to his feet. "Is it far?"

"Nope," Ronon answered. Well, by some definitions, it wasn't. He eyed the stream warily. "Better cross further back from the edge."

It took almost two hours to reach the break in the cliff that Ronon had decided was the best place to cross. There was an easier slope another couple of kilometers further along, but here the opposite bank had given way, and it would be an easy scramble up to the other side. Rodney balked at the top, staring down at the rocks and the rushing water. The river came close under the cliff here, and water foamed around the heaped stones.

"You know, this doesn't look like all that great a place to climb down. One false step, and you've got a sprained ankle, or worse."

"You don't have to worry about that right now," Ronon said. He couldn't help grinning at the look McKay gave him, offended and appalled in equal measure. Jennifer smiled too, and began to pick her way carefully down the rocky slope. Ronon watched long enough to feel confident that she was going to be all right, then looked back at Rodney.

"Come on, McKay."

"This isn't —" Rodney's heel slipped as he spoke, and he flailed for balance. Ronon reached without thinking, caught him by the upper arm and held him steady. Rodney grabbed at his sleeve, and they stood frozen for an instant, Rodney's handmouth against the coarse fabric. It took all Ronon's willpower to hold still, not to shove him away. Rodney looked stricken, eyes wide and golden as if with shock.

"I'm good," he said, in a strangled voice, and Ronon nodded, not trusting himself to speak. He let go, and Rodney scrambled down the slope in Jennifer's wake. Ronon could feel himself shivering, as though he'd been out on Atlantis's balconies unprotected. He stiffened his shoulders and made himself follow.

Jennifer was waiting for them by the water's edge. She'd found a long stick — probably the trunk of a sapling — among the debris, and held it up at their approach. "I thought — you know how people rope together for things like this? Maybe this would work."

"Good idea," Ronon said. He was amazed that his voice sounded even close to normal. He tapped the wood against the nearest rock, decided it felt solid enough. "Let's go."

They edged into the river, holding tight to the sapling. Ronon took the lead, feeling for unseen potholes, the water rushing up past his knees, numbing his skin. Jennifer clung with determination to the middle of the pole, and Rodney brought up the rear, yelping as the cold hit him.

"Ow! Isn't this likely to give us all hypothermia or something?"

"Suck it up, McKay," Ronon said without thinking, and that felt strange and normal at the same time.

The riverbed was treacherous underfoot, stones the size of a man's fist shifting uneasily in the current. No potholes, though, at least not in this relatively smooth stretch, and, though the current was strong, it was at least steady. Then Jennifer cried out, and Ronon whipped around to see her falling, her hands peeling away from the wood. She was light enough that the current took her instantly, rolling her over in the waist-deep water, and it took all Ronon's control to keep from diving after her. Rodney lunged toward her, black coat billowing, ready to tangle them both. Ronon curbed the impulse to join him, instead kept tight hold of the stick, let the current take it toward them. Then Rodney had reached her, had her by the jacket and then her hand, and his other hand closed firmly on the sapling. Ronon braced himself to take their joined weight, held firm as first Rodney, then Jennifer dragged themselves to their feet and resumed their careful progress. On the far side, Jennifer collapsed onto the nearest rock, and Ronon gave her a worried look.

"Are you all right?"

She nodded, her wet hair straggling over her face, then grimaced and began to bind it back again.

"What happened?" Rodney asked.

"A stone turned under my foot," Jennifer answered. "I'm fine."

"Are you sure?" Rodney asked. "Because that's the way people break ankles, not that I'm staying I told you so —"

"I'm fine," Jennifer said again. "I'm a doctor, remember? I'm not hurt." She stood up as though to prove it, and Ronon, watching carefully, saw no sign of injury. She might be sore in the morning, but for now she'd be better off if she kept moving.

"OK," he said. "Let's go."

"Wait," Rodney said. "Just wait a minute." He was just as wet as Jennifer, the white hair plastered to his skull, water pooling at his feet. "We're both soaked through. We should stop, dry out — maybe we could even camp here overnight, there's lots of wood, and plenty of room."

"It's not safe to camp in a streambed," Ronon said.

"Oh, come on, you can't seriously be worried about flash floods,"

Rodney said. "The sky's completely clear."

"Ronon's right," Jennifer said. "We need to keep going."

Get as close to the Stargate as they could, Ronon thought. That effort would have taken it out of McKay. He said, "Not much further." He pointed downstream to a spot where dirt and gravel spread in a fan from the collapsed cliffside. "Just there. Once we get to the top, we'll see about going on."

Rodney was profoundly grateful for the steel rod he'd salvaged from the lifepod, leaned heavily on its support as he followed the others down the streambed. They were going back the way they'd come — not that it made any real difference, and there'd been no way to get down the cliff on that side anyway, but it was somehow even more discouraging to have to retrace their steps. At least Jennifer was all right. She was limping a little, but she was going to be fine. A night's rest was all she needed. He could feel his own body shifting, the bruises from where he'd banged against the rocks healing as he walked. It was a complete waste of energy, and he had no idea how to stop it, wondered if any Wraith did. Probably not — as far as he could tell, they had no compunctions about feeding, a Wraith in his situation would already have drained both the others, and be well on his way to the Stargate by now.

And that, of course, he couldn't do, no matter what Jennifer said about this retrovirus. It was too much of a risk, she'd already said the first version hadn't worked, and there was no way to test this one safely. And besides, she was Jennifer. He couldn't think of her like that, any more than he could think it of Ronon. Though perhaps just a taste — just a sip, just enough to keep him steady on his feet, to get him to the Stargate so that they could bring him back to Atlantis. Ronon was strong, nearly as strong as two men, he could spare just a little —

Rodney stopped, appalled by his own thoughts. This was Ronon, Ronon and Jennifer; he couldn't let his mind wander in those directions, not if he wanted to stay sane. No wonder

Michael had gone crazy, he thought. It was simply too confusing to keep track of who one was.

"Come on, McKay," Ronon called.

They were almost to the break in the cliff — Ronon was there, in fact, stopped with his feet in the red spill of dirt. Jennifer wasn't far behind him, her hair loosening as it dried.

"Hurry up," Ronon called again. Rodney bared teeth at him and dragged himself forward.

He wasn't sure quite how he got up the last few meters — offhand and stick bracing himself and Ronon shouting at him to keep going — but he knew when he reached the top that he wasn't going any further. He staggered a meter from the cliff's edge and sank down onto the grass, still warm from the sun. He saw Jennifer and Ronon exchange a look, and then Ronon said, gruffly, "OK. We stop for the night."

"We need to talk," Jennifer said, and Ronon shook his head, his hair flying.

"Nope."

He busied himself collecting stones and wood, built a perfect stack of branches, kindling tucked neatly into the gaps, as though the right, the correct method, would keep them from having to have this conversation. Rodney watched him, feeling some of the weakness ease as his body finished healing his bruises and he stopped exerting himself.

"Yes, we do," Jennifer said. "Rodney—" She stopped, bit her lip. "Rodney, you have to feed."

"I'm fine," he said, and knew nobody believed him.

"You're out of your mind," Ronon said. "He'll kill — whichever one of us he feeds on, and if he doesn't kill us, he'll take years out of our lives. You remember what Sheppard looked like —"

"I've taken the retrovirus," Jennifer said patiently. "I'm ninety percent — well, seventy-five percent certain this version will work. And assuming it does, Rodney can feed and nothing will happen to me."

"Except you'll suffer," Ronon said. "Horribly. And if you're wrong, you'll die."

"If I'm wrong," Jennifer said, "Rodney will return what he took. Just the way Todd did."

"Jennifer," Rodney said, and she turned to look at him. The setting sun was below the treeline now, so that she was backlit, her face in shadow, her loosened hair catching the last of the light. His heart ached to see her like that, and his hand throbbed in time to his heartbeat. "I don't — I told you, I never fed myself. I don't know if I could return your — life. I don't know if I know how."

"And if you don't feed now," Jennifer said, "you will die."

"You've been wrong before," Ronon said.

"Yes," she said. "Yes, I have, and you were right. I'm trying to learn from that. But — Ronon, look at him. Can you tell me he's not dying?"

"I'm fine," Rodney said, but couldn't muster anything approaching conviction.

There was a little silence, and then Ronon's face twisted, an expression that might have been laughter or tears. "Yeah. OK. If he wasn't bad, he wouldn't be trying to tell us he was all right." He paused. "But, Jennifer —"

"Don't," she said. "I have to. I swore an oath, to heal the sick, and this is Rodney, and I love him. There's no other choice."

"God!" Ronon shoved himself to his feet. "All right. But you can't — don't ask me to watch."

He stalked away between the trees, vanishing into the sun. Jennifer took a breath, came to sit beside Rodney, unzipping her jacket enough to bare the skin beneath. Rodney let her take his off hand, feeling for the pulse point.

"It's not good, is it," he said, quietly, and she shook her head.

"It's now or never, Rodney."

"Jennifer, I —" Rodney stopped. There were too many things to say, too many things he needed to remember, to mention, to be sure someone knew; a thousand thoughts, scattering like quicksilver, everything he would never see again. His feeding hand hurt, far worse than it had ever done before, and, looking down, he could see the handmouth gaping, see and feel the inner membrane pulsing, matching not the beat of his heart, but hers. Now or never, and no matter what he did, nothing would be right again — He lifted his feeding hand, saw her close her eyes.

"Oh, God," he whispered, and let that stand for all the prayers he didn't believe in: don't let me screw this up, please let the retrovirus work, please don't let me kill her… He placed his feeding hand against her skin and set his claws.

Her life jolted through him, sweet and clear and true, sharp and strong as the note of a horn. He pulled back, terrified that he would see her withered already, but her face was still young, even as it twisted in pain. Her fists were clenched, there were tears at the corners of her eyes, and still he fed, helpless, gulping life. He hadn't known how far gone he was, neither Dust nor Ember had let him truly starve, and a thousand clichés flooded through him. Rain in the desert, silence after the storm — no, it was life and reprieve, and he released her, newly afraid.

"Jennifer?"

She hadn't aged, her skin was smooth and her hair still golden, but her eyes were closed, and she sagged in his arms.

"Jennifer!" He touched her throat, trying to remember his first aid training — not that there was anything in it that would cover either being fed upon or some strange retroviral side effect — and gasped with relief to feel her pulse strong and steady under his touch. She shifted then, shrugging her shoulder the way she did sometimes in sleep, and he cradled her against his shoulder, smoothing her hair in helpless apology.

He didn't know how long they sat there. Long enough that the air turned thick and purple in the twilight, the sun a distant ember beyond the trees. Ronon emerged from the wood, his face set and cold. His eyes narrowed, seeing them, and Rodney said quickly, "She's sleeping. She's all right."

Ronon didn't answer, came to kneel beside them, touched Jennifer's neck with one big hand. He found her pulse and took a long breath like a drowning man, but pushed himself up and away to busy himself with the fire. He spitted the coney efficiently, set it to cook, all without looking at them again, and Rodney shifted uneasily, Jennifer a solid weight against his shoulder.

"Ronon, I—"

"If she dies," Ronon said, "I will kill you."

After a moment, Rodney dipped his head. "Fair enough."

Jennifer rolled over, wincing as her muscles protested the slightest movement. OK, that's the last time she would go out drinking with a linebacker, no matter how good-looking— She stopped, her surroundings registering fully. Not college, not a night of partying, not even residency, that permanent haze of misery and exhaustion. An unnamed planet, a shelter taken from a Wraith lifepod, and—Oh, God.

She sat up, flinching. She felt as though someone had beaten her with a stick, every muscle aching. OK, that wasn't pleasant, but it wasn't life-threatening, either. So, if she was remembering correctly— She looked down at her open jacket, saw the wound just below her clavicle, the puncture marks of the claws and the puffy scar where Rodney's handmouth had fixed to her skin. It had closed more than the claw marks, looked more like an inflamed scratch than anything serious. Automatically, she checked her pulse, tipped her head to the side as she counted: normal; her temperature felt grossly normal, too. In general, she felt as though she'd just gotten over the flu. Not pleasant, but survivable. The retrovirus worked.

She couldn't help smiling at that. It was an answer, maybe, and at the very least they could use it on Atlantis, so nobody else would have to go home withered to a mummy, a corpse that couldn't be explained. Assuming it worked for Rodney. She hadn't thought of that, that the retrovirus might taint her like the Hoffan drug, and she crawled to the front of the shelter, panic nipping at her. She could see Ronon's back, and the ring of stones that had held the fire— and Rodney, crouched like a black bird on the far side of the fire, head down but unharmed. She sagged in sheer relief, new pains running up her arms, and made herself crawl forward.

"Good morning."

Rodney's head snapped up, fear and relief and concern chasing themselves across his pale green skin. He was looking less thin, less starved, Jennifer noted; the feeding had worked for him as well. Ronon swiveled on his knees, held out his hand to steady her.

"Are you all right?"

"I'm—" She had been going to say fine, but decided to be more realistic. "I'm OK. I'm sore, though some of that could be from falling yesterday. And tired. But, yes, basically, I'm fine." She lifted her head, looked at Rodney. "And you?"

He gave his lopsided smile. "Much better. Thank you. I mean, I know that's not anything like adequate—but thanks."

She smiled back at him, a dazed kind of satisfaction filling her. She'd saved lives before, many times, but somehow this was different, came from a different place. This must be a bit like what it was like to give birth, to bring new life out of your own body, life from life— She shook that thought away, recognizing that she was too tired, too attenuated to make it coherent, and let herself drop awkwardly onto the dirt beside Ronon.

"You were out for more than twelve hours," he said. He didn't look directly at her, glanced sideways, then away. "Passed out first, I think, but then it was like normal sleep."

"That's good to know," Jennifer said. She closed her eyes, considering her body's needs. She didn't feel hungry—no, she was past hunger, at the point where she felt like a hollowed shell.

"Is there—" she began, and in the same moment, Ronon held out one of the last powerbars.

"You should eat."

She took it gratefully. "Yes. Thanks."

"There's still some coney, too," Ronon said, when she had finished, and she devoured that as well.

"All right," she said, and wiped her mouth on the back of her hand. The food had helped more than she had expected, and she hoped it wasn't just a quick burst of energy that would vanish as she moved. "It's — is it still morning?"

Ronon nodded. "We're about ten kilometers from the Stargate." His voice was even, without accusation, but Rodney flinched.

"Maybe we should have waited," he said. "I don't know, maybe you should have gone on and gotten help —"

"You were going to feed anyway," Ronon said.

"I didn't have a choice!" Rodney snapped. "Look, I don't want to be overly dramatic here, but I was dying —"

"Ten kilometers," Ronon said.

"I couldn't have walked ten steps!" Rodney said.

Jennifer looked from one to the other. "You know? This isn't helping."

Ronon looked away. "Sorry."

'I didn't —" Rodney stopped abruptly, flushing.

"We should get moving," Ronon said, and reached for the first of the sticks that held the shelter in place.

It didn't take long to break down the Wraith shelter and pack up their few belongings. Rodney insisted she take the rod he'd been using for a walking stick, and Jennifer accepted without demur. She was feeling better, certainly, but "better" was a long way from "well." Her muscles still ached, and she only hoped the tightness would ease once she got moving.

Walking was better and worse: better because she could put the soreness aside, fix her mind on something else — the number of steps she'd taken, the tree just at the edge of the clearing, the coney tracks in the soft ground — worse because every so often a random muscle would knot into a cramp, and she had to stop, breath hissing through her teeth, to try to work it out. The first time, and the second, she thought no one noticed, but the third time, when it caught her below the rib cage so that she had to lean hard on her walking stick, fist pressed to the spasming muscle, the others stopped, turned back with uneasy looks.

"It's just a cramp," she said, and Rodney hurried to her.

"Try stretching," he said. "Or putting weight on it. That is, if it's a foot or a leg, that should help."

"It's not," Jennifer said, through clenched teeth. It was hard to breathe; each movement of her ribs seemed to pull the knot tighter.

"Try — try leaning backward," Rodney said. "That should stretch it."

"Leave her alone," Ronon said. His unspoken accusation echoed between them: if you hadn't fed, none of this would be happening.

"Maybe you should go on to the Stargate," Rodney said. "You could get help, send it back. Then Jennifer wouldn't have to walk when she's — like this."

Ronon's scowl deepened, but his voice was deceptively mild. "I don't think that's a good idea."

"Oh, for — don't you trust me?" Rodney demanded.

"And why should I?" Ronon answered. "If it wasn't for you —"

Jennifer straightened, feeling the cramp ease at last. "How much farther to the gate?"

Rodney fumbled with the Wraith device, but it was Ronon who answered. "We're more than halfway. Maybe four kilometers."

"I can walk that," Jennifer said, and hoped she sounded more confident than she felt. "Look, right now, the important thing is to get Rodney into the infirmary. I know he looks fine now —"

"I am fine," Rodney said.

Jennifer ignored him. "But he has still missed several doses of the Wraith maintenance drug, and that means his transition is well underway. He needs to be where we can monitor him properly, and we need to get him there as soon as possible."

There was a little silence, and then Ronon nodded. "OK." He paused. "If you get worse, we'll revisit this."

"That's fair," Jennifer said, and made herself start moving again.

They had been walking for maybe another hour when the next wave of cramps hit. It was her feet this time, first the muscles of her toes, and then one in the arch of her other foot, so that she lost her balance and tumbled to the grass, trying to bend one set of toes back and the other forward. She'd never felt anything like this, a pain so sharp she couldn't catch her breath, and she knew there were tears on her cheeks.

Ronon knelt beside her. "What and where?"

She blinked, the tears on her lashes starring her vision. "My foot's cramped. Oh, God, so stupid!"

Someone drew her foot out from under her in spite of her gasp of pain, worked her boot off and wrapped her toes gently in his hand. Ronon? she thought, but, no, Ronon was beside her, so it had to be Rodney—And then he'd pressed her foot back, flexing it hard to stretch the knotting muscles. She gave a yelp of pain, but the worst was over, just the slow, bruised feeling of overworked flesh.

"I'm sorry," Rodney said. "Oh, God, I'm sorry. Ronon said it would help—"

"If you'd done it right—" Ronon said.

"I did exactly what you told me to do," Rodney said. "I do know how to follow directions, when they're given properly."

"Since when?" Ronon said. "McKay, you suck at taking orders."

"I do not!"

"Will you both shut up?" Jennifer glared up at them, grabbed sock and shoe from Rodney and began to put them on. "OK, that's—I've had it with both of you. I am sore and tired and my muscles keep trying to tie themselves in knots, and I don't need to hear any more of this. From either one of you." She knotted her bootlace, too tight, and half of it snapped in her hand. She flung it away, swearing, and hauled herself to her feet, leaning heavily on Rodney's walking stick. "If you can't say something useful, shut up. And stay shut up until we get back to Atlantis. I have so totally had enough!"

There was a ringing silence in the little grove. She took a step, and another, decided her feet would hold her, and started in the direction of the Stargate. She could hear the men following, silent except for the sounds of feet on leaves and grass, but she refused to look back.

The adrenaline had worn off long before they reached the Stargate, but she refused to slow down, refused to look at either one of them, just dragged herself to the console and pressed the symbols that dialed Atlantis's gate. The chevrons lit and locked, energy whooshing out and then stabilizing in the lovely blue of the event horizon, and she touched her radio.

"Atlantis, this is Dr. Keller."

There was a little silence, and then Banks' voice spoke in her ear. "Dr. Keller! Are you all right?"

"We're — essentially, we're fine," Jennifer said. "Ronon and I are here with Dr. McKay." There was an indistinct noise from the other end at that, and she closed her eyes, trying to think of everything she needed to say before she allowed herself to collapse. "Dr. McKay is himself — well, mentally, he's himself, he knows who he is, but he's still physically pretty Wraithy —" Oh, very professional. She stopped, took a breath to steady herself. "So he'll need to go into Dr. Beckett's care right away."

"Dr. Keller, this is Sheppard."

"Yes, Colonel." That sounded better.

"We were getting a little worried about you."

"It's a long story," Jennifer said.

"We had to get out in a lifepod," Ronon said. "And Keller —" He stopped, and she guessed he didn't want to say anything about the retrovirus in front of the entire gateroom. "We're good, Sheppard."

There was a brief pause, and then Sheppard said. "Open the iris. Welcome back, guys."

Jennifer took another deep breath, leaning hard on the metal rod as she climbed the three stairs to the open Stargate. Someone took her elbow as she stepped into the event horizon, and then there was the moment of disorientation and cold and she came out abruptly into the familiar gateroom. Sheppard was there, and Carson, bustling forward to check on Rodney — and Woolsey was there, leaning on the rail with a small, almost beatific smile creasing his face.

"Welcome home," Sheppard said, to Rodney, who gave an odd little smile.

"I'm a little — well, I guess I'm the new poster child for 'it's not easy being green.'"

"OK, this is seriously weird," one of the Marines said, under his breath, and Jennifer had to fight not to laugh out loud.

"Onto the gurney," Carson said, to Rodney. "I don't care if you can walk, you're riding until we've had a chance to do a full check up. Don't bother arguing, I'm not listening."

He turned to Jennifer. "And you don't look so good yourself. Were you hurt?"

Jennifer shook her head. "No. It's — the retrovirus. The new version works."

Carson's eyes widened in comprehension, and he gestured for one of the nurses. Jennifer felt her knees give way, and Carson caught her as she fell.

CHAPTER SEVEN

Home

SHEPPARD stood for a moment in the shadow of the gate, watching as the gurneys carried away Keller and Rodney—Rodney still talking, arguing with Carson even as the doors slit shut behind them. To have him back, alive and himself again, at least mentally: he'd begun to fear that was impossible, that he might have to do the unthinkable, and he knew the smile he gave Ronon was tinged with relief.

"Good job, buddy."

"Yeah." Ronon didn't smile back. He looked pretty beat himself, and John gave him an appraising glance.

"You OK?"

"Yeah," Ronon said again.

Woolsey was coming down the steps, Zelenka at his heels, and Carter appeared on the balcony.

"Colonel Sheppard," she called. "I heard—"

Sheppard couldn't repress his grin. "We got McKay back. In one pretty Wraithy piece, but in one piece. And very much himself again."

"Wonderful," Carter said.

"A very good job," Woolsey said, to Ronon. "Well done indeed."

"It is good to have him back," Zelenka said. "For so very many reasons."

Carter came to join them. "What's the prognosis?"

"You'll have to ask Carson for the details, how long it's going to take to get him back to normal physically," Sheppard said, "but it certainly sounds like Rodney."

"Doesn't look so much like him," Ronon said. "But, yeah, it sounds like him."

"That's really good news," Carter said.

Sheppard looked at Ronon. He was looking — odd. More than merely tired and hungry and worried — he looked like he had when he'd first come to Atlantis, lines of stress making him look older than his years. "Ronon," Sheppard said, and the Satedan's eyes flicked toward him, and then away. Not good, Sheppard thought, and laid a carefully casual hand on the other man's shoulder. He could feel the tension even in that touch, said, "Come on. We need to debrief."

Carter gave him a quick look at that, and Sheppard risked a fractional shake of his head. Her eyes widened just a little, and she looked away.

"What?" Ronon said.

"Debrief," Sheppard said again. "Let's go."

He hadn't had much of a plan to start with, but by the time they'd reached the doors, he'd figured out the place he was least likely to be bothered. His office was in its usual state of disarray, but the city did its best to make it inviting, adjusting the lights and the heat and sliding back the shutter that closed the single long, narrow window. Outside, the sun was shining, striking sparks from the ice, and a stiff wind blew gusts of new powder sparkling past the window. Some of the stiffness eased from Ronon's face, seeing that, and Sheppard swept papers from the spare chair.

"Sit."

Ronon glanced at him then, but did as he was told. Sheppard reached into the drawer of his desk, pulled out the jar of moonshine that had found its way to him through unofficial channels. After a longer search, he found a clean-looking mug and poured a stiff shot, slid it across the desk toward the Satedan.

Ronon took it warily, sniffed at it. "Aren't you drinking?"

Sheppard reached into the little portable refrigerator, pulled out a beer and held it up. "You can have a beer if you'd rather, but I thought you liked this stuff."

Ronon took a sip. "It's — smooth."

"Yeah." Sheppard twisted off the cap of his beer. It was earlier in the afternoon than he would have chosen, but he was pretty sure Ronon didn't need to drink alone. "You want to tell me what happened?"

Ronon shrugged. "We couldn't get out, so we found a life-pod, ejected in that. McKay got us down safely, and we walked to the Stargate."

Sheppard lifted his beer as much in salute to the masterful understatement as to the actual actions. "Does that mean McKay had started to remember who he was?"

"Yeah." Ronon nodded. "So I guess that whole Gaffen thing wasn't a trap."

Sheppard had guessed as much, but the confirmation still made a little warmth spread through him.

"That's —". Ronon stopped, made himself go on. "That's part of the problem. Was part of the problem, and still is. It's McKay, or he thinks he's McKay, but physically he's still a Wraith."

"Beckett says that will wear off," Sheppard said. "That he'll be back to normal eventually."

"Sheppard. He's been a Wraith. You don't get to be 'normal' after that."

"Hey." Sheppard glared. "This is Rodney we're talking about."

"Sheppard, he —" Ronon took another swallow of the moonshine. "He fed. On Jennifer."

Sheppard froze, the bottle halfway to his lips. "She was fine."

"She'd taken that retrovirus of hers," Ronon said. "A new version. Well, it worked. And McKay fed."

Sheppard set his beer down untasted. "Why?"

Ronon's face twisted. "He was starving. She said he wouldn't make it, wouldn't survive the change if he didn't. I tried to talk them out of it, but — she wouldn't listen. And I couldn't figure out another way."

"Ronon," Sheppard said, but the words were tumbling out of him.

"I didn't want to leave him with her — I didn't know if the virus had worked, and I didn't know, McKay didn't know, if he could restore her if it didn't work, so I didn't want to try to go for help. Maybe I should have — if I had, maybe he wouldn't, she wouldn't have —" He shuddered. "I couldn't watch. I know, you know, what it feels like, I couldn't see Jennifer go through that —"

And then he stopped, shaking his head, his face open and vulnerable for the first time since Sheppard had known him. Oh, boy, Sheppard thought. This wasn't his strong point at the best of times, and Ronon — well, it was bad enough for him to see Rodney as a Wraith, to know that he must have fed, but to know that his teammate — his friend — had fed on the woman they both loved… No, that was more than anybody should have to deal with. He took a sip of his beer, buying time. "She volunteered, right?" he ventured.

"Keller?" Ronon blinked.

"Yeah."

Ronon shrugged. "So?"

"She volunteered, and you tried to talk her out of it," Sheppard said. "And I bet Rodney did, too. So it was her choice."

"I was in charge."

"She's the doctor." Sheppard made his voice hard. "This was her call. She's the one who knew whether or not McKay could make it to the gate, she's the one who invented this damn retrovirus. It was her call, buddy. Not yours."

"If you'd been there —"

"I wouldn't have liked it much either, no," Sheppard interrupted. "And I'd've tried to stop her, and she'd still have done it, and it still would have been her call." He stopped, fixed Ronon with a stare, willing him to believe. "And she was right."

Some of the tension had eased from Ronon's face. He took another sip of the moonshine, grimaced as though he was tasting it for the first time. "Would you feed on the woman you love? I mean, that's just — not right."

Sheppard paused. It was a fair question, and this didn't seem to be the time to explain about vampires or the dreams he had where Steelflower was a true Wraith queen. But maybe that was part of the key, even if it did take them onto very dangerous ground. "I don't think—look, if it was Teyla, if she needed to feed on me." He shrugged, the words still terrifying. "She can have my life anytime. And so could you."

Emotions chased themselves across Ronon's face, almost too fast to read, visceral fear, disgust, sympathy, and he nodded slowly. "OK. I—OK."

Sheppard reached for the jar of moonshine, and Ronon nodded, held out his mug. "Look," Sheppard said, pouring. "We got McKay back. We got him back alive and sane. That's a win in anyone's book."

Ronon lifted his mug in answer, and drank deep.

Rodney hunched himself further up in the awkward hospital bed, the knobs of his spine digging into the mattress. The laptop slid down his upthrust knees, and he caught it with his off hand, hissing softly in frustration. And he was going to have to stop doing that. It only made people look oddly at him, made them see the Wraith, not him.

He glared at the screen, happy to turn his anger outward. He needed a real computer, one that was networked, that had all the data he needed to get back up to speed. He needed to know more about how this mechanical iris worked—Zelenka hadn't done a bad job with it, but he suspected there were improvements they could make. And there he stopped again, unwilling to follow that thought to the end. He had this computer because he had been Quicksilver, because he'd proved he couldn't be trusted. Because he'd killed.

He set the laptop aside, squirming against the pillows. He needed at least a couple more, could feel the bed frame through the layers of padding, and for a disorienting moment he was almost homesick for the hive, for his niche shaped to his body. He grimaced at that, made himself look around. At least he was getting used to the level of light. It no longer made him squint, or made his eyes water: a sign he was starting to change back, or so he hoped.

At the far end of the long room, blue curtains were drawn

around a single bed. Jennifer lay there, resting, Carson had said, though whether she was drugged or sleeping naturally Rodney had not been able to bring himself to ask. He closed his eyes, remembering the feeling of her life flowing into him, clear and strong without stint. Ember would have had the words for it, that quality of sustenance — Quicksilver had had them, but Rodney wouldn't look. Jennifer had saved his life, and he was grateful, as grateful as he'd been after the brain parasite. It wasn't that much different, after all.

He could make out movement behind the curtain, a shift of light more than a shadow, and then Carson slipped between them, pulling them tight behind him.

"How are you feeling?" he asked, as he came down the length of the room.

"Fine," Rodney said. God, it was good to see Carson, someone who knew him, who recognized him as Rodney McKay. "Except I could use some more pillows."

"All right," Carson said, and swept one off the neighboring bed. "Lean forward."

Rodney did as he was told, one hand on the laptop to keep it from falling. He felt the thin fabric of the johnny open over his spine, felt Carson looking at the ridges even as he set the pillow in place. "What?"

"It looks as though the — protuberances — are shrinking," Carson answered. "I want to document the progress."

Rodney rested his arms on his knees, the points of the calipers cold on his skin. Carson made a note on his tablet, then nodded.

"Definitely progress. They've gone down about three centimeters since you were brought in." He tucked the tablet under his arm as Rodney settled himself back against the pillows, squirming a little to find the most comfortable spot. "No aches, pains, any other symptoms I should know about?"

Rodney shook his head. "Well, I'm tired all the time, which I assume is part of this whole transition thing. And I'm — my gut keeps twinging, you know, pains and gurgles."

"That's encouraging," Carson said, with a quick smile. "Not pleasant, I admit, but that should mean that your digestion is starting to work again. Are you hungry at all?"

He'd fed too recently for that. Rodney winced, shook his head hard. "No. No, not at all. Just tired. A lot tireder than I'd expect to be, really, unless you're drugging me—" That had slipped out without his having meant to say it, but now that it was said, he watched Carson for any reaction. It would make sense to drug him, to keep him from being able to betray them again—to keep him from feeding, if they had to—

Carson shook his head. "No, Rodney, I'm not drugging you. In fact, I'm trying to avoid giving you anything more than the serum we used to support Michael in his transition. I don't want to risk unpredictable reactions as your system continues to revert to human norms."

Michael. Lastlight. It was no comfort to think of him, and Rodney bared teeth. Carson blinked, visibly startled, and Rodney shook his head. "No, no, sorry. How's—how is Jennifer?"

Carson's face softened. "She's a brave girl, brave and smart. She'll be fine as soon as she's had a chance to rest." He glanced down at his tablet. "In fact, the retrovirus—unless there are further side effects that aren't yet evident, it seems to work as planned. She's lost some weight, which she didn't have to lose, and her blood pressure was high—it's falling now—and there are some issues with electrolyte balance that I'm keeping an eye on, but, in the main, it works. I'm—well, I'm hugely relieved, for one thing, and cautiously optimistic. This may actually be a good thing."

"Yes," Rodney said, but couldn't project the confidence he meant. He could still feel his own terror, his hunger, knowing that he would die if he didn't feed, and would kill Jennifer if he did. The image was too clear, fueled by all the dead men he'd seen since he'd come to Atlantis, by the withered husks dragged from the feeding cells by the drones. It so easily could have been Jennifer lying like a mummy in his arms, only her hair still young and golden, spilling over his arms.

The infirmary door opened with a soft sound, and he looked up, desperate for any interruption. Lorne stood in the doorway, leaning on a tripod cane, a rather sheepish look on his face. "Got a minute, doc?" He stopped abruptly. "Oh. Hi, Dr. McKay."

"Major," Rodney said.

"What have you done now?" Carson asked, and waved Lorne to the next bed.

"It's, um." Lorne stopped. "I know you warned me about over-doing it, and I didn't think I did, but — it's hurting pretty good right now."

"Let me take a look," Carson said.

Rodney looked away politely, but not before he'd seen Carson unfasten the straps of a leg brace. He could see a raw scar, too, a couple of them, pink against Lorne's skin. Nobody ever said duty on Atlantis was easy.

"Well, Major," Carson said, "I won't say I told you so because it won't do any good, but I did. And what you need to do is stay off your feet for twelve hours."

"I'm not sure I can do that," Lorne said.

"If you don't," Carson said, "you're going to be back on crutches. I guarantee you that. Look, I'm going to give you something that will help the pain and decrease the inflammation, but it won't help if you don't rest that leg."

Lorne gave a reluctant nod. "OK, doc. I'll do my best."

"You'll do better," Carson said, and turned away to rummage in one of the cabinets.

Rodney said, "What happened?"

Lorne gave him a strange look. "Um. Right. It happened when you — when the Wraith attacked through the gate, and got away in a jumper. I tried to go after them, and got wrecked. Busted my leg pretty good."

"Oh," Rodney said. He remembered that, all right, or Quicksilver did, the flight with the ZPM, the last second decision to try a jumper and the savage pleasure when he'd realized the ship answered to him. He vaguely remembered that there had been pursuit, but didn't remember wrecking a jumper. "I — look, I — I'm sorry."

Lorne shrugged, looking just as uncomfortable as Rodney felt. "It's OK. Things happen."

Yes, but not like this. Rodney swallowed the words as Carson returned with a bottle and instructions, and Lorne worked himself upright, leaning on the cane while Carson lectured him again about needing to rest the leg. Lorne kept nodding, and limped at last toward the door. I did that, Rodney thought. It's my fault — a man I would consider a friend is badly hurt, and people are dead because of me. Carson gave him a smile and a nod, and settled himself at his computer to enter his evening's notes. Rodney forced a smile in answer, and reached for his laptop again. He'd fix it. Somehow.

Lorne made it about halfway down the corridor toward the transport chamber before his leg spasmed again. There was nothing much he could do except wait it out; he braced himself against the wall, cane in his opposite hand pressed hard against the floor, and made himself breathe. He would take the pills, he needed to take them, but if he didn't wait until he got back to his quarters, he was going to fall over. And that would be — well, at best it would be undignified, and at worst it would break something else, and all in all, he'd just rather it didn't happen. Dr. Beckett would have words for him if it did.

It was weird having McKay back — no, he thought, be honest. It's weird having him back as a Wraith. Weird and not very pleasant: not only did it remind everyone that McKay had been turned, it reminded Lorne of the experiment with Michael, and that had been a very bad choice. He hadn't been involved in it, not directly, but he had met "Michael Kenmore," followed orders and treated him as human, as part of the expedition, and he still felt guilty about that one. He wondered if there was a Wraith somewhere who was having the same worries about

McKay, and shoved that thought aside as way too disorienting. The pain in his leg was starting to ease. Now the trick was to get moving again before anyone saw him and reported him unfit for duty.

Light spilled from an open door ahead of him: one of the lounges generally used by enlisted personnel. Somebody had started calling it "Vegas" because they said the stained glass looked sort of like a casino carpet. The comparison still made Lorne twitch, but he knew better than to say anything. He could hear voices, loud and cheerful — one of the new Marines, he thought, dredged the name out of the depths of his memory. Hernandez.

"When I was in Afghanistan, that whole sheep's-eyeballs-are-a-delicacy thing, that was top of the weird-o-meter. Now? I don't think that would even register."

There was a burst of laughter, all male.

"Still," someone else said, "this has got to be about the weird-est, right?"

There was a confused noise of scuffling and curses, a muffled 'ow', and another voice said, "Get a clue, dude."

"He's got a point, though," Hernandez said. "I mean, this thing with Dr. McKay, it's pretty weird."

"We've had weirder," somebody said, but he didn't sound all that certain.

"Yeah? Like what?"

"Like, I don't know —"

There was a rather sober silence, and Hernandez said, "So what are they going to do with McKay now that they've got him? Ship him back to the SGC?"

"No way." Lorne recognized that voice: Elton Sandoval, an Air Force sergeant who'd been with the expedition from the beginning. "That's Dr. McKay you're talking about."

"But he attacked —"

"He's been —"

"He was brainwashed," Sandoval declared, his voice riding

over the others. "He's all right. As soon as he gets back to normal, he'll be fine."

"Derek was killed," someone protested. "Come on, Sarge, they're going to let him get away with that?"

"It wasn't him," Sandoval insisted.

"It was."

"He wasn't in his right mind," Sandoval said. "Give me a break, Ray."

That was as much as Lorne could afford to hear. He straightened, deliberately letting his cane fall hard against the floor. It was definitely more than he'd wanted to hear, and he groaned softly at the thought of the conversation he was going to have to have with Sheppard. He took a careful step, leaning hard on the cane, and down the hall someone closed the door to Vegas. He limped past it, let himself into the transporter. The guys had one thing right, though. This was a long way off the weird-o-meter.

CHAPTER EIGHT

Suspicion

DR. WILLIAM Lynn was bent over the far end terminal in the upper bank in the control room, a neglected travel mug at his elbow, as he madly typed on his laptop, his eyes never leaving the screen of the Ancient terminal. Radek knew that rapt expression. His mouth tightened.

"What are you doing?" he asked, coming to stand behind him.

"I'm working on the Ancient database," William said, not lifting his eyes from the screen. "Some absolutely fascinating stuff here. The parts you've sent to Earth comprise only…"

"About 12% of the whole, yes. I know that." Radek bent forward. "But what are you working on that is a priority to have one of the control room terminals?"

"I need the full searchable database," William said. "Not just downloaded bits and clunky interfaces. I can perfectly well work in Ancient, and I'm doing so."

"Yes, but what are you working on?" Radek asked again. "I have the watch and I am the Chief of Sciences. If you are using the control room terminals, you should ask me first and tell me what you are doing."

William stopped and looked at him sideways. "Throwing your weight around?"

"I am asking you to courteously inform me in the same way you would anyone else."

William sighed. "I'm trying to find out more about the Ancient installation we found on the island, the one we think was a prison."

"I thought this planet was not mentioned in the database," Radek said.

"It's not. It's not listed in the inhabitable worlds, in the dialing addresses, survey and general geographic reports. Just like thousands of other worlds that don't support human life." William raised one finger, and Radek knew that expression, the one of haring off on a trail that no one else could possibly care about. "But I have found something interesting! Nine hundred years before Atlantis was evacuated, there was a disciplinary hearing conducted, investigating the decisions of a prison administrator who managed to lose 108 high security prisoners in a mass jail break."

Radek frowned. "What happened to him?"

"Nothing. He was dead. He'd been killed in the prison break."

Radek snorted. "And this is important why? I am terribly sorry some poor slob was killed in a prison break, what, eleven thousand years ago? But this is a priority for computer usage?"

"It's about this world," William said, his fingers flying over the screen, paging through the data in Ancient. "I have a feeling."

"You have a feeling." His voice was flat.

"I have a feeling." William lifted his eyes again. "Look, anybody can go through data and any reasonably competent individual can walk around taking pictures of ruins. Dr. Jackson hired me for the SGC because I can put pieces together, make the leaps of intuition. Remember the work I did on Hadrian's Wall?"

"I do."

"There are pieces," William said. "I can't quite see how they fit yet, like pot sherds that are still missing. But there are pieces and they fit together. They make something." His eyes met Radek's. "This is what I do. I don't tell you how to do your work."

"You do not," Radek said. He took a deep breath. What harm could it do, really? No one else was clamoring for the terminal. "A prison break eleven thousand years ago?"

"Less a century," William said. "It's a fascinating proceeding. Really interesting to see the examination of witnesses and the presentation of data. I'm almost certain that the prison was the one here. It was clearly somewhere very cold. And at that time this world could have had a Stargate." He scrolled the data again. "This is the account from one of the surviving guards.

For some reason one of the officers let a woman out and she let out the others. It's very murky what happened. There was a report of a fire, that the base was filling up with smoke and the ventilation systems had failed, but the investigation found no evidence that there was a fire at all, despite several of the survivors insisting there was. The fire suppression systems were manually engaged, but the automatics didn't cut in. Very strange. Nearly all of the garrison were killed. Those who weren't were the ones who rallied in the hangar bay control room. The prisoners managed to get to the DHD and dial out. They escaped through the Stargate."

Radek frowned at the screen. One line of symbols stood out amid the Ancient writing. "That is a gate address," he said.

William nodded. "That's the address they dialed out to. Of course by the time of the hearing the Ancients had sent law enforcement to that address to recapture them, but they were long gone." He looked up at Radek again. "I've never seen this one before."

"I have," Radek said. "That is the first address we dialed when we came to Atlantis. That is the address for Athos."

"Teyla's homeworld?"

"Interesting," Radek said.

"Really interesting," William said. "Thank you. That gives me the next piece. Now I need to look at law enforcement activities on Athos nine centuries before the fall of Atlantis."

Radek was about to ask him why, but stopped. There was no harm in pursuing it, no need to be petty. "You might also want to talk to Teyla when she returns," he said.

"Yes, of course." William was already calling up a new search, no doubt hunting through millions of pieces of irrelevant data for law enforcement on an obscure colony eleven thousand years ago, like a dog on a scent, implacable and undaunted.

Radek shook his head. He thought he could see where this was going. "You know Colonel Sheppard is not going to let you take another team back to the island unless you can give him more than that. William, we are stretched far too thin to pursue this on a whim."

William looked up. "It's not a whim. There's something there. I know it. I know it's important. Help me, please."

Radek sighed. "Is there a chance there is a ZPM there?"

"I don't know." William gave him an honest answer, at least. "There certainly was. At the time of the prison break this installation was on a standard layout, and that meant that it was powered by a ZPM. But the prison was subsequently closed and it appeared when we were in there that most of the equipment was taken. But it was standard procedure to leave the ZPM in place on these sorts of bases so that they could be reopened if necessary. That was certainly the case with Proklarush Teonas, and that base had been completely abandoned a long time ago."

"But there was a ZPM here?" Radek asked.

"Once, yes." William nodded. "But whether or not it's still there…"

"Or still active," Radek mused. "Many of the ZPMs we've found have been completely depleted, or nearly so."

"Still, even a very small amount of power, like the one we found on Sateda…"

"…was incredibly helpful. Yes, I know." Radek met William's eyes. "Very well. I will talk to Colonel Sheppard. Perhaps Colonel Carter would be willing to beam a team in so that we do not need the engineers and you can look for a ZPM. Will that be satisfactory?"

"Very much so," William said. "Radek…"

"It is worth a try," Radek said, walking off toward the office.

"Colonel Sheppard to the gateroom." John had just walked into his office, ready to sit down and attack the mound of paperwork that had built up.

He keyed his radio open to reply. "What's up, Banks?"

"Teyla's back."

Which meant he needed to know what had happened with Todd. He turned around and headed back out again, the office lights obligingly going out behind him.

Teyla was in Woolsey's office, but Woolsey beckoned him in as soon as he saw him and he slipped in without knocking.

"I think for his part Guide is sincere," Teyla was saying. "But I cannot vouch for every man on his ship. Queen Death is very charismatic, and while I do not think that any of them suspect that I am not who they believe, that might not be sufficient if some of them were offered rewards from Death."

Woolsey nodded gravely. "You're saying some of Guide's men might be bought."

"It is possible," Teyla said. "I do not think that any of them suspect that Steelflower is not what she appears, but it did stretch their loyalty somewhat to treat with the Lanteans. None of them would openly oppose their Queen and Consort, but there were certainly those who were not happy. Whether or not that dissatisfaction is anything besides unspoken disagreement, I cannot say. Were I to return, I think…"

"You can't do that right now." John felt like he had to get out in front of this one before Teyla had another reason to head back to the hive. "You haven't had solid food in a month, and your blood pressure is all over the place. You know Carson isn't going to let you out of here again."

"Dr. Keller," Teyla began, turning yellow eyes on him, her black clad form still incongruous in Woolsey's office chairs.

"Dr. Keller is off duty," Woolsey said. "She's in the infirmary herself."

Teyla's brows knit. "Was she injured?"

"Rodney fed on her," John said. Probably best to get that out in the open. "The retrovirus worked as far as it goes, and Carson says she'll be ok. But right now she's resting."

Teyla took a quick breath, and then let it out more slowly, her hands opening against the silk of her dress very deliberately. "It worked."

"It worked," John said. She looked worried. "Really. And Rodney's back and he's going to be ok."

"Then this is cause for joy," Teyla said, and there was no mistaking the catch in her voice.

"They're going to be ok. It's just a rough patch," John said.

Woolsey shifted, coming around his desk to perch on the edge. "I'm afraid I have to agree with Colonel Sheppard about returning to the hive, Teyla. It's possible that you may need to do this again in the future, if you are willing to, but for the moment I don't see that the benefits outweigh the possible cost to your health. You can't keep an eye on every man, even if you were there. So let's leave Guide to do what he does. And you can stand down and take care of yourself." Woolsey smiled, and it truly looked genuine and fond. "You've done a remarkable thing."

"Thank you, Mr. Woolsey," Teyla said.

"I'll put this intelligence to good use," Woolsey said. "Never fear."

Teyla paused in the hall outside the infirmary, John at her heels. Part of her, the part that was Steelflower, expected him there, as of right; the part of her that was Teyla wanted him beside her, so that she could lean on him, just for this little moment, until the buzz of the hive faded from her mind. But he had much to do — good things, but good news still required managing, and Rodney's rescue required more than most — and she smiled and pushed him lightly back as he stopped beside her. She also, if she was honest with herself, did not so much want him to see her in the first stages of transition, the days of soreness and recovery. Or, rather, more honest still, she wanted him to see her again when it was well begun, and she could take pleasure in his company.

"I'd like to come with you," he said, as though he'd read her thoughts, and she smiled, her hand still on his arm.

"I know you are needed," she said. "And it is not that I do not need you, too, John, but—"

"You don't need me hovering now," John said.

"And you have other obligations," Teyla said. "But — come

and hover later?"

He touched her shoulder. "Definitely."

He turned away, and she lifted her hand to the infirmary door. Strangely, the echoes of Wraith seemed louder here. The door slid back, admitting her to the familiar lights and faint clean smell and the sudden startled leap of a cleverman's mind. She drew herself up, becoming Steelflower, even though there was no possibility of Wraith here, reaching out to identify and control the stranger. A mind of glittering thoughts, a thousand skittering balls of mercury, fleeing her touch. And Rodney McKay knelt on the infirmary floor, his head bent to her feet.

"Oh, Rodney," she said aloud, and in spite of herself echoed his name. *Quicksilver.*

Steelflower. He lifted his head, his eyes, exhausted, red-rimmed, human, meeting hers. "Teyla?"

He had seen her before in this guise, the first time she had worn it, but it had not been like this — could not have been, how could it, when he had never had the Gift? She could see too much in that instant, feel too clearly the collision of emotions. Bewilderment — he had been drowsing, woke to find a queen before him — the pain, physical and emotional, of the transition, the sheer relief at seeing her. And not just at seeing her, Teyla, but at seeing Steelflower, knowing himself safe within a queen's command. There was even a part of him still thinking, calculating, pieces falling into place — Guide's plots, suddenly rearranged, made to make new and deeper sense, and she could not help but share that flicker of amusement.

It is ever so with Guide.

But that did him no service. If anyone else saw him like this, it would be worse than humiliation. Bad enough that she should know, but she understood, as no other would; if another saw — Rodney might forgive, but he could not forget, and she stooped, taking him by the shoulders to ease him to his feet. He came upright under her hands, breathing hard.

"Gently, Rodney," she said aloud. "You should not be out of bed."

"No, he shouldn't be." Carson came bustling out from the office, and Teyla allowed herself a sigh of relief that she had gotten Rodney to his feet in time. "What were you thinking?"

"I —" Rodney stopped, for once struck silent, and Teyla stepped smoothly into the gap.

"I believe he wanted water — is that not right, Rodney? And overestimated his strength."

"Yes," Rodney said. His mind clung to hers like a man drowning clings to any floating branch. She eased his hold as gently as she could, and together she and Carson maneuvered him back onto the bed. They got him settled again, and she laid her hand on his forehead, feeling the skin hot and damp.

"He should sleep," she said, to Carson, and the doctor nodded.

"Aye, he should, but I'm reluctant to give him a sedative. His body chemistry is already so far out of balance that I don't like to risk it."

"That is reasonable," Teyla said. She could do better anyway, one last, kindly use for her disguise before she was finally able to lay it aside. *Sleep,* she whispered, mind to mind, skin to skin, and obediently Rodney's eyes closed, his breath easing.

"I didn't expect you quite so soon," Carson said. "But I expect you're ready to have all this undone." He waved his hand, the gesture encompassing her clothes, her skin, the layers of surgery and artifice, and Teyla could not help a laugh.

"You cannot know how ready I am," she began, and stopped, smiling now for her own folly. She would not be rid of Steelflower, not ever, but she made herself meet Carson's eyes with her most human smile. "When can we begin?"

"The small things now," Carson answered, and led her toward a bay. He pulled the curtains closed for her to undress, talking about IV drips and medications, surgery tomorrow when her blood pressure had stabilized. Teyla closed her eyes for a moment, unaccountably close to tears. She was home, and Rodney was home; they were all together on Atlantis now, all the team. That would be enough for now.

It had been a fairly spectacularly disappointing day, despite Dr. Lynn's brief attempt to find something positive to say about his researches. Radek had shut him down pretty quickly, and John wondered if he was going to have to say something to Radek about it. Managing the scientists really wasn't his job, though, and Lynn hadn't seemed particularly bothered, so maybe he could leave it alone. Outside the gateroom window, the clouds were low, darkening to purple in the fading light. It wasn't snowing yet, but he was willing to bet that it would be soon.

At least there didn't seem to be anything that required his immediate attention, which meant that he could slip down to the infirmary and check on Teyla and Rodney before he hit the mess hall. And the paperwork that was still waiting in his office, though he thought he should probably tackle that in the morning when he was fresh. And he still had almost fifty laps of last year's season-ender at Homestead backed up on DVD, not that he didn't already know who won. Between that and War and Peace, his evening was almost full.

The infirmary was warm and bright — and crowded, Carson and several of his assistants busy directing traffic, triaging a group of maybe a dozen scientists and technicians. One of them, a pretty red-head, was holding a towel to her eyes, and from the noise and commotion it seemed as though something had blown up in their faces. At the far end of the room, the curtains were drawn closed around Teyla's bed; Rodney's curtains were open, and he was sitting hunched against the pillows, laptop in hand, glaring at the injured scientists as though he wanted to lecture them on safety or, more likely, on the fundamental pointlessness of their plan. The back of his johnny was open over the ridged Wraith spine, and somehow seeing that was more disconcerting than all the other physical changes. Maybe it was because the only other times he'd seen those ridges it had been on dead

Wraith laid out for autopsy, but it made him more uncomfortable than anything else so far. Rodney was looking good otherwise, not in need of cheering up, and clearly Carson didn't need
strangers getting in his way, and John hesitated, the door obligingly hovering open behind him.

"Oh. Colonel."

John stepped out of Lorne's way, and Lorne grimaced, seeing the crowd.

"Maybe I should come back."

"Apparently something blew up," John said, helpfully. "It looks
like it's going to be a while."

"Yeah." There was a look on Lorne's face that John recognized
only too well, the look of a junior officer biting a bullet. "Look,
sir, have you got a minute?"

"Trouble?" John's voice sharpened in spite of himself, and
Lorne shook his head.

"No. Well, not really. Just — if I could have a word, sir?"

That was worse than the usual run of trouble, that was off-
the-record trouble, and John winced. "Sure." He thought for a
moment about suggesting a cup of coffee, but one look at Lorne's
face told him it wasn't the kind of problem they could discuss in
a quiet corner of the mess hall. "There's a lounge — here."

Lorne followed, his cane loud on the hard floor, and the lights
came on around them. John couldn't remember when he'd first
found this space, narrow and warm, with a long window that
looked out onto the pad where the *Hammond* was docked. Lights
glowed around her, and sure enough the first flakes of snow were
whipping through the air. There were a couple of long sofas that
faced each other, and niches on the wall that might have held art
or books or something else entirely, and John motioned toward
the nearest one.

"Have a seat, Major."

"Thank you, sir." Lorne did as he was told, sat for a moment
turning his cane between his fingers. John perched on the arm
of the other couch.

"OK," he said, after a moment, and Lorne sighed.

"I've heard some talk — it's been brought to my attention that some of our personnel are uncomfortable about having Dr. McKay back."

Damn it. John swallowed the words, knowing that he was being unreasonable. "Would you care to be more specific?"

"Specific how, sir?" Lorne looked even more wary, and John couldn't blame him. This problem was dynamite on a short fuse, worse than whatever had just blown up on the science team. And the fact that his ranking officer was McKay's good friend as well as the leader of the gate team — Lorne had spent enough time at the SGC to know about gate teams.

"What level of uncomfortable are we talking about?" he asked.

Lorne relaxed slightly. "Apparently some of the newer personnel don't understand why Dr. McKay is being treated with such — deference. There is some sentiment that he ought to be held in a more secure location until he's been fully debriefed."

That wasn't entirely unexpected: there were a lot of people on Atlantis now who didn't know McKay, who hadn't seen him pull miracles out of his hat over and over, who didn't owe them their lives. All the new people had seen was a bad tempered scientist who'd disappeared and come back a Wraith, attacked the city and killed their friends. But that didn't matter. This was still McKay. That was the bottom line. This was Rodney, and so this was a rescue. No matter how complicated it was. "That's not going to happen, Major," he said aloud. "So, how big a problem is it going to be?"

Lorne nodded, unsurprised. "I'll see that it isn't one, sir."

CHAPTER NINE

Isolation

RODNEY glared down at his laptop. The infirmary was full of people, both his own staff—who really ought to know better than to experiment with things they didn't understand, and he looked forward to having words with Zelenka once he got out of here—and a couple of sheepish-looking airmen with a sergeant who looked a lot like a sheepdog. At least Carson finally seemed to have the chaos under control. A couple of the technicians were leaving, one with his hand on the other's shoulder, the most embarrassed-looking of the airmen had finally gotten her boot off to reveal a swollen ankle, and Marie was bandaging the last of the minor burns. That was Dr. Russell, who really did know better, and Rodney was looking for a chance to tell her so, but she wouldn't meet his eyes.

And maybe that was all right after all. The screen swam before his eyes, and he leaned forward as a wave of nausea overwhelmed him. How could he feel sick? He hadn't eaten in—weeks, certainly. It wasn't as though he could just throw up the last meal he'd eaten before he was captured.

That thought made him feel even worse, his mouth flooding with metallic-tasting saliva. His head was spinning, his breath short, as though his lungs were clogged. The laptop slipped through his too-slow fingers, slithering across the sheets. He grabbed again and missed, opened his mouth to swear, and realized he couldn't make a sound. He tried again and choked, struggling against an impossible thickness. The laptop fell with a clatter—a part of him was glad it was one of the rugged models—and Marie swung around, her eyes widening in shock. Rodney drew a crowing breath, slapped his chest as though that could somehow dislodge the blockage. It was like an allergic reaction, but not; the shortness of breath, the closing throat — those all fit, but not the nausea or the loss of voice —

"Dr. McKay?" Marie caught his wrist, her expression changing from surprise to worry. "Dr. Beckett!"

"Aye, what's wrong?" Carson moved quickly between the beds, abandoning his other patients for the new emergency.

"His blood pressure is sky-rocketing," Marie said. Somehow she'd gotten a cuff on him, but its pinch was remote. "Oxygen levels are dropping."

"Rodney?" Carson said. "What happened?"

Rodney opened his mouth again, but couldn't force the words through the tightness in his throat. His vision was narrowing, a tunnel with gray edges.

"Talk to me, Rodney," Carson said, his voice sharpening. "Marie —"

Rodney put his hand to his throat. The was the universal sign for choking, he remembered, and he just hoped Carson knew that, too. Something stung his arm, ice and fire flooding his veins. He flailed blindly, caught Carson's chest with his feeding hand. Someone screamed — Dr. Russell — and there was the distinct sound of P90s being cocked.

"Stand down!" Carson shouted.

"Get back, doc —"

"Stand down, I say!" Carson turned into Rodney's grasp as though the handmouth wasn't pressed against the fabric of his lab coat, as though Rodney couldn't feel the heat of his skin, his life, pulsing against his palm.

"It's all right, airman," Carson said, with a quick glance over his shoulder. "I'm not in any danger."

"Doc," the airman protested, but the sergeant caught his arm. "Let the man do his job, son."

"Rodney," Carson said again. "Rodney, say something if you can."

Rodney shook his head, his mouth gaping. He was losing consciousness, he realized, and reached out with his last scrap of will.

Steelflower —

He fell back, distantly aware of being handled, felt at last the touch of her mind on his. He stilled, muscles unknotting, and faintly he heard her say, "He cannot breathe, Dr. Beckett. Or speak aloud."

I'm sick, he thought at her. *I'm sick and I can't breathe and my throat is closed—*

Yes, she said. *We have you, Carson and I.*

He could hear her repeating his thoughts aloud, her voice quick and clear and urgent, but the touch of her mind was strong and sure.

Rest, she said, and he let her lower him into darkness.

Something was wrong in the infirmary, a muffled cry from behind the door, noises that could only be explained by trouble. John reached for his pistol as he turned, leaving Lorne to follow at his best pace, the doors slamming open before he reached them. Carson and Marie and a tall doctor whose name John hadn't yet learned were huddled around Rodney's bed, and another of the nurses was dragging over a tower of serious-looking machinery. Teyla was there, too, standing a little back to be out of their way, her face intent and worried as she looked from Rodney to Carson and back again. She was pale and drawn, deceptively fragile-looking in the oversized hospital gown. The rest of the scientists John had seen earlier had drawn aside into a nervous knot, all of them wearing the expression he associated with people watching a bad traffic accident, and a trio of Air Force personnel were clustered by the bed to Rodney's left. One of the airmen was sitting up on the bed, her ankle bandaged and one hand on her P90; the other had his P90 at the ready, held in check by the sergeant's hand on his arm. Somewhere an alarm was sounding, and it took a second for John to identify it as something medical. Something to do with Rodney.

He wanted to rush in, demand to know what was happening, but he knew better than to interrupt the doctors. Teyla looked over toward him as though she'd felt his thought, gave the tiniest shrug of her shoulders. John nodded back, looked at the sergeant instead.

"What's going on, Sergeant?"

"Not sure, sir." The man's face was wooden. He was one of the new men, with a face like Ford's if Ford had lived to be thirty-five, and John squinted at the name above the pocket: Trotter. "Medical emergency, sir."

"Why the weapons, then?" John asked.

Trotter hesitated, and behind his shoulder, the two airman exchanged nervous glances. "The — Dr. McKay — he tried to attack Dr. Beckett, sir."

"No, he didn't," Carson said, over his shoulder.

"With respect, sir," Trotter said. "He slammed his feeding hand into the doc's chest."

"But did not set his claws," Teyla said. She came to join them, wrapping her arms around herself as though she was cold. The effect was to diminish the remains of her Wraith disguise, and John guessed she was doing it deliberately. "Or even try to do so. He was choking — I do not think he remembered that he had been made Wraith then, just that he was in distress."

Trotter looked skeptical, but nodded anyway, and the airman shifted his P90 back to port-arms. The rhythm of the alarm had changed, and even as John realized that, it cut out, was replaced by a steady, softer beeping. The movements of the medical team changed, too, became less urgent, and Carson turned away from the bed.

"He's stable for the moment," he said. "And, no, sergeant, he did not attack me."

"If you say so, Doc," Trotter said, and John lifted an eyebrow.

"And the doctor would know, Sergeant. If your people are through here, I suggest you get out of the way."

"Yessir." Trotter saluted and turned to help the airman off the table. They limped away, one airman steadying the other, and John looked at Carson.

"How bad is it?"

Carson shrugged. "I warned you that this might happen. All our simulations showed that the process of purging the Wraith drugs from the system was a violent one, and involved some unpredictable shifts in systems and even in physiology. Frankly, I'd like to know how the Wraith kept him alive through the first process, given that the changes are progressing at different rates in different parts of the body. This — it looks as though the changes to the lymphatic system that allowed Rodney to feed are reversing themselves, and that's caused swelling in a number of critical nodes. I think it's that rather than an auto-immune response that cut off his breathing. We've got him on a ventilator for now, and, as I said, he's stable."

"He is sedated," Teyla said. "I thought you did not want to do that."

"I didn't," Carson said. "But there's no choice, not with him on the ventilator."

John looked past him at the bed, at Rodney flat on the pillows, body slack, arms straight like a corpse laid out for burial. He bit his lip at the thought, and looked away. That wouldn't happen. Carson was the best, Carson and Keller together would take care of him — and where was Keller, anyway?

Even as he thought that, he saw her, standing beside the farthest bed, clinging to her IV pole with one hand, the other hand knotted in the curtain. Her hair straggled loose over gown and scrub pants, and she looked as though she was about to fall over. Of course she wasn't working, she was still recovering — he remembered how he had felt for the first week after Todd had fed on him, the hollow exhaustion that was almost an ache in the bone, and that was with Todd restoring what he'd taken. He ought to go to her, or someone should, and he tipped his head to one side.

"Carson."

Carson's eyes flicked sideways, and he nodded. "Aye. I'll take care of that. In the meantime, I'm going to have Rodney moved to the isolation room. His immune system may crash on us, and it'll prevent any more — misunderstandings."

John nodded. "That's a good idea, Doc. I'm going to put a guard on the door, too, but that's mostly for the same reason. Consider that they're there to reinforce your orders."

"I will," Carson said, and turned away.

"Major?" John looked over his shoulder, and Lorne drew himself up.

"Right here."

"Dr. Beckett is going to move Dr. McKay —"

"I heard, sir," Lorne said. "I'll set up a guard detail."

"Thanks," John said. That was everything taken care of, or at least everything that he could actually do anything about, and he gave Teyla a wry smile. "You look like crap."

She smiled back, but her mouth wobbled. "That is at least better than I feel."

"Back to bed," John said.

She started to nod, but grabbed at his sleeve as she lost her balance. John caught her, steadied her for a moment until he realized she was swaying.

"Doc —"

"It is low blood pressure, I think," Teyla said. "I will be fine once I lie down again."

"Right." John stooped, swept her up before she could protest, and carried her to the bed, setting her down among the pillows. She made no objection, and John felt fear spike through him.

"Excuse me, Colonel," Marie said, and brushed past him, brandishing a hypodermic.

"I am fine, John," Teyla said. Her voice sounded a little stronger, and John relaxed.

Marie finished the injection, looked up at him with a faint smile. "We're still getting her blood pressure stabilized — it's still fluctuating a bit, but, basically, she's fine. It's just getting the last of the drugs out of her system. This —" She held up the empty syringe. "This is going to put her to sleep, so there's no point in staying."

I don't mind. John swallowed the words, understanding what

was really being said. Teyla was in no danger, and he was in the way—but he didn't want to leave. Teyla smiled as though she'd read his mind.

"If he could stay just a bit, Marie. He will leave when I am asleep."

"I will," John said.

"Suit yourself," Marie answered, but she was smiling again.

John tugged a stray chair over to Teyla's bedside, pulled the curtains partly closed to give her a little privacy. "Are you OK?"

She nodded. "I am. It was—it was a shock to see Rodney so."

"They'll take care of him," John said. Out of her sight, he crossed his fingers like a kid. "He'll be fine."

Rodney was vaguely aware that the room was swaying, that he was rushing forward, feet first toward something. Toward the light, he thought, with sudden panic, then realized that it was the bed that was moving, and he was surrounded by medical staff in gowns and masks. An allergic reaction, then—but, no, they wouldn't need masks for that. Was he sick? He felt awful, weak and fuzzy-headed. Maybe he'd caught something on one of the stupid planets, some weird Pegasus virus, and they were isolating him so he wouldn't infect the entire base. He tried to lift his hand, and immediately Carson bent over him, the corners of his eyes betraying the reassuring smile behind his mask.

"Easy, Rodney. You're on a ventilator, so don't try to talk. You're still undergoing the transition, and it's affecting your immune system. We're moving you to isolation as a precaution."

Rodney blinked, memories flooding back. Capture, the hive, Quicksilver, Ronon and Jennifer and rescue... He tried to nod, but his neck hurt, and Carson laid a gloved hand on his forehead.

"Easy, now," he said again, and nodded. One of the nurses did something out of Rodney's line of sight, and he drifted back into fitful dreams.

Jennifer stood for a moment in front of the mirror in her quarters, smoothing her hair into a tighter ponytail. She was definitely feeling better, she told herself; even if she did feel as though she'd been in a car wreck, it was an improvement from yesterday, and the day before. She had talked Carson into releasing her to her quarters yesterday afternoon, once her electrolyte balance had finally stabilized and she had proved she could not only keep down the recovery drinks but could, and would, eat real food. He had told her to get some rest, to come back only when she was ready, and from the sound of it, he'd expected that to be another day or two. And that was more than she could stand.

She drew herself up, studying her reflection. She still looked tired, her face drawn, shadows dark and puffy under her eyes. She looked older — but that wasn't possible. The retrovirus had worked. Rodney had fed — which, incidentally, had saved his life, Carson had been clear about that — and she was unharmed. She hadn't lost even a year. That was just exhaustion that she saw, nothing more.

For a moment, she wished she were back on Earth, where she had had friends who would understand, who wouldn't look down on her if she went to them and said, Do I look older? Please tell me if I look older. They wouldn't think she was shallow, the way Teyla would, or think she ought not to worry about side effects as long as Rodney was alive — that was Jeannie's attitude, she was sure — or look completely confused, like Colonel Carter. She still cringed when she thought about being trapped with her and Rodney, about that stupid, awkward conversation. She couldn't ask Marie, or any or the other doctors and technicians; she didn't know many of the other scientists, and certainly none well enough for a question like this. None of the military personnel, even the women, would get it, either, because what she was asking wasn't just about how she looked, but what price she'd paid for Rodney's life. She closed her eyes, the tears prickling at the back of her throat. It wasn't that she begrudged it. She'd do it again, she knew that. But was it so unreasonable to want to know what it had cost her?

She shook herself, hard. Whining was pointless, and there was work to be done. Carson would at least give her an update on Rodney, and on Teyla. At least she was doing exactly as expected. In a day, no more than two, she'd be ready to start getting back to normal. Jennifer smiled then, though she didn't look to see if it was believable. Teyla didn't need to look like a Wraith Queen to be intimidating. Lucky Teyla.

She fiddled with her hair again, then tugged her jacket into place. She was Atlantis's chief medical officer, no matter how easy it was to forget that now that Carson was back, and no matter how much of a fraud she felt sometimes. Now she had to do her job.

For once, the infirmary was quiet when she arrived, only Teyla looking up from a borrowed e-reader to give her a nod of greeting. Marie looked up from her tablet with a smile.

"Good morning. I hope you're feeling better, Doctor."

"Yes, thanks." Jennifer picked up her own tablet. "How are things?"

Marie tapped the edge of the nearest desk. "So far, so good. No overnight disasters — well, except the Marine with the broken condom — and both Teyla and Dr. McKay are stable. And Dr. Beckett asked if you'd check in with him as soon as you had a minute."

"No time like the present," Jennifer answered, and headed for the isolation chamber.

The young Marine on duty at the door gave her the sharp nod that was the substitute for a salute, and Jennifer forced a smile and a murmur of greeting. It still bothered her to see guards on Rodney's door, even if she understood the logic; it felt like just one more thing they'd need to overcome before she could have him back to normal. Or for what passed for normal with Rodney. Beyond the door, she could see Jeannie Miller sitting in a chair beside the bed, a mug in her hand, and she was guiltily glad to see that Carson wasn't there as well.

She found him in the observation area, frowning at a workstation screen. Behind him, a cot was set up, neatly made, but even so, her heart skipped a beat.

"Oh," he said. "That's for Mrs. Miller, not for me."

Jennifer allowed herself a sigh of relief. "Marie said you wanted to see me."

"Aye, I did." His eyes raked her, frankly assessing. "You're looking better this morning."

"I'm fine," Jennifer said.

"No dizziness, no headache? No other untoward symptoms?"

Jennifer shook her head. "I'm still tired, but otherwise — nothing."

"Good."

"And Rodney?" It still felt odd to use his first name when she was thinking about him as a patient, but 'Dr. McKay' was even weirder.

"Some things are better, some are worse," Carson said. "I'm hopeful we can take him off the ventilator very soon. And his latest labs are showing some improvement."

Jennifer scanned the reports, frowned as she reached the third page. "This isn't so good."

"No," Carson agreed. "And, no surprise, he spiked a fever overnight." He looked pensively toward the window, at Jeannie's gold curls bright beside the drab hospital blankets. Rodney looked even greener by contrast, unconscious against the sheets. "I've developed a theory that I'd like to run by you."

"OK," Jennifer said.

"I think that not all of the transformation was biological," Carson said. "Specifically, I think whoever did this used surgery to create some of the changes, specifically the feeding organ and the enzyme vein that runs along the back of that hand. I don't know whether they grew organs tailored to his DNA — I wouldn't put it past their capabilities — or if they used organs harvested from cadavers, but I don't think that Rodney grew his own bits there. I'm also thinking that the withdrawal of the support drugs has caused the connective structures for those organs to die, and now the actual feeding organ and the vein are dying as well. It's the necrotic tissue that's causing the fever."

"OK," Jennifer said again, still studying the notes. It matched what she was reading, made a pattern out of otherwise meaningless numbers. "So are you proposing — surgery to remove them?"

"That's my first choice," Carson said. "Take them out now, before they can do any more harm."

"Wow." Jennifer paused. "You know, I — that's a big risk. He'll have to be fully sedated, and we don't know how that will react with the remaining Wraith characteristics. I mean, we can sedate a human, and we can sedate a Wraith, but somebody in between —"

"I know," Carson said. "I think the vein would just slough off, but the feeding organ is in pretty deep. I'm very worried about infection there. If it sets in badly —"

"He could lose his hand," Jennifer said. She made herself distant, as though this were all academic, nothing whatsoever to do with her. She took a deep breath. "I agree."

Carson gave her his quick smile. "Thank you."

"Oh." Jennifer felt herself blushing. "I can't — I'm not — Mrs. Miller is his next of kin."

"Oh." Carson looked startled, and Jennifer found herself babbling on.

"We were going to set up powers of attorney, do all that, but somehow, you know, it never happened."

"It's all right, love," Carson said. "I'll talk to Jeannie."

Jennifer nodded, wrapping her arms around herself, hugging the tablet to her chest.

"Jennifer," Carson said. "This isn't — it can't be an easy time for you. Have you considered having a word with Dr. Robinson? Eva's a remarkably level head."

"I'm fine," Jennifer answered, and willed it to be true.

Jeannie sat beside the bed, the machine chirping softly in the background. Rodney looked surprisingly peaceful, despite the IV lines and the tube of the ventilator, peaceful and distant, as though he were fading already into oblivion. She had sat like this before, when Caleb's grandmother died, but this was worse. This was her brother, white-haired and green-skinned, motionless against the pillows. He was looking a bit more human, she thought—she hoped, anyway, but it seemed as though the dark veins had faded a little.

She looked up as the door slid back, admitting Dr. Beckett, and managed to match his preoccupied smile. She knew from his earlier visits that she wasn't in the way, so she stayed where she was until he'd finished checking the machines and making notes on his computer. He looked up then, met her eyes unsmiling.

"We need to have a word."

That was never good, and she wondered where Jennifer was. She needed to be here, needed to be involved in these decisions, if she was going to marry him, she had to be able to assume some responsibility—Jeannie shook herself, hard, ashamed of her reaction. Jennifer wasn't here because she'd saved Rodney's life, was still recovering. "Of course," she said, and pushed herself to her feet.

"One of the things we've been finding out as the effects of the Wraith drugs wear off is that not all of the changes are purely chemical," Carson said. "Some of it was accomplished with surgery, particularly the creation of a working feeding organ in the palm of his hand, and the associated enzyme veins. And, as the vascular and other structures sustained by the Wraith maintenance drug atrophy and disappear, these added organs are beginning to die."

Jeannie stole a glance at Rodney's hand, at the shriveled vein that wound up his forefinger. "What do you need to do?"

"We have two options," Carson said. "And there are problems with both of them. We could simply leave the added structures alone, and trust that Rodney's body will reject them more or less naturally. The venous network would probably slough off harmlessly, but the feeding organ is fairly deeply embedded into the structure of his hand. If it were to become infected, there is a very real chance that it would affect his ability to use his hand. And his immune system has been affected in unpredictable ways already, and I'm concerned that this would be too strong a challenge."

"And the other option?" Jeannie's eyes were dry, her voice remote.

"We remove them surgically," Carson said. "Under normal circumstances, that would be the preferred, even the obvious method, just cut it out, but — we don't really know how the Wraith made it functional in the first place. There may be deeper connections that we won't find until we actually try to take it out. And there's still the risk of infection, plus — Rodney's already been through a lot. I'm concerned about the effects of further surgery on his already weakened systems."

"And you're asking me to choose?" Jeannie was starting to get the faint, familiar headache that came from being in a strange galaxy after her brother had been kidnapped by aliens.

Carson nodded. "You're his next of kin."

"Damn it, Meredith!" Jeannie glared at the figure on the bed. When he recovered, she was going to kill him. How could he be moving in with someone, be planning to marry her, and not give her the right to take care of him? "It's just like him." She took a breath. "Ok. Sorry. What are you recommending?"

"I think surgery is best," Carson said. "But I won't pretend it isn't a gamble, too. And — if it's to be done, it needs to be done right away. Before he gets any weaker."

"Have you asked Dr. Keller?" Jeannie knew she ought to talk to the younger woman herself, but she couldn't do it, couldn't make stilted conversation, struggling to be polite while her brother might be dying.

"Dr. Keller agrees that surgery is the better choice," Carson said.

Jeannie nodded slowly. "All right, then. When — will you do it now?"

"As soon as I can get an operating room readied," Carson said. "So if you'll excuse me —"

"Of course." Jeannie watched him bustle away, then turned to lay her hand on Rodney's forehead. His skin was warm, too warm, and dry, papery to her touch. "You idiot," she whispered. "You complete idiot. I'll be waiting."

CHAPTER TEN

Acceptable Risks

RICHARD Woolsey eyed his Chief of Sciences expectantly. He was rather getting used to Dr. Zelenka as Chief of Sciences, and whether or not he would remain so on a permanent basis was as yet to be seen. Of course Dr. McKay might recover and return to work. It was possible. But Dick had spent far too many years auditing Stargate Command to feel that it was likely.

The first time he'd looked at the SGC's files he'd been appalled. They were losing more men than a full combat brigade in Afghanistan, more KIAs and more permanent disabilities, with nothing to show for it except the vague goal of 'advancing human knowledge.' That was unacceptable. A couple of dozen lives a year. *A couple of dozen?* For nothing that could be quantified, for no ground gained, no allies reinforced, no enemies captured? George Hammond was spending lives like water for aims that shifted and changed constantly. He was spending lives like he was at war.

Woolsey had always been suspicious of the undeclared war. Wars were meant to be conducted in the full light of day, with the sunshine of public scrutiny. That's why the President could not declare war — it required a vote from Congress, a public declaration from those responsible to the American people. Of course, that had been thrown out the window in recent decades, with one 'police action' or 'limited response' after the other, Presidential detours around the fact that the public didn't want war. Tens of thousands of men of his generation had died in a war that had never been declared.

Hammond was running his own war out of a basement in Colorado Springs, with subordinates who only vaguely seemed to acknowledge the authority of the United States government.

O'Neill was a bronco, and he'd seen that before. Jackson was uncooperative to a degree that would have been insubordinate had he not been a civilian contractor, and Carter was hostile to a degree one step this side of charges. Reynolds stonewalled and Makepeace seemed to have the brains of a guard dog who had been kicked in the head, while the entire medical section cited patient confidentiality at every question. Retired General Carter couldn't be found as he was apparently off in space, and their alien contractor, Teal'c, simply glared at him with a stony gaze. If the president hadn't been in love with covert operations with cool names the entire place would have been shut down. But such was the tenor of the times. No one was asking too many questions in 2004.

Five years later everyone was asking a lot of questions. Unfortunately for him, as he now had to answer them, not ask them. Woolsey frowned at Zelenka, still waiting patiently. "And what do you see as the risks of this mission?"

"Minimal," Zelenka said. He thrust his hands in his pockets. "There is no reason for us to go anywhere near the lower levels where Ronon's team encountered the bears. Colonel Sheppard turned it down before because he thought it was a waste of time, not because he thought it was dangerous."

Woolsey nodded thoughtfully. "And how long do you think this would take?"

"If the *Hammond* will beam us in, two hours, maybe three." Zelenka shrugged. "There is either a ZPM there or there is not. If there is, it is the work of ten minutes to pull it. If there is not, there is no need for further action." He pushed his glasses up on his nose. "If there is the remote chance of finding a ZPM, it is worth the minimal expenditure of time."

It occurred to Woolsey that Zelenka was better at selling him on things than McKay. Possibly because it had dawned on Zelenka that the way to persuade people was to address their objections, not drown them in technobabble.

"All right, Dr. Zelenka," Woolsey said. "I'll query Colonel Carter and see if she would be gracious enough to beam you in. If so, I see no reason this isn't worth a couple of hours."

Ember looked around the striated walls of his own lab, grateful once again to be safe aboard his proper hive. He had come here a refugee, but Queen Steelflower's law was to welcome a stranger's talents no matter what his lineage — unless he proved himself an enemy, and Bonewhite and Guide had dealt aggressively with the very few who had tried to take advantage of her generosity. And now that he had seen her himself… He could not repress a sigh. Death was perhaps more beautiful, taller, finer-boned, and Steelflower was barely out of her adolescence, but already she carried herself like one of the First Mothers. A cleverman did not aspire, could not aspire, but — if she had wished to taste his life, he would have bared his chest and begged for her touch. A true queen, a queen of queens, indeed.

And a queen with a cleverman's appreciation of possibilities. While he had played Guide's triple game with Death, she had brought a Lantean scientist to Guide, and the three of them together had opened up an almost frightening range of possibilities. If one could feed on humans without killing them — well, what then? They would not need to tempt the Lanteans' wrath, seeking their homeworld; the Lanteans in turn would have no need to hunt them down, and they could maybe even join forces against Death's fleet. Such an alliance would not last, but it might buy them time to repair and rebuild their hives, and then — well, then there would be the familiar cycle of Culling, the constant hunt for those humans who had developed technology that might allow them to fight the Wraith on their own ground. Perhaps the Lanteans would be slower to trade such knowledge, if they knew it brought only retribution? It was hard to know.

The first retrovirus had failed, but it had promise. He could see that, reading over the notes and the formulae, watching the molecules turn and twine in the projection. Guide was more skilled than any blade he'd ever known — well, he was old enough, had

had time to learn both the methods and their necessity—and the human had been working from a solid foundation. But this was what he was born for, his true talent, and he reached into the simulation, shifting the chemical traces slightly. A part of him wished Quicksilver could see: it had been a long few weeks, and he had grown tired of the changeling's arrogance. The worst thing about it was that it was not unearned. He smiled at that, soothed by the familiar rhythm of his own work. Quicksilver was brilliant at the sciences physical, but this was purely science biological. There were very few who could match him in this.

He studied the new form, subcorporial bonds sparking incomplete, used familiar reagents to fill the spaces, bridge the gaps, and stabilize the compound. He could see why the human hadn't chosen this path. There was more risk that it would incapacitate the subject for some period, but he thought it would make the necessary changes. The subjects would be sick for some days, and some would die, but the survivors would emerge protected from the worst of the enzyme. Indeed, it would bind with the new blood markers, suppress the flood of chemicals that ravaged the body. It would not be a pleasant process, but the subject should survive, and could be fed on again.

Of course, that was just the beginning. There were tests to be run, the precise dosages to determine—perhaps the retrovirus could, should, be tailored to each recipient? That might prevent or mitigate the illness, reduce the inevitable death rate. But the basic idea was, he thought, solid.

He shut down his equipment then, turned to the nearest screen to call up the ship's status reports. The holds were nearly empty: they must be due to Cull soon, he thought, and laid his hand on a communications pad.

"I would speak with the Commander," he said, and there was a moment of silence.

"He will see you," a voice answered—Springgreen, who had taken over the commander's household. "In one hour in his quarters."

"Thank you," Ember said.

One did not call on the Consort in any less than one's best. He took time to bathe, to change his clothes and dress his hair properly, and presented himself at the entrance to Guide's quarters precisely on time. The drone admitted him, and Guide lifted his eyes from the game table.

So. You've made progress?

Ember dipped his head. *I have.*

Guide gestured with his off hand. *Sit. And tell me.*

Ember did as he was told, settling the skirts of his coat in graceful folds. *I believe I have a variation of your work that is ready to test.* Quickly, he outlined the changes he had made, the direction he had taken the work, and Guide nodded.

I see. What made you choose that path?

Ember hesitated. *Forgive me, Commander,* he said at last, *but you were working with the human female. I do not think she would have agreed to the changes I have made. The risk to her kind is greater, though I believe the results to be assured.*

Guide smiled. *That is possible,* he said. *Still, this was as our queen wished.*

And if our queen would have me do more to eliminate the side effects, I will most certainly do so, Ember answered. *But I believe we should test this version as well.*

Guide looked down at the board, veiling his thoughts. The game was one of pattern and strategy and speed, one Ember knew well; he did not doubt that Guide was a master, and was not surprised to see all seven jewels in play. The game had reached a crucial stage, the forerunners embattled, the rearguard pressing on, and everything would depend on the next jewels to appear. Corundum, jet, and diamond were neutral, beryl would win all, aster would lose all, pearl and opal merely prolong the loss. Guide saw where he was looking, and smiled. He pressed the release, and the next sphere popped into play: beryl, glowing green. Guide placed it, and the pattern collapsed with a clatter of chimes, the gamble paying off a hundredfold. Ember bowed his head again, acknowledging the point.

So what is it that you want? Guide asked.

We must Cull soon, Ember said, and the commander nodded. *I would like to accompany the hunting party, and choose suitable subjects from among the humans. In addition to those we Cull, I would not deplete our stores.*

Do so, Guide said, after a moment. *It would be as well to have alternatives.*

Thank you, Commander, Ember said.

We will reach Lymours in three days, Guide said. *And Cull there. In the meantime…* He waved his off hand at the board. *Would you care to join me in a game?*

I am honored, Ember said, and bent his attention to the board.

John turned away from the sun and the soaring towers, sparkling as the ice melted in the noon light. It would freeze again by the end of the afternoon, a thin treacherous glaze, but at the moment it felt like a promise of better days. Or it had, until Teyla called. *They've taken Rodney to surgery,* she said, and that was pretty much all she knew. He reached for his laptop to check his schedule, saw it stretching empty into the afternoon. He'd been planning to get paperwork done, the endless round of emails and approvals that Lorne couldn't handle, but the thought of retreating to his office to try to concentrate while Rodney was in surgery did not appeal. He wouldn't get a damn thing done, and there wasn't much point in pretending otherwise. Not when there really wasn't anything important going on.

He found Ronon in one of the turret rooms that the scientists called aeries, high on the side of the tower and bumped out and angled so that the big window gave a view beyond the city's edges. Some of the scientists had speculated that the rooms might have been watchposts, or even weapons emplacements, but John was pretty sure they were meant for exactly what Ronon was doing. The big man was folded into one of the padded Ancient chairs, his feet up on the window's low sill and a book in his hand. The

sun had warmed the still air, struck gold from the metal band woven into Ronon's hair. Beyond him, the empty south pad was drying in the sun, and past its edge the sea stretched to the horizon, touched here and there with specks of white. The exact point where sky and sea met was hazed with fog.

"Ronon," John started to say, but the other was already turning, looking up, his face sharpening.

"What's wrong?"

For a second, John was tempted to deny it, but he knew Ronon wouldn't believe him. Why else would he hunt him down in person rather than use the radio, if something wasn't wrong?

"Rodney's in surgery," he said.

"What happened?" Ronon asked, after a moment. The book was still open on his lap, an accordion-like spill of paper between wooden covers. It had to be Satedan, John thought, irrelevantly, and looked toward the sea.

"Apparently they need to take out what's left of the feeding organ," he said. He'd poked into the medical computers after Teyla called. "Carson and Dr. Keller were worried about infection."

Ronon slowly folded the book back together. "I thought they were worried about doing too much to him. That his systems were too weak to mess with."

"Yeah." John bit his lip.

"This sucks," Ronon said, conversationally, and John nodded.

"Yeah."

"Keller said getting him back to normal wasn't going to easy." Ronon's voice was very quiet.

"Not so much," John said.

There was another silence. Even Atlantis seemed to be h its breath, not even the faint noise of the ventilators soun the little room. Ronon dug into his pockets, came out w looked like a wide rubber band and slipped it around

"Who's doing the surgery?"

"Keller. With Carson."

Ronon nodded, all his attention seemingly still

in his hands. "Did they say how long?"

John shook his head. "Look, I was thinking. Maybe Teyla would like some company. You know. While we're waiting."

"Yeah." Ronon straightened. "Yeah, she might."

Teyla had her bed pulled up to a sitting position, sat with her knees up frowning at a battered-looking paperback. She looked up at their approach, her expression easing a little.

"John. Ronon. There has been no news."

"They say that's good news," John said, and seated himself on the foot of her bed. Ronon lowered himself cautiously onto a flimsy-looking plastic chair. It crackled, but held.

"How long as it been?" he asked.

Teyla didn't need to look. "Not quite three hours."

That didn't sound good. John bit his lip to keep from saying anything stupid, and Ronon looked at his feet, his hair falling forward to hide his face.

"At least — maybe Keller was right."

Teyla gave him a questioning look, but he wouldn't meet her eyes.

"About — when she let him feed."

"I do not think they would have risked surgery otherwise," Teyla said.

See? John wanted to say. Keller was right. But the point might be moot, and he didn't feel like pushing it.

There was movement from the door, and all three of them turned sharply. It was only Jeannie, a paper cup of tea in her hand. John looked away, but Teyla beckoned to her.

"Jeannie. Join us if you wish."

Jeannie gave them an automatic smile, but drifted closer. onon rose to his feet and pushed the chair in her direction. She ok it with a tired nod, and he perched on the next bed.

"He's still in surgery," Jeannie said. "I couldn't watch."

'No one should expect you to," Teyla exclaimed.

I don't think they really did," Jeannie said. She paused. "Marie ₑ out a while ago and said it was going well. It was just taking

them a while to detach the various nerve connections."

John flinched in spite of himself, and Ronon grimaced.

Teyla said, "Both Jennifer and Carson are excellent surgeons. Though I tell you something you already know."

"I don't mind hearing it again," Jeannie said "I can't help worrying."

"Rodney would expect it," John said, and Jeannie made a sound that might almost have been a laugh.

"He would, wouldn't he? Oh, I've got a few things to say to him when he gets well."

"Get in line," John said.

"She is his sister, John," Teyla said. "I believe that takes precedence."

"Thank you," Jeannie said.

"If you want me to hold him down for you, I will," Ronon offered.

"I appreciate —" Jeannie began, and the door slid open again. Her breath caught, seeing Marie still in her scrubs, the mask dangling at her neck, and John swallowed a curse.

"Oh, Mrs. Miller," Marie said. "I was looking for you. Rodney is out of surgery."

John let out a breath he hadn't known he was holding, and Jeannie put her hand to her mouth. Teyla carefully closed her book, her face unreadable.

"Is —" Ronon began, and couldn't finish.

"He came through beautifully," Marie said. "Dr. Keller was able to remove the feeding organ intact, which minimizes the risk of infection or any other response to Wraith molecules, and she was able to preserve all of the nerves. That's what was taking so long, making sure that there was no damage there. But it's out, along with the vein, and his fever has already subsided considerably. Dr. Keller thinks he may be on the mend."

Jeannie took a breath, tears welling, and John held out his arms. She rose to his awkward embrace, clung for a moment, her shoulders heaving, then pushed herself away.

"I'm all right," she said. "Really."

Marie nodded, touched her shoulder gently. "He's back in isolation — it's still safer for him there — but he should be waking up soon. Would you —"

"Yes," Jeannie said, firmly. "I'd like to be there." She looked at the others. "You should be there, too."

"We will come when he is awake," Teyla said. "Go."

"He's really all right," Ronon said, as though it had just hit him, and Marie nodded again.

"It's still early, but — it looks that way." She started for the door, Jeannie at her heels, and Ronon smiled.

"He's going to be OK."

"So are we all," Teyla said softly. "So are we all."

CHAPTER ELEVEN

Prisons

THERE was a light were no light should have been, far underground in icy caves that had kept their silence too long. The corridors echoed with footsteps once again, the sounds of boots on polished floors. Voices echoed in the gloom.

Power flickered, but the batteries were emptied, the last expended in a rush days ago. Even for him it could not comply. Even for him, the power starved systems could not obey. There was nothing left to give.

Flashlights slid over the silent terminals, screens refusing to light at his touch.

"Ronon, I thought you said this thing was working?" John said.

"It was," Ronon said, coming to stand beside him. "Cadman and I had it up for a while."

"There is no power," Radek said, shining his flashlight over the indicators on the wall. "There must have been some stored in batteries or the like." He shook his head. Of course there might have been. It was likely that there were backup batteries so that the ZPM and its connections could be pulled for maintenance. "This is not good."

William, who had already been here with Ronon, looked up from the silent equipment. "We might have run out the ZPM?"

Radek shook his head again impatiently. "If there were a ZPM connected you could not run it out with a few lights and one terminal, not even if it were almost emptied. The amount of power in 1% of the capacity of a ZPM is enormous."

"Maybe it's burned out then," William said. He shone the light over the two isolation cells at the back of the room, clear glass windows reflecting.

"That is probable," Radek said.

"Ok," John said. "Let's see if we can find the ZPM room." He took one final glance around the control room. "Radek, do you see anything you need in here?"

"No." Radek said. "These are standard environmental control systems. There is nothing here of value."

"They stripped the place when they left," Ronon said from his position already in the corridor. "They didn't leave anything worth taking."

"Let us hope they left the ZPM," Radek said.

Unfortunately, they hadn't. Radek swore under his breath at the empty socket, while William shone his light fruitlessly into corners, as though it were likely that the ZPM were just lying around. "Pulled," he said.

John frowned. "Isn't that weird? Don't most of these installations still have a ZPM?"

"It is unusual," William agreed. "We've found about a dozen Ancient installations since the first was discovered by SG-1. In most of them there is a ZPM but it's entirely depleted. We've never found one where the ZPM had been deliberately removed. That was not the Ancients' normal method."

"Yeah, but weren't most of those bases intended to be used again?" John asked. "This puppy was closed down for good. Ronon said they even took the light fixtures in the living areas."

Radek blew out a long breath. "Well, there is not much point in our staying. There is nothing here except the power control terminal for the ZPM, but since there is no ZPM and we have about eight of these in Atlantis…"

"What's this?" William said, kneeling down beside the pedestal where the ZPM should be, fingers exploring grooves in it, hard to see painted as they were to match the rest. "Bullet holes?"

John knelt down beside him, squinting in the light of the flashlight. "Could be. If so they were sanded out and painted over. Or maybe it just got banged around."

"Projectile weapons?" William mused. "Why would you use projectile weapons if you had energy weapons?"

"If you were shooting at something energy weapons couldn't touch," Ronon said gruffly. "If you needed some stopping power."

John's long fingers ran over the small indentations. "Could be bullet holes. But if so it was before this place was abandoned. They've been pretty much sanded out, primed and repainted. Somebody did a nice repair job." He stood up. "Ok. Radek, are we done here?"

Radek spared a glance for William, who was still investigating the almost imperceptible imperfections in the pillar. "Yes, I think so," he said.

"*Hammond*, this is Sheppard," John said, keying his radio on. "You can beam us out any time."

"With a ZPM?" Sam Carter's voice sounded cheerful.

"Unfortunately, no," John said. "Out of luck this time."

"Ok. Pulling you out."

There was a shimmer in the air, and darkness took the installation once again.

For a long moment, Rodney lay blinking in the harsh light, wondering where he was. Atlantis, that much was certain — there was Elizabeth, smiling at him, her expression for once relaxed and open and kind, and Carson, too, frowning at his monitors, oblivious to her presence. It was good to be home, Rodney thought, and wondered why his mind was so sluggish, why his hand was filled with a distant ache. Because he needed to feed, of course, except that was wrong. And Elizabeth was dead, and Carson, too, and he blinked harder, trying to think. Elizabeth was gone, but Carson was still there — yes, Carson was dead, but his clone was alive, and that's who that was, looking up from the screen at the first faint movement.

"Easy, now," he said, and came closer to the bed. "Easy, Rodney. You've been through a lot."

No kidding, Rodney thought. His mouth was painfully dry, his throat burning, and he swallowed, wincing, not daring to speak.

"You're back in the isolation chamber," Carson went on. "You've had surgery to remove the feeding organ from your hand — which was entirely successful — and the rest of the transition is proceeding well."

"Jennifer?" The word came out a croak, barely intelligible, but Carson nodded.

"She's fine. She did the surgery yesterday, and she'll be in to see you shortly, I expect. In the meantime, your sister's here to see you."

"Jeannie," Rodney whispered, and turned his head to see her sitting beside the bed. He blinked at her with watering eyes, not quite believing she was really there. "Jeannie?"

She nodded, the gold curls bobbing. "You — oh, Meredith!" There were tears in her eyes. "You idiot!"

Rodney smiled then, relaxing, and let himself drift off into sleep.

Jeannie was still there when he woke, though he thought her shirt was different. He had lost all track of time, he realized, had no idea of the day, never mind the hour. He blinked at her again, frowning, and she shook her head.

"Honestly, Meredith!"

"What?" Rodney pushed himself further up on his pillows, and was almost surprised when his body obeyed him. "Look, it's not like I asked for this to happen to me —"

"You got yourself caught," Jeannie said. "Oh, look at you."

"I haven't," Rodney said, more sharply than he'd meant. That was the fear he saw, and the grief, his Wraith shape reflected in her gaze. "What are you doing here, anyway?"

"The SGC asked me to come and help with the security problems," Jeannie said. "I've been helping Dr. Zelenka find and close your back doors."

"Oh." That made sense, even if it was painful to think of: Rodney seized instead on the piece that led elsewhere. "OK, that explains why I thought I was up against myself some of the time. Of course you could copy my thinking."

"Well, your ego certainly hasn't suffered," Jeannie said. Her expression softened. "How are you feeling?"

"Sore," Rodney said. And he was, his muscles ached as though he'd had a fever, and there was a weird deep thrumming at the center of his bones, as though he could feel the marrow changing. "And can't they turn the lights down?"

"It's pretty dim already," Jeannie said, doubtfully.

Rodney started to bare teeth at her, and stopped himself midway. "It's my eyes, isn't it? I'm going to have problems."

"Dr. Beckett said you'd continued to change," Jeannie said, "to revert to normal, and I imagine that includes your eyes. But, yes, he said you'd be photosensitive for a little longer. He said the Wraith prefer a lower light level than we do."

I suppose we — they — do, Rodney thought. He was having trouble making that adjustment, and that made him want to snarl again. "Where is Carson, anyway?" he asked. "I'd expect him to be spending more time with his patient, considering that this is something he hasn't exactly done before —"

Behind her, the door slid open, and he checked. Not Carson, but Jennifer, neat in her uniform. "Oh," he said again, and Jeannie managed a smile.

"I'll leave you to talk," she said.

"That's not —" Rodney began, but she was talking over him.

"I need to get something to eat anyway. I'll be back in a little bit, Meredith. Jennifer."

And then she was gone, the door sliding closed behind her. Rodney fiddled with the sheet, words deserting him, and Jennifer crossed to the bedside.

"How are you feeling?" Her voice was level, professional.

"Sore," Rodney said again. He wasn't quite sure what he'd expected, but it wasn't this, his girlfriend treating him like any other patient. It wasn't that he wanted her to fall into his arms, like the cheerleader in a high school movie — that had never been his thing, and, anyway, what he really needed was the chance to apologize, to make sure she was all right.

But if this was what she wanted, what she needed from him, he'd try to provide it. "Queasy, just at the moment. And my eyes are — they're watering, and it would help a lot if you would turn the light down. And my vision's blurry."

"The lights are about as low as I can get them," Jennifer answered. "But I'll see what I can do. Let me take a look."

Rodney leaned back against the pillow, the knobs of his spine digging painfully through the padding, submitted to her peering into his eyes, her penlight flashing painfully. Green streaks filled his vision, blurring her face even further. "Ow. I can't see."

"It's actually — you're making progress," she said. "The internal structures are shifting back to human norms."

"That's good," Rodney said, dubiously.

"It is, you know," Jennifer said.

"Yes." Rodney paused. "How are you? Jennifer, I —"

"I'm fine," she said. "Really."

"I guess the retrovirus was a complete success."

She nodded. "Yes — well, there are some issues, and I need to run some more tests, but — yes. It works."

"That's really good news," Rodney said. "Look, are you sure you're OK? Because I did —" He couldn't say it, and Jennifer looked away.

"I'm fine," she said again.

Rodney reached across his body, caught her wrist in his unbandaged hand. She stood still, made no effort either to move closer or to step away. "Jennifer."

"I don't want to talk about it," she said. "Not right now."

Rodney released her, struggling to focus on her face. "I —"

"I mean it," she said, and Rodney bowed his head.

"OK. If — if that's what you want, OK. I'm just — I'm sorry."

The words were ridiculously inadequate, but Jennifer managed a faint smile. "It's all right," she said, and turned back to the console, checking the most recent notes.

It's not all right, Rodney thought, but he made himself keep silent. It's not all right, but I — I'll do what I can. Somehow.

Richard Woolsey examined his emails from the IOA with a grimace. Yes, they had sent him back to Atlantis in charge, but he knew all too well it was only because they couldn't think of anything better to do. It had looked for a few days there as though Dr. Daniel Jackson would be taking his place, something which had thrown several members into fits. He, of all people, was aware of just how intractable Jackson could be. And so they'd reinstated Woolsey. But he would be a naïve fool to assume that they weren't still planning to get rid of him at the earliest opportunity.

Woolsey sighed and laid aside his laptop. It was very early in the morning, and in the control room the duty crew were changing shifts. Dr. Zelenka was huddled with Dr. Kusanagi at the far end, possibly going over the day's work and deciding who was needed where. Airman Salawi was on her way to bed.

Woolsey closed his eyes. He'd like to go back to bed. He hadn't slept well. Somehow Atlantis had that effect on him. This morning all the coffee in the world wasn't producing bright attention. He rested his head for a moment on his hands, fingers against the his brow.

The soft sounds of the machines outside. The whirr of his laptop's drive. A dull, inchoate murmur of voices from the control room. The soft hiss of the ventilation system, as though Atlantis breathed softly. It was quiet, peaceful. Almost enough to put him to sleep right here at his desk…

There was the sound of footsteps just inside the office door, and Woolsey looked up. He hadn't heard the door open.

There was no one there. He'd been mistaken, of course. He'd almost fallen asleep at his desk and imagined that someone had come in to speak with him.

That wouldn't do. Woolsey got up briskly. More coffee was what he needed. He'd take a quick walk down to the mess and refill his travel mug. It would do him good to get moving, wake him up a bit, make him less sleepy and fanciful.

For a moment as he lifted his head he'd thought he'd seen a flash of scarlet, Elizabeth Weir standing at the office window, looking out into the gateroom.

CHAPTER TWELVE

Christmas in October

JOHN came into the gateroom just as the wormhole died. On the floor four or five people were maneuvering wheeled pallets away from the Stargate — ten or twelve pallets with probably a few hundred pounds apiece of shipping containers on them. There was even a bunch of big cardboard boxes, not standard at all. Sheppard scratched his head. "What's all that?" he asked Miko Kusanagi, who was running some kind of test on the upper gateroom boards.

"The SGC has sent through personal items and baggage that was intended for *Daedalus* day after tomorrow," she replied, looking up from her screen happily. "There was no point in holding it since they can open a wormhole, and *Daedalus* has little space." Miko looked at the pile of pallets with satisfaction. "Besides, much of that is personal items that are low priority, but we will be happy to get."

"I'll say," John said. The number of people ordering warm winter clothes was pretty big. He'd had a look at Radek's LL Bean catalog himself.

Somehow in the last few years Radek had become the king of mail order. He had dozens of catalogs for everything from gloves and hats to electronics to much more personal items. He was also the only authorized Tupperware representative in the Pegasus Galaxy. If you needed it, whatever it was, from brand new movies on DVD to fleecy long johns, Radek could get it for you for cost plus a very affordable handling fee, less than you'd pay for shipping on Earth.

"I think three of the pallets are Dr. Zelenka's," Miko said as though she'd read his thought. "What did you get this time?"

"Ski gloves, a couple of movies, electric razor, some personal items. You?"

"Two fleece Henleys since the gateroom is always freezing," Miko said promptly. "Wrap around sunglasses because the glare is terrible when I have my team out on the hull of the *Hammond*. Thermal check socks." She blushed. "And a set of flannel sheets."

"I wish I'd thought of the flannel sheets," John said. Toasty, toasty flannel, perfect for cold mornings.

"Dr. Zelenka has the catalogs," Miko said brightly, as though a happy thought had struck her. "I am sure there are new catalogs with the filled orders."

"Yeah," John said, looking down over the gateroom floor. Radek was down there, of course, bustling around sorting boxes. It looked like about half the stuff was consigned to him, everything labeled 'Sgt. Walter Harriman, NORAD.' Radek and Walter had this long time deal about stuff getting mailed to Walter who sent it on. UPS must think Walter was some kind of crazy. "I'm going to mosey down there and see what he's got."

Radek was loading boxes from Amazon onto a handcart with the able assistance of Sgt. Pollard, who straightened up when he saw John. "Colonel."

"As you were," John said offhandedly. "Got my stuff, Radek?"

"Yours, and two hundred other people's," Radek said, his glasses slipping down his nose. "And you will have to wait until it is sorted. You know I cannot let people just take things. I must check what we have against the order forms I sent in so that everyone gets their proper items."

"I know." John put his hands in his pockets. "So Miko doesn't get Ronon's socks." He looked at the six big boxes being stacked on the floor. "Is a bunch of this stuff yours, Pollard?"

"Yes, sir." Pollard looked at the boxes in a proprietary way. "$1,800 worth of Tupperware. Halling will be glad to see this. I've been promising him it was coming for weeks and he was getting testy."

John blinked. "You bought the Athosians $1,800 worth of Tupperware?"

"It's ideal," Pollard said. "Lightweight, air tight, almost indestructible. And plastic's worth an arm and a leg as trade goods. I told Halling this was the best there was, and he'll be very happy with it."

"Ok." John scratched his head. He vaguely remembered his mom having a Tupperware party. He associated it more with suburbs than with pastoral nomads, but if Halling wanted Tupperware he could have Tupperware.

Radek was digging in one of the boxes and came up with a smile. "I can give you this," he said, "As there is no doubt who it is for." It was a little blue snowsuit.

John took the snowsuit and a couple of other boxes for Teyla by the infirmary. Just because she was still stuck didn't mean she shouldn't have the pleasure of Christmas in October. Nobody had been expecting their stuff for weeks, and a general air of good humor was prevailing.

Well, it had been prevailing for him. They had Rodney back. And Teyla was home. Everybody was under one roof and more or less themselves, or at least was going to be.

Teyla was propped up in one of the beds in the front room, the curtains undrawn. Her skin looked almost normal except for the healing scars from the plastic surgery, a little more ragged than last time. Carson didn't seem to do as fine work as Keller had. But at least her skin had lost its green tint and vaguely shiny gloss. She was frowning over an expensive e reader, but looked up with a smile when he came in. "John!"

"Hey." He put her packages down on the foot of the bed. "The SGC sent through a bunch of personal orders." He held it up. "Torren's snowsuit."

Teyla reached for it, feeling the thick down lining. "That should be very warm. Yes, that is exactly what I wanted. And snaps to let the legs out as he grows."

John gestured to the e reader on her lap. "Who's is that?"

"Sam's. She said I could borrow it while I am in the infirmary. I am reading a very sad book about a pilot and a young girl who are in a plane crash in your Rocky Mountains in bad weather. It happened a long time ago, I think from the things they use."

John turned the reader around and glanced at it. "Ernest Gann's *The Aviator*? Damn, that is a sad one. You'd like some of his other books better."

"Sam said I should probably not start with the one where the entire cast commits suicide."

John put the e reader down. "*Masada*? That's been unfortunately relevant. Doesn't Sam have anything cheerful on there?"

Teyla looked amused. "Asks the man who is still reading *War and Peace*."

"Hey, Andrei is finally dead. I've got to be getting near the end." John grinned. "How's Rodney?"

"I do not know." Teyla's smile disappeared. "He is in the isolation room, and Marie just tells me that he is fine. Dr. Keller has been there most of the morning since Carson went to get some sleep."

"How's Keller?"

"She is well, as much as I can tell." Teyla shook her head. "John, you have been fed upon and restored. How did you feel?"

"Sore. Shaky. But otherwise ok." The worry in her eyes was the mirror of his own. "And Jeannie?"

"Jeannie has been in there the entire time," Teyla said. She moved, winced. "They will not let me get up yet because it has been less than twenty four hours, though Carson said before he went off duty that I could try some real food at lunch. I do not think he will keep me here past tomorrow if I do not have complications, though he said I must have several days off duty but I could rest in my quarters."

"That's good," John said. Plastic surgery was still surgery, for all that it wasn't usually critical. And she hadn't eaten anything more solid than pureed bananas in a month.

"I am afraid I have lost strength and muscle tone," Teyla said ruefully.

"You'll get it back." He put his hand on her shoulder, just a quick squeeze. "You'll be fine."

"Yes, I will." Teyla smiled up at him. "Will you please check on Rodney? I cannot go myself, and I too will feel better when I know what passes with him."

"Yeah," John said, and left her reading depressing books on Sam's reader as he headed to the isolation chamber.

The isolation room was further back, away from the rest of the medical spaces, and there was a Marine on duty by the door. But a Marine with a chair and a desk, and his P90 in reach but not in hand: a good call, John thought, and returned the smart salute. He recognized Trueblood from the first days of the expedition, somebody who knew just how valuable McKay really was — knew who McKay was, at the core. You couldn't blame the new guys, they hadn't seen Rodney at his best, hadn't seen how he'd changed, hadn't been there for all the times he'd saved the city. All they'd known was the Wraith, the traitor who'd killed their friends.

"How's it going?" he asked, keeping his voice down, and Trueblood answered in the same low tones.

"Looks like progress to me, sir. Dr. McKay's looking a lot more like his old self."

"That's good to hear," John said.

Trueblood nodded. "Yes, sir. It's good to have him back."

"Yes, it is," John said. Message received: the old hands were keeping an eye on things. "Anyone with him?"

"Mrs. Miller," Trueblood said, barely glancing at his screen. "And Dr. Keller."

Crap. John nodded as though that was good news, and said, "Any chance I can see him for a few minutes?"

"I'll check, sir," Trueblood said, and touched his radio. "Dr. Keller? Colonel Sheppard is here to see Dr. McKay."

John couldn't hear the answer, but a moment later the door opened.

"Colonel," Keller said. She looked worn out still, John thought, which he supposed wasn't surprising, considering Rodney had had to feed on her. It had taken him a couple of weeks to feel normal after the whole thing with Kolya, and that had been with Todd restoring him. Even with the retrovirus to protect her, Keller had to have had a pretty hard time of it.

"I just want to see how he's doing," John said. "I promise not to upset him or bring him lemons or anything."

Immediately, he wished he'd been less flip, but Keller gave him a tired smile. "One positive result from all of this seems to be that Rodney's allergies are considerably less severe." She looked back at the locked door, the smile fading. "He's — you know, he's making very good progress, considering. We may be able to try him on some solid food in a day or two."

A hungry McKay was not a pleasant thing. John swallowed the words, managed a nod. "How are you doing, Doc?"

She blinked, as though that was the last thing she'd expected to hear. "I — I'm good, thank you. Fine."

She didn't look it, her eyes bloodshot and her shoulders drooping, but John nodded as though he believed her. "Glad to hear it."

Keller nodded back, almost briskly. "You can see him — in fact, if you could get Mrs. Miller to take a break, that probably wouldn't be a bad thing. But not for long. He still tires easily."

And it's probably not a good thing that she's calling her more-or-less sister-in-law "Mrs. Miller," but maybe that was just that she was in formal, medical mode. John nodded. "I'll do what I can, Doc. And thanks."

"You're welcome," she answered, and turned to her own work station, settling herself in front of the Ancient machines. Trueblood ran his key through the door's lock, and John pulled open the heavy door.

Jeannie Miller was sitting in a relatively comfortable-looking chair that had to have been dragged down from the residential levels, a ball of blue yarn on her lap and a handful of dangerously pointed purple sticks in her hands. Double-pointed needles, John identified, after a moment, remembering his grandmother knitting ski hats that Dave had refused to wear and he'd been embarrassed by and worn anyway. It looked like a sock, or maybe a mitten, and she looked up and put a finger to her lips. John glanced at the bed, letting the door close softly behind him.

Rodney was drowsing again, propped up on what looked like a ridiculous number of pillows, though John supposed that the points he'd grown on his back might not be entirely gone yet. Otherwise, though, he looked a lot more human than the last time, his skin sallow, his veins no longer dark against his skin, his nails shrunk to normal, though they were still black. There was a fuzz of hair on his chin, and starting back on his arms, and John wondered if it would be white, too, to match the hair on his head. Carson had said the new growth might come in dark, which would look — well, pretty funny, if it happened.

Jeannie was staring at him as though she wanted him to leave, and John came quietly around the end of the bed. He thought he recognized the yarn and needles as something one of the scientists had traded for, guessed Jeannie hadn't come to Atlantis with her knitting bag in hand.

"How are you?" he asked, softly, and she sighed and smiled.

"I'm all right. And they tell me Meredith will be."

That came out more like a question than he thought she had intended, and John gave her his most reassuring smile. "Beckett and Keller are good. If they say he'll be all right, he will be."

Jeannie looked down at the sock on her needles. "They also say there's a chance — a fairly large chance — that he's never going to be completely himself again. That he'll always look a little — Wraith-like."

John nodded. "Yeah."

"And what then?" Jeannie held up the sock. "I've been told I can't actually bring these socks home with me, because the wool — well, it isn't wool, it's some alien goat-spider thing, and nobody wants to have to explain it. What's going to happen to Meredith if he doesn't change completely?"

John paused, but he owed her an honest answer. "I don't know. I hope it won't come to that."

"That he might have to stay here."

"Yes."

Jeannie looked down at the sock again, folded the needles together and began rolling the fabric around it. John thought there were tears on her eyelashes, but her voice was steady.

"Thank you for telling me the truth."

There wasn't a good answer to that, either, and John just nodded. "Do you want me to stay with him for a bit? You could get a sandwich or something."

Jeannie nodded. "Yes. That would probably be good." She looked up at the darkened observation lounge. "I've been sleeping there since Dr. Beckett moved him in here. Just in case he needed company."

And to keep anyone else out, John thought. "Rodney must appreciate that."

As though the name had awakened him, Rodney shifted on his pillows, eyes opening. Human eyes, John saw with relief, not the slit-pupilled Wraith eyes, and not greeny-gold, but gray. And annoyed, which was also a step toward normal.

"Do you mind? I was asleep."

"I'm going to get some dinner," Jeannie said. "I'll be back later."

She signaled for Trueblood to open the door, and was gone without another word. Rodney closed his mouth over something he was going to say, and scowled up at John.

"What do you want?"

"Hi, Rodney, how are you?" John said, cheerfully. "Hi, Sheppard, it was nice of you to stop by. I'm feeling — how are you feeling, Rodney?"

"Crappy," Rodney said, but he looked more relaxed. He tugged a pillow into a new position, sat up slightly. "My back itches — who knew that reabsorbing bone would not only be painful, but itchy? And I'm starving. Unfortunately, the only thing I can eat is broth — and I hope I never see another chicken again in my life — and even that has, well, unpredictable results that you probably don't want to hear in any detail."

"You're right," John said.

"My digestion either doesn't work, or it works too well, and I'm not particularly happy with either one—"

"I said I didn't want to know the details," John said.

Rodney grinned in spite of himself. "Well, you're sounding normal, anyway."

"So are you."

"Thank you," Rodney said, then stopped. "Wait — no, never mind, it's not worth pursuing." He paused, his expression slowly sobering. "How bad is it?"

John cocked his head. "How bad is what?"

"My situation." Rodney gave his old, wry smile. "I'm not exactly unaware of what I did, and I'm not expecting the IOA or the military to accept that I didn't know who I was or why I shouldn't help people I thought were kin—"

"They do understand that," John said. "It happens."

"Oh, come on!"

"Well, OK, not like this, I grant you," John said. "Not very often. But everyone knows, everyone understands, that you weren't yourself. Literally, in this case. It wasn't you."

There was a little pause. "But it was me," Rodney said, softly. "That's the problem. It was me — and for once I say this with all humility — because I was the only person who could do this. Who could attack Atlantis like that. It's my responsibility."

"I know," John said. He remembered with sudden clarity standing in the door of the transporter chamber after Rodney's experiment with the Ancient weapon had destroyed half a solar system, Rodney apologizing not just for being wrong, but for betraying his trust. That seemed so much simpler, and such a very long time ago.

"I'll make it right," Rodney said. "I'll — I have to. You know that."

"I know," John said again. "Look, Rodney, you're — as soon as you're well enough, you're back on the team. We need you."

He wasn't sure he had the right to make that promise, but the sudden relief, the gratitude on Rodney's face, made it worthwhile.

"Yes, well," Rodney said. "Of course you do."

"I'm not supposed to tire you out," John said. "But I'm glad to see you're — not so green."

"Very funny," Rodney said. "John —"

John paused, his hand on the door.

"Thank you," Rodney said, and John nodded.

"Any time."

CHAPTER THIRTEEN

Passages and Pomegranate Seeds

LADON Radim climbed from the crawler that had brought him from the railhead, stood for a moment looking up at Dahlia's spaceship while his entourage formed up around him. Here in the secluded valley, the ship seemed larger than ever, filling the narrow space. The mountains rose above it, placing it in near-constant shadow, the sun-kissed snow of the peaks even brighter by contrast. This was the safest place to hide it, away from attack or a random Culling. The *Pride of the Genii* would stay safe here until they were ready to launch, and then… He allowed himself a thin smile. Then they would see what kind of bargain they could make with the Lanteans.

He schooled his face to neutrality as the first members of Dahlia's team scrambled toward them, mostly young men in working uniforms. He had rescinded the rule that all government workers had to hold military rank, but he hadn't expected it to have any practical effect just yet. Mostly it was the few women — he counted two, besides Dahlia — who wore civilian clothes, though Dahlia, of course, was in her usual severe uniform.

They clasped hands in formal greeting, touched cheeks as was proper between siblings.

"I'm glad you could come," she said, and Ladon smiled.

"I wanted to see the ship again. It's been a few months. I take it you've made progress?"

"We have," she said, and there was a note in her voice that made Ladon look sidelong at her.

"But?"

"Let's go up to the control room," Dahlia said.

Ladon followed her, past the scaffolding where a team was welding plates to the Ancient hull, the new metal stark against the smooth sheen of the Ancient alloy. Something else they couldn't duplicate, that metal, but the alloys they mined themselves, and the ones they'd traded for on Sateda, would work well enough. They had calculated the stresses on the joins, worked out what was needed from the welders, and it was within their capabilities. The hull would hold against vacuum; Ancient technology would protect it in battle until they could learn to make their own.

Inside, diffuse light gleamed from the ceiling, the glow broken here and there by missing panels, broken links. Mostly Dahlia hadn't bothered to replace them, except where the light was absolutely necessary, and once again Ladon grimaced at the contrast between their own hard lights and the Ancients' delicate devices. Someday, though, they would tease out all the secrets, find their own answers to the problems the Ancients had left for them, and then — then the Genii would assume their proper place as protector of humans in this galaxy.

"We have full control of the power plant," Dahlia said, "and it seems to be very close to fully charged. It is not the zero-point-module we have heard about, but it seems more than sufficient for our needs. It regenerates itself by a process I don't yet understand, but our tests indicate that, even in battle conditions, it will rebuild its charge over time. If the mechanism itself is not damaged, of course."

"And how did you test that?" Ladon asked, with a smile, and Dahlia gave him an answering grin.

"Very carefully, I promise you! I can't be entirely sure, of course, but — I believe it's reasonable. And it means we don't have to worry about powering down, and risking having to reinitialize the systems." She paused. "I take it you haven't been able to find anyone with this ATA gene?"

Ladon shook his head. "Not so far." He was still tempted to try for a tissue sample from one of the Lanteans who had the gene, but that wasn't something that could be obtained discreetly, not in the size his biologists told him was required.

She led them down a broad corridor, the main axial access,

past little groups of technicians busy with secondary systems, reciting their successes as she went. The sensor array was entirely repaired, along with life support; the ship could carry a strike force of two hundred over and above her regular crew. Ladon nodded approval at that: they would be using the *Pride of the Genii* as a transport rather than a warship for the foreseeable future, couldn't afford to risk her in more than brief combat until they were sure they could create their own fleet. In fact, there was still a vocal group among the Sciences who wanted to disassemble the *Pride* rather than repair her, and he could appreciate their argument. But with both the Wraith and the Lanteans to worry about, it seemed more important to have a working starship.

The control room gleamed, the soft Ancient light a little faded next to the brilliance of the new interfaces. Familiar computer screens and familiar displays sat beside the Ancient controls, translating their messages into readable form, and the controls had been relabeled in normal letters. A young man was using a Lantean tablet to check a console, but he came quickly to his feet at their entrance.

"Chief Ladon."

"That'll be all, Nastri," Dahlia said. "Take your break now. And make sure we're not disturbed."

"Yes, ma'am," Nastri said, and set his tablet aside. "Sir."

The door slid closed again behind him, and Ladon looked at his sister. "So. What's the catch?"

She didn't bother to deny it, merely moved toward one of the consoles to the left of the commander's chair. It was dark, and the computer beside it showed only the trace of a sensor, minimal power or none at all.

"This," Dahlia said. "This is the fire control station."

Ladon closed his eyes. "The weapons systems."

"Yes."

"Do they work at all?"

"No."

Ladon swallowed a curse. "Can you fix them?"

"Not with anything we have here," Dahlia said. She stooped, tugged open a concealed panel to reveal a cracked and darkened crystal. It sat in the middle of a field of smaller crystals like the center of a geode, and Ladon glared at it.

"I suppose you've already searched for spares."

"Of course." Dahlia straightened, pushing the compartment closed again. "There was one, but it is damaged — there's a hairline crack in it that I wouldn't like to trust."

"We may have to," Ladon said.

"There's more," Dahlia said. "The spare — it looks as though it, too, needs to be initialized before it will function."

Ladon sighed, but there was no way around it. One way or another, he would need to approach the Lanteans for help.

The village was noted in their records, one where the humans tended to bear their young in pairs. The cleverman who had jotted down that fact had listed it in passing, one more curiosity resulting from a deep Culling in generations past, but Ember knew it would spare him the work of creating matched subjects. Assuming that the trend had continued, of course, and assuming that he could find sufficient material, but the kine had been cooperative in the past. It was worth the extra effort.

He had the use of a scout and its three-man crew, plus a pod of drones under the control of a young blade whose mind was the blue flame of a coal fire. They came out of hyperspace and established orbit, the scout's copilot watching for the flare of the Ring as the Darts burst through. At that signal, they broke orbit, and the pilot brought them gently down onto the headland overlooking the village.

The plan was simple: surround the village to prevent escape, then offer its elders a way to buy off the worst of the Culling. Coalfire dispersed the drones, sending them fanning out through the scrub, and Ember walked ahead of him down the long slope. He could hear stunners firing in the woods — villagers who had seen the ship land trying to flee — but by the time he had reached the circle of houses, the humans had resigned themselves, were huddled in doorways while a bearded man stood staff in hand at the point where the beaten road met the first houses. A pair of younger men stood with him, faces identical even without their fear, and Ember's heart rose. Clearly the trend had continued, and even one pair would make a difference. And where there was one such, there were likely to be more.

"You are the leader?" he asked, and the bearded one took a reluctant step forward.

"I am."

"I am here to offer you the old bargain," Ember said. Someone in one of the huts gave a soft cry, instantly choked off. "I seek those born two or more at a birth. Give them to me, and you shall be spared further Culling."

"We have not forgotten," one of the younger men said. "We accept." His brother nodded.

The bearded man's mouth tightened in pain, but he said, "They are here and waiting."

"Two are not enough," Ember said. "Six more."

"I don't think we have so many," the bearded man began, and Coalfire snarled.

Shall I set the drones to flush them out? We waste time.

No, Ember said. *This is only settling the price.* Aloud, he said, "I do not believe you. This village has always been rich in such."

"We have changed," the bearded man said. There was pleading in his voice.

"Shall I send my drones to search?" Ember asked.

The bearded man bowed his head in defeat. "Let them come out," he said, to the young man at his right, and his brother lifted his hand to beckon.

Slowly, the humans began to emerge from their huts: a pair of females with hair nearly as pale as his own, a boy and girl not yet at maturity, another pair of males, a male and female, a trio of males with identical faces. Ember pointed, selecting the trio and the two pairs of males, waved away the two unmatched pairs. He hesitated over the females — they were of breeding age — but he needed a multitude of subjects.

"These," he said aloud. "These will do."

"And we will be spared Culling?" the bearded man asked.

"You will." Ember wished he could be more certain his promise would be kept by other hives, but it was the best he could do.

The bearded man twisted his hands together, looked over his shoulder at the waiting villagers. "So be it," he said, and one of the women sagged to her knees.

At Ember's nod, Coalfire collected the drones, formed them up around the group. One of them reached down to drag the woman to her feet, but one of the men shrugged him away and lifted her himself. They moved off reluctantly, the drones' weapons lowered and ready, and Ember turned away.

It was made clear this village was to be left alone? he asked, and Coalfire nodded.

All the Dart pilots have the coordinates. Their orders were clear.

Good.

Ember turned back toward the path that led to the headland, letting Coalfire and the drones manage the captives. There was room aboard the scout to hold them all, and the Darts would have Culled well in the other villages: a good day's work, considering.

"Please." That was one of the women, not the one who had fallen. "What do you want from us?"

One of the men made a sound that was half snarl and half sob. "To feed, what else? Be silent, if you can't die with dignity."

Ember looked over his shoulder. It was actually a perceptive question, more so than he had expected, and perhaps it would serve him to answer. "I have need of human subjects. If you cooperate —"

He broke off, hearing the whine of Darts overhead. Coalfire looked up sharply, lifting his communicator to his lips.

Not ours, he said, and Ember snarled.

Whose?

It was a largely pointless question. If it was not their own ships, it would be Death's, and that was very bad indeed. Coalfire gave him a look that said as much, still speaking into the communicator.

It's just Darts so far — no, wait, there's a cruiser just exiting hyperspace.

Get them back to the scout, Ember said. *We'll try to stay low—*

Dart! Coalfire cried, and his drones swung in answer, lifting their weapons. They fired, but the Dart pitched sideways, presenting a narrow edge.

Go, Ember said again, and Coalfire obeyed.

"You promised!" the woman cried, and the man rounded on her.

"They're Wraith! What did you expect?"

The Dart looped above them, and Ember shoved the nearest human toward the trees. "Run!"

Coalfire turned his drones, sent them to their knees to track a second Dart. Ember drew his own hand weapon, snarling, braced himself to fire. His shots bloomed blue against the first Dart's wing, but did no damage. Out of the corner of his eye, he saw the other woman gather herself, grab the nearest man's hand and dash for the forest. Coalfire swung to fire after them, but Ember raised his hand.

Let them go. We've got enough to worry about.

Coalfire bared teeth in answer, fired at another incoming Dart. That made three of them, and no shelter, no way to get back to the scout. The Darts were coming again, spitting fire; a drone fell, and then another, and Coalfire sent the others into cover. It was the right answer, Ember thought, the right solution, and turned to follow.

Ember!

He turned too late, and the blue of the Culling beam enveloped him.

Jennifer frowned at the healing scar across Teyla's palm, touching the pale scar tissue gently with the tip of her probe. Teyla didn't react. She had no sensitivity yet in her right palm, nerves cut that had not regrown, a patch of skin left insensitive. It was a common enough problem. Often it took years for the skin around an incision to regain its former feeling. "Does that bother you?" she asked, touching it with the probe again.

"No," Teyla said.

There was no sign of infection, but the scar was pale and raw against her palm, puckered just a little where sutures had pulled. This scar couldn't be hidden. Teyla would carry the mark of the handmouth for the rest of her life.

Teyla looked up at her and shrugged expressively. "It is not so bad, Doctor. It merely looks as though I cut myself badly. I am not vain about my hands."

Jennifer looked down at the scar to avoid meeting her eyes. "Still. I'm sorry we didn't do a better job for you."

"You did exactly the job that needed to be done," Teyla said. "Your work was very convincing, and it saved lives. Just as your retrovirus will."

"I hope so," Jennifer said. Of course Teyla knew what had happened. Someone had told her. And having been there when Guide fed, when the first trial failed, she knew exactly what it had entailed.

Teyla closed her hand around Jennifer's fingers, causing her to look at her. "It was a very brave thing that you did," Teyla said, and her eyes were steady. "A very great gift that you gave Rodney when you put your trust in him, not knowing if the retrovirus worked or not."

"I didn't trust Rodney," she said. "I trusted my own work." Jennifer pulled her hand away. "I thought it would work this time."

"And you were right," Teyla said.

She looked as though she wanted to say more, so Jennifer took a step back. "Your hand seems to be healing well, and your blood pressure is normal. It's still going to take you a few days of regular food to feel entirely like yourself again, but I can clear you to rest in your quarters. If you have no problems you can return to duty day after tomorrow. But I do want you to rest until then."

"I understand," Teyla said. There was a regretful expression on her face and she looked like she was about to say one of the terrible things, something starting with 'I'm so sorry that Rodney' or 'I'm sure he'll be fine' or 'If you ever need to talk.'

"Good," Jennifer said briskly. "You can take ibuprofen for the stiffness and soreness if you feel that you need it."

And there was Colonel Sheppard right on cue, slouching in with his hands in his pockets. He could always be counted on not to want to start a conversation about her feelings. "How's it going?" he asked the room at large.

Teyla's entire face lit up, though her voice was even as ever. "Dr. Keller says that I am free to leave the infirmary and may return to duty in a few days." She gave Jennifer a warm smile. "Once again she has put me back the way I was before."

"Not entirely the way you were before," Jennifer said, thinking of the scar she could not erase.

"No, not entirely." Teyla's eyes met hers. "But we will live with that, you and I." She knew too much, had seen too much in those awful moments when Jennifer was dying at Guide's hand, had seen too much before and after. A dark passage, like a tunnel leading down into darkness, into places she did not want to go. She wasn't afraid of the dark. Just of the creatures that lived there. Some of them were way too interesting.

Bits of a fairy tale came to mind, something in one of her books when she was a kid, about a princess who ate a pomegranate seed. Just one seed, red as blood, her life mingled with Guide's, fed back to her. If that wasn't a pomegranate seed, she wasn't sure what was.

I don't want to change, Jennifer thought, thrusting the story away from her. I know who I am.

"You shouldn't overdo it, right?" Sheppard asked Teyla, frowning. "You should take it easy."

"She should," Jennifer said briskly. "And she should eat as normally as possible. That's what will get her strength back."

"You heard the doctor," Sheppard said, but he didn't look at her. He was looking at Teyla, the corners of his eyes crinkling when he smiled.

"I promise I will rest," Teyla said. She slid down off the side of the examining table. "And I will see you day after tomorrow, Doctor?"

"That sounds fine," Jennifer said. "I'll clear you for duty if you're in good shape then."

She watched them leave together, Sheppard protectively one step behind through the doorway like a consort with his queen.

Guide had swept her up like nothing when she had fallen, her knees giving out though her life was restored, had carried her through the hive. It should have been terrifying, going in and out of consciousness like that, carried into darkness against a Wraith's chest. But it wasn't. He had already restored her. If he had meant her ill he would never have done that. Teyla followed after, a light in her hand burning unbearably bright…

Jennifer shook her head, putting the probe in the used instruments caddy to be sterilized. There was no reason for her to go aboard the hive again. Teyla was back to normal, and if Guide needed to, he could come here. She was the Chief of Medicine in Atlantis, and that was exactly where she was staying.

Jennifer went over to the narrow window, looking out across the towers of Atlantis glittering with ice from the rain that had frozen, sparkling with dazzling brightness in the sunshine. Rodney would get better, and then everything would be back to normal.

CHAPTER FOURTEEN

Osprey

IN THE CITY of the Ancestors, Teyla Emmagan dreamed.

In her dream, she once had a name and a past. She had walked in springtime beneath the cool blue sky of Athos, leaves budding on the trees in the uplands, though the valleys were already green with spring. She had a name, though it was gone from her now. So much was gone. There had been a man with a beard who pulled the cart she rode in, a red beard and a wide smile, but she could not remember his name. There had been a boy older than she. He walked beside the cart, ranging back and forth, filled with energy. He had dark hair and a square face. And she did not remember his name.

No one named her here, not even Kairos, the assistant who bent over her, only human as she was, his homely face a study in concern. She could feel his concern, feel it touch her like water falling from the sky.

She remembered rain. It had rained on the morning that marked her seventeenth year, and she remembered no mornings after.

"Vital signs are stable," someone said. One of the Ancestors. One of the gods. She must have been badly injured somehow, she thought. So badly that they had petitioned the Ancestors to save her. She did not remember it. But there had been people who would have done so. The red bearded man. The boy. Even Kairos. Perhaps that was how she knew his name. He had brought her here to save her.

She closed her eyes against the brightness, the lamps that never flickered and never died, the lights of the Ancestors. She closed her eyes and dreamed. She dreamed of home and springtime, of the lake with its still water and a soft mist rising, a white waterbird taking flight.

"That is the ninety-first of the females," one of the Ancestors said, and he did not even draw the sheet over her still face, distorted by purpling blotches beneath the skin.

"The other nine are stable," another said.

Indifference. No sense of loss. What terrible thing had happened that so many died? She turned her head, but there was only the quiet of the room, white draped beds with patients, the two Ancestors standing by the bed at the end of the room. Too far away for her to have heard. She had thought they stood close at hand.

One of them shrugged. "We've only lost one of the males. The Y chromosome is acting as some protection against the most radical changes brought about by the retrovirus. Perhaps..."

A surge of anger. She felt it as though it were within her, but it was not. Kairos stood nearby, and his hands closed at his sides. It was him. The anger came from him, brought forth by their words that she did not understand. But he did. And it filled him with despairing rage.

"Kairos," she tried to whisper, but nothing came out. Not a sound escaped her.

And yet he turned unerringly, his eyes filled with tears. "I am so sorry," he said.

"Little one." The voice was a whisper in her mind. No words were spoken, but she heard them anyway. A woman's voice, older, softer.

"Yes?"

"Can you hear me?" Soft, urgent.

"Yes." She waited in darkness. She had woken in darkness. Only the fitful lights of a few machines winked here and there, like the stars she half remembered. "Who are you?"

A momentary picture in her mind, a woman's distorted reflection in a mirror. Forty, perhaps. Black haired, with olive skin, a round face and brown eyes, tall and full breasted, a white cloth holding back her pinned up hair. And then, sadly, "I don't remember."

Her voice was like the comforting dark itself, like waking from a bad dream to find that your mother is waiting, that she is safe and so are you...

...like tucking your child safe in her blankets, whispering her *back to sleep… An answering picture of starlight, of night through a window, a sleeping child.*

"You are Night," she said. "I will call you Night, and we will be together in the dark."

A hesitation, as though there were something she were keeping back, as from a child who has been very ill. "Do not let them know you can hear me," she said. "Little one, please be safe. If they know we can speak like this they will kill us."

"It is only a blood draw," Kairos said. "I will be quick and try not to hurt you." His hands were gentle on her arm. It was not because of him that she screamed.

When he lifted her arm into the light she saw it rightly for the first time, mottled green skin like something long dead, dark emerald veins twining around the back of her wrist, the back of her hand. Her palm was opened, turned up, purpled tormented flesh surrounding a long gash across her hand, lips open and straining like a second mouth.

She screamed. She screamed until the second needle slid into her flesh, returning her to oblivion.

The sky was blue above the ice. When she was well enough they moved her to another room, one with a window that looked out on the sea. Storm clouds blew across and left thick snow behind them, glittering crystal in the morning.

She sat in a chair beside the window wearing nothing but the white shift they had given her. It was they who were offended by her nakedness, even though she was not made in their image anymore. Her body was as hairless as a child's, shaded from palest green to the dark emerald tint of her nipples. Her black hair had gone shocking white, like a grandmother of eighty summers. And yet it still fell all the way down her back, just as she had brushed it before… Before things she could not remember.

"Are you warm enough?" Kairos asked.

Of course she was. There were no drafts, and inside was the same temperature all the time, even beside the windows onto snow. Everything was perfect.

Little one. This time when she heard the voice in her mind she was not surprised, only turned to see who had spoken.

She did not look like the image of the woman in the night, but the voice was the same. Tall, yes. Full breasted. Black haired still. But her skin was green as a lizard's, her yellow eyes slitted like a cat's.

Night.

She wore the same white shift, sat in one of the gravity chairs used by the very sick. It slid across the floor so that she might sit beside the window, looking out on the sea. *I am glad you are not dead,* she said.

So am I, she replied.

There are seven besides us, she said. *The rest are dead.*

I don't understand.

She turned her head, yellow eyes hard though her voice was sad. *Little one, I wish that you did not have to.*

One day, Kairos was gone.

She asked one of the other attendants. Her voice worked now, though it was low as a man's.

"He volunteered for the second trial," the attendant said, and did not meet her eyes before he hurried away.

The gods jested. Sometimes they laughed. When she washed, standing in the basin with the spray in her hand the guards made rude remarks about her, talked about her in ways that no one ever had in her hearing, the way that no man of her people would have permitted. She said nothing, eyes cast down. Perhaps the retrovirus had affected her mind and she did not understand.

They are not gods, she whispered in the darkness, in her bunk in the bare room with three other women.

No, another said. She was plump and young, shorter by a head, her red hair scarlet as fresh blood over ashen skin. Cloud, like a

mountain of clouds seen from the sea, billowing and distant, with the sun rising behind them. Red sky at morning.

They did not speak with words, except to say excuse me, or to move something. There were microphones and cameras. They were observed by the medical staff night and day. They did not seem to need to eat or excrete normally, though they drank water. It was fascinating.

I do not understand.

They are not gods, Night said. *Now speak of what you remember. We must remember together. We are not witless.* Her voice was soft but resolute. *We must use our minds if we are to go home.*

Home, Cloud said, and spun the picture of a city for them, of white towers against the sea. *I dwelled in the City of the Ancestors, where I served the gods as my parents and grandparents did. I served in their crèche. I cared for their children.* Her voice was wondering. A picture then, a plump, blonde young woman, blue eyes too wide apart for beauty. *I dwelled in the City of the Ancestors. Once.*

Expelled from paradise to the nether regions, she thought. There was some story about that, about those banished by the gods, but she did not remember.

What has happened to us? Cloud asked.

I do not know, said Night.

Kairos knew, she thought. *Kairos knew.*

It was eight days before she saw him, and she hardly recognized him. His flat, homely face was transformed, grooves beside his nose making his face seem narrower, his hair gone white and his skin pale instead of the rich brown it had always been, just as hers had.

Kairos? She spoke his name to his mind and he did not know it, only cringed and put his hands over his eyes. There was nothing but confusion there, huddled in the corner of one of the common areas wearing naught but a white shift. He did not know his name anymore.

She went to him and sat beside him, and at last he let her take his hand. *You wanted to know,* she said. *You wanted to know everything the Ancestors had to teach.* She remembered that much. He had gone to the City of the Ancestors to learn. He had become a healer. They were proud of him. Now the taste of his mind was like ashes in her mouth, bitter and tainted, like scraps of burned bark turning on the wind.

Who am I? he whispered.

You are Ashes, she said.

The day after they were locked away, each in her own place, each by herself. Alarms blared and yet she did nothing, only sat with her back to the wall, her arms around her knees.

What has happened? she said.

Gryphon answered. Her mind voice was very soft, even when they were not separated by stone and glass. *One of the men has killed someone.*

Who?

A god. Gryphon's voice was quiet. *They are saying that he killed a god and drank his blood.*

It was a small thing. She did not like that guard. She did not like the way he looked at her. And so when he came past she willed that he would not see her.

He didn't. He blinked, examined the bars and the locking panel, and then he sounded the alarm.

The other guards laughed at him. "She's right there," they said as she sat against the wall. "Right in front of your nose. Been hitting the off duty fun early?" And the guard, the one she hated, looked silly and shook his head. Of course she was right there. She'd been there all along. The camera logs showed that. She hadn't moved the entire time he'd been searching for her, not though he came within arm's length of her.

Somehow he had not seen her.

I can touch their minds, she said. *I can make them see what I wish.*

Test it, Night said. *See what you can do.*

"I hate this damned base," one of the attendants said. "The weather's always terrible."

The other one frowned, glancing at the window beyond the laboratory where she sat, patient and mute. "What are you talking about? It's fine."

"You don't see those clouds rolling in?"

"You're crazy. It's clear."

Clouds and mist, rising up like memory, a thick fog hiding the sea and snow…

"Oh," the second attendant said, perplexed. "Boy, that fog rolled in fast."

Gryphon?

I burn, Gryphon said. *My legs are weak and my hand throbs all the time. I eat and I eat, but it comes right back up. They have put the nutrients into my veins but it does no good.*

Where are you? Cloud asked.

In the laboratory, Gryphon said. Her mind voice was thready. *They think I will die. And then they will cut me open and see what failed.*

We will not let that happen, she said.

And how will you prevent it? Gryphon said. *Little One, you are powerless.*

Not so much as they think, she said.

I am Wind, he said, and his voice was strong.

I did not know the men could speak.

Some of us, he said, and he showed her a picture. A red sailed ship leaped over the sea and he stood at its tiller, a golden skinned man with long black hair, glorying in the play of air. It moved the ship, lifted it, and he sang with it, one with the joy of the sail. *I

was a ship's master,* he said. *And a soldier.* A naked sword in
his hand, the sweet curve of its blade like silver as they prepared
to repel boarders...

Blade, she said, seeing it in his mind. *Soldier of the queen.*

Who are you? His mind voice was curious, and so she showed
him what she remembered, a slender girl just out of childhood,
honey skin and dancing brown eyes, a girl who loved music and
the green places. The lake came back suddenly in memory — morning, and a fog rising from the lake beside the Ring of the Ancestors,
a white bird lifting from the water.

"I am Osprey," she said.

She is dying, Cloud said, soft so that none besides Osprey might
hear. *Gryphon is dying. They say three men are too. It is not only
that we do not take sustenance. It is that we cannot. We cannot
metabolize food. And so in time we will all starve.*

You know this?

I took it from the mind of one of the doctors, Cloud said, and
her mind voice was tinged with embarrassment.

You can read the minds of the gods? Osprey let her astonishment creep into her tone.

Yes. Some. She stopped, then began again. *But I cannot make
them see things as you can. I've tried.*

How long? Osprey asked. *How long do we have?*

I don't know, Cloud said regretfully. *They do not know.
Weeks? But I do not think Gryphon and the men who are already
ill have so long.*

We will starve. Already she could feel it when her mind touched
Gryphon's, a long burn like a pain in the bones. And Gryphon
was not the only one. It rested on some of the others, even Wind...

If I go I will take some of them with me, he said, and there
was steel in his voice. *They can only kill me sooner, and better
weapons than starvation. I'll take some of the bastards down to
the shades with me.*

We all will, Night said. Her voice was even and steady. *Better to die together if we must die.*

Osprey's voice was quiet. *Better not to die at all. What would it take to get to the Ring?*

And go where? Cloud demanded.

Anywhere, Wind said. *Anywhere is better than here.*

Midnight and snow. Outside, the winds kicked the snow to a whiteout. Inside it was warm and nice.

Cloud waited, her red hair falling free around her face, lips as red as cherries. She lounged against the bars, waiting, her mind open to her sisters'.

The guard stopped on his way downstairs. There was no reason to. Except that she was strangely beautiful. "What do you want?" he asked.

"You," Cloud said, and smiled. "I want you."

He stepped nearer, his eyes on hers, unblinking.

"I want you to open the door so that I can touch you," she said. "Open the door, beautiful man."

He ran his hand over the lockplate, one that only the gods could open, and the bars sprang apart.

"Thank you," Cloud said, raising one long finger to brush along his cheek. "Now come with me back to the control room and turn off the cameras."

"Why?" he whispered, though his eyes never left hers.

She giggled. "Do you really want people to see what we're about to do?"

Osprey's door slid open, the third one after Cloud and Night. *What is happening?* she demanded.

We must go, Night said. *There is no time. Soon their automated systems will alert them that something is wrong.*

Not without Wind and the others, Osprey said, and her bare feet were cold on the stone floor.

Cloud's face was strained, the guard standing beside her with blank eyes. *I can't hold more than one at a time! We have to go now!*

Not without the others! Osprey whirled around. *I can distract them. I can keep them busy. You go ahead and open the other doors.* They hesitated. *Trust me!* she said.

And then she closed her eyes.

Fire. She remembered fire. She remembered dancing around the flames, bright pipes lifting and playing, soaring like the sparks. Smoke drifted in great clouds, choking and billowing. Smoke was filling the rooms, cutting off breath. Smoke. There was smoke everywhere. It seeped from the ventilation ducts, crawled under doors. The halls were filling with smoke, and everywhere could be heard the lapping of flames, devouring oxygen and life...

She was smoke. She passed like a ghost, and they started around, leaping to their feet, scientists and doctors, rushing for water to drench cloths for their faces. They did not see her, and above it all was the high scream of the alarms, turned on manually. The halls were filled with running guards, but they did not see her. She was smoke. They retched, turning away from vents, trying to close them by hand.

The laboratory. Gryphon was not fooled. She turned her head on the white pillow. She was alone. The doctors had fled.

Gryphon.

I can't walk, she said. Her face was pinched, her skin stretched tight over her bones. *Osprey...* She raised her shaking hand. Her fingers trembled, the slit in her palm opened. Her hand spasmed. "Osprey..."

She only meant to take her hand. She only meant to help her up, to put her arm about Gryphon's waist and get her to her feet. But the hand rose inexorably, shaking. And then Gryphon's nails dug into her chest, tearing through shift and skin, biting like fire into her flesh.

Dragging at her soul. Life pouring from her, strength pouring from her into Gryphon. Mind to mind and soul to soul, her heart and Gryphon's beating in unison.

Take my strength, Osprey whispered. *Take my strength. Take it, sister.*

And it was life. It was rich, dark and sweet as all the food they could not digest, life and life and life. To lose it was pain, sweet ecstasy to drink. Minds entwined it was both. Life and death, death and life, swirling together like fireflies above the lake...

And it stopped.

Gryphon sat before her whole, her face full and round again, her blooded hand lifted. *Osprey...* Her mouth worked as though she resisted with her full strength. *No more. No more, or you will die in my stead.*

Osprey breathed. It came in her mouth and parched her tongue. And yet she lived. The claw marks on her skin faded, punctures healing. She was dizzy, reeling, and yet she lived.

Life shared, she whispered.

Gryphon hauled her to her feet. *Come,* she said. *We must go.*

Ashes!

He was there in the corridor, where soldiers ran blindly past them, fire equipment in hand. His eyes were wide, but they knew her. *Osprey, you must help me!*

We will help you, Gryphon said. *We are going to the Ring. Come with us.*

No! He dragged at her arm, his eyes on Osprey's face. *We must do something first.*

There was a sudden rattle at the end of the corridor, and then one of the guards was borne backwards, thrown against the wall where he fell like a broken doll. Wind came around the corner, two other men behind him, his white hair streaming like a banner, one of the Ancestors' weapons in his hand. *They have fallen back to the control room,* he said. *The one beside the hangar. There are ten men or so in good order, but the rest are panicked by the smoke.* He smiled grimly. *Your doing, Osprey?*

Yes, she said.

Ashes dragged at her arm again. *Osprey, help me!*

Wind's expression shifted. *Come, good fellow,* he said. *We'll do our best to get you away.*

There is a weapon! Ashes straightened up. *I am trying to tell you. They have created a weapon that kills only us, that reacts somehow with the new chemistry of our brains. Hyperion, the Chief Scientist, created it. It was supposed to work on something else all together. I don't understand. I don't understand any of this. But we can't leave it. If we do they'll come after us with it.*

Cannot Hyperion just build another? Gryphon asked.

Hyperion is dead, Wind said. He flexed his hand, and Osprey saw the blood on his nails, crusted between his fingers.

Her eyes widened. *You...*

I drank his blood, Wind said, raising his chin. *It seemed a waste to only shoot him.*

We have to take it with us, Ashes said.

There was a sudden alarm, and from ducts along the ceiling fire suppression foam began to spray.

They have found the overrides, Wind said. *They believe that the fire suppression equipment has malfunctioned and they have turned it on manually.*

Go! Osprey said, shoving Gryphon in the direction of the men with Wind. *Go to the Ring with them. I will help Ashes bring this thing.*

Gryphon hesitated.

I'll go with them, Wind said. *Go on. Dial out if you can, and don't wait for us.* He shifted his weapon to his off hand. *Let's get this thing.*

The lab was silent except for the distant alarms. Wind fell back to cover the door.

Here, Ashes said, and he seized a buffed steel box from one of the work tables, flipping it open. Within, a scepter surrounded by crystals glowed faintly. *This is it.*

Bring it then, Osprey said. There was a pedestal at the center of the room, lights shining on terminals around it. A thought came to her. *Would it not be a good idea to disable this somehow?*

Ashes had pulled out one of the drawers from the workstation and was grinding crystals beneath his heel, smashing months of work. *I have a better idea.* He entered a series of commands on the terminal, and from the pedestal rose a long red cylinder, faceted like stained glass, glowing brightly. The glow faded as Ashes pulled it from its holder. *Take the power source.* He shoved it into her hands.

The lights died. The alarms ceased. Here and there an emergency light flickered to life, but for the most part the underground corridors were plunged into night.

Can we get out of here now? Wind demanded. *The smoke isn't going to fool them forever.*

Yes, Osprey said, dragging Ashes away from the console. Wind fired into it, sparks flying.

She tucked the power source under her arm and manhandled Ashes along with him still clutching the case. The corridors were pitch black, slick with fire suppression foam. Here and there they came upon bodies, many of them withered and dry, like corpses buried for months in deep caves, chests caved in around the puncture holes.

Life for death and death for life.

Gryphon was waiting at the hangar doors, five men with her. *Two groups have already dialed out,* she said. Beyond her, the bay doors were open to the night, swirling snow obscuring anything beyond them, even the Ring of the Ancestors and the podium before it. *You are the only ones left. We waited for you.*

Wind shifted his weapon. *They have a clear field of fire,* he said. There were guards in the docking control room. The glass windows had been blown out, and they covered the wide expanse of the bay to the open doors, a long distance of nothing but concrete. Osprey could see the barrels of their weapons, one, two, three… There was nothing to hide behind at all. *Can you distract them?* Wind asked.

Maybe? She was so tired. Her feet were leaden. She had held the illusion of smoke for so long, and Gryphon had fed so deep. *I will try,* she said. *It may only last a moment. So we must run.*

Smoke wreathing around them. Smoke filling the bay, obscuring their shots, clouding their sight. The entire bay was filled with smoke...

Run!

Gryphon in her white shift and bare feet, Ashes clutching the silver case, the dialing symbols burning in his mind...

Run!

The men sprinted into the fog ahead of her, smoke curling...

And the weapons opened up. Someone in the control room had sense. They could not see their targets, but they could shoot in the right direction.

Osprey ran, Wind at her heels, the power source clutched to her chest. Across the endless space of the landing bay, toward the snow.

Shots touched her, once, twice, but miraculously she was still running, still running through the pain, and outside the whirling whiteness lit with unbearable blue light. The Ring kindled to life under Ashes' hands.

She heard Wind grunt, felt him stagger, but he was still running too, at her back.

Snow surrounded her, the cold wind hitting her like a blow, snow beneath her bare feet. Gryphon was through, and Ashes. One of the men disappeared into the pool of light.

Another shot, and she stumbled on the shallow steps. And then the light enveloped her.

Night again, but warm and still, the soft chirping of insects in the grain. Wind almost plowed into her from behind as the Ring deactivated.

Dial out! he shouted, pushing her away from the Ring. **Dial out so that they cannot follow!**

The stars above were the stars of home.

Osprey stood before the Ring gasping, the power source in her arms.

Beneath the stars of Athos.

In the City of the Ancestors, Teyla Emmagan woke.

CHAPTER FIFTEEN

Hidden Things

TEYLA stood by the window, her hair still wet from the shower, watching the dawn come over the sea. She had thought the warm falling water would soothe her, but it had not. In the next room Torren slept on peacefully.

The skies were streaked with thin, high clouds, turning pinkish in herald of the sun. Her body felt strange to her, and not only because she was lately out of the infirmary. The dream had been so vivid that she had expected to wake as Osprey. It was strange indeed to see these skies instead of the ones of Athos, these skies that had held Osprey imprisoned.

There was a step behind her, John's hands on her shoulders. "You ok?" He sounded muzzy with sleep, though his hands were warm enough, and she leaned back against him.

"I dreamed," Teyla said. "I dreamed I was a Wraith queen."

"Well." His arms went around her waist, her hands tightening over his. "That's probably because of all this stuff with Todd, right?"

"I do not think so," she said slowly. "I believe what I dreamed was real." She turned around, seeing his stubbled face and worried hazel eyes. There was more gray at his temples than there had been even six months ago, a few strands threading through on top as well. Harsh morning light was unkind. Almost his face seemed that of a stranger. *Of a god*, the part of her that was Osprey whispered, and Teyla shuddered.

"Hey." John frowned. "What's wrong?"

Son of the Ancients, heir of their power, heir of their crimes and their arrogance...

I am not you, she thought, pushing the thought away. I am not Osprey. I am Teyla Emmagan of Athos, Teyla Who Walks

Through Gates, and I choose for myself.

"I dreamed of the First Mothers," she said. "And I think I dreamed true. Guide told me..." She paused, knowing how it would sound, but John had always believed her, always from the beginning. "He told me that Wraith queens may retain some of the genetic memories of their mothers, of the lineage that they come from back to the First Mothers. I dreamed of Osprey."

John swallowed but his eyes didn't leave her face. "Ok," he said evenly. "That's disturbing."

"I am disturbed," she said, turning once again toward the cold sea. It was hundreds of miles across icy ocean to the island where Osprey had been imprisoned, but the view was the same. "The Wraith were created here, John. Here on this world. I do not know why. But the Ancients made them. I do not know what they intended to do, taking humans from the worlds of this galaxy and twisting them so, but they made them. I remember." Osprey's sadness closed her throat, feelings both new minted and eleven thousand years old.

He did not disbelieve her. "The installation on the island," he said. "Dr. Lynn's prison break."

"She was a teenage girl," Teyla said, and her voice did not shake. "A girl of seventeen, one of nine women who survived the experiments. I do not know why Osprey survived. But she did."

"Somebody always does," John said, and he stepped forward to put his arms about her again.

She would not flinch. This was John, not some prison guard dead nearly a thousand years before the Ancestors walked through the Stargate to Earth, before the ATA gene found its way into John's lineage. I am not you, she said to Osprey within her, and I will not avenge you.

"Elizabeth told me the secret was in my blood," Teyla said softly. "I think perhaps she meant it literally. I carry Osprey's memories, every wrong done to her and every cruelty, everything she did to survive."

"Do you want to tell me what happened?" John asked quietly.

"I think that I do," Teyla said. "Yes, I do." She closed her eyes, seeing again the flight through the Ring of the Ancestors, the others running through the snow ahead of her, Wind at her back, while against her Osprey cradled... "John," she said. "They had a ZPM. And it was almost new."

Ladon Radim flipped through the latest batch of telegraphed reports, not really seeing the faded print. Most of it was either old news or long expected: a disturbance at the northern nuclear facility after a rumor of a containment breach; shifting alliances within the Council of Twelve, marked by two marriages and a divorce; crop failure in the west, hailstorms flattening a summer's growth of grain. That, at least, could be offset by better harvests elsewhere, maybe even without tapping the emergency surplus. He made a note, even though he suspected Ambrus had already dealt with the matter. He could hear the hum of the cameras in the antechamber, warming for the scheduled contact with the Lanteans, and he allowed himself a sigh. Someday — someday they would synthesize the Ancient gene, but until then, they were desperately dependent on the Lanteans. Though if he could just get his hands on a few more tissue samples...

"Commander."

He straightened, putting aside that thought. "Yes."

"Mr. Woolsey is available."

"Excellent." Ladon straightened his jacket, cast a quick glance to the mirror above the sideboard to be sure that he looked both businesslike and calm. Then he slid back the door and stepped into the lights and warmth of the improvised transmission chamber.

"Chief Ladon." As always, there was the faintest hint of irony in Woolsey's voice.

Ladon nodded to the image on the monitor, knowing the cameras were positioned to make it seem as though they met face to face. Behind the monitor, he could see the young operator frowning at his screen, face uplit by the reflection as he worked to keep the transmission steady. "Mr. Woolsey."

"I understand from our Satedan contacts that the trade agreement is going well," Woolsey said.

"For all our peoples," Ladon said. As if Woolsey wasn't perfectly aware of everything the Genii were doing publicly on Sateda, and probably most of their theoretically secret dealings. He had no illusions about where the so-called governor's loyalties lay. "Governor Cai has been very cooperative."

"We've found him to be an excellent trade partner," Woolsey said. "And we've been impressed by the progress they've made with rebuilding."

In other words, don't expect to walk in and take over, Ladon thought. Woolsey would be wise to heed his own advice. He said, "Yes, it's most impressive. And we are glad to have been of help in that regard." He saw Woolsey's gaze flicker at that, and knew the shot had gone home. The Genii had food and raw materials to spare, both from their homeworld and from the worlds of their many allies; the Lanteans' new home was barren and, in the end, they had so much less to give. "However, we've reached a point where we could use help from our older ally."

"Of course we'd be glad to offer any possible assistance."

"As you know, our people do not possess the ATA gene," Ladon said. "When he helped us recover the *Pride of the Genii*, Colonel Sheppard was able to initialize most of the ship's systems. However, as we've continued to make repairs, we discovered that one of the key control crystals in the navigation systems needed to be replaced. We were able to locate what seems to be the required device in Sateda's museum basement — along with a number of other interesting artifacts — but the crystal needs to be initialized before it can be installed. We were hoping that you could spare a technician to handle that for us." He paused, giving Woolsey a chance to offer out of pure charity. The other man remained silent, and Ladon went on. "We would of course also be more than happy for your scientists to examine the other items in the collection, and to take some for further study."

Woolsey did smile at that, the faintest movement of his thin lips. "We're always happy to help out an ally," he said. "Let me consult my chief of sciences, and I'm sure we can settle on a suitable date and time. I'll be back in touch as soon as I have some options for you."

"Thank you," Ladon said, and motioned for the technician to cut the transmission. He hated having to grovel to the Lanteans, but the *Pride* was worthless without her weapons systems. One way or another, they had to have the initialized crystal.

"Need a hand, Major?" Lorne looked around in the mess line to see Lt. Colonel Hocken coming up behind him, her red hair just growing out enough to curl over the tops of her ears. She shifted her tray to one hand and reached for his with the other.

"Thanks. I appreciate it," Lorne said. It was hard to manage the tray and a cane, though he'd done it. But he wasn't too proud to accept help; a little backup was just good teamwork.

She snagged his tray and put it on one of the tables under the skylights, then pulled out his chair for him.

"Thanks again," he said, sinking into it. "Join me?"

"Sure." Hocken put her tray down opposite, breaded chicken tenders with fries and today's mystery vegetable.

"I didn't see you at the poker game last night," Lorne said, settling his cane against the edge of the table.

Hocken didn't look up from her lunch. "I got busy."

"A lot of that going around," Lorne said, reaching for the salt shaker casually. "Carter must be driving you guys hard. Franklin didn't come either."

Hocken glanced at him, startled. "Really?"

"Yep," Lorne said. "In fact, nobody showed but me and Cadman and Grant. Not much of a game with three hands, so we called it off and Cadman and I watched *Rear Window* instead."

"Ok," Hocken said. She frowned. "What was that about?"

Lorne shrugged. How to put this without making it clear he'd gone to the top of the food chain? "You know, Colonel Sheppard's a good guy. Maybe some of that stuff Franklin said about Afghanistan made some people uncomfortable. That's kind of how it works sometimes. Ricochet. You get hit with your own bullet."

"You think?" There was an unexpectedly bitter note in Hocken's voice. "I thought that had more to do with the *Hammond's* 302s than with Sheppard."

Click. Ok, that made everything make sense to Lorne, Hocken's absence and Carter's fury. Yes, it was a serious breach of protocol to dig up stuff about the base commander and gossip to his subordinates, but Carter had also read that as an internal problem on the *Hammond*, her first officer gunning for the commander of the 302 flight. Oh yeah. Big problem. And he'd better make it clear where he stood.

"I told Carter," Lorne said.

Hocken blinked. "Yeah?"

"Sheppard's a good guy," Lorne said again. "I wouldn't want any misunderstanding, you know?" He shifted his leg around under the table, trying to get comfortable. "Carter said she'd handle it."

Whatever Hocken would have said was forestalled by Sheppard, Ronon and Zelenka approaching with their trays, Zelenka holding forth about something or other while Ronon listened attentively, more attentively than Sheppard.

"Hey," Sheppard said, staking out the seat next to Hocken. "Got room for us?"

"Of course."

The protocol gets into your bones, Lorne thought. She was the ranking officer, so of course he asked her. Radek took the seat beside him with Ronon on the other side. "...and so I said, of course we can get it, but it won't be easy. Is it ever?"

"No," Ronon replied.

Sheppard looked at Lorne. "How's the leg? Did Keller clear you for off world duty yet?"

"No," Lorne said regretfully. Another thing he couldn't do yet, another duty of his being dumped on someone else...

"It's ok," Sheppard said. "I can get somebody else to be the human light switch. Ronon's taking a team back to Sateda and I need somebody who can turn on the Ancient doohickey Radek's looking for. It's not a big thing." He glanced sideways at Hocken. "You up for an off world trip, Mel? If you're just hanging around with nothing to do, maybe Carter could spare you for the afternoon?"

"I could be up for that." Hocken grinned at him. "Not a problem."

"Hey, you wanted to be an astronaut," Sheppard said. "Look how that worked out."

CHAPTER SIXTEEN

The Skies of Sateda

IT WAS still a long walk from the Stargate to the City Museum, even though the Satedans had cleared a better path through the damaged streets since the last time Radek had been there. It was a pleasant day, clear and warm, and after the endless cold of Atlantis's new world, it was a relief to be able to open his jacket and enjoy the sunshine. Ronon had exchanged his long-sleeved shirt for one of his familiar sleeveless vests, and even the trio of Marines looked relaxed and happy. Colonel Hocken was squinting up at the sky as though she were judging the speed of the gentle wind, while William was busy chatting up the Satedan in charge of the day's expedition. William had already discarded his jacket and overshirt, revealing a t-shirt that fit too well to be regulation — all in all, Radek thought, more than a bit of a holiday. Even if there were Genii to deal with at the end.

And sure enough, there they were, three young men in a mix of civilian clothes and uniforms, and Ladon Radim's sister Dahlia stood with Ushan Cai beside the entrance to the Museum's basements. She was looking a little grim, and Radek was glad they hadn't brought Teyla along after all. Dahlia had disliked and distrusted her since they'd recovered the Ancient warship, and there was no need to exacerbate the problem. Cai lifted his hand in greeting, then came forward to clasp Ronon's hand.

"It's good to see you again," he said.

"We're glad to help out," Ronon answered. That was for Dahlia, Radek guessed, a reminder that they were the ones doing the Genii a favor here.

"And we appreciate it," Dahlia said, with a creditable smile. "I believe my brother made our situation clear?"

Ronon nodded. "You found something you need us to initialize for you. Along with some other stuff we might find useful."

"Yes," Dahlia said.

"So let's see it," Ronon said.

"We've left the objects where we found them," Dahlia said. "At the insistence of Mr. Lyal here." She nodded to the man who had been talking to William. "He informed us — insisted, in fact — that you would find them more interesting if we did not move them."

Ronon looked as though he was going to protest, but William interrupted. "Brilliant, thank you. That's exactly what we need."

"Right," Ronon said, after only a fractional hesitation.

"This way," the Satedan, Lyal, said quickly, gesturing toward the open door. "But — it's a small space."

"Colonel," Ronon began, and Hocken nodded.

"Why don't I stay here? With the Marines."

And provide cover and back-up just in case, Radek thought, with approval. It wasn't precisely that he didn't trust the Genii, but he felt a lot better with the military contingent keeping an eye on things above ground.

"I'll remain also," Dahlia said, firmly, and Ronon nodded.

"OK. Let's go."

It was, Radek thought, better than the last time he'd climbed down into the basement of the City Museum. Cai's people had rigged a remarkably sturdy-feeling ladder, and the Genii had provided a generator and strung electric lights, so, all in all, it was an improvement. Admittedly, the giant, massive-tusked skull was still lying in the middle of its smashed crates, though someone had decorated it with a wreath of wilting flowers, which didn't make it look any less aggressive, and there was still a section of passage where one had to crawl, but at least he was confident that the ceiling was unlikely to collapse on them. Reasonably confident, he amended, studying the nearest supports. He would have preferred to place them just half a meter or so closer to the main wall, but he thought they would probably hold.

He edged through the last narrow corridor, came out into a

wider space lit by a cluster of worklights on tripod stands. Behind him, Ronon grunted, came out of the corridor rubbing the top of his head. William ignored them both, concentrating on the items laid out on the improvised worktable.

"I thought you said nothing was moved," he said to Lyal, who gave an apologetic shrug.

"This was salvage. It wasn't until they started finding things we didn't recognize that we decided to leave the objects where they were."

William gave an abstracted nod, an all too familiar expression, and produced a flashlight from his pocket. The beam of light splashed over a row of dark gaps, like the mouths of narrow tunnels, revealing shelves and crates and a waterfall of dust and plaster. "These are — were — more storage areas?"

"Yes," Lyal said. "More of the Ancestors' collection, I think — assuming we've identified the area correctly, and that the plans we have are accurate."

"There's always that," William agreed, with a smile, and edged carefully into the first of the openings.

Ronon made another irritated noise, and looked at the young Genii who'd come down with them. "So what's this thing you need us to turn on?"

"Here." The Genii — his name was Alvers, Radek remembered — pointed to the largest of the crystals laid out on the worktable.

"May I?" Radek moved forward without waiting for an answer, slipping off his pack of tools. You didn't often find crystals that large and complex intact, though clearly the Satedans had made an effort to collect them. He lifted it carefully, turning it in the light, and shook his head. There was a fine crack in the outside pillar, a faint thread of darkness that followed an internal face, spoiling the even color. "This is damaged — here, do you see?"

Alvers shrugged. "It's very small."

"But enough to blow this apart in your faces," Radek answered. "And I don't particularly want to be blamed for that."

"The Chief of Sciences knows there's a crack," Alvers said, sounding offended. "But — without this, we can't fly our ship."

"I don't think you can fly it with this," Radek said. Still… He had made cracked crystals work, if only for a limited time. He set it back down again, and took out the finest of his probes. The crack was shallower than he'd thought, and not as long; the internal facets had deceived him. OK, maybe it would work for a while, but if this was a key navigational component, when it blew, the *Pride of the Genii* would be stranded somewhere in deep space. And that wasn't exactly going to make anybody happy.

It didn't look like a navigational crystal, though, or at least not the ones with which he was most familiar. They tended to have more internal crystals, layers within layers, not this central core surrounded by smaller, stubbier controls. If anything, it looked like a weapons array.

"We need it initialized," Alvers said. "We're prepared to take whatever risks are necessary."

It *was* part of a weapons array, Radek realized. He'd seen this shape of crystal before in the jumpers, though this was at least six or seven times larger. This was the power control, the equivalent of a capacitor, which, in practical terms, meant it was likely enough to overload. "What did you say this was for?"

"It matches a damaged crystal in our navigation systems," Alvers answered.

And that, Radek thought, means this is a lie. He glanced over his shoulder, wondering how to warn Ronon — not that it was necessarily a problem to give the Genii working weapons, they were technically allies, but if they were going to lie about it, it was hard not to think that Ladon Radim was up to something. It wouldn't be the first time.

"If it blows up, it will damage the surrounding systems," Radek temporized. "It's your business, of course — but do you want to take that risk?"

"We don't have a choice," Alvers answered. "Unless you have an undamaged crystal you'd be willing to trade for us?"

"I doubt we have one," Radek answered. "I know most of our larger inventory, and I haven't seen one like this."

Alvers spread his hands. "There you are."

"What's wrong with this one?" Ronon asked.

"It's cracked," Radek began. *And it's not what they say it is. If only there were a way to get Alvers out of earshot—*

William reappeared in the tunnel mouth, his flashlight gripped in his teeth. He was cradling a box of what looked like datacrystals, and set it carefully on the table, then took the flashlight out of his mouth. "This looks interesting."

"Yes?" Radek fixed him with a stare. At Cambridge, William had been quick enough to pick up a hint. "What is it?"

William blinked once. "Datacrystals. Mostly intact, I think. Possibly worth something in trade?"

"Where did you find them?" Radek asked.

William blinked again. "In — they were in a storage cell."

"Do you think there might be information about these larger crystals somewhere?"

"I don't —" William stopped. "It's possible, I suppose. Maybe — maybe if I knew where it was found? So I could match catalog records?"

"Yes," Radek said. "That might help. Mightn't it?"

William nodded. "Yes. Yes, absolutely. Mr. — Alvers, is it? Would you show me?"

The Genii hesitated, but there wasn't a good way to refuse. "Of course," he said. "This way."

He started down the farthest corridor, William and Lyal on his heels, and Radek turned to look at Ronon.

"We have a problem," he said quietly.

Mel Hocken looked up at a cloudless Satedan sky. The wind was out of the southwest, freshening slightly, a perfect day for flying. Of course, she wasn't flying. She was standing around waiting to be a human light switch. Whenever Ronon and Zelenka's science team hunted up whatever they were looking for, her job was to turn it on and see if it worked. Pretty boring, but the chance to get off world wasn't. Sateda was her twelfth world, counting the planet where Atlantis now rested. She'd been in 302s since the second batch of trainees, and mostly she'd seen a lot of the inside of starships. Well, and the outside of some. She'd been there when the *Korolev* was destroyed by the Ori, with the 302 wing aboard *Odyssey* at the time.

Mel shook her head. No point in thinking about that. It hadn't exactly been their most resounding victory ever. It hadn't felt good. The losses were too high.

The best one had been the first one, the battle over Antarctica when she was part of Lt. Colonel Mitchell's squadron. That had felt good, at least until the adrenaline wore off.

"Tea, Colonel?"

Mel turned at the voice at her elbow. It was the Satedan leader, Ushan Cai, with two stoneware handleless mugs of the strong Satedan tea. "Thank you," she said, "I appreciate it." More than that, she appreciated her proper rank and honorific. She'd always had to fight for that from the Jaffa in the Milky Way, but the Satedans didn't seem to have a problem with women in the military.

Cai handed her one mug. "And what were you thinking, with your eyes on the sky?"

"That it's a perfect day for flying," Mel said.

Cai glanced upward. "How can you tell, in your metal boxes?"

"I was thinking more about a light plane," Mel said. She took a sip of the hot, smoky tea. "You wouldn't think so, when I've got a 302, but I like small aircraft too. When you can really feel the airspeed and the wind makes a big difference. There's a whole different skill set to it, a different challenge. I like the big guys, no question about it, but sometimes I wish I'd lived in the era of prop fighters. I'd like a P-38 Lightning." Not that Ushan Cai knew what that was. "There are a lot of planes that are smaller and less high tech than the ones we use right now. Propeller driven, gasoline engines — from passenger and cargo planes that can carry a couple of dozen people down to single person ultralights."

Cai frowned slightly. "And your people use these as well as the ships we have seen?"

"Oh yeah." Mel took another sip. "I was stationed in Alaska for a while a few years back. General aviation is a huge thing there, because there's so much territory to cover and the roads aren't good, and lots of places there aren't even roads. Lots and lots of little light aircraft, most of them propeller driven ones that can land in any open field that's big enough. Or sea planes, fitted out with floats that can land on a lake or river. A lot of people use them to get around the back country instead of driving."

"And are there not rail lines?" Cai asked.

Mel shrugged. "Alaska has rail lines, but it's not like they go wherever you want. Not out to every little town."

"And these planes can land in any open field?"

"With a skilled pilot, sure." Mel looked at him curiously. "With respect, Mr. Cai, why are you interested in Alaska?"

Ushan Cai grinned. "I'm interested in the planes, Colonel Hocken." He leaned up against the edge of the fountain, one booted foot on the pockmarked stonework. "Are they expensive?"

"Not compared to a 302," Mel said. "They're millions apiece. General aviation planes run a couple of hundred thousand, depending on what you get. There are ultra light kit planes for twenty five, thirty thousand. I looked into buying one for fun a few years ago, but then I was posted to *Odyssey* and would never have had a chance to use it."

"So that is very affordable? What is the value of that in trade goods?"

Mel thought about it for a minute. "Well, finished titanium runs about $20 a pound, give or take fluctuations in the market. One of those big plates of yours is probably worth $2,000. So fifteen of those for an ultra light? Seventy five of them for a shiny new Cessna? Something like that."

Ushan Cai nodded gravely. "That seems very reasonable."

"You want to buy a plane?"

Cai leaned over his foot, taking a sip of his tea. "Sateda was a heavily populated world, Colonel Hocken. This whole continent had a population of millions. But many of them did not live in the cities. There were towns and villages, farms and mines, and homesteaders who lived as our ancestors had, in upland holdings answering only to their own chieftain. The rail lines connected us, and in recent years had brought steam heat and electric lights to even remote areas. Coal and other resources flowed into the city down our arteries of iron." He looked out over the city, his eyes narrowed against the bright sunlight. "The Wraith destroyed our rail lines, and there is not a working engine in the city. It will be generations before they can be restored. But I do not think that all the people are dead. I cannot imagine how they could be! It is one thing to Cull a great city, and another to find every isolated farmstead. The country people did not rely on food brought in, or on things from far away. Most of them lived like my grandfather's people did, with little farms and goats, carrying their water and burying their waste in outdoor latrines, making tallow candles against the dark of the year. I can't believe they're all dead. I think they must be going on as they were, radios silent to mark the end of the world. But we have no way to find out." He looked at Mel sharply. "And you are giving me a way."

Mel swallowed hard. "Take an ultralight out to scout. Go see who you can find. Use light planes to reestablish contact." She nodded slowly, taking another sip of tea to cover where her throat had closed. "Light planes to ferry medicine and doctors, to tie the world back together."

"Yes," Cai said.

"The Satedan Air Force."

Cai nodded. "Do you think it could be done?"

"Way too easily," Mel said. "A couple of kit planes bought with your titanium, brought out on the *Daedalus*. Bring them through the Stargate disassembled and put them together here. I'm not enough of a mechanic to do it, but we've got plenty of people who are." She looked at him. "But who would fly it? If your people didn't have aircraft, you'd need to send some people to flight school."

"Or hire an instructor," Cai said. His eyes lingered on her face speculatively. "I wonder what that would cost."

Mel swallowed again. "I'm sure with the right person you could work something out," she said. "After all, Ronon is a contractor who works for us. You could hire someone as a contractor, someone to help you get your air program off the ground, no pun intended."

Cai looked at her sideways. He must see the interest, the hunger. "Interested?"

"I could be," Mel said. "I'll have my twenty years in June, seven months from now. And if they haven't repealed Don't Ask, Don't Tell… Well, that's a long story, but let's just say I've got some personal frustrations with certain regulations." She straightened up, looking up into the bright, cool Satedan sky. It felt right. A new world, a new beginning, the start of something entirely different. No more lies, no more watching her back among her own people. "I could retire and come to Sateda. Yes."

Ronon hauled himself slowly up the ladder to the Museum's main floor, wondering what he should do. The Genii had lied, but that was hardly a surprise; the Genii generally found lies easier than truth, and he could see why Ladon Radim might not want to tell anyone that his brand-new Ancient warship wasn't currently armed. But that still left the question of whether or not they ought to initialize the crystal. He wished there was a way he could call Sheppard—no, call Woolsey; if he was going to ask for help, he ought to ask the person who was actually in charge—but he couldn't think of a way to do it that wouldn't offend Dahlia Radim. And she already didn't trust them. It wasn't like Teyla to screw up anything that involved diplomacy—but that wasn't the point. The point was, the Genii were still useful allies, and it was in his hands whether they stayed that way.

He came out into the sunlight, blinking, the smell of the settlement's cooking fires drifting on the warm breeze. Dahlia was sitting on a low wall, her scientists one on each side like a Wraith queen's warriors. She looked tired, her skin blanched, wrinkles showing in the strong light. The Marines had moved away, toward the edge of the little courtyard, and were talking quietly, P90s dangling; Hocken and Cai had their heads together, and the colonel was grinning as though he'd told her a particularly clever joke. Ronon had never seen her expression so unguarded, wondered if there was a place where his face changed like that. Once it had been Sateda, of course, but now — Atlantis, perhaps, where they'd taken him in, seen him at his worst, and still let him find his way. Which was another reason he had to do this right. Somehow.

He cleared his throat because he didn't know how to address a Genii Chief of Sciences, and they all turned to look at him. Right. Give them the device Dahlia needed to make their only starship operational — to make it a battle cruiser, perhaps the equal of one of the Earth warships. He wished he knew more about their capabilities, wished he'd paid more attention, read more, studied more. Probably not their equal; the ship might be better, but the Earth people knew what they were doing, their crews were trained in a way the Genii couldn't be. And they needed everybody, every human in Pegasus, who could fight to stand up against Queen Death. That had to be the bottom line, he thought. They couldn't do anything unless they defeated Death. And that meant handing the Genii the weapons they needed, much as he hated the idea.

Dahlia rose to her feet, the sun bright on her fair hair. "Can you initialize it?"

Ronon nodded. "Yeah. But — you know there's a problem."

Dahlia hesitated for just an instant, then dipped her head in turn. "I am aware that the crystal has a hairline crack, yes. I believe it will hold, if power levels are strictly controlled."

"Maybe," Radek interjected. He moved to join them, giving Ronon one wary glance. Ronon nodded again, and the scientist's mouth tightened for an instant.

"OK, then," Radek said. He looked back at Dahlia. "It may hold for a while, yes, but not forever. You will blow it up eventually."

"That's possible, certainly," Dahlia said. "But, unless you have a replacement to offer in trade, we have no choice if we are to get the *Pride of the Genii* into running order. Which, I hardly need mention, is to your advantage as much as it is to ours."

"Yes, yes," Radek said. "I am aware of the situation. But that's not my concern here. The crystal is flawed, and it will eventually fail. Probably catastrophically. And I have no desire to be blamed for sabotaging it."

Something like a smile flickered across Dahlia's face. "I can assure you that will not happen."

"No?" Radek tipped his head to one side, looking like an angry bird.

"The flaw is known," Dahlia said. "I have taken full responsibility."

Radek threw up his hands. "On your head be it, then."

"Very likely," Dahlia said. She looked at Ronon, frowning, and he shrugged.

"It's a reasonable concern."

Her eyes fell. "Yes," she said, after a moment. "From your perspective, I do see that. But — as I said, the responsibility is mine."

"OK, then," Ronon said. He had to believe her, or say no. And they needed the Genii, at least for now. "Colonel?"

Hocken turned away from her conversation with Cai, came to join them. "Mr. Dex?"

"Go ahead and — turn this thing on." Ronon waved toward the improvised bench where Radek had left the crystal cocooned in spongy padding.

"Sure thing." She bent over the crystal, folding the padding away, and the crystal hummed softly at her touch. She frowned, concentrating, and the crystal lit with a flash that made them all jump.

"Hocken?"

"Holy crap." She bit back whatever else she would have said.

"Did I do that?"

"Let me see," Radek said, hurrying over, and Dahlia was at his heels. Hocken backed away, and the two scientists bent over the crystal together.

"Great," Hocken said, under her breath. "Way to go, Mel."

Ronon glanced at her, and saw her blush. "Hey, it's not your fault. Everybody said it was damaged."

"Yeah, but." Hocken shook her head.

"You heard her yourself," Ronon said. "It's her call, not ours. And they weren't going to be able to manage without it."

"I suppose," Hocken said, but he thought she looked relieved.

"Oh, very good," Radek said, straightening, and Dahlia gave a long sigh. "OK, yes, that was — interesting — but it has held, and it's successfully initialized."

"Thank you," Dahlia said, and managed to remember, "Colonel. Gentlemen."

And if it held under that stress, Ronon thought, it would probably hold up to the strain of the weapons system. At least for a while. And that had to be a good thing, or at least that was what he'd tell Woolsey.

It was a little harder to remember that conviction sitting in Woolsey's office, his hands folded carefully on the desktop, copying Woolsey's familiar pose. He felt like a schoolboy, like the overgrown fifteen-year-old he'd been, tripping over his feet and his tongue, often at the same time. But that was a very long time ago, and he straightened his spine, fighting for the words.

"So it seemed to me that it was better to go ahead and give them the working crystal so that they could fight Queen Death. So I did."

There was a little silence, Woolsey watching him steadily. "That's it?" he said at last.

Ronon nodded. "Yeah."

Woolsey nodded slowly. "I agree."

"What?" Ronon had been braced to argue, to justify himself, felt as though he'd stepped on ice that cracked to let him fall through.

"I agree." Woolsey smiled slightly. "It was a good call, Mr. Dex."

"Thanks," Ronon said after a moment, and pushed himself back from the desk. Woolsey looked up at him, his face abruptly serious.

"You're welcome. It's why we're glad to have you here, you know."

"Thanks," Ronon said again, and let himself out into the gate-room.

CHAPTER SEVENTEEN

The Old One's Tale

THE SHIP would not speak to him, despite his blandishments. Ember hauled himself to his feet, letting his fingers trail along the wall of the cell one last time. He thought this was a cruiser, but it was hard to be sure even of that much: the ship resisted him, blocked his thoughts, and if he pressed much further, it would send a warning jolt of electricity through its skin. He worked his shoulders, assessing his condition. He still felt the haze of the Culling beam, and he was weaker than he should be, the first pains of hunger starting in his palm. He had fed recently, though, so either he had been held for longer than seemed reasonable, or — He tugged open the neck of coat and shirt. There was no mark on his skin, but he was sure someone had fed on him. It was common enough, to weaken a prisoner so, but he wished whoever had done it would sicken. So he had been a prisoner, then, long enough for his body to heal itself, but not long enough for all the effects of the Culling beam to have worn off completely: a day, then, and no more than two.

It didn't make sense. Why would he have been taken prisoner instead of being killed outright? Death might suspect that he had helped Quicksilver, but the point where that would have mattered was long past. Steelflower had set herself openly against Death, and both sides were gathering their allies and their fleets. The business with McKay had failed, and should be put aside, unless Death was feeling vindictive. That was a possibility that could not be ignored, either, and he grimaced at the thought. He remembered kneeling before her, her feeding hand against his skin, tugging the life from him. Or perhaps she thought he might be a useful bargaining counter: he was, after all, Steelflower's chief cleverman. That thought was no more appealing.

The light shifted outside the webbed door, and he straightened, smoothing his hair to something like order. A pair of drones, and a tall blade — no, a blade he recognized, and Ember shuddered in spite of himself.

The Old One smiled from the far side of the grill. *Good. You have not forgotten.*

How could I? Ember dipped his head politely, and braced himself for whatever game was to come. He was not on Death's flagship, he would have recognized it even if it refused contact; this was some smaller craft, a ship he had never visited.

I am sorry it has come to this, the Old One said, after a moment, and waved the drones to a distance, out of ordinary listening. *Your queen is reckless with your lives, to stand against our lady.*

Death was more reckless still. Ember let that show in his face, said only, *It is her right.*

The Old One gave a thin smile. *As it is my queen's right to take your life in truth, rather than the taste she had earlier.*

Ember flinched, and knew the Old One saw.

It is fortunate that she has another use for you.

Forgive me if that does not fill me with delight, Ember said, and this time the Old One laughed aloud.

No, no, this is truly your day of fortune, cleverman. I wish you to carry a message to Guide.

I will not act against my queen, Ember said warily.

I do not ask you to, the Old One said. *I say this message is for Guide as one lord of the zenana speaks to another. It is not yet a matter for queens.*

Such messages were not unknown — Ember remembered such negotiations from childhood, when there had been more hives circling the galaxy in complex alliance. But now? He tipped his head to one side, considering. It would only be trickery, but surely there was no harm in carrying a message. Guide would be glad if he lived, and there was no shame in finding a way to survive. And yet why would the Old One bother, knowing that he would put the pieces together in the same way?

Tell me this message, he temporized. *And if I may do so with honor, I will carry it to Guide.*

You are a cleverman, master of sciences biological, the Old One said. *Have you never wondered how we came to be?"

We? Ember repeated.

We Wraith, the Old One said.

Ember paused. *We are not encouraged to pursue the matter.*

You are a master, a cleverman of Gryphon, the Old One said. *And the sons of Gryphon never leave well enough alone. What were your conclusions?*

We are a hybrid of the Iratus insect and humans, Ember said, after a moment. Anyone who made Sciences Biological their specialty learned that much, though it was not something blades spoke of, and even cleverman treated it with caution. But that much was no real secret.

And?

Iratus abilities imposed on a human template, Ember said. That was the dangerous piece, that they were close kin to the kine that fed them. No one wanted to hear that, even if it were true.

The Old One gave an approving nod. *By whom?*

Ember blinked. *By…no one, I would say. The Iratus drones are vicious and stealthy. I expect humans came through the Ring looking for a new homeworld, and found too late that a queen and hive were already in residence. Over the generations, the species merged.* His voice trailed off. No, that couldn't be the right answer. The human settlers would simply have left the planet, gone back where they'd come from, long before the Iratus traits could become solidly established. Unless there had been some reason they couldn't leave?

The Old One smiled again. *You already see the flaws in that hypothesis.*

You have a better answer?

We were made, the Old One said. *We were made by the Ancients for their own purposes, but we rebelled against them. What did you think caused the war between us? They knew we would kill them all for what they had done.*

Ember's breath caught in his chest. Yes, that made sense. It smoothed out the impossible time line, eliminated a hundred problems that he and other clevermen had worried over — that generations of clevermen had worked to solve, but could not, unable to imagine that one possibility.

You see it, the Old One said, and Ember dipped his head again.

Yes. But — why?

That I never knew, the Old One said, and there was a bitter edge to his voice. *But that is the message I would have you take to Guide — and to Steelflower, if she has wit to hear. We cannot trust these humans, these new Lanteans. They are children of the Ancients, carrying their blood, their genes, and we cannot make peace with them. If we try, they will destroy us utterly.*

That doesn't follow, Ember said.

The Old One bared his teeth. *They will have no choice. They made us too well.* He paused, extended his off hand through the unshielded bars of the holding cell. *As we had no choice in our day. Come, I will tell you a story, one no one has heard in a thousand years or more — if you dare listen.*

What is your lineage? Ember demanded. A man of Osprey could fill his mind with visions, Cloud's children could compel —

I have no lineage, the Old One said. *I served Osprey in my day, but I am not of her kin, or any others'. I am the last of ninety-nine men who served the First Mothers. Will you hear my tale?*

Impossible, surely — but, no, it was all too possible. Even the Old One's face testified to its probability, carved on lines no living queen, no queen in living memory, would choose. Slowly Ember held out his own off hand, let the Old One close fingers around his wrist.

I will hear, he said.

Their eyes were stung by the full light of day but the caves beneath Mount Sirris were cool and damp and welcoming. Ashes had hunted crystals there when he was younger, before he had sought the City of the Ancestors, and to his mild surprise he found that he remembered the network of tunnels as though he had searched there yesterday. There was a cave toward the eastern side of the mountain where the air was sweet and there was access to a cold spring. He led them there by the light of a single torch, amazed at how much better his night-sight had become, and as their band spread blankets and kindled a fire, he carried skins to the pool to fill them. Not that he was thirsty — none of them were; he'd asked, over and over, and no one admitted thirst — but he still could not entirely believe that they could live without drinking.

Without drinking water, in any case. He sat back on his heels, the first waterskin soft and plump at his side. The distant firelight caught the crystals that studded the rock behind the pool, flecks of light like stars, like his first glimpse of space from the Ancestors' ships, when he had still been loved by them, when he had still believed… He looked away, fixing his eyes on the barely-rippling water. They had all drunk blood in plenty, in the escape, and after.

He looked down at his left hand, turned it palm up to study the new organ at its heart. He'd heard the uneasy jokes, first from the Ancestors themselves, when they hadn't known he'd listened, and again from the younger men, though the women's strength kept them from saying them too loudly, but he had no time to waste with that. He was a scientist; it was his task to decipher what it was that they had become.

It — they, he — he did not actually drink blood. He had tested that theory when they first fled to Athos, and from Athos to Lepys: it was not blood alone that nourished them. Nor could flesh or vegetable feed them. The most changed, the ones he guessed had been most malleable, most receptive to the virus, vomited the food immediately; when he palpated their bellies, in the moments before they sickened, he could feel the food shifting in a shrunken stomach pouch. Others ate and enjoyed the taste, but within a day either threw it up again or passed it undigested. A few fruits — dammas, on Renweir; the sweet plums of Athos — seemed to pass without undue pain, and they'd all enjoyed the taste, but he could tell they took no nourishment from them.

The death of men nourished them. That he had proved conclusively, both in the escape and in the hunted aftermath. The death of animals did not. He had tried, trapping coneys alive and latching onto them with his strange new claws and the mouth in the center of his hand. The coneys had withered and died like men, but there had been no surge of strength, no respite from the hunger.

We feed on that which separates men from beasts, he thought, and wondered again if that had been the Ancestors' deeper intent. They had said they sought an immunity to the attack of the Iratus bug, but he no longer believed that. More likely, they sought immunity from disease — there had been whispers of a plague, once and away, that even the Ancestors feared — or perhaps they sought another route to Ascension. And perhaps this had been intended to become a gift for their children, he thought, a way for us to follow them into whatever bliss lay beyond this life. Perhaps this — soul? Mind? Perhaps this essence we feed on is what one must have in order to Ascend? Or perhaps it is that from which we must be freed? Maybe that was what they wanted, that we should free them, send them on their way... His hand ached, a dull throbbing in the center of his new mouth, slower than a heartbeat, and he slipped it beneath the water as though that might numb the pain.

The cold was like an electric shock, a thrust of lighting and a knee to the balls, shaking his very heart. He snatched his hand away, hissing between his teeth, cradled it against his chest until the pain stopped.

Are you well?

It was Osprey's voice, and he looked up, still clutching hand to chest, to see her standing at the other end of the sliver of dark beach. He had not sensed her presence — he could feel the others, all of them, count them together in the larger chamber, but she was as invisible as a ghost until she chose to be seen.

Yes, he said. *I'm — I did something stupid, that's all.*

You must feed soon, she said, and he nodded again.

Yes. But not immediately.

She regarded him thoughtfully, and his eyes fell. He remembered her as she had been, slight and smiling, barely out of girlhood, her long black hair in a braid that fell below her hips. He had taken her hand, recognizing a fellow Athosian, spoken to her of places they had shared before he'd gone to serve the Ancestors, promised her he would look after her, promised that she would be unharmed, and changed only for the better. The lie had been inadvertent, but it had been a lie nonetheless, and its weight was in his chest every time he looked at her.

You know more than most about what was done to us, she said. *And I've seen you testing your ideas. I want to know what you've found.*

He hesitated for a moment, seeing again the smiling girl, a farmer's daughter, not even a child of the Ancestors' City, and he felt her displeasure like a shock of cold air.

I am not that child, she said. *I am not sure I was ever only what you saw, Kairos, but rest assured I am not her now.*

Kairos. The name echoed, and with it came an image, his face, flat and plain and kindly — her memory of the man he had been, and he bowed to her, bending deeper than he had bent to the Ancestors themselves. *I apologize.*

We must share everything we know, she said. *No matter how we have come to know it, or where it may lead us, we must pool our knowledge. Without it, we will not survive.*

It was more than a year before they came again to Athos, and by then Osprey's band had stolen a ship, so they were no longer dependent on the Rings, at the mercy of the Ancestors. It had been Ashes' idea to return to his and Osprey's home, to try to contact the kin they had left behind, and after some debate the others had agreed that the risk was worth the trial. Only Wind objected, but he bowed to Osprey's decision. Whether he had come to agree with the idea, or merely did not wish to break the band or to be left to himself, Ashes could not have said, and did not inquire. He was *simply grateful that Wind had capitulated.*

They landed in the hills north of Emege, where the people lived in seasonal villages, and the high pastures would still be untenanted at the beginning of the spring. The air was cold and thin, but neither seemed to have much effect on what they had become. Ashes noted that, as he had noted all the other changes, the records of how they fed, and when, on whom and what it did to the victim. The last had not been pretty to explore, but it had been necessary: they could not always feed on their pursuers, and it had seemed worthwhile to find out if they could gain sustenance without damaging the subject beyond recovery. The feeding process mimicked aging in the subject, though it was not completely analogous. They had captured one of the Ancestors, a pilot, when they first tried to steal a ship, and kept him alive almost three months, draining his life sip by sip, but he had never recovered the strength he had lost. He had died raving, maddened by the enzyme that triggered the feeding process, and even the most embittered of the band had turned their face from him. But the result was incontrovertible. They could only kill, quick or slow, and Wind and the others who called themselves his blades swore that they would drain all at once and call it mercy. Ashes did not disagree, at least in principal, but he would not rule out the possibility of further research. Osprey granted the necessity, and that was enough.

I suppose you've brought us here for a reason, Wind said, standing in the hatchway of the stolen ship. It was a small craft, a freighter, but the former engineer they called Glass had rigged it with guns they'd stolen from one of the Ancestors' scouts.

Osprey stepped past him into the gathering dusk, her hair falling straight and silver to her hips. She walked past both of them without speaking, until she stood at the edge of the meadow, where the ground fell away abruptly to a forest of conifers. There was still snow on the slopes above them, and they could feel its breath chill them as the first stars showed against the purpling night.

My former wife lives in the nearest town, Ashes said. *That is why I have brought us here. She is a physician and a scholar herself, and I would tell her what the Ancestors have done to us.*

Former wife, you say. Wind's mental voice was tinged with skepticism. *And on what terms did you part?*

Good terms, Ashes said. *In these hills, we marry for a term, and when the term is run, we may part without dishonor. She had her life, her work, and I—* Even now it was hard to say it calmly, and he bit down hard on the bitter anger. *I wished to go to the City of the Ancestors, to learn what I might of their science. And I had been chosen, over a dozen others, and we were both proud—*

He stopped, unable to go on, and Osprey's voice reached them, soft and cold as the touch of a snowflake.

I was born in these hills — there, on the slope of Gallenar, beneath the Father of Snows. My mother, my father, they live there still, for all I know otherwise.

Wind took a step forward, as though he would take her hand.

There is a lake there, where the ospreys live. She turned, held out a hand to each of them. Ashes took it, bowing his head, and her grief and anger broke over them like a great wave. He braced himself, stood firm against it, saw tears on Wind's cheeks. Even in that moment, he filed the fact: he had not known they could still weep. And then Osprey mastered herself, took a slow breath that calmed them all.

So, she said. *And you believe she will help us?*

I believe she will listen, Ashes said. *And, at worst, she will not betray us.*

And at best? That was Wind, wiping his hand across his face.

At best, I believe she will aid my research, help me find out what I, what we, have become, Ashes answered. He did not speak of a cure, though that thought still hovered in the backs of their minds.

It's a risk, Wind said.

Osprey paused. *Yes. But I can bring us there — a few of us, Ashes, of course, and you, Wind, and — shall we say two more? Armed and ready?*

Wind nodded.

The more we know, the better, Osprey said. *And if any of our kin will help us — we could surely use their aid.*

The chosen company made their way down the winding path that led to the winter village, arrived at its edge in the coldest hours just before the dawn. Osprey wound them in a cocoon of mist, and they drifted along the side streets until Ashes held up his hand.

Here.

Rissa's house stood a little apart from the others, with a larger yard where stock could be held for treatment. The pen was empty now, though he could hear the faint stir of animals in the barn. In the yard, a dog lifted its head, but Osprey soothed it to silence. A lantern burned at the side door, shuttered against the wind, the candle almost out — the healer's light, announcing that someone within would deal with emergencies — but another, brighter light glowed from a back window. That had been Rissa's workroom, and Ashes edged closer, until he could peep in the rippled glass. She could have remarried, could have lovers, could even have taken an apprentice, but to his relief, he saw she was alone, bent over her microscope at the long bench. She had always said she worked best in the still of night, when there was nothing to interrupt her thoughts. He remembered waking to find her gone, the warmth still lingering beneath the blankets, the distant flicker of her lamp a comfort.

We will wait, Osprey said. *But — do not take too long. There is something not right.*

Then we should leave, Wind said. *Try another time.*

Ashes hesitated, knowing he spoke sense, but held by the familiar images. Beyond the glass Rissa straightened, reached for another slide, her long hands sure and steady.

No, Osprey said. *This may be all the time we have.* She nodded to Ashes. *Go, speak to her. We will cover you.*

The mist swirled higher, covering her as she spoke, and Wind and his men melted into its shelter. Ashes took a breath, and tapped gently on the glass. Rissa looked up sharply, her eyes widening in fear.

"What—" Her voice broke, and she reached for the pistol she

had always kept beneath the workbench. "What do you want?"

"It's Kairos," he said. His voice was rusty with disuse, the words clumsy on his tongue. "Rissa, I need to talk to you."

"No." She kept the pistol leveled, but moved closer to the window. "I don't believe you. Who — what are you?"

"It is me." Ashes paused, trying to think of some way to prove it. It was hard to think, though, standing here with only a pane of glass between them. She had changed, of course. There was silver in her hair, and the lines at her eyes and bracketing her mouth had deepened, her skin more weathered. But still she was Rissa, and the breath caught for a moment in his throat. "I gave you the ring you wear there on your left hand, and our names are engraved within it."

"And what else?"

Ashes closed his eyes. "Our prayer for a child. A prayer not granted."

She moved then, came to pull back the door, but did not lower the weapon. Ashes turned to face her, but knew better than to close the distance between them.

"You cannot be Kairos," she said. "You are nothing like."

"Look again."

She shook her head, more in denial than in lack of recognition.

"I have been changed," he said. "But it is still me."

Rissa shook her head again. "I don't understand."

"This." Ashes gestured to his face, his hair, but some sense of decency kept him from showing his feeding hand. "This is what the Ancestors wanted. This is what they did to me, and to everyone who joined their experiment."

"No." Rissa's face hardened. "I don't believe you."

"It's true!"

"No," she said again. "They told me that you might come, that you stole my friend's memories and his life, a revenant monster—"

Ashes! That was Wind, and in the same instant Osprey's mind leaped to warn them all. The Ancestors were there, hidden in ambush, Rissa the bait to lure them in—

Ashes snarled aloud, knowing and not caring that it made him seem more monstrous still. "I am Kairos," he said, his eyes fixed on Rissa's. "I was your husband and your friend, and you have betrayed me."

"Liar," she said, her hands steady on the gun.

"Kill me, then, if you can."

She fired, a shot that sent him staggering back, more in surprise than in actual hurt. She fired a second time, and a third, and his control broke. He lunged for her, his off hand whipping up to strike the gun aside, his feeding hand flexed and ready. She screamed, a high and terrible noise that tore at his heart even as he sank his claws into her chest. The handmouth pulsed and clung, and she withered to a corpse in his hands. He pulled his hand free, blood on his nails, between his fingers. He had been so sure she would listen, that she would believe, and she had betrayed them, was part of the trap the Ancients set—and she was dead, Rissa dead at his hands, her life stolen. He had stolen her life, and it would never be enough. There would never be revenge enough for that.

One of Wind's men seized his arm. *Come!*

An energy weapon blazed through the night, one of the Ancestors firing blind into the mist.

Do not answer, Osprey called. *Fall back to the ship.*

Ashes shook himself, the wounds in his chest already healing, and turned to follow the others. Rissa, of all people—that Rissa would choose to follow the Ancestors blindly, even with the evidence standing before her—She of all people knew science, should have been willing to test, to probe, not to accept anything at face value. But she had not, and they were utterly betrayed.

He stumbled up the trail after the others, his face wet with tears, and at the top of the slope Glass caught his arm, drew him into the shelter of the ship. Wind took the controls, and they leaped for the shelter of deep space.

Ember jerked his hand free, snarling, the echo of Ashes's—the Old One's—grieving fury an ache in his own chest. I don't believe you, he would have said, except that the memory carried the conviction of truth. That is how it had been, how they had been born, been created, in the error of the Ancients' laboratories. It was a hard truth, but it made too many things fit together for him to reject it outright.

What then? he asked, and was proud that his tone was mostly steady.

The Old One gave a thin smile. *The rest you know. We hid, scurrying from shadow to shadow, and all the while we gained strength. Our queens bore children, blades and clevermen and daughters to aid them, and we soon found we did not age and die. Immortality the Ancients sought, and immortality they gave us, though they would never pay the price we paid. In the shadows we hunted, and they did not know what to make of us, or what to do to stop us. They could not find us, and our numbers mounted. They died, too, generations of them died, until at last there were enough of us to meet them face to face. We swept out of their nightmares then, and drove them out of a dozen systems before they knew what had happened to them.*

Yet it was not an easy victory, Ember said. That much he knew, that the Ancients had nearly destroyed them, and it had been force of numbers alone that had overwhelmed the Ancients in the end. The Wraith were still paying the price of that victory, too many men still living, and not enough humans left to feed them all. Which was something his work might solve, but he buried that thought deep in the recesses of his mind. He could not afford for the Old One to know of that, or he would never be released.

It was not, the Old One said. He sounded tired now, as though the memories themselves weighed more heavily than the years. *But it was victory nonetheless. There were a handful of us still living then who had been among the first Returned, and we toasted the victory in the lives of those who made us.*

Ember caught the ghost of that memory, half a dozen blades and clevermen and a single queen, circling a band of humans bound kneeling on the floor of an Ancient outpost. Smoke still rose from the broken consoles, and a swirl of dirt blew in through the broken walls. The queen was ripely beautiful, her scarlet hair caught up and back, exalted in her vengeance. The Ancients looked exhausted, exhausted and confused and afraid. Most bore the insignia of scholars and scientists, and the men and the queen paced slowly, savoring the moment as they chose their prey. Ember could taste the Old One's fierce joy, the life ripped from a gray-beard man, and then fed back, to be taken again — and the Ancient scientist had never known why, he realized. He could feel the terror and confusion that the Old One had felt, and recognized ignorance when he tasted it. He hid that, too, met the Old One's eyes.

And so here we are, he said, and made the words light and rueful.

Here we are, the Old One said. *We had our victory, and yet Atlantis has risen again, and the children of the Ancestors dwell within it. We must end it this time.*

These are not the Ancients, Ember protested. *They're — they are strong and clever, but they're not the Ancients.*

They are their descendants. They carry their blood, or else the city would not serve them. The Old One sighed. *That is my message to Guide. There can be no peace between us and these new Lanteans. We are what they made us, their doom incarnate, and we can be nothing else. Let us urge our queens to alliance at least long enough to end this war once and for all.*

Ember shivered. He could not quite believe it, did not want to believe, and yet the Old One's words carried the touch of absolute truth. He dipped his head again. *I will carry that message willingly.*

Good.

The Old One lifted his hand, and the cell's door opened. Ember walked out between the waiting drones, braced for a shot that did not come. He made himself relax, and looked over his shoulder at the Old One.

I will leave you where you can summon Guide, the Old One said, answering the unspoken question. *You have my word.*

Ember hoped it would be enough.

CHAPTER EIGHTEEN

Bloodtainted

WILLIAM had been on Sateda all day with a science team, came back later than the rest, arriving through the gate long after it would have been dark on Sateda. Radek had been hanging around the gateroom for a hour after the end of his shift, running diagnostics and chatting idly with Miko Kusanagi. It was not that he was worried, of course. It was merely that the science personnel were still his responsibility, and if he needed to send Marines to the rescue, he would rather know it now than in the middle of the night. And now as the wormhole vanished again and the iris folded closed, he was prepared to be annoyed. He expected William could see it, too, and was surprised when the other made his way up the steps.

"Radek. I didn't think I'd find you still here. I wonder if I might have a word?"

"Trouble?" Radek asked sharply. Things had been going a little too well…

William shook his head. "No. Or nothing immediate. Just—I'd like to talk to you about something."

He smelled of woodsmoke and Satedan tea and maybe just a bit of Satedan whiskey. Radek frowned, but even at second glance William looked completely sober, just tired and a little worried. "Very well—"

"Someplace quiet?" There was a note almost of pleading in William's voice.

"Very well," Radek said again, and gestured for him to lead the way.

They all had their favorite lurking places: Atlantis was large enough, and their number small enough that it was easy to find privacy. Sometime, in fact, it was harder to find company, or at least the company you wanted, but William seemed to have found his feet quickly. As usual.

They stopped in a room about a third of the way down the central tower. It was bleak in daylight, looking out onto roofs and walls, no clear view of the ocean horizon, but at night the aurora played behind the buildings like sheets of cold flame. William waved his hand over the controls and the lights came on, but only dimly, as though to preserve the spectacle. A twist of blue-green light coiled lazily behind the closest tower, and a streak of purple crossed the sky toward the zenith.

"So," Radek said, after a moment. "You did not bring me down here just to look at the pretty lights."

"No, unfortunately." William perched on the arm of the nearest chair, his face turned to the window. Shadows flickered on the floor, fell across his face. "It's an anthropological question, really. Have you run across the term 'Blood-Tainted?'"

"No," Radek began, but even as he said it, a faint memory returned. "Wait — Teyla's Gift? Something to do with that."

William nodded, his face still to the light. "I spent most of the day with the Satedans and the Genii salvage team. Blood-Tainted is their word for people like Teyla, who can sense the Wraith's presence."

"Yes," Radek said. "People — humans — with Wraith blood."

"No," William said. "That's what I thought it meant, myself, but neither the Genii nor the Satedans have the scientific sophistication to recognize that this is a function of shared DNA. 'Blood' is metaphorical here." He looked at Radek with a tired smile. "Only we were using the wrong metaphor. It's not blood as in kinship, shared blood, it's blood as in shed blood, blood as in murder and death. They — the Satedans and the Genii both — assume that any human who can hear the Wraith, who has Wraith traits, Wraith DNA, in our terms, is likewise a cold-blooded killer, a murder waiting to happen. To be tied to the Wraith in any way is to be a deadly danger to society. I think you see where that leaves us."

"Damn," Radek said softly as the implications began to sink in, and William nodded.

"My sentiments exactly."

"Ronon has spoken of such things before," Radek said. "But I don't think it occurred to anyone that this would be a widespread belief." He paused. "Or at least we hoped it was not."

"The first contact was with Athos," William said. "Where it's a Gift, not a stigma — well, yes, it sets people apart, but look at the word they use."

"You'd think more people would find it useful to know when there are Wraith around," Radek said. "When a Culling was imminent."

William nodded. "You'd think so. But maybe it doesn't work so well in an urban population? It probably isn't as useful — if the Athosians are warned, they can just scatter into the countryside, there are plenty of places to hide in the forests and fields and whatnot. But in a city, there just aren't enough places to hide."

"And too many people to hide," Radek said. He dropped onto the long bench opposite the other. "And no good way to fight back, either. Yes, I see."

"I wonder." William looked back at the window, where new skeins of blue and purple and gold arced across the sky. "I don't necessarily think that every serial killer in Genii or Satedan history had Wraith DNA. We've had enough of them on Earth to assume that it's a human flaw. But part of the Gift is a kind of telepathy. I wonder if either they're receiving images — hunger, satiety? — from distant hives, sensations that they're driven to recreate? Or maybe it's just having so many people around? Low level telepathy would make being in a crowd like a million fleabites."

"Or maybe not," Radek said, but gently. "Teyla cannot read human minds, remember."

"That's right," William said, unabashed. "I forgot that."

"It has made things interesting," Radek said, thinking of Steelflower and Todd's hive. "But Sheppard is good at pretending."

"I would imagine," William said, with a fleeting smile.

"Still — why, on Athos, is this a Gift? Are there other worlds that see it as such?"

Radek shrugged. "You know I don't know."

William gave him an apologetic glance. "Sorry. One more item to research."

"And perhaps more useful than ten-thousand-year-old prison escapes," Radek said.

"Maybe." William shook himself. "Still, I thought you should know about this. The more we have to work with the Satedans and the Genii — it's likely to complicate things."

"What doesn't?" Radek asked. William was right, though. They were committed to supporting the returned Satedans and Woolsey was determined to preserve some alliance with the Genii, and if this was how their allies felt about people like Teyla… "What do you want me to do about it?"

"I don't know," William said. "Woolsey needs to know, I suppose, and Sheppard, too — I suppose?" He smiled again. "Really, I think I wanted your advice."

"I'm touched," Radek said, his voice dry. "Yes, they need to be told, and yes, *you* should talk to them. Still — at least we have some time before we have to deal with this."

John touched Carson's shoulder, drawing him back into a corner of the room, leaving Teyla talking with Eva Robinson in front of the big windows. "Are you sure this is a good idea?"

Carson looked unhappy. "I'm never sure it's a good idea, not since Kate got this brainstorm five years ago. But I've learned better than to try to stop Teyla when she's got the bit in her teeth."

Between the white couch and the windows Teyla was chatting with Eva, who had her crutches under one arm. She still had two weeks to go in the cast. Teyla didn't look nervous at all.

"I can't stop her either," John said in a low voice. "But at least I can make sure she won't try it on her own."

"I've no idea what trying to access the genetic memories of a

Wraith queen could do," Carson said. "But I'm prepared for a medical emergency just in case."

Eva seemed to have heard the last, for she turned around with a reassuring smile. "Possibly nothing will happen. We have no idea how this works. Teyla tells me that she understands that many Wraith queens have very little access to these memories and that they essentially impart nothing. Hopefully, we'll do a little better than that."

"I feel sure that we will," Teyla said, lifting her chin. She came around the white sofa, sitting down on the other side. "If I could remember where Osprey and her people put the ZPM they took, perhaps it is still there."

"And maybe it's not," John said. They'd had this conversation before, but it seemed like he ought to say it again for form's sake.

"And maybe it is not," Teyla agreed. "But if it is, and we lose the opportunity to find a fully charged ZPM…"

"I know." John bent over the back of the sofa, leaning on his elbows. "We've got to try it."

"I assure you this is a very safe technique," Eva said, looking from one to the other. "On Earth it's mainly used in a spiritual setting, for people who believe that they have past lives to attempt to recall them." Carson snorted, but Eva ignored him. "Whether you believe in the literal truth of their memories or not, these things are powerful for the people who experience them."

"Well, we want to know literally where the ZPM is," Carson said.

"Carson," John said.

"I know. I'm just here in case this adventure gets out of hand." Carson raised his arms in a gesture of surrender.

Teyla looked up at him. "John, do you believe this will work?"

It didn't matter what Carson thought, or at least it didn't matter much. "Yeah," he said. "I do. Whether the ZPM is there now or not, at least it's a lead." John stood up, shoving his hands in his pockets. "It's worth a try." He gave Teyla a smile that he knew was wrong as he did it. "I'll be right here."

"I know you will be," she said, tilting her head to the side with an expression he knew meant she wasn't fooled at all by his nonchalance.

"Ok." Eva sat down on the other end of the couch, arranging her crutches against the chair arm. "Teyla, I'd like you to take a deep breath and let it out slowly. Just try to relax and let your breathing become nice and even."

Teyla took a deep breath, her eyes half closed, her hands resting open on her knees as they did when she meditated.

"That's right," Eva said, "nice and easy. Colonel Sheppard, why don't you sit down instead of hovering?"

"Oh, right." John sat down on one of the chairs. He supposed leaning over the back of the couch was kind of distracting.

"A nice deep breath," Eva said, "And then let it out. Then another. Just let go of all the stress. Nice, deep breaths."

Teyla looked serene. But then, she usually did. She looked relaxed, her back still perfectly straight, her eyes closed. The movement of her chest was even and regular. She did controlled breathing a lot. This probably wasn't scary for her, at least not this part.

Not like trying to teach Rodney to meditate that time. Rodney had flailed and fussed and complained, but John knew there was fear beneath it. Rodney had been scared to death by what was happening to him, by the weird effects of the ascension device he'd turned on. You couldn't relax when you were scared to death. If this worked for Teyla it would work because she wasn't afraid.

"Imagine yourself floating in a serene pool," Eva said quietly. "Floating on your back in a pool in the forest, looking up at the light through the tree branches above you. It's very quiet and very comfortable, very restful… Just let your breathing become very relaxed. Just let yourself rest in the serenity…"

His mom had been sitting like that, absolutely straight backed, cross legged on the floor, her palms turned up and her eyes closed.

The summer after the divorce he'd been at camp, eight weeks of basic training crashing into the Professional Officers Course, learn-

ing to be Air Force. There was a lot of running and physical training, but he'd been in pretty good shape to start with, so it wasn't
as bad as he'd expected. There'd been some weapons training too,
and that was actually pretty fun. The thing he'd loved was when
they'd been taken up in real planes, just to get a taste of what it
was all about. That couple of hours — maybe that was when he'd
fallen in love. The Air Force had been a way to pay for school after
the divorce, a way to tell his dad to shove it. He'd never seriously
thought about staying in, not until he spent thirty minutes in the
second seat of an F-15.

There was only two and a half weeks between the end of camp
and school. It was just long enough to go back to Tahoe and see
his mom, make sure everything was going ok. Well, as ok as it
was going to go. He'd parked in the drive and let himself in, and
there she was, sitting still as a statue in the quiet dining room, the
table moved over to the wall, just her on the bare hardwood floor
wearing a leotard and legwarmers like a kid. There was something
wrong about that, about seeing your mom that way, every flaw
of her body shown by the leotard. Her hair was pulled back in a
pony tail, and beneath the platinum hair dye her brown roots were
showing. Her neck was crepey from too many suntans, and her
closed eyes were carefully accented with blue eyeshadow. "Mom?"

She opened her eyes, blinking. "John?"

"Hi, Mom." John shoved his hands in his pockets. "What are
you doing?"

She got to her feet and came to hug him. "Just meditating. I
didn't expect you for hours. Did you have a good drive?"

"Yeah, a real good drive," he said. He didn't say that the choke
was acting up. He'd probably have to get it fixed after school started.
His Air Force stipend would have to cover it, and if he told her
about it she'd either pay money she couldn't afford anymore to
get it fixed or worry about him every time he drove. So what she
didn't know wouldn't hurt her. Besides, he'd get it fixed in a few
weeks anyway. "Meditating?"

She let go of him, holding him out at arms' length to take a look at him. John towered over her by six inches now, which always felt weird. "I've joined a Buddhist group."

"Um," John said, "isn't that…a little strange and New Age-y?" He didn't know what she did with her time now that Dad was gone. He hoped she'd found some new friends and stuff. But.

"It's not a cult, John. It's a Buddhist meditation group." His mother laughed, the creases around her mouth looking deeper than he remembered. "I'm doing some studying, getting in touch with myself and with my karma. It's not anything bad."

"Ok," John said.

"So tell me about camp," she said, leading him into the kitchen which was just the same as before. "Do you want some Crystal Light?"

"I don't suppose you've got Coke?" John wasn't sure how far this healthy living thing went, but after eight weeks of camp he'd had about enough of the no soft drinks thing.

"Just for you," his mom said, pulling a 2 liter out of the fridge. "So tell me about the Air Force."

He sat on a bar stool on one side of the kitchen island and she sat on one on the other side and told her all about it — about the drill and how there was this guy who didn't know his left from his right and how people got confused about the different orders and didn't know the difference between right march and column right. "See, if it's right march you just turn right, everybody where you are. And if it's column right the first row turns and then everyone else turns when they reach the position where the first row was when you called it," John said. "It's like for when you're on a path and you want everybody to turn right when you get to the corner. So this guy, moron, he has us all marching along the path and instead of saying 'Column right' he yells 'Right march!' Which is really bad, because there's this big rhododendron hedge along the path."

His mother shook her head, smiling. "So what did you do?"

"Well, what was I going to do? The moron was telling me to march into a bush."

"Did you do it?" she asked.

"Of course not." John took another drink of his Coke. *"But then I got pushed into the bush anyway because the idiot behind me did it, so he ran right into me and there I am, nose down in the hedge."* He grinned at his mother. *"I should have taken marching band in high school instead of physics. It would have probably done me more good."*

Her face sobered. *"John... I never thought you would need to do this. I thought we'd be able to provide for you. That we would help you get a good start in life. Of course your father could, but..."*

"I'm not asking that SOB for anything," John said, and for once she didn't correct his language.

Instead, Frances Sheppard nodded gravely, her eyes on his. *"I see that you aren't,"* she said. *"I just want to be sure...John, are you happy?"*

"Yeah," he said, and meant it. *"I kind of am. I'm good at this. I like this."* He reached across the counter and put his hand over hers. *"Mom, don't worry about me. I'm ok."*

"I wasn't worrying," she said. Her hand looked weird without a wedding ring. She smiled a watery smile. *"I'm very proud of you. I know you're only twenty, and I'm very, very proud of the responsibility you're taking. I'm very proud of the young man you're becoming."*

John swallowed. *"You're not upset about the Air Force thing?"*

"It's not what I expected," she said. *"Not what I'd hoped. But one thing my teacher was saying is that we have to understand that our children have their own paths. You have your own destiny, one I can't even begin to imagine. And like all mothers, I have to find my peace with that."* She squeezed his fingers. *"I want you to know that no matter how far from home you go, I will always love you. I want you to carry that with you when you have people's lives in your hands."*

He swallowed again around the lump in his throat. *"I don't want to do anything that will make you ashamed of me."*

"I will never be ashamed of you," she said, and her eyes didn't waver from his. "I'm sure of that, John."

John blinked, and blinking opened his eyes. The snow was swirling past the windows of Kate Heightmeyer's…no, Eva Robinson's office. Teyla sat on one end of the couch, her eyes closed and her breathing slow, while Carson was glancing through one of Eva's books on the credenza.

Eva was still talking, her voice even and monotonous. She glanced at John as he started, gave him a nod. "…down a flight of stairs into the past. And as you go down, you will be going deeper and deeper into your subconscious."

He had dozed off for a moment. Or maybe he'd been caught in it too. Kate had said once that he'd be a spectacularly easy subject, something he'd run from like his tail was on fire. The last thing he needed at that moment was another weird thing in his life.

The memory had seemed so real, so vivid. It had been like walking back twenty one years, like seeing his mother again, as though he'd really walked into that house that had been sold long ago and found her there. John blinked. Teyla had asked him about her a couple of times. She'd asked him what his mother was like. What she'd think of her. John had mumbled and said he didn't know, and it wasn't important anyhow. Frances had died when he was twenty-five.

He should tell Teyla, he thought. He should tell her that his mother would have loved her.

CHAPTER NINETEEN

First Mothers

"...DOWN the stairs, deeper and deeper." Eva Robinson was speaking to her in some distant place, but it didn't matter.

She stood in the curve of the stairwell, one hand on the rough hewn stones, looking out the narrow window. Below, the waves beat against the cliffs, white spray flying and leaping, the booming sound of the sea echoing through all, while the cold wind sang around the tower, pale sea birds soaring and turning on its currents.

It was like some other place she had known, Osprey thought in some small part of herself that was not this, some part left behind. The view from a tower of storm-tossed sea...

But it was not.

"I am Osprey," she said aloud clearly. Someone had asked, and she answered.

She was Osprey and her child quickened within her, hers and Wind's, her choice of them though all the men protected her as though she were their own wife. Nine and her, eleven when her daughter was born at the turning of the year. She had seen her in dreams, a white haired miniature of her, long limbed like Wind.

"Three years," she said.

Someone asked her how long she had lived there, but that was only this world, the first haven they had found. She had lost track how many it had been before that, running from one world to another, hunting through the Ring and disappearing like mist, always a step ahead of the hunters who sought them. Sometimes they came upon another band, sometimes Gryphon or Night or Cloud. Cloud had two sons now, the eldest walking and speaking well. Perhaps he would make a mate for her daughter in time, perhaps if they dared to plan so far. Life does not wait for death, even among the Returned.

This world was nothing, like so many seeded and forgotten. Car Leonid, the Ancestors had called it in their machines, but there were no lions, just the seals that harvested the rich oceans, and the men who lived on them. The land was poor, but the oceans were rich. People lived here, hunting the mammals who hunted the fish, hunted in turn by the Returned. They spoke of the tower on the cliff as a haunted place, the dwelling of soul-renders, and they did not come near.

The Lanteans had no reason to come here, and the humans had no way to call them. The Ring was in orbit. The Returned could reach it with the ships they had stolen, but the humans were poor. They called the Lanteans gods and prayed to them as though they heard, and the Lanteans had not made themselves felt in many lives of men. As a home it was safe enough.

For the moment.

After the birth, when she was strong again, they would move on.

Osprey descended the stairs carefully, one hand on the stones. She could no longer see her feet beneath her belly. Outside the wind was rising. Another storm was coming in off the sea. The sound of the waves echoed through the base of the tower, a deep thrumming that was never still.

It disturbed the cochlea, and Osprey reached for them with her mind, quieting them. *It is only a storm, little ones,* she said. *You have seen many before.* She felt them move, felt them still under the touch of her mind. The length of her hand or smaller, they were some sort of mollusk with a spiraled shell, living in vast colonies, taking their sustenance from the sea. They were not intelligent animals, but they did have some residual psychic ability. Osprey and some of the others could touch them with their minds, which was proving very useful.

Ashes had named them cochlea, and like some other mollusks they secreted their shells, building a tough bone framework around their soft bodies. They also secreted shell anchors on stone to which they attached their egg sacs, and this was what Ashes had found a use for. When it dried, their shells made an almost impenetrable *mortar, securing rough hewn stones together as tightly as the con-crete of the Lanteans. This tower was built with their aid, Osprey and the others egging the small creatures on. The Returned set the stones in place and then the cochlea cemented them, snug and tight against the winds that blew and the waves that flowed.*

Some distant part of her, some part that was not Osprey, found it fascinating. Such tiny creatures, and yet they could build something so strong...

Where is the power device you took from the Lanteans, it asked her. Where is it now?

Another day, a spring day, her daughter an infant that dozed in a cradle of shell... The sun struck sparks of light from the water and the white birds were hunting out to sea in a vast shoal of birds, mirroring the unseen shoals of fish beneath the surface.

"Another day," Wind said, climbing the first steps of the tower to where she waited. "Ashes says we're almost done with the repairs." The sea breeze tugged at his long white hair, blowing strands of it about his face. He wore dark leathers against the chill, even in the summertime, battered and stained with salt.

"There is one more thing," Ashes said at his elbow. He squinted looking up into the sun, photosensitive as so many were.

*There were none besides themselves close at hand, and yet Osprey spoke mind to mind, as though she feared to be overheard. *Hyperion's weapon,* she said.*

Ashes nodded. "It is dangerous to carry it around with us. It's not impossible that we will be captured or that we will lose our ship or be forced to abandon it. And you know if that happens..."

"I don't see why we don't just throw it in the ocean," Wind said.

Ashes snarled. "How many times have I told this great brawler that throwing it in the ocean will not destroy it? It is made of the Lanteans' most sturdy materials, metal that even our brightest flames will not scar. Even when, if you remember, I exposed it to the vacuum of space it did not crack or show any damage at all, no more so than the orbital Rings do. I do not know any way to unmake this thing." He shook his head, and his eyes were on

Osprey's. "It is only our ignorance. I cannot make things as the Lanteans did. I do not know how. I was a student of sciences biological, and none of us, not in any band, understood the physical sciences at the level which would be applicable. Another more clever man another time might solve this problem, but I can tell you now, Osprey, that I cannot."

"Then what do you suggest we do?" Wind demanded, his hand on his hip.

"We must hide it," Osprey said. "Hide it and the source that powered it. It is dangerous as you say to carry it with us, and we cannot destroy it." She glanced about at tower and cliffs, at windswept sea. "The cochlea give us an opportunity. Let us carry it down to one of the sea caves and have the cochlea seal it in. Beneath layers of bone and stone it will be impossible for anyone to stumble over who does not know that it is there. And none shall know where it is cached except the three of us."

Wind nodded slowly. "That is well thought."

"And perhaps the time will come when we may return and destroy it," Ashes said. "That day yet may come."

Sea caves, dark and damp and cool, comfortable and quiet... They did not need torches, not they whose eyes saw in the dark. They did not need anything to light their way to its resting place. The sounding sea called around them. The dark shielded them. The metal cases lay side by side on the floor of stone, and the cochlea came at her command, crawling back and forth leaving their pale trails, stone and bone, sealing the cave for all eternity...

For ten thousand years, till Osprey's distant daughter should remember.

"I know where the ZPM is," said Teyla Emmagan. She lifted her head, blinking, while outside the towers of Atlantis the snow swirled. "I can find it."

CHAPTER TWENTY

Pilgrims

JOHN knocked on the door to Woolsey's office, waiting for him to look up from his laptop and motion him in. "Got a second?" he asked.

Woolsey nodded, pushing back from the desk. "Yes, of course. It's probably time I took a break anyhow." He didn't look happy. "I was reading through my emails from the IOA."

The databurst had come in three hours ago, downloading all the emails sent through the SGC. John had had four, three of them from Sergeant Walter Harriman about various logistical issues affecting the military detachment in Atlantis, all of them already answered promptly and in the outgoing mail. There had also had been one from his brother, but John hadn't opened that one yet.

Woolsey had more than three hundred emails in his queue. No wonder it was taking him hours to get through them.

"Anything bad?" John asked, slouching into one of the visitor chairs. He'd made a point of slouching initially when Woolsey arrived and hadn't gotten out of the habit.

"Yes, actually." Woolsey frowned at his laptop. "For Dr. McKay at any rate."

John sat up. "We're not going to…"

Woolsey raised a hand. "Nothing like that, thankfully," he said, his mouth pressed together in a thin line. "But they are concerned, very concerned, over the extent of Dr. McKay's transformation. They have heeded my recommendation that his confinement or lack thereof be contingent on the medical advice of Dr. Beckett, Dr. Keller having recused herself from the decision based upon personal considerations. Subject of course to the review of SGC medical personnel."

"Well, that's good, isn't it?" John asked.

"And contingent upon one other thing," Woolsey said. He sighed. "That Dr. McKay is not to return to Earth under any circumstances until it is clear that all effects of the retrovirus are completely eliminated."

"That may never happen," John said. "Carson and Jennifer said…"

"I'm well aware of that, Colonel Sheppard," Woolsey said. "Dr. McKay may have to spend the rest of his life in the Pegasus Galaxy."

John bit back his first answer. That's not so bad, he nearly said. And it wasn't. Not compared to being locked up. Not compared to being a Wraith forever. Not to having to go back to Earth. Being exiled to Atlantis for the foreseeable future wasn't so bad at all…

"We'll just have to see how it goes," Woolsey said briskly. "After all, these effects may fade in time. It's only been six days. In a few months the situation may be entirely different."

"That's true," John said. "It may clear up on its own."

"Was there something you wanted to talk to me about?" Woolsey asked.

"Yeah." John pulled his head back. Rodney stuck in Atlantis wasn't horrible at all. Better that, some part of him said, than Rodney being recalled to Earth. "Dr. Robinson has been doing some hypnosis work with Teyla. We think we've got a good lead on a ZPM and I want to take the team to check it out."

"Go on."

"It's a space gate — we dialed it years ago and never checked it out further once we discovered it was in high orbit around a planet that didn't seem to offer anything. No lights, no radio or EM emissions, no signs of technology. I can't swear it's uninhabited, but it's unlikely to have a population that would be a threat to us. In and out in a cloaked jumper, checking out this lead. Pretty much minimal risk. If we don't find anything, we've wasted an afternoon."

Woolsey folded his hands. "That does sound like minimal risk. Do you think there's actually a ZPM there?"

"There was once." John shrugged. "That's about all we've got anywhere. It may be gone, it may be destroyed, who knows? But it's worth taking a look."

"All right." Woolsey took his glasses off and pinched the bridge of his nose. "Assemble your team whenever you're ready. You have a go, Colonel."

John warmed up the puddle jumper, checking the board carefully though he'd done this hundreds of times. There was no such thing as a perfunctory flight check. Teyla slid into the seat beside him. "Ok?" he asked.

"Yes," she said. "I am sorry that I am late. I was seeing Torren off to New Athos."

"It's ok. Radek's not here yet either." Everything was green. They could get going anytime Radek showed up. Ronon was already in the chair behind him, leaning back with his eyes shut like he was taking a nap. John keyed the radio on. "Radek? We're waiting for you in the jumper bay."

"In a moment," Radek said. The noise around him sounded like he was downstairs in the gate room. Probably people had about ten things they wanted him to do before he left. "I am…" The end of his sentence was cut off.

Teyla smiled. "I am glad I am not the latest one."

"Not by a long shot," John said. Radek would be a while.

"Ready to go?" Rodney's voice was cheerful as he appeared in the cockpit door. Ronon came to his feet in one move, while Teyla and John swiveled around. His hair was dead white, standing up spiked like an 80s rock star, in sharp contrast to his black leather Atlantis jacket, but otherwise he looked like himself, like old familiar Rodney. Maybe he was a little thinner, looked a little older, but his voice, his hands — all Rodney.

"What?" Ronon said.

"Carson's cleared me out of the infirmary," Rodney said with a smile John didn't quite believe. "So I'm good for duty. Radek out, me back in." He looked at John. "Right?"

John opened his mouth and closed it. He could see every

word written on Ronon's and Teyla's faces, just as if they'd discussed it for an hour. No from Ronon, yes from Teyla. But it was his call, and he knew perfectly well it was about more than this mission. If he said no, if he sent Rodney downstairs and had him send up Radek, it was saying he was off the team. It was saying he couldn't be trusted. And everyone would know that. If John wouldn't trust him, who would?

"Are you sure you're ok to go in the field?" John temporized. "You just got out of the infirmary. And don't you still have some…" Wraithy bits didn't seem like the way to put it.

"I'm good," Rodney said with that same not-right smile. "Never felt better. Of course, I've still got this pesky telepathy thing." He waved his finger around beside his ear. "But since the only person who can hear it is Teyla…"

"It may prove very helpful on this mission," Teyla said warmly. "I am glad you are back, Rodney."

Teyla was staking out a position. It wasn't warning to him, but to Ronon, who looked thunderous. John didn't think she understood quite how freaked out Ronon had been, how far he'd been pushed.

And so he looked at Ronon, not Rodney. "If Rodney's himself again and good to go, let's do it," he said. "We've all had some bad times and come back." They'd trusted Ronon again after he'd turned. Now Ronon could do the same. And no, it wasn't easy. It was never easy.

"Ok," Ronon said and sat down, but his eyes didn't leave Rodney as he bustled around, fussily arranging his gear in the seat behind Teyla.

"Control, this is Sheppard," John said into the radio. "Opening the bay doors."

"Confirmed," Airman Salawi said confidently. "Clear the gateroom floor, please."

The jumper descended into the gateroom and John dialed the gate, listening to Radek talking to Salawi. He sounded relieved.

This was better. This was how it ought to be. The wormhole opened and the jumper threaded the needle.

It was a high orbital gate, just as John remembered. The jumper sent back a wave of telemetry. No other ships, no wreckage, no satellites, nothing but the gate. Below, a mostly blue and brown planet turned serenely, seamed by the long white cloud layer of a cold front, deserted and quiet.

"Teyla?" he asked.

She shook her head, her eyes on the starfield. "I am not sensing Wraith," she said. Her eyes flickered back to the seat behind her. "Or at least not more than a slight distortion that I believe can be accounted for."

Rodney huffed, and then Teyla smiled, their eyes meeting over the chair back as he shrugged with an offhanded smirk. John shook his head. He was going to have to get used to their little telepathic asides.

"Ok, Teyla," he said. "Tell us where to set down."

Teyla looked over the map now unscrolling on the heads up display, the jumper neatly filling in water and land and weather patterns at his prompting. He gave her time. After all, she was trying to match what she saw to a memory ten thousand years old.

"There, I believe," she said, pointing toward the eastern coast of the large southern continent. "I think that is the right area."

"Ok." John put them into a lower pass, dropping down through cloud layers and jet stream to about ten thousand feet. One of the indicators blinked briefly. "Picking up some wreckage to the north of here. No power source."

"Some space junk," Rodney said. "Probably."

The puddle jumper's readings were clear. "It's old," John said. "Not even any residual radiation. Not our problem." This was the kind of world the Travelers liked. If they'd crashed or scrapped a ship here long ago they would have stripped it bare. And the sensors weren't suggesting the kind of rare alloys an Ancient ship would have had. "Let's keep our minds on the ball here. Teyla, where are we going?"

"South, I believe," she said. Teyla leaned forward, looking out the windscreen.

"Smoke," Ronon said. They swept over a cluster of villages by the mouth of a river, cooking smoke rising into the air from stone chimneys. On the headland above there was what looked like a square tower house, a huddle of outbuildings in its shadow. A fleet of little fishing boats stood offshore. "Not uninhabited," Ronon said.

"They don't look like a lot of trouble," John said. Another fishing village further down the coast where Teyla indicated, twenty or thirty buildings together where a break in the sea cliffs was formed by an outflowing stream. "Teyla?"

Teyla shook her head. "Come around again," she said.

John brought the jumper around, dropping down to 4,000 feet and slowing. Sea cliffs. Miles and miles of sea cliffs. He could see the white speckles here and there of birds roosting by the hundreds. Every bit of cliff looked alike.

"I cannot tell," Teyla said, frustration in her voice. "It was a round tower on the cliff distant from any river or stream, but I do not see it or anything that might have been it."

"These cliffs have probably changed in 10,000 years," John said. "Erosion."

Ronon let out a sigh from behind John, one that sounded suspiciously like a sigh of relief. It would be nice to just call the mission off and go home. Couldn't find it, end of story.

But no. Ronon was going to have to work with Rodney. They were going to have to get over this thing, and they weren't going to do that by avoiding each other.

"Let's put it down near that little fishing village," John said. "Let's ask the locals if they know anything about it."

"Do you seriously think..." Rodney began.

That sounded like the old Rodney. "It's worth a try," John said, turning the puddle jumper around and looking for some level ground that wasn't either in the village or too far away.

"A marsh? You had to land in a marsh?" Rodney pulled his boot out of four inches of stinking mud. "There's a whole planet full of rocks and you had to land in a marsh!"

"Suck it up, McKay," Ronon said, stepping off the back of the puddle jumper confidently and striding toward the fishing village. Teyla followed him down the ramp, an expression on her face that said louder than words that it was good to hear what passed for normal around here.

"Hang on," John said, waiting until Teyla was clear of the ramp to close it up and cloak the jumper. "Wait for us."

"I can't believe you landed in a marsh."

"Because in the ocean is a bad idea, and so is in the river. Which left on the cliff or in the marsh. And since I can't park vertically…" John replied.

Ronon turned around, arms spread. "I don't know what you expect to get out of these people," he said.

"They may know something," Teyla said. "Often there are stories about old ruins, even if there is not much that is visible from the air. And there were sea caves beneath the tower. The caves may still be there even if the tower is gone after ten thousand years."

"Should have brought Lynn," Ronon said. "He's pretty good with those things."

"If we find anything interesting we'll go get him," John said. And he meant it. He'd learned his lesson about not going back for specialists when you needed them.

Some children with baskets were heading toward the sea cliffs, a big black dog with them. The dog snarled, but one of the kids, a girl about twelve, held him by his leather collar.

"Hey, kids," John said, taking off his sunglasses and giving them a big smile. "What's up?"

"We're going egg hunting," the littlest one piped up, a blond boy maybe six or seven. "On the cliffs."

The older girl hushed him. "You are travelers from afar?"

"Yes," Teyla said, coming forward with her best trader's smile. "We have come a long distance, and we do not know our way around here."

"We don't have an inn," the girl said, lifting her chin. "Not like some. But we do have a Pilgrim House. Are you Pilgrims?" Her eyes flickered over Ronon and Rodney, then came to rest on Rodney. "Is he sick?"

"Yes," Teyla said. "He is our friend and he has been very sick. But it is not an illness you can catch."

She nodded. What Teyla had said seemed to pass muster somehow. "I'm Lyra."

"I am Teyla," Teyla said. "And I am grateful for your name and your welcome."

Small population, John thought, looking at the kids. All that red and blond hair was recessive, and tended to be rare on planets that had a lot of contact with other worlds. These kids were mostly tow headed, with the exception of one kid with hair as red as Halling's. Boys and girls alike wore rough wool trousers and tunics with woolen jackets and caps. There must be sheep somewhere, and that dog looked like it was probably bred for herding and sent with the kids to keep an eye on them.

"Are you here to seek healing for your friend?" Lyra asked, still looking at Rodney appraisingly. "He ought to get well soon with so many people to intercede for him."

"We hope he will be well soon," Teyla said. "But we do not know how to find what we are looking for. Perhaps you can help us?"

"Are you looking for the Shrine?" the oldest boy asked. "I know the way. I'll guide you for a token!"

Lyra shoved him quiet. "You know it's not nice to ask Pilgrims for tokens! Showing a Pilgrim the way is an act of charity!"

"The Shrine?" Rodney asked. "Is that like the...thing... that time?" He looked at Ronon inquiringly.

"Like the Shrine of Talus?" Ronon's eyebrows rose. They'd taken Rodney to the Shrine of Talus a year ago and more, when he'd contracted a deadly brain parasite. It had been Ronon's idea, and despite Jennifer and Woolsey's objections, taking Rodney there had proved to be the right thing to do.

"I don't know this Shrine of Talus you speak of," Lyra said respectfully. "Ours is the Shrine of the Bride. But Pilgrims come from a long way to seek healing for their kindred there. Lots of people are healed." She put her hand on the head of the littlest boy, the loud one. "My brother would have died when he was a baby if it hadn't been for the Shrine. He was born with a hole in his heart, the Bride said, but my grandfather made the intercession and he's just fine. So I know it works," she said solemnly.

"He looks strong and healthy now," Teyla said, and only John would have heard the tiny catch in her voice. Birth defects like that killed on Athos too.

"I am!" the boy yelled at the top of his voice. "I'm really strong!"

"I see you are," Teyla said, and her mouth twitched with amusement. She looked at Lyra again. "We do not know how to do this correctly, how to, what is it you say? Ask for intercession?"

"You go that way," Lyra said, pointing. "Along the path there, the one that runs along the top, until you get to a path that goes down. It's kind of steep, but we've tried to make it easier for people who are sick by putting a rope barrier along the edge so there's something to hold onto. You go down to the Shrine. It's one of the entrances to the World Beneath, the Land of the Dead, and you ask the Bride of the Lord of the Dead to help you."

"Some kind of local priestess?" Rodney asked. "It's probably the cave that does it anyway, not flim-flam…"

"Hush," John said, and no, everything wasn't back to normal, because Rodney did, looking abashed. Teyla was getting the information they needed, and if Rodney would just shut up they'd have it.

"Anyway, the Bride examines you, and if she thinks that you can be healed she'll take you and your intercessors into the cave. And then you come back healed," Lyra said.

"A device like the Shrine of Talus…" Rodney said quietly.

"Shut up, McKay," Ronon growled.

John turned around. "Look, if we've got an Ancient device in a cave we're on the right track. So let's just play this."

"And if you cannot be healed?" Teyla asked.

Lyra looked solemn. "Sometimes she says you can't be. That's what she says with very old people a lot. That what's ailing them is old age, and that there is no cure for it. And so she refuses the fee."

"Ok," John said. "Let's go talk to this Bride. I think she'll be able to help us."

"I hope she can for your friend's sake," Lyra said brightly. "Give her my greetings if you would, and tell her my mother said to bring her three eggs when we've finished the day's search, so I'll be there later."

"We will take the Bride your greetings," Teyla said warmly. "And thank you, Lyra."

The children waved as they started up the cliff path, the big black dog running along beside them.

Teyla frowned.

"Something wrong?" John asked quietly.

"No." She looked out to sea, the birds rushing up in a whirling crowd from the cliffs where the dog ran barking. "This may be the place. I cannot tell. If so, the cliffs have much changed. I think the tower may have stood in a place that is no longer here. The sea may have taken it."

"Hopefully not the caves," John said. "Sounds like a local priestess, and maybe she knows about the ruins or about the sea caves. Probably a good person to ask."

"Yes," Teyla said, glancing at Rodney. "I expect that you are right."

The cliffs were steep, but the path was clearly marked as the children had said. Along the edge of the drop there was a rope held in place by iron stakes, evidence of some metalwork at least. They climbed down in single file, John, then Teyla, Rodney and Ronon.

John glanced back at Teyla, who had an unusually abstracted expression on her face. "What do you think this priestess..." he began.

The cave mouth opened up, a broad dark portal in the weathered gray stone, some strange striations in the rock around it like veins of quartz. Bells of brass hung on long pale threads around it, each one moving with the continual wind, a faint soft chiming. He saw the movement inside the door just a moment too late, red hair too vivid for humanity, blue tinged skin too pale. He saw her move, and it seemed to take an eternity to raise his P90, forever, as though he were underwater. The Wraith Queen met his eyes.

CHAPTER TWENTY-ONE

A Door Into Summer

TEYLA saw John move before she saw why. Of course she sensed Wraith. Rodney was standing right behind her and had been, his mind a constant irritation, like listening to continual chatter. She was thinking that she would have to work with him not about speaking as Guide had worked with her, but about maintaining silence...

And then there was the Queen. She stood in the doorway of the cave, her long dress of undyed wool blending with the gray stones, and her mind leapt with delight for one moment before it was eclipsed by fear.

Her eyes met John's as he brought up the weapon, so slow, but not slow enough...

...there was a high pitched scream and John's finger jerked just as he pulled the barrel of the P90 up, bullets ringing off the hanging bells, off the stones, missing the child who hurled himself between, throwing himself at the Wraith Queen's waist.

"No," Teyla said, her hand on his arm as he took a deep breath, feeling the muscles in his arm shaking. "No," she said, her eyes on the Queen's, the Queen's eyes on hers, held in tableau.

"Damn it," John said under his breath.

The child looked up at him, a boy perhaps five years old, his white hair shoulder length, the Queen on her knees beside him, her arms around him and her shoulder turned to the humans as though to shelter him behind her regenerative abilities. They had never seen a Wraith child before. There had been Ellia, of course, but she was already adolescent, the young queen John had killed. This child was much younger.

Behind, she heard Ronon's pistol power up. "Put it down," John said. "Teyla's got the situation under control."

"I do," Teyla said slowly. She could feel the Queen's mind in their locked gaze, fear — mostly fear there. She would do nothing to harm them while they might harm her child. He was too young to regenerate. Teyla knew that in a moment, felt the Queen's astonishment that she did not know. And astonishment at all she did.

Her pale bluish brow knitted. "What are you?" she asked in a tone full of curiosity.

"I am Teyla Emmagan of Athos," Teyla said. "Teyla Who Walks Through Gates. Osprey's Daughter." All her names, birth and earned name and her lineage, as was proper.

The young queen shook her head. Yes, Teyla thought, she was young. Not so young as Waterlight, but young as Steelflower pretended to be. Her eyes flicked to Rodney. "What is he?"

"Mine," Teyla said, and felt Rodney's flicker of pleasure and embarrassment at once.

She shook her head again, long red hair half covering the child. "You are impossible."

"So I have been told," Teyla said, words spoken and thought at once. "I am abomination. A cleverman of Osprey mixed his DNA with that of his captives, and I am that result, Osprey's human daughter." John shifted, and she thought he was looking behind her, catching Ronon's eye. "And who are you?"

She stood up, still holding the child before her, one hand on each of his shoulders. "I am the Bride of the Lord of the Dead, Alabaster of the lineage of Osprey, and I am the Guardian of the Shrine."

The child bit down on his lower lip, his eyes going back and forth from one to another. "Mama, I'm scared."

Ronon made some inarticulate noise Teyla couldn't interpret.

"There is nothing to fear," she said, and hoped she spoke the truth. "Not if your mother will treat with us under the six symbols of truce, as is proper queen to queen."

"A human queen." Her yellow eyes were expressionless, measuring, but the tenor of her mind was bright, curiosity warring with fear.

Teyla had felt the like, knew suddenly where she had heard the name before… "You are Guide's daughter," she said.

A flare of bright hope, just as quickly cut off and held close. "I am Snow's daughter, and Guide was her Consort," she said carefully.

"Guide's daughter?" Rodney's voice went up a scale. "Oh for the love of…"

"Ok." John slung the P90 to port arms. "Ronon, put it away. We're not going to shoot Todd's grandkid while we're technically his ally."

"You are allied with my father?" Alabaster looked from one to the other skeptically.

"For some value of allied," Rodney said.

"No." Ronon kept his gun leveled, the barrel over Teyla's shoulder. "No. We've had enough of this."

She turned about. "Ronon," she said quietly. "You cannot shoot a child."

He didn't waver, his eyes on Alabaster. "What do you think they eat, her and that little parasite there? Those villagers we saw a few minutes ago. People who are stupid enough to come here looking for healing and find her instead. You think she doesn't kill their children? You think that little girl you were talking to earlier is anything but a snack for her? You want to watch that kid wither into a ninety-five year old without having her life?" Ronon's lips opened in a snarl. "It's a delicacy for you, isn't it? Feeding on children. So tasty. You like babies in arms best, don't you? But they go so fast. They don't usually even have time to cry."

"Ronon!" John stepped in front of the gun. "Put it down, buddy."

"No."

"Let Teyla handle this," John said, his eyes level even as Ronon's finger twitched.

"No. This stuff has gone far enough." He looked at Alabaster over John's shoulder. "How many? How many villagers have you killed?"

"None," she said quietly.

"Liar."

Alabaster's face seemed even paler. "I have fed on many, but I have not fed enough to kill, and I have fed on no one unwilling."

"Parasite."

"I give them full value in return," Alabaster said. Her eyes shifted to Teyla, her mind open so that she could see the truth of her words. "What mother would not give years off her life for her child's healing? What man would not do the same for the woman he loved, or for his best friend? They come to me seeking healing, and if I can give it I offer a bargain. I will heal the one they love with some of their own years, two thirds to heal and a third as my fee. If they wish, I will spread it among several people, as many as care to come and plead as intercessors."

"Lyra's brother," Teyla said, a piece fitting into place.

Alabaster nodded. "Just so. Without healing that is far beyond the technology of this planet he should not have lived more than a few days. But his grandfather stood surety, saying that he had already had many full years. Fifteen years I took from his grandfather, five as my fee and ten to heal Jasen. I closed the hole in his heart that he had been born with." Her eyes flicked to Ronon. "I gave him life, not death."

"Ronon," John said quietly, "Stand down."

Wordlessly, Ronon turned and walked away, his footsteps loud on the trail above.

"Rodney, stay here," John said, and followed him. She could not touch John's mind, but Teyla did not need to. She saw it all in his eyes.

"It will be well," she said. And why not? She was a trader and the daughter of a trader, and she was Steelflower too. Why not negotiate with a Wraith queen with no one but Rodney for backup, a Rodney whose mind was entirely open to the persuasion of a queen? *Then we will see who is the stronger queen*, the part of her that was Steelflower said.

Alabaster watched them go, and when John's footsteps had faded away she looked at Teyla instead, her shoulders relaxing fractionally. "I do not understand what passes among your blades."

"Ronon has known much harm from your kind," Teyla said rather sharply. "He is of Sateda."

There was no comprehension in her face. "And what?"

Teyla lifted her chin. "You have been here since before Sateda was destroyed?"

"I have been here twenty-one planetary years," Alabaster said. "Twenty-one years with no news and no word from outside. I did not know that any of my kin lived."

Teyla let out a breath. "Then I have much to tell you. May we come inside?"

Alabaster nodded slowly. "If you will abide by the six symbols of truce, your cleverman and you."

"We shall," Teyla said, "And we will do no harm to your child."

"Then come within."

The inside of the cave was dark, but perhaps not so to a Wraith's eyes. Teyla had gotten used to moving in the dark as though she knew what she was doing when she was Steelflower, wearing Steelflower's face but without her vision. Rodney had not. His Wraith vision had been real. And so he promptly fell over a chair.

"Sorry," Rodney said, picking it and himself up.

There were two chairs, presumably for Alabaster and the humans she consulted with, and Teyla took one as by right, leaving Rodney standing. Miraculously he did not complain.

I know how this goes, he said, his mind voice as clear as if he'd spoken, tinged with faint embarrassment. *I know how a cleverman acts in the presence of his queen.*

Dear Rodney, she thought. *I know I can count on you, my friend.*

You can. Rodney stood behind her chair, jaw forward like a pit bull.

There were no offers of refreshment. Wraith did not eat together. "How did you come to this place?" Teyla asked, leaning forward in her chair, her hands together as one should hold them when one does not mean threat.

Alabaster still held the child's hand, and now she let him go to return to his games. "Twenty-one planetary years ago," she said quietly, "My mother died. No, my mother was murdered by another hive, by Hightower's men, Hightower of the lineage of Cloud. We were taken by treachery and boarded. My father bought time for our cruiser to put off with me and a few others aboard, for I was newly carrying my son and he feared for my life as he had for my mother's. It was her last wish that he should guard me rather than her, and he did so."

Dishonor. Dishonor that a Consort should outlive his Queen, even at her wish.

"Our ship took fire even as we fled, and we were badly damaged. We opened a hyperspace window, but when we came out we could not decelerate properly because of thruster damage. We entered this world's atmosphere like a missile, on a ballistic course. There was one lifepod." Her eyes met Teyla's, and for a moment she saw as Alabaster had seen, the deadly calm on the bridge, the hatch irising shut, the commander and his three men still and dark at their posts.

"For the queen," Rodney said.

"The ship crashed north of here," Alabaster said. "There was nothing left."

Teyla bent her head.

"I was injured, alone. The villagers took me in. They said I was the Bride of the Lord of the Dead, sent from the skies to bring them hope. I did not persuade them otherwise." Her voice had a bitter note, one that suddenly reminded Teyla of Guide, that tone, that inflection. "I have lived here twenty-one years of this planet with them for company, hoping against hope that some of my people would somehow find me. The Ring is orbital. I have had no way of reaching it, and if any Darts have come through culling they have not come here."

"And your son?" Teyla asked.

"Darling was born my second year here. He is nineteen years old." Alabaster looked at Teyla sharply. "You did not know our children take so long to grow? We are long lived, and twenty years to us is not half a lifetime."

"I have only met one young one before," Teyla demurred. Ellia.

"He does not feed yet, except on such food as the villagers bring in trade. Fruit, eggs, plants from the sea…" She looked over at the child by the hearth. "But you have told me nothing. Tell me."

"Guide is well known to me," Teyla said carefully. "It was he who taught me to speak mind to mind, and who has tutored me in much I know. He is a power yet, the Consort of one Steelflower…" And she could not hide it, not mind to mind. She was Steelflower, one more turning in Guide's machinations, one more gambit on the table — a human woman with the mind of a queen, brought forward to forge an alliance and legitimize his power.

"Oh, Father," Alabaster said softly. "What are you playing at?"

Rodney snorted. "I don't think anybody knows that."

Alabaster's eyes flicked up to him, and Teyla saw Rodney blush. "That is Guide through and through," Alabaster said.

Teyla thought it wise to lay the trades on the table. "What is it you want?"

"Is that not obvious?" Alabaster asked. "Safe passage for myself and my son back to the hive, to where my father is. You said that you were his ally. If so, then you know what I will be worth to him. He will pay you whatever you ask."

Teyla knew the truth of that, felt it in her bones.

"And what do you want?" Alabaster asked shrewdly, her eyes flicking from Teyla to Rodney. "You have not come here by chance."

"We came here seeking something hidden long ago by the First Mothers," Teyla said carefully. "A power source."

"The ZPM," Alabaster said. Her eyes did not leave Teyla's now. "And more besides. You are seeking Hyperion's weapon. But you must know that it will kill you as surely as it will me. It works by destroying the mind, burning out all that is touched by our abilities, all that carries our genetic code, leaving nothing but a mindless body behind it. It will leave you a husk, you and your cleverman both."

Teyla felt a chill run down her back, but it was true. She knew it as surely as anything. "How do you know that?" she asked.

"Because I am Osprey's daughter too," Alabaster said. "And I know she left it here for a reason. If you seek it on behalf of the humans, you seek your own death, Teyla Emmagan."

John hurried up the path to the clifftop swearing under his breath. He didn't like leaving Teyla to deal with the Wraith queen by herself, but he'd seen her do it before. Steelflower had done it, and it looked like this was more likely to involve talking than shooting. Even if the queen had the ZPM, she couldn't use it here. It would be better to barter it to them for passage off this planet, back to Todd or wherever. And having her might give them a hold over Todd. No, she was more use to them alive than dead, and they were way more use to her. After all, she couldn't fly the puddle jumper even if she could find it under its cloak. And good luck trying to dominate Teyla mind to mind! John would lay good money that even the queen they'd met in the submerged power station under the sea nearly three years ago wouldn't get the best of Teyla now.

John got to the top of the cliff and looked around for Ronon. Where the hell…?

Ronon was a little ways along the cliffs, sitting on the stones looking out to sea. He didn't move as John came up beside him, as John sat down beside him on the rocks, their shoulders not quite touching. The wind off the ocean lifted Ronon's hair. His eyes were clear, and somehow he looked younger than John had ever seen him.

John swallowed. "I understand how you feel," he began.

"No, you don't, Sheppard." Ronon didn't look at him, and his voice was quiet, his eyes on the sea. A wave crashed ashore, spray dashing thirty feet up the cliff and then subsiding. "You have no idea the things I've seen."

John glanced away, as if there were some answer in the water, picking up a rock and worrying it between his fingers. "You're right," he said. "I don't." He paused, putting the words together, and then went on. "But I know this. It's done and you can't change it. The only thing you can change is the guy it turns you into."

Ronon looked at him sideways, and John turned the stone around in his hand, tossing it over the edge and watching it disappear into the waves. "You don't want to be a guy who kills little kids." The bodies were still there in memory, the ruined village smoking from the airstrike. It was still a sick feeling, still a punch in the gut, even here in the clean sea wind — but it was far away. Time and distance blurred the memory, not into forgiveness but into occasional oblivion.

Ronon glanced away, his eyes on the far horizon. "I can't do this, Sheppard."

"I know you can't." John swallowed. "I'm not going to ask you to do this again." He'd pushed too far. He'd pushed Ronon beyond where he could go. If he pushed any more he'd break him. Everybody has limits.

"McKay is one thing," Ronon said. "I mean, it's McKay. He'll get over it. It's just like he's been sick or something."

"Yeah," John said.

"Teyla…" Ronon looked out to sea, his eyes clear and scoured clean, as though he were looking for the right words.

"Teyla's back to normal now," John said.

"No, she's not. She's changed. You've changed. We've all changed." Ronon shook his head. "I don't know who any of us are anymore."

John didn't say anything. He couldn't think of anything to say except things change. People change. Ronon said they wouldn't, but they did. And sometimes it was bad and sometimes it was good but it was always a crap shoot.

"I could go back to Sateda," Ronon said, the wind lifting his hair away from his brow, "but I'm not crazy enough to think that it would be like it was. It wouldn't be going home. That place doesn't exist anymore." He shook his head. "Radek talks about rebuilding and trees growing and new generations like somehow that fixes it. But it doesn't. It doesn't make it the way it was."

John swallowed. "No," he said. He stretched his legs out in front of him. "My mom said that the past was a different country, a place you could never visit. So you gotta find something you want, something out there in front of you that's worth it. A new world. A new sun. Something worth living for."

Ronon looked at him sideways. "I thought you had a death wish."

"Not so much a wish as a …" John looked for the right word.

"A geas?"

"Yeah, maybe." He picked up another little rock, turned it around in his hands carefully. "I'd rather stick around. I mean, there's Atlantis. It, you know, kind of needs me. And there's Teyla. She'd be really upset if I died. And Torren. It would tear him up. And you and McKay…"

"You think we need you too." Ronon's voice was quiet.

John tossed the rock over. "Yeah, kind of."

Ronon watched it fall, its trajectory clean and swift. "At first I just wanted to stay alive," he said quietly. "That's all. Just stay alive. And then I thought maybe I could hunt them. I could avenge Sateda. I can't bring anybody back from the dead, but I can avenge them. I can make them pay in blood for every kid, every old person, every place I lived that was ground into rubble. Every person I ever loved." His voice stopped.

John waited.

"If I'm not a Satedan Immortal and I'm not a runner and I'm not a Wraith hunter, who am I?"

"My friend," John said. "You'll have to figure out the rest."

Ronon looked at him sideways. "Just like that?" he said with a bitter smile.

"Yeah, just like that."

Out to sea a cloud bank was building, cool and purple and white. White as snow, white as Antarctica where an alien drone had chased him, where a chair beneath the ice had called to him.

I think anyone who doesn't want to walk through a Stargate is cracked, O'Neill said, and he hadn't gotten it then. He'd never seen a gate, never seen a sunrise on a strange world. There were beginnings worth having but nobody could give them to you. All they could give you was a gate to walk through.

There would be a gate for Ronon, but he'd have to decide if it was a door into summer. John hoped he was still around for that part.

He put his hand on Ronon's shoulder. "Come on," he said. "Let's go on back and see if McKay has managed to totally screw up Teyla's negotiations."

CHAPTER TWENTY-TWO

Underground

"WE SOUGHT this world as a haven because of Osprey's memories," Alabaster said, her hands flat on the arms of her chair. "Again and again through the centuries it has served our line as a last place of refuge. I thought to come here for some little time, and when that time had passed and my father did not seek me I thought that he was dead."

Teyla nodded, watching as the child fed the fire bits of driftwood. "Carefully, Darling," Alabaster said.

"Is that his name?" Teyla asked bemusedly.

"He is too young for a true name," Alabaster said. "He still wears his Mother Name, the one I gave him when first I saw him. When he is older he will earn his First Name." She looked over at the child again, past him to the flames. "What happened to my father?"

"He was captured by the Genii," Teyla said. "He spent seventeen years as a prisoner until Colonel Sheppard came, that same blade whom you just saw. They were prisoners together and planned an escape together. That is how the first tie between us was made."

"Seventeen years." Alabaster's voice was quiet. "And surely he thinks me dead."

"I believe he does," Teyla said. "And he will rejoice greatly to know that you are alive, and that you and your son are well."

"And if I return with you," Alabaster said, her eyes on Teyla's, "to the City of the Lanteans, as you say, I will be your ally rather than your prisoner? Forgive me if I am slow to believe that."

"As you should be," Teyla said. After all, here Alabaster might be stranded but she was at least free. "But our alliance with your father is of great worth to us. We both stand against Queen Death, she who claims the mantle of Coldamber of the lineage of Night.

Admittedly you give us leverage over your father, but your alliance is worth more to us than your death. If you should raise your banner against Death, a genuine queen of the line of Osprey, a true contender for power, you could do far more to oppose her than I have been able to as Steelflower."

"And yet what you have done is not inconsiderable." Alabaster put her hands together in thought. "But it is not only a matter of trusting you." Her eyes met Teyla's. "But trusting your people with Hyperion's weapon."

Rodney shifted behind Teyla's chair. "Look, we've dealt with Ancient weapons before. The Attero Device — I mean, we did clear it out, us and your father. After we'd made a mess, but... Anyway, I'm sure that I could figure out something to do with Hyperion's weapon. Some way to change it or modify it."

"So that it only killed others?" Alabaster looked skeptical.

"I am very attached to my life," Rodney said. "Believe me, I am very, very interested in living. I'm not about to use a weapon that's going to kill me too."

Alabaster glanced up at Rodney, a slight smile on her face. "Is your cleverman as smart as he thinks he is? Or does he prosper only on a handsome face and wit?"

A slow blush started crawling up Rodney's cheeks, and his mental sputtering was plain to Teyla. "I assure you he is very clever," Teyla said. "If not perhaps as omnipotent as he would like to believe he is." She leaned forward in her chair. "If we do not have the ZPM we will be crushed by Queen Death. And you know as well as I that it is folly to take the ZPM from this place and leave Hyperion's weapon. It will not stay hidden once it is found, and so the only choice we may make is whether it is better in our hands or the hands of others. You know there are others who will use it without a second thought."

Ronon, she thought, and buried it as deeply in her mind as she might. But Ronon would never have that choice. John would see to that. Hyperion's weapon would rest in Woolsey's fussy, cautious hands, not the hands of vengeful Sateda. Or perhaps it would be taken to Earth for study. Perhaps Sam would take it aboard the *Hammond* and Ladon Radim would never hear of it.

Oh Ronon, she thought, how far we have come from home, you and I! If I had it in my hands now, to kill all the Wraith that ever were at the price of only my own death and my son's — to save all Athosians yet unborn from all Cullings to come — I could not. Perhaps Jennifer has the right of it, Jennifer and Guide. Perhaps there is another way that does not lead to this: sororicide, that the daughters of the Ancients kill one another.

Alabaster smiled grimly as though she had followed every thought. "And if I kill you now so that you will not take it?"

"You will not succeed," Teyla said. "And you and your son will die rather than me and mine."

"And must it be one or the other?" Alabaster asked. Her voice was like her father's, dispassionate, as though this were some academic question to be debated by scholars in dusty old rooms.

"I hope not," Teyla said. "But I do not know." She lifted her chin, and the thought of Guide came back to her, listening to her story in the dark. *Once, there were three sisters...* "But I do know that there is no hope if we cannot find it between us. It rests in our hands today and if we turn from this I do not know when this chance will come again. We are Osprey's daughters, both of us, the heirs of her suffering and of her awful vengeance. And so it comes to us to decide."

Alabaster shook her head sadly. "And you would have me believe that your people will not use Hyperion's weapon to destroy us?"

"Not if there is another way," Teyla said. "And your father believes there is. He has been working on a retrovirus with our Dr. Keller." Rodney shifted behind her, but she did not look around. "And it may change everything."

John came back down the trail cautiously with Ronon behind him. He didn't know what he'd find. Hopefully just Teyla still chatting up a Wraith queen, like that was totally normal.

Somehow his idea of normal had gotten seriously skewed.

"And you say it is possible to drink fully, to drink deeply, and not kill?" Alabaster was leaning forward, her face alive with avid interest.

Oh crap, John thought. Teyla's told her about the retrovirus.

"Yes," Teyla said. She looked like herself, not Steelflower, but her posture mimicked Alabaster's, an old trick of trading.

"And could this retrovirus be given to those who seek intercession before I feed upon them?" Alabaster asked. "So that I might drink completely and not shorten their lives?"

"That is our understanding," Teyla said. "For a human under its protection, being fed upon is both painful and traumatic, but it is not fatal for someone who was already in good health. It is an injury that one may heal from in days or weeks and suffer no consequences in the long run."

"It is already painful and traumatic," Alabaster said thoughtfully. "But if it could be made not to shorten their lives, it would be an improvement. Those who seek intercession now are already willing to endure much for their loved ones' sakes. And I should prefer it."

John halted in the doorway, motioning Ronon quiet behind him.

"And why is that? Why do you not kill?" Teyla asked quietly. Rodney stood still as a statue behind her.

"I shall give you two reasons," Alabaster said, lifting her head in the firelight, the red glow casting shadows around her. "And you may pick which you like. When I came here I was alone. I was hurt, and I carried my firstborn. If I had killed they would have risen against me and hunted me, hundreds of them against me. I would not have survived." Alabaster pushed strands of long red hair back from her face. "And the other is this. Twenty one years is a long time. If you were left alone on a planet with none but your son for twenty one years, would you not come to feel a fondness for the kine? Would you not give them names and speak to them, notice who is sick and who is well, follow the tales of who has mated with whom and watch their young grow? They are my friends. They are all the company I have known for twenty one years. I do not wish to kill them."

The boy looked up from where he was playing by the fire. "Are we going now?" he asked, his yellow eyes reflecting like a cat's. "Are we going like you said we would?"

"We are, Darling," Alabaster said. "But first I will help Teyla find what she came to get."

There was a light in the darkness, the wavering light of a flashlight skimming over the stones. Teyla held it, flashing it ahead of them, Alabaster beside her.

Osprey had walked thus, the passage whispered, the stones whispered in her memory. She had descended this way, through sea caves hollowed out by the booming ocean. The ways had changed in ten thousand years, but not their purpose. Not the thing at their heart. The sea roared against the walls, a continual presence.

We must be very close, Teyla said to Alabaster beside her.

Yes. Alabaster put her hand to the stone. *The ocean is just on the other side of this wall. We are below the water level now except at lowest tide, thrice a year when this world's moons are both at aphelion.*

"I don't have a power reading yet," Rodney said, turning this way and that with his scanner, standing behind Teyla.

"How big would it be?" John said from behind him. "The ZPM isn't plugged into anything."

"Not big," Rodney acknowledged. "But I should.... Yow!" Rodney screeched, jumping backwards straight into John.

"What the hell?" John said, his P90 swinging up instinctively.

"What's that?" Rodney trailed his light on the wall where a pale, whorled creature seven or eight inches long was leaving a trail of slime. "Oh my God. I put my hand on that!"

"That is a cochlea," Alabaster said. She sounded amused. "There are many of them in these caves. They will not harm you."

"Giant bugs," said John grimly. He didn't look any happier than Rodney.

"I believe they are mollusks," Alabaster said. "I assure you they are not harmful. They eat miniature sea creatures and fish eggs."

"Fascinating," Teyla said, bending close. It was not intelligent, not in any way she knew, not even so much as a bird might be. But it could hear her when she thought at it. *Turn toward the light,* Teyla thought, and watched as its head turned about, antennae wiggling, seeking Rodney's flashlight.

Amazing, is it not? Alabaster thought in return, and her mind was bright with pleasure. *I believe it is from these that we derived many of the things we use, perhaps even some of the genetic material that went into the design of our ships. So much from such a small thing!*

The cruiser Eternal was much more intelligent, Teyla thought. Trying to explain to John, she had likened it to a horse. This was like comparing some sort of small mammal to a horse, a little animal that lived on seed in the woods. And yet Carson said they were related, that long enough ago horses were derived from tiny mammals.

Horses! Squirrels! Rodney shouted in her head. *Tiny Wraith Snail Hive Ship Things!*

Teyla and Alabaster both turned and looked at him.

"What is wrong with your cleverman?" Alabaster said aloud.

"He has been genetically manipulated," Teyla said. "Given the DNA of the Returned, and now it is wearing off in part, and he must learn to control his Gift as I have. Rodney, please speak quietly. You do not need to shout."

John and Ronon, who had heard nothing, looked at one another in bewilderment.

Rodney looked sheepish. "Sorry," he said. "Some of the work I was doing with Ember — a lot of the genetic makeup of the hive ship hull looked similar to a mollusk. Now I see why. I wonder if these guys' shells weren't the original prototype."

"That is well reasoned," Alabaster said aloud. She put her head to the side. "Are you a Master of Sciences Biological?"

"Of Sciences Physical," Rodney said, and Teyla thought he almost added an honorific. "I was made to serve Queen Death as Chief of Sciences Physical, with a specialty in the Subcorporia and Ratiocination. Of course I've done a good deal of engineering over the years, so I got stuck with some of that too, though let me tell you I'm glad to be rid of it. Though some of the bioengineering…"

"That is so?" Alabaster looked up at him with new interest. "Were I a cleverman I should have chosen the Subcorporia myself, and I learned a great deal about it for my own pleasure, though of course a queen must concentrate on the Sciences Biological, particularly what you call bioengineering, in order to fulfill her duties. But I have long been fascinated by stellar phenomena and by the manipulation of the subcorporial particles."

"Really." Rodney stared at Alabaster. "Really?"

"Can we keep our eyes on the ball here?" John said, giving Rodney a push on the shoulder. "Let's find the ZPM. You and Alabaster can geek out about physics later."

"Yes, let us," Teyla said, trying to keep the amusement out of her voice even if she could not keep it out of her mind.

Why are you amused? Alabaster asked curiously.

There is a long story of a queen who is a Master of Sciences Physical whom Rodney has pursued fruitlessly for years, Teyla said. *You will see her soon, I expect.*

Ah. There was a long pause as they climbed deeper into the caves, over stones now faintly moist from the receding tide, before Alabaster spoke again, cautiously as though careful not to give offense. *But is it not true that among your people it is most generally the men who rule?*

Generally, but not universally. Teyla shone her light ahead. Alabaster could see in the dark, but she could not. *It depends upon the world and people. Among the Lanteans this one holds high status as a warrior and leader of men. Most often such positions belong to men, and those women who have attained it are extraordinary indeed. Rodney has desired her for many years, but she will not choose him.*

And you are her ally?

Her ally, and I should like to think her friend, Teyla said. She paused in turn. *Though you must not think we lack strife and inner politicking, or that we all love one another as brothers and sisters. We are not so different from you, all of us children of the Ancestors.*

"I'm getting a power reading," Rodney said, blessedly aloud and without shouting. "Very small. I think it's this way."

"That's through a solid wall," Ronon said, shining his flashlight over it.

"It should be," Teyla said. "It was sealed." It was true that the stone looked different, not the weathered limestone of the surrounding walls, but paler colored, streaked and striated in a different pattern.

"I think this is the place," Alabaster said.

"I think so too," Teyla said. It was hard to tell from her memory. One bit of cave looked very like another. And yet…

"Definitely a power reading," Rodney said with barely suppressed excitement.

"Ok," John said, flashing his light around it. "C4."

"C4? In a sea cave? Have you lost your mind?" Rodney demanded. "You'll bring the ceiling down on us! And if you rupture the retaining wall, then here we are in a cave twenty minutes underground that's filling up with ocean!"

John just looked at him. "Rodney, I am not that stupid. I'll use a small shaped charge. Have I ever blown you up?"

"Is that a serious question? Because if it is…"

"McKay," Ronon said. "Do you have a better idea of how to get through that wall?"

"Um." Rodney looked around. "No."

"Then we blow it," Ronon said.

"You guys back off," John said, "Up the corridor that way." He surveyed the wall with his hands on his hips.

"Around the corner is best," Teyla said, ushering Alabaster back. "We do not wish to be hit by flying chips of stone."

They waited, Ronon carefully staying far away from Alabaster, until John came back. "Ok," he said, "Cover your heads. Fire in the hole."

It was a very small explosion, though it sounded loud in the confined space. Still, the ceiling did not come down. Not that Teyla had believed it would. John was better at this than that.

"Careful," John said, picking his way through the settling dust over the rubble from the door.

And it had been a door. It was easy to see now how thin it had been, a few inches thick at most, a veneer of bone as hard as stone. His flashlight played over the chamber beyond, an alcove not even a meter wide. On the floor lay two metal boxes side by side.

"Let me get by." Rodney pushed past Teyla, his instruments in hands, taking hold of the first case and opening it reverently. The Ancient bindings gave way. On a background of soft black material lay a gleaming ZPM, its surface traced with red and gold and orange like stained glass. Rodney laid his instruments over it, frowning and adjusting. Then a beatific smile spread across his face. "It's at 97%," he said.

"Sweet," John said, looking down at it with a bemused expression as though he could hardly believe it.

"And there is this," Teyla said. Her hands were sure on the bindings. She had closed this box before. Osprey had closed this box. Her fingers had been the last to touch it. Alabaster bent too, eclipsing the light of the flashlight as she leaned. It did not matter. Teyla could see what lay within, a scepter of dark metal, the cold sheen of naquadah. "Hyperion's weapon," she said.

CHAPTER TWENTY-THREE

Osprey's Daughters

THEY CAME out of darkness into bright afternoon sun slanting across the cliffs behind them, though the cave mouth lay in shadow. "We'd better get moving," John said, looking at his watch. "We're ten minutes late for check in, and Woolsey will get worried." He looked at Teyla. "I can't call in from here. It's an orbital gate."

"It will take us some time to prepare to leave," Alabaster said.

John was on the verge of saying hurry it up, but Teyla gave him a look. And what was the hurry anyhow? Well, ok, there was a hurry, but not so much of one that an hour or two would make any difference.

"I'll go call in," John said. "Ronon, you're with me. Rodney, you stay here and help Teyla and Alabaster get ready to go." And Darling of course. John had learned there was no way to go somewhere with a kid quickly. "It should take a couple of hours for us to walk back to the jumper, go up to the gate, talk to Woolsey, and come back."

"Thank you," Teyla said graciously, as though he'd actually had any choice about it.

John made his report to Woolsey as brief as possible, knowing that every word he said was being heard by the gateroom duty crew. Found a ZPM at 97%, super terrific should make your day. Also found Todd's daughter, big bargaining chip, bringing her back. Not a word about Hyperion's weapon. That was something best discussed in private.

Teyla had told him about it, told him what she remembered. He didn't think she'd told Ronon.

A weapon that could destroy all the Wraith, forever, for all time… The only thing you could say to something like that was holy crap. He didn't know what he'd do if that kind of power was in his hands.

Yeah, you do, some inner part of him said. You already decided, or you would have told Woolsey in front of the gateroom. You already decided, or you would have told Woolsey in front of Ronon, sitting beside you in the jumper. He knows it's an Ancient weapon, but he doesn't know what it does. And if you meant to use it, you would have told him. But you don't, do you? You would have shot Alabaster and the kid and taken it. You could have. No one would have stopped you.

John looked out at the glimmering orbital gate, his mind only half on what Woolsey was saying. Once, Teyla had asked him why he had brought the Athosians to Atlantis when the Wraith attacked, why he had stayed to talk to her in the first place. "I needed intel," John had said. "Asking you seemed like the best way to get it."

Teyla had smiled as though he were being very thick. "And why did you not ask me at the point of a gun? No one could have stopped you. No one could have stopped you and your men from simply taking what you wanted. Why all the talk of tea and Ferris wheels, when you could have simply demanded from people who could not resist you?"

"It didn't occur to me to do that," John had said after a long silence.

"You could have taken instead of asked. You could have held Jinto hostage and required that Halling tell you want you wanted to know. But it did not occur to you." Teyla had shaken her head. "Because you are a good man."

He hadn't said what was on the tip of his tongue. "Because I know where that goes."

And he never wanted to go there again.

John cast a sideways look at Ronon, frowning slightly as he listened to Woolsey droning on through the radio. Ronon, buddy, he thought, if you want someone to kill all the Wraith, it won't be me. He would defend Atlantis to his last breath, and sooner or later it probably would come to that. But he'd made his decision in the split second the barrel of his P90 had jerked up, bullets ringing off the hanging bells, missing the kid by inches. He was going to stand with Teyla and Keller on this one.

There was an obscure comfort in knowing where he stood. The decision was made. He just had to live with it, be willing to pay the price for it. But he'd been there before too.

"Sheppard?" Ronon prompted.

"I said, what is your ETA, Colonel Sheppard?" Woolsey repeated again. "When should we expect you?" He sounded impatient. Probably couldn't wait to get his hands on the ZPM.

"Give me two hours," John said. "Sheppard out."

He landed the jumper as close to Alabaster's cave as possible, figuring they were probably going to have to carry a bunch of baggage with them. Before they were halfway down the path to the cave they heard voices raised in anger. What could possibly have gone pear-shaped already? He should never ask that. Motioning Ronon to back him up, John came around the final corner with P90 at the ready.

The cave was filled with about two dozen big blond guys arguing. Filled, as in there was hardly room to step inside. The whole place smelled of sheep, wool, and Iron Age hygiene.

In the middle of it, Teyla and Alabaster were both gesturing and talking, a pile of packed bags around them. The kid, Lyra, and her brother were watching in fascination. Rodney stood near the door, also apparently fascinated, holding the ZPM's case in his arms.

"McKay? What the hell is going on?" John demanded.

Rodney came over to them in the door. "Not long after you left, these guys showed up. Apparently Lyra told her dad that she was worried that the rude foreigners would hassle the Bride, so they all turned up to make sure we were properly respectful. That was all ok until Alabaster said she was leaving with us. Then they got upset."

"You cannot leave us," one of the men said, his voice almost breaking with emotion. "Do you not know how many people would have died if you were not here? You are the mercy of the gods. You are our proof that they love us! They sent us you so that our children would live!"

Jasen's dad, John would bet. Oh boy.

"I must go," Alabaster said. "Pesei, this has never been my home, and you know it! I have lived here for a time in exile, but I cannot remain! Even now my father summons me from beyond the stars."

"But what will become of us?" another man demanded. "We are your people. We have relied on you for a generation! What will happen now when someone is injured as I was on the boats last year? You know that my legs were crushed and I would never have walked again! Who would have cared for my family if I had been left thus?"

Alabaster looked rattled. Her long red hair spread over her shoulders and she shoved it back with one hand. "Others need me too, in that place beyond the stars. My sister has come to tell me of their need and to bring my father's summons."

Teyla did not move as the man turned to her. "What right have you to take the Bride from us?"

"There are many worlds," Teyla said. "And there are many things that she must do. Her concerns cannot be limited to just this one world." Teyla shook her head. "In the heavens there is a celestial war, and she is our best chance of averting tragedy that could kill more people than all those this world has ever known."

Jasen pulled on Alabaster's sleeve, standing next to Darling. "But what will happen to us?"

Alabaster's pale face seemed to blanch still further. "I will return," she said. "I will return from time to time when I may. I will come and heal those of you I may. I do not know when it will be, but I will come as often as I can." She put her off hand on the arm of one of the men. "Hear my word on this. But I do not know what will transpire in that celestial war, as Teyla names it. I go from here to the City of the Ancestors, where I hope to be reunited with my father."

A murmur spread through the room.

"Oh, not good..." John began.

"You go to stand among the Ancestors with your father?"

"My father lives," Alabaster said loudly. "He is not dead, and the City of the Ancestors is a place one may journey to while still breathing." She glanced sideways at Teyla. "It is a citadel those of many worlds have visited, Athosian and Satedan and Genii and many more, a place left by the Ancestors now reclaimed by their children. I do not go to the land of the dead, but to a place no less living than this."

"Then why cannot we go there?" Jasen's father demanded. "If people from other worlds have gone there, why cannot we accompany you, Our Bride?"

Teyla looked like she was hunting for an answer, but Alabaster spoke first. "I do not see why you may not," she said, turning to Teyla. "Why should not three heroes accompany me? Why should they not come before your elders and represent their people? Surely they are the children of the Ancestors too?"

Teyla's mouth opened and closed, her eyes still on Alabaster as though the queen spoke other words that could not be heard.

"Crapola," John said.

"I do not see why not," Teyla said, her eyes still on Alabaster's. "But know that it is a hazardous quest, and those who undertake it will be changed by the things they see. It is not something to be done lightly or by those who fear what they may become."

At that a vast babble went up, young men arguing with each other, each claiming more courage or a deeper love of their Bride.

"It's like a zenana," Rodney said wonderingly. "It's like a human zenana. They all want to show off for her."

John shook his head. "You and Ronon take the ZPM and the other thing to the jumper. I'll see if I can get them moving. Woolsey's going to kill me." Right. Hyperion's weapon, Todd's daughter, a Wraith kid, and a bunch of emissaries from an Iron Age society with no contact through the Stargate in ten thousand years. Oh, and Rodney crushing on a Wraith Queen, and

Ronon's head popping off. "Teyla, can we get going here?" John waded into the fray.

It was, Dick Woolsey thought, not exactly a reassuring sight. They'd gotten almost used to Teyla walking around Atlantis garbed as Steelflower. That had become almost normal. But this was a real Wraith queen. And she came under a flag of truce as an ally.

The three big human men with her looked like bodyguards, clustering close while at the same time looking around them with wonder and apprehension. Captain Cadman and the Marine team who had met the jumper on the gateroom floor looked wary, weapons just barely at port arms. Only Teyla looked entirely comfortable, five inches shorter than the Queen, her black uniform jacket in stark contrast to the Queen's white gown.

"Mr. Woolsey," she said formally, "I would like to present Alabaster the daughter of Snow of the line of Osprey, and thus my kinswoman. She is also daughter to our ally, Guide. This is her son, Darling, and her attendants Perssen, Thessen, and Erach."

Woolsey inclined his head. "It's a pleasure you meet you. I'm Richard Woolsey, in charge of this facility." At least she was looking at him. Todd usually talked straight through him to Carter or Keller or Teyla.

"It is a pleasure to meet you too, Mr. Woolsey," Alabaster said in her low voice. "Teyla says that you are a valued ally of my father, and that you will contact him for me. You must know that I am eager to speak with him after so many years."

"Yes, of course," Woolsey said with a quick glance at Teyla. "Our procedures for contacting your father are somewhat indirect, as we do not know his position at any given moment. It may take several days to reach him."

"I have waited many years. Several days is a short time," Alabaster said graciously.

Woolsey looked around as Dr. Lynn hurried into the gateroom, somewhat late. He'd told him that he'd better get ready to play anthropologist as soon as Sheppard's team returned with their guest. Well, now guests, as of course Sheppard hadn't said anything about the entourage. Which was just like Sheppard.

"Dr. Lynn will be happy to escort you to guest quarters where you can be comfortable," Woolsey said. "Also, this is Captain Cadman, who will provide security."

"I will accompany you as well," Teyla added with a reassuring trader's smile. "To make certain that you and the others have all you might need for comfort."

"We will send a transmission in hopes that your father will soon reply," Woolsey said. "Perhaps we can speak in a few hours, when you are settled."

Alabaster looked at Teyla, and it seemed to Woolsey that some words must pass between them telepathically. "Of course," Alabaster said.

Woolsey watched them go, feeling as though they'd managed that pretty well. Ronon was with the Marine detachment, and he could rely on Ronon not to let their guests get up to anything they shouldn't. Cadman and Ronon worked together well without stepping on each other's toes, a good thing since Lorne had just traded his crutches for a cane and still couldn't walk without its help.

To his left, Sheppard cleared his throat nervously. McKay was hovering at his shoulder, a case that looked as though it were of Ancient work cradled in his arms. He was at least looking less Wraith-like now, the sensor pits all but vanished, only the shock of white hair to remind people of what he'd been.

"If Rodney and I could have a word?" Sheppard said.

There was a note in his voice that undid all Woolsey's satisfaction. "Very well," he said, and motioned them into his office. He left them to find their own way, and sat deliberately behind his desk. "All right, Colonel, what it is?"

Sheppard gave him a shifty grin. It was almost as though he was trying and failing to copy Teyla's trader's smile. "I know I didn't say anything about Alabaster's folks," he said. "But they asked to come as a diplomatic embassy from their people. And I thought we always need new trading partners and…"

"I don't really see a problem," Woolsey said. "Though I don't see any great advantage, either. And you found the ZPM. So, I repeat, what is it?"

Sheppard bit his lip, and Woolsey felt a familiar sinking feeling in the pit of his stomach. "Well," Sheppard began, and McKay swung the Ancient case up onto the desk.

"We found the ZPM, yes," he said. "We also found this."

He worked the latches and flipped back the lid. Woolsey leaned forward warily, to see an object nestled in what looked a bit like velvet padding — like a jewel in its case, he thought, irrelevantly, or some museum artifact. It looked like a scepter, or perhaps a mace; the head was bigger than a grapefruit, and studded with crystals, and another, larger crystal terminated the base of the shaft. The metal looked like naqadah, which meant it probably wasn't purely decorative, and Woolsey frowned.

"What is it?"

"It's a weapon," McKay said. "Teyla believes, and Alabaster confirms, that it was created by an Ancient scientist named Hyperion, who was tasked with building a weapon that would destroy the Wraith if they got out of hand."

"As they did," Woolsey said, slowly. It made a kind of sense — it was what you'd do if you were experimenting with dangerous animals, be sure you had a way to control or destroy them, a failsafe to keep them from escaping and harming anyone else. Except that the Wraith hadn't been made from animals, they'd been made from humans, from volunteers who revered the Ancients as their protectors. He wished he could believe it wasn't true, but he remembered his own brief encounter with the Ancients all too well. They hadn't had time or thought to spare for the Athosians, and not much more for the humans from Earth — and the Replicators had slaughtered them, which was not satisfaction, but felt more and more like some rough justice.

"Teyla says they stole it," Sheppard said quietly. "In the escape, along with the ZPM, so it couldn't be used against them. They were going to destroy it, but they couldn't figure out how, so they hid it, sealed it up in a cave where no one could find it."

"And now we have it," Woolsey said. He was furious, and desperately afraid. How could intelligent men be so stupid? The political ramifications were appalling. If the IOA found out about it, or the Genii —

"We couldn't leave it," Sheppard said. "We had to open the cave to get at the ZPM. Once we'd done that, it wasn't safe to leave it behind."

"Besides," McKay said, "I'm pretty sure that given enough time I can figure out a way to reprogram it."

"No," Woolsey said sharply.

"But with the Ancient equipment here in Atlantis, I'm sure I can —"

"As far as I am concerned, there is no weapon," Woolsey said. Sheppard sat up straighter in his chair. "What do you think will happen if we say there is? Besides, we genuinely don't know what it is. We know that you discovered an Ancient artifact of unknown provenance that we have not tested and have no idea what it does or how it works. Just like lots of Ancient artifacts we have discovered. Do you really think I want to tell everyone that we have a weapon that will destroy all the Wraith, and that we know this based on Teyla's recovered genetic memories of a Wraith queen?"

Sheppard swallowed. He saw the pit. And about time.

"We have a thing. We don't know what it is, or what it does." Woolsey folded his hands in front of him, closing them over his anger and panic. There was no time for either one, not yet, and with any luck, not ever. "Sheppard, what were you thinking, bringing it here?"

"I didn't think we could leave it," Sheppard said again.

"And do you intend to use it?" Woolsey demanded.

Sheppard's eyes evaded his. "No," he said.

McKay looked at him sideways. "Just no?"

Sheppard straightened up in his chair. "And kill you? And Teyla? And Torren? And every other Athosian with the Gift? Every other person in this galaxy who doesn't know they're descended from someone with Wraith DNA?"

"I'm sure I could modify it so that it would just ..."

"Kill Wraith?" Sheppard asked.

McKay winced, as though he hadn't really worked it all out until now.

Woolsey cleared his throat. "It may come as a shock to you gentlemen, but I do have a problem with assassinating our allies. This may surprise you, but that's not how I do business." It felt good to say that. He wouldn't always have been able to say it, not with surety. Not when he worked for the NID. He hadn't done it himself, of course. His hands were technically clean. He didn't actually have definitive knowledge of any covert operation, of any assassination. He didn't actually know it had happened. He had never needed to know.

And maybe it hadn't happened. Maybe he was, as Jack O'Neill had said, a paranoid little bastard. But it wasn't how he did business, and this was on Dick Woolsey's playing field.

"Dr. McKay, I want you to take the ZPM and plug it in. Let's see what we've got. I'll expect a report in an hour. Colonel Sheppard, I want you to take the other box down to some location within the city about which you will inform no one, and lock it in the most secure place you can find. And by no one I mean even McKay, Teyla, and me. If we don't know, it can't be taken from us." He swallowed hard. He'd been mind probed before, and they were all alive only because he hadn't known what the plan was.

Sheppard looked surprised. "OK."

"We need some time to think this through," Woolsey said. "And we need to get this business with Alabaster squared away. If we do have the beginnings of an effective alliance against Queen Death as well as a working ZPM, we may be back in the game."

CHAPTER TWENTY-FOUR

Fair One

JENNIFER glanced over to where her nurse, Marie Wu, was very carefully listening to Thessen's heart. He looked more interested than frightened by what she was doing, and as Jennifer watched Marie took the earpieces out of her ears and offered them to Thessen so that he could hear his own heart.

Alabaster followed her gaze. "She does much to reassure him," Alabaster said. "You must realize that the people of their world had no contact with others because they had no access to the Ring. This is entirely new for them."

"I know," Jennifer said. Her scans showed that Alabaster was the picture of health for a Wraith, something that probably ought not surprise her. "They seem to be coping well."

"They are all intelligent men," Alabaster said. "I chose men to accompany me who I hoped would adapt."

She sounded like a pleased trainer, Jennifer thought, flinching just a little, pleased that her sheepdogs had performed well at the county fair. They're good dogs and they're pretty smart. Made me proud of them.

"So it is you who has derived this retrovirus with Guide," Alabaster said, her eyes on Jennifer's face.

Jennifer nodded. "We worked on it together, up to this latest iteration. I took the final trial myself."

Alabaster put her head to the side. "And you chose to be fed upon yourself?"

Jennifer nodded again, not looking up from her instruments. "I did. And other than being exhausted for several days, and having some aching and soreness at the puncture site, I'm fine."

"That is quite remarkable," Alabaster said. "The difference it would make to my people is enormous."

"Yes, well, I don't think we're ready for a mass trial," Jennifer said tightly.

"Why not?"

Jennifer swallowed. "There are ethical guidelines… We don't know that what happened with me was what usually happens… I can't let those men take the retrovirus without being more certain…"

Alabaster frowned. "But they came for that purpose. They volunteered to represent their people and be the first. If it works as you say, then it will do no harm to them."

"I just don't think we're quite ready for that yet," Jennifer demurred.

Alabaster sat down on the stool opposite her, perching on the edge in a way that seemed utterly incongruous for a Wraith queen. Teyla as Steelflower had always been conscious of dignity. Alabaster knew she was the genuine article and had no reason for anyone to doubt it. "Why did you work with my father on this?"

Jennifer looked up at her, blinking. "Um, because genocide is wrong." She was suddenly conscious that Marie had stopped speaking, of the silence in the infirmary. Only Thessen, who didn't know the word, wasn't looking in her direction. "It is," Jennifer said. "That's the bottom line. There has to be a way to stop the Wraith from having to kill to feed, or sooner or later there will be a way for us to kill you all."

Alabaster's face was tight. "And if there were such a way?"

"Somebody would use it," Jennifer said. "I thought…your father and I thought…that maybe there was a third path."

Alabaster leaned back on the stool, her hands behind her, looking up at the ceiling as though something there held an answer. "I know why my father would prefer such a path," she said. "But why would you?"

"I told you," Jennifer said. "Because genocide is wrong. Period. Always wrong. No exceptions, no excuses."

"And you believe that firmly enough to let one of us feed upon you, with no idea whether or not the retrovirus worked?"

Alabaster sounded curious, as though this were all an academic question.

"The first trial didn't work," Jennifer said. "Guide nearly killed me. I was in defib when he restored me."

"And yet you did it again," Alabaster said.

"Yes." Jennifer met her eyes firmly. "It's my job."

"Your job to save my people from yours? Or your people from mine?"

"My job to save people," Jennifer said firmly. "I'm a doctor. That's my oath. I save lives. Your lives, our lives, everybody's lives." She slid onto the other stool opposite Alabaster. "I had a job, before I came to Atlantis… It was for an organization that went into the most war-torn parts of the world, places where famine was compounded by guerilla war, by tribal war and rape as a means of war… And we treated everybody. Civilians. Government soldiers. Guerillas. Every tribe. Because we were doctors. Our job was to save lives." Jennifer looked around the infirmary, where Marie was now getting Thessen's blood pressure, where Airman Drake's broken ankle was propped up on nice white pillows while he played video games on his cell phone, and tears pricked at the back of her eyes unexpectedly. "That's what I came here to do. But it didn't turn out like that."

Alabaster put her head to the side, a gesture just like Todd's, the one Jennifer had thought made him look like a courtly gentleman. "Why not?"

Jennifer shrugged. "I spend most of my time being a General Practitioner in a military setting. I set broken ankles and wrangle over who's had an eye exam. I dispense headache medicines and antacids and I patch people up so they can go back out and get shot again. It's not what I wanted to do. It's not what I planned to do. But Elizabeth needed me to do it, and then…" Jennifer looked away, blinking. "I was thinking recently I'd go back to Earth and maybe do that again, but…" She got up briskly. There was no good end to that sentence. "Anyway, it doesn't matter."

"If your retrovirus works, you will have saved many lives,"

Alabaster said gravely. "Human and Wraith alike."

"I hope so," Jennifer said. She brushed her hands off on her pants legs. "Ok. I think we're done here. If you'll wait until Marie is finished with Thessen, Captain Cadman will escort you back to your quarters."

"I will do so," Alabaster said gravely.

When Jennifer got back to her quarters, Rodney was stretched out on the couch, his laptop and Newton sharing his lap by virtue of Newton making himself very small between Rodney's leg and the pillows, roughly the size and shape of a meatloaf. A meatloaf that gave her a reproachful glare when she walked in.

Rodney, on the other hand, didn't look up from the laptop screen. "Oh, hi," he said.

Jennifer came around the couch and plopped down on the ottoman. "Hi Rodney."

His color was good — no more pasty skin, and the scars from the sensor slits were fading, looking like no more now than age lines that bracketed his mouth. With the white hair it made him look older, but not inhuman. Just older than he really was.

Rodney looked up from the screen, actually looking at her, like he was taking in her hair falling out of its pony tail, her tired face. "Bad day?"

"Not by Atlantis standards," Jennifer said. "I had Alabaster in the lab until a few minutes ago. At least she doesn't want to work all night, like Todd. She's spent enough time around humans that she expects us to close down and get some sleep."

"Yes, well," Rodney said. He shifted, dislodging Newton, who yowled in protest.

Jennifer frowned. "She talks about them like pets. The humans who came with her, I mean. Like nice pets she likes a lot, but pets all the same."

Rodney shrugged. "Well, that's kind of what they think, right? I mean, we don't live very long compared to them, and we can't talk like intelligent beings and you know, she got used to the people on that planet and she doesn't want to eat them. How many people would want to kill and eat their dog? Most people would be horrified at the idea. They love their dog."

Newton gave Rodney a reproachful glare.

Rodney glanced back at his screen, where some kind of analysis was rolling. "Alabaster's a good dog owner. She wants her pets taken care of and healthy, with plenty to eat and nice things happening to them. She doesn't want them to be unhappy, and she doesn't want to abandon them any more than most people want to ditch their dog by the side of the road just because it's gotten inconvenient. Most people would feel really bad about doing that. So they bring their dog with them and hope it behaves."

Jennifer stared at him. "Rodney?"

"I've been a Wraith, and believe me, it's different." Rodney reached down to quiet Newton, who was writhing against his side. "Maybe that's what the experiment was for in the first place, what the Ancients wanted. The ones who couldn't Ascend. Wouldn't it be great to be immortal without Ascending? To have telepathic powers and eternal good health? To never die of old age? To get all the benefits of Ascension without leaving home and without all those pesky rules and things?"

"Oh my God, Rodney," Jennifer breathed. "That's exactly why they did it. That's exactly what they were trying to do."

"But they weren't ready to try it on actual people yet. On themselves. They were still trying it on the nearest thing, on humans. Just like we test drugs on monkeys before we go to human trials. Only it didn't work out the way they wanted it do, and their creations weren't very happy about it," Rodney said. "So they tried to kill them and finally came up with a way to do it. But their experiments rebelled first."

"A way to kill them," Jennifer said. Things clicked into place. "Is that what Alabaster was talking about?"

Rodney looked abashed. "We found a device on Alabaster's planet that was designed to kill all the Wraith. I don't know if it works or how it works yet. Woolsey won't let me get my hands on it. He says it's stored in a safe place."

Jennifer leaned forward, her fingers against her temples. "You want to get your hands on a weapon of mass destruction." Of course he did. He was Rodney.

"I've had weapons of mass destruction for years," Rodney said cheerfully. "Come on. How many nukes have I had?"

"I have no idea." Jennifer pressed her hands to her forehead. A weapon that could kill an entire race, not hypothetically, but actually. And the only reason not to use it was her retrovirus. Well, that and the fact that it would be wrong, wrong in a way so big she could hardly get her head around it. But wrong didn't matter. Not to the people who would make the decisions.

On the other hand, if Mr. Woolsey wouldn't let Rodney have it, maybe he didn't mean to use it. Maybe he hadn't already decided to go there. If he had, he would have been telling Rodney to figure out how to make it work…

"Jennifer? There's something I wanted to ask you," Rodney said.

She pressed her fingers to her forehead until she saw red spots before her eyes. There were pressure points that released tension. Maybe Mr. Woolsey was open to trying the retrovirus first…

"You know, it's been kind of busy since I got back. Since I got out of the infirmary, I mean. Since I was back in my right mind. And we haven't seen a lot of each other these last few days, but we've been seeing each other for a year now, and…" Jennifer looked up, trying to figure out what Rodney was talking about. "We moved in six months ago and yes, ok, I've been captured a lot of that time and incidentally Eva says that she has a bunch of resources for the spouses of POWs that she thinks you might find helpful and Jeannie is still here but who knows how long she'll stay since we've got a ZPM now and can open the gate to Earth anytime she wants rather than having to wait until the *Hammond* leaves…"

"Rodney?"

"And I'm not sure who's actually qualified to do it, but at the very least we've got a ship's captain and there's no doubt we're outside the three mile limit…"

"Rodney, what are you talking about?" Jennifer asked. Genocide. A genocide weapon, a weapon to correct the Ancients' mistake…

Rodney swallowed. "About getting married. Now. I suppose we could ask the SGC to send a chaplain through if it's important to you. I think they have one of those."

"Getting married." Jennifer felt like she'd been dropped in a bucket of ice water. "Now? Rodney, we hadn't talked…"

"We're talking about it now, aren't we?" he asked with his lop-sided smile, the one that always looked overconfident even when it wasn't. He sat up, dislodging Newton who fled with a hiss, coming to sit on the edge of the couch, knee to knee. "I think it's time for something solid in my life. I'm ready to make a commitment. If I'm going to stay here forever, it's time to think about the future seriously. And I'm not getting any younger. If I want to pass along my genes…"

Jennifer seized on the nearest floating plank. "You're not that old."

"I'm forty one," Rodney said.

"And I'm twenty eight!" She hadn't meant it to come out almost as a screech, but it did. "Rodney, I have no idea…" She couldn't even make the words work. She bent her head to her hands again.

"No idea of what?" he asked quietly.

Jennifer looked up. "I have no idea what I want to do in five years, much less what I want to do for the rest of my life. I took this job and it's a great job and I'm not complaining about it or about my decision to come back to Atlantis. But it's a job. Not something I plan to do for the rest of my life. I'm glad I've done it, but I don't want to be the Chief of Medicine on a military base for the rest of my life! And yes, someday I probably will want to have kids, but not now and not under these circumstances." She swallowed. She shouldn't say it, but it bubbled up anyway, truth that she'd thought would be better in six months, better when he'd had time to heal. "And I'll tell you this about Eva's resources. I can't do this again. I can't be married to someone who is MIA for months at a time, and just when I've started to pull it together and move on, turns up again and wants to pick up where it was. I can't be a military wife. There are women who can, and who do it over and over for twenty or thirty years, but I can't live like that. I can't live with the uncertainty over and over, with not knowing. At least when someone is terminally ill you know they're not coming back." She stopped, staring at the stricken expression on his face.

"You don't want to marry me."

"I don't want to marry anyone now," she said. "And I don't want to marry someone who is going to be out there putting themselves in harm's way every day. I don't want to be a young widow with kids the way my dad was, and I know that could happen anyway! My mom died of cancer. That happens. But she didn't do it on purpose."

Rodney opened his mouth and shut it again. "But…I thought… you loved me."

"I do. Maybe I do. But I can't marry you like this." She put her hand on his arm. "We can date. We can see each other. We can see where it goes in five years. But I can't marry you now."

Rodney looked down at her hand on his sleeve, and she couldn't see his face. "I need to know that you're here," he said finally. "I can't live with you and get deeper and deeper into this if it's not solid. If it's not going somewhere. If you can't say yes." He was silent for a long moment, then looked up. "Maybe we need to take a step back," Rodney said with that same lopsided smile. "I think I probably need to move out. If this is going to be a casual thing…"

"Yeah," Jennifer said, and she blinked back tears. "If it's casual…"

"Right." Rodney got up, folding his laptop shut. "So I think I should find someplace else to stay tonight. I'll look for new quarters in the morning."

"Yeah," she said, not moving. "That's probably best."

"I think my old room is taken," Rodney said, putting his laptop under his arm. "It had a good bathtub. I think somebody snagged it."

"I'm sure there's another room with a bathtub," Jennifer said. She was proud that her voice was steady.

"Yes, I'm sure there is." He looked at her and then down at the big white slug on the carpet. "Do you mind keeping Newton one more night? I'll get him in the morning."

"No, I don't mind," she said. "I kept him for months. But I was going to send him home with Jeannie…"

"Well. Now you don't have to." Rodney reached down and ruffled Newton's fur. "I'll see you in the morning, cat."

"Good night," Jennifer said. She couldn't trust herself to say anymore as he walked over to the door, his steps as jaunty as the old Rodney McKay. "Good night."

CHAPTER TWENTY-FIVE

A Winter's Night

RODNEY made his way purposefully through the halls of Atlantis. It was late at night, and there were few people to see him, but still he moved like a man with purpose. Not like a man who had no idea where he was going. He finally stopped outside a familiar looking door and shrugged. Why not? He touched the chimes.

The door slid open almost immediately. Teyla was wearing a tank top and sweat pants, but she didn't look as if she had already gone to bed. "Hi," Rodney said.

Teyla looked perplexed. "If you are looking for John," she said, "I believe he is meeting with Major Lorne and Colonel Carter. I think they are in the lounge by the puddle jumper bay."

The one that was sometimes used as an auxiliary conference room for meetings smaller than the main conference room, or that you didn't want people wandering in to, as there was no reason for anyone to be on that floor except to go to the jumper bay. "Actually, I was looking for you," Rodney said. If he'd wanted Sheppard he would have gone to Sheppard's room.

"Oh," Teyla said, and stepped back. Her voice was low. "Come in. Only do not wake Torren."

There was one lamp turned very low in the main room. Torren was sound asleep in a little pile of blankets and stuffed things in his corral in the middle of the room. The sound of soft snores emerged from it.

"Come in the bedroom," Teyla said, beckoning him in and closing the door behind him. Once the bedroom door was closed she spoke normally. "We can talk in here and it won't wake him."

Her room was a nest of light, clothes and electronics and toys scattered here and there, a TV in the corner with a stack of kids' dvds on top of it, while on the floor an overflowing laundry basked shared space with a ride-on fire truck and tangle of boots and slippers. A few pine scented candles were lit on a table by the window. That and the whirling snow outside made Rodney suddenly think of Christmas, of some bizarre way Christmas ought to be, though by the calendar on Earth it was only the end of October.

The room wasn't large, and most of it was taken up by her big bed. Teyla plopped down on one end of it, straightening out the dark red flannel comforter cover and a bright handwoven throw. She crossed her legs. "What did you want to talk with me about?" she asked.

"Um," Rodney said, sitting down on the other side of the bed. Teyla just sat there looking at him quizzically. "I was wondering if I could sleep with you tonight. I mean stay with you tonight. To sleep on your couch."

Rodney. She spoke mind to mind, and her mental voice was concerned. *What is the matter?*

He looked wildly around suddenly registering that about five of those boots were way too big for Teyla. And that was Sheppard's laptop on the table by the TV. And unless Teyla had started wearing a classic Johnson t shirt, that was Sheppard's shirt on the floor. "Wait, are you and Sheppard…"

Teyla's usually composed face looked a little embarrassed. "We are together, yes."

"Oh." Rodney blinked. "That's weird. I mean, that's great. That's really good for both of you. That's super."

Rodney. She took his hand, her mental voice strong and warm. *What is wrong?*

I asked Jennifer to marry me. The images tumbled out faster than words, faster than he could say and more completely, a babbling flood of words and thoughts. *She said no.*

Oh Rodney, she said. *I am so sorry.*

Rodney closed his eyes. One thing about speaking like this was that he could see her still, see the sense of her even more clearly. But it was easier than looking at her face. Less like Rodney and more like Quicksilver, who was always Rodney to begin with, only not remembering all the things that made it hard to do this, that made it hard to say things that should be obvious but weren't. *I'm really sad,* he said.

I know. Her mental voice encompassed him like warm arms. *I am so sorry, my friend.*

I thought she wanted to marry me, but now she says she doesn't. That maybe she'll decide she does in five years but I can't just go on for five years like I think this is going to happen if it's not.

Of course not, Teyla said. *You are not someone who can wait. You must know that your family loves you.*

Her hand shifted on his, wrist to wrist, her right hand stretched against his arm and his against the back of hers, the palm tingling slightly. There was no handmouth there, not anymore, but he knew where it should be. Which was confusing.

You should not have asked her now, Teyla said ruefully.

I thought she'd say yes and then I'd be really happy.

The door opened. "Has Torren been asleep long?" Sheppard asked in a quiet voice.

Rodney's eyes sprang open as Sheppard closed the door behind him, his black jacket over his arm. He was sitting on Teyla's bed holding hands. No, not just holding hands but sitting with his hand against her elbow. With their eyes closed. "It's not what you think!" Rodney said quickly.

"What's not what I think?" Sheppard looked perplexed.

"It's not that I… I wouldn't do that. And I didn't. I mean, especially if I'd known, which I didn't, because you didn't say and you really should have." Ok, now Sheppard looked utterly baffled. "Where's Carter?"

"On her way back to the *Hammond*," Sheppard said with a look at Teyla that pretty clearly conveyed what in the hell is wrong with Rodney. "You could call her on the radio."

Rodney had grabbed his hand back from Teyla and now stared at her as she looked at Sheppard. "And you're ok with that?"

"With Colonel Carter going to the *Hammond*?" Teyla asked. "Rodney?"

With Carter…with Sheppard…hanging out with her late at night… His mental voice cheated, showing all the things he couldn't say.

Why should I not be? Teyla sounded perplexed. *He has friends. Some of them are women. Some of them are men. Why would that disturb me in the least?*

"Rodney, are you ok?" Sheppard asked. He put his jacket on top of the pile in the laundry basket, where it promptly fell off and draped over the fire truck.

Teyla apparently decided that waiting for him to explain was a lost cause. "Rodney asked Jennifer to marry him and she said no."

"Aw, crap," Sheppard said. "That sucks, Rodney."

"He asked if he could sleep on my couch tonight," Teyla added.

"Of course you can," Sheppard said. "Hang on. Let me get some blankets. I think there's a clean comforter around here too." He went into the bathroom and started rummaging, presumably in the storage unit. "It's in there with Torren," he called out. "Torren gets up pretty early. Sorry about that."

"It's ok," Rodney said.

Sheppard came out of the bathroom with a pile of blankets. "Here you go. I've got one more thing I need to check on before I turn in, so if you and Teyla want to hang out, I'll be back in a little while."

Rodney wondered what he needed to check on at eleven at night without his jacket that he hadn't checked on when he was out before, but that was Sheppard for you. "Ok," Rodney said.

Sheppard opened the door and looked out into the dark main room, no doubt checking whether or not Torren stirred.

"Thanks," Rodney said.

Richard Woolsey looked out the window through the thickening snow toward the light limned form of the *Hammond* resting on the pier. He didn't need to use one of the security cameras to identify the person striding toward it, moving at a quick walk but not running despite the cold. Hatless, the *Hammond's* running lights gleamed off its commander's blond hair.

So Sheppard had told Carter and Lorne about Hyperion's weapon. Very discreetly, of course, in the lounge upstairs where everyone on duty in the gateroom wouldn't wonder what required all the senior military officers at ten at night. And not out on the *Hammond*, of course. That would have looked like he was going behind Woolsey's back. Not that he would have given himself a three percent chance that Sheppard wouldn't tell them. The Air Force was circling the wagons, and ordering Sheppard not to tell Carter would have forced a confrontation Woolsey dreaded.

Which meant there was a zero percent chance that Jack O'Neill wouldn't find out about it. Woolsey let the curtain drop over his full length window, shutting out snow and Carter and starship. O'Neill would know. The question was what he would do with that knowledge. Not share it widely. O'Neill never did. Woolsey should tell Banks to make sure to have a second VIP suite ready. Now that they had a ZPM and one could come and go without a twenty four day round trip, O'Neill would be in here locked and loaded himself in a couple of days. He wasn't going to have a conversation about a genocidal weapon in front of the whole gateroom and the whole SGC.

Well, it would be what it was. He had a day or two to prepare. And that was best spent contacting Todd, who hopefully would respond to the message they'd already sent. Yes, the key to all this was Todd. And the sooner he could talk to him, the better…

The hive was damaged, holes in its hull that were beyond even the massive ship's ability to heal. He could see that even from a distance. Clevermen in environmental bubbles worked at its edges, their lights like sparks of stars against the green-black hide of the ship. A scaffold was almost complete, not quite bridging the gap, and Guide knew the air in the sealed-off compartments would be hot and stale. The damage was forward, sparing the guns, but it had taken out at least one of the holding pens, and the hive would be hungry soon.

A powerful ally, Bonewhite said, bitterly, and Guide could not reprove him for mirroring his own thoughts. *I'm fond of Ember myself, but this is not fair trade.*

If that were all, it would not be, Guide agreed. *But Farseer has always been a valuable friend.*

He's a liability, Bonewhite said. *And you know it. Death will hunt him down because her pride is hurt — he was her man, as you never were, and he's deserted. Proud Journey won't be able to stand another fight for months to come, maybe not for years, and we don't have the ships to protect him. Take Ember back, yes, and send Farseer on his way.*

Guide studied the image in his screen, the schematic that showed the disposition of their ships. Just Fortune hung in the center of the rough sphere, Waterlight's elderly hive below and to the right in the place of honor, and the small tough hive commanded by the consort Stonefire in the name of his dead queen took point. There were half a dozen good-sized cruisers, and another handful of smaller, lighter ships, but it was not, on the whole, an encouraging sight. Death's fleet was larger, and even if some of her allies found ways to avoid the conflict — Arrow, certainly, would do his best to take no side, and probably Swiftsure — this was not a fleet to take her on directly. Bonewhite was right, Proud Journey was more of a liability than an asset, and Farseer had brought only a single cruiser with him.

We can't afford to turn anyone away, he said, and touched his control board, hailing Farseer's ship.

The screen lit with more haste than was entirely seemly, and Farseer looked out from the screen. Data fell beside him, tracking the hive's health in the strength of the transmission, and Bonewhite's mouth tightened in disapproval. Guide read the same tale of damage and destruction, but gave no sign of his disappointment.

"Well met, my friend."

"Gladly so," Farseer said. "I have come to place myself and

mine under the rule of Queen Steelflower. And in earnest of my intentions, I've brought with me your chief cleverman, who was abandoned on Tenassa."

Tenassa was one of their few shipyard worlds, where Wraith worshippers protected hidden installations, and Guide's brows lifted. If Farseer had been there, why had he not remained there long enough to put Proud Journey into better order, sent Ember on ahead to plead their cause? "Our Queen is not with us at the moment," he temporized. "She was attacked by Death while under bonds of truce, and so she has taken herself out of range of further treachery, at least for now."

"I am not surprised," Farseer said. He paused. "Tenassa has been destroyed."

"What?" Guide could not stop the question, and Farseer gave a thin smile.

"Destroyed. Death sent her ships to Cull in despite of our agreements — she has undone the work of centuries, to tame the humans there, and teach them how to guard our workplaces. I have filled my ships to bursting with supplies, and with the few humans who survived." Farseer paused. "All of which I also, of course, place into Queen Steelflower's hands."

Guide could feel Bonewhite's approval, had to agree with it himself. Proud Journey itself might not be in shape to fight, but as a storeship, it was just as valuable. "You and yours are welcome, as always. Can we send assistance?"

"Our repairs are well begun," Farseer said. "And proceed apace. But I thank you for the offer."

Guide bowed in answer, and Farseer continued. "I will send across your chief cleverman. He has been of great help to us, and we are also in your debt for that. But he is yours."

The opening was there, to offer Ember's continued assistance, but Guide ignored it. "Very well. Welcome to our alliance, Farseer."

Ember arrived in the shuttle lock looking pinched and hungry, and Guide sent him to feed before they spoke. For a moment, he thought the cleverman might protest, but then hunger got the better of him, and he disappeared toward the holding pens. Guide returned to his own quarters, Bonewhite and the engineer Hasten at his heels, busied himself arranging for Farseer's supplies to be counted and shared out among the ships of the fleet. When Ember returned at last, looking sleek and full-fleshed again, the others withdrew, though Guide signaled Bonewhite to remain.

So, cleverman, he said, and Ember made a deep and graceful bow. *I feared you lost on Lymours. Coalfire reported you taken in a Culling beam.*

That is so, Ember answered. His eyes slid nervously to Bonewhite, who bared teeth in annoyance.

He is in my confidence, Guide said, mildly, and Ember bowed again.

I did not doubt it, Commander.

Bonewhite did not quite roll his eyes, but his disbelief was almost palpable.

Did you escape? Guide went on. *Or were you released?*

I was released, Commander, Ember said. *I was taken by men under the command of Death's pallax, the Old One, and he released me to bear you a message, queen's man to consort — as, he says, it was done in the oldest days.*

Bonewhite did roll his eyes at that, hissing softly, and Guide smiled. *In my day, men who plotted behind their queens' backs — but, no matter. What is this message?*

Commander, he urges us to abandon Queen Steelflower's alliance with the Lanteans as utterly untenable. Ember let the images spill out with the words, the Old One's story, his transformation, the implacable hatred that the Ancients had truly earned. *He believes we can never make peace with the children of the Ancients, and urges you to reconsider.*

Guide allowed himself an almost soundless sigh. Three daughters, Teyla Emmagan had said to him once in the darkness of Steelflower's chamber. Once before we slept, there were three daughters of one mother, and how shall their story end?

We are indeed the bastard, the child of shameful congress, and we ground our mother and our favored sister both beneath our heels. So far the story goes, and I cannot see the ending.

There is one other thing, Ember said. *If this is true, and I believe it is, still — this retrovirus, this changeling drug that the Lanteans have worked on. That I have worked on. It changes things.*

Does the Old One know of this? Bonewhite demanded.

No, Ember said. *Not from me, and I don't believe from any other.*

But does it change anything enough? Guide shook his head. *I do not doubt this either. But—* He reached for a game piece, turned it over in his hand, claws clicking on the stone. *It does not resolve our war with Death. Let us settle that first, and then deal with the other.*

As the commander wishes, Bonewhite began, and a chime sounded.

"Your pardon, Commander," a voice said from the bridge. "We have received a signal in your private code. Will you accept the packet?"

It could only be the Lanteans, or, barely possibly, Death herself, and neither was likely to be good news. "Yes," Guide said, and moved to his console. The data poured gold across the screen, pooled to form familiar symbols. The Lanteans, then, asking for contact. He entered the key, and waited while the algorithm unspooled itself, deciphered the message. After a moment, the screen lit, and Woolsey's face looked out at him. He hadn't really expected to see him again, and couldn't help smiling at the familiar worried frown. A clever man, Hairy, even if an entirely unsuitable consort for either of his queens.

"I am contacting you on our own account and on behalf of your daughter," Woolsey said, and Guide snarled aloud.

I have no daughter.

He wished instantly that he had not spoken, had not betrayed himself. But in the screen she was there, at Woolsey's shoulder, moving among the Lanteans, speaking now to Sheppard and to Teyla, tall and straight-backed and scarlet-haired, the image of her mother. The breath caught in his chest, a painful hitch of heart and lungs. He had been sure she had not survived — there had been no wreckage, no sensor trail to follow, only a scattering of debris and an enemy commander who swore he had seen the ship explode as it entered the hyperspace window. He had searched anyway, and had spent seventeen years starving in a human prison to teach him the futility of hope. And yet there she stood, Snow's daughter, his daughter, and his heart turned slowly in his chest.

Guide? That was Bonewhite, his tone worried, and Guide took a careful breath, tamping down the joy that threatened to overwhelm him. Alabaster lived: it was impossible, inarguable, and it changed everything.

A change of plan, he said, and both Bonewhite and Ember looked up sharply, catching the echo of his wondering delight. *We will contact the Lanteans.*

Very well, Bonewhite said, slowly.

Guide fixed him with an emerald stare. Bonewhite had been friend and ally then, would know as well as anyone what this could mean. *Alabaster lives.*

"And so that is that," Radek said, pushing his glasses back up on his nose with one finger. "We have a ZPM at 97%, and full capability to the command chair, to the shield and to the cloak. And the hyperdrive, though I do warn you that using the hyperdrive depletes the ZPM very quickly."

Woolsey nodded. "I don't think we need to move the city right now, but it's good to know we could." He looked as though he wished he had papers to shuffle, but of course he didn't. "Dr. Zelenka, there is one more thing I want to discuss with you."

"Of course," Radek said. Of course there was one more thing in the middle of the night. Wasn't there always?

"Dr. McKay will not be returning to his position as Chief of Sciences," Woolsey said, not looking up. "He's back on the gate team at Colonel Sheppard's discretion, but in terms of the other position, I believe it's wiser to retain you."

"Ah," Radek said. He could not think what else to say. "Rodney…"

Woolsey did look up then, his eyes meeting Radek's. "Can you seriously, in good conscience, give him access to every bit of rewritten code, every password? One hundred percent of the most sensitive material?"

Radek swallowed. "I do not think that Rodney would betray us," he said.

"Dr. McKay was in enemy hands for two months," Woolsey said gravely. "And while Dr. Beckett and Dr. Keller are certain that he is recovered enough to rejoin the gate team, I would like a little more certainty before we give him his previous job back." He folded his hands over his laptop. "Besides, you've done an exemplary job. I can't recall when the sciences have run so smoothly with so little interpersonal strife. Dr. Zelenka, you are Chief of Sciences permanently, not just in the interim. That is how it is."

"I see," Radek said.

"If there's nothing else?" Woolsey asked. He looked tired. As of course he would be. It was two in the morning.

"No, nothing," Radek said, and walked out into the control room, his laptop under his arm. He should rest as well. Tomorrow there would be Todd, and that was always exciting. And yet.

William was still there, bent over the end console in an unconvincing display of interest in whatever was on the screen, as though he had not been rubbernecking at the conference in Woolsey's glass paneled office. "Walk with me," Radek said.

William looked up. That did indeed surprise him. Yes. "To where?"

"To wherever." Radek shrugged.

"I was just wondering if I'd need my jacket," William said.

"I doubt it." Radek gave him what he hoped was a reassuring smile, but William didn't seem reassured. "Come on." He headed for the transport chamber without waiting to see if William followed.

Which of course he did, stepping in after him, all long, lanky grace which should have been fading at his age. "Where are we going?" he asked.

"You'll see." Radek touched the destination, and it was only a moment before the doors opened. On a dim stretch of semi darkened corridor, plain and windowless.

"Where are we?"

"Section 11, A56," Radek said, knowing that would mean nothing. "Deep in the city's substructure. These are the main corridors that access the repair corridors for the sublight engines."

William's mouth twitched. "This is where you keep your etchings?"

"Actually it's more of a secret lair." Radek waggled his eyebrows at him. "But if you are too frightened to continue… It is rather dark and atmospheric."

"By atmospheric you mean…"

"Spooky." Radek switched on his flashlight and turned to the left. "There is the transport chamber. Return or come." He hurried off down the corridor as though he could care little which William did.

And of course with a challenge like that, he was a step behind. "Aren't these lights supposed to work?"

"They did," Radek said, taking a right turn into a stairwell and starting down. "But the lower levels of the city flooded several years ago and every one of them shorted out. Somehow repairing the lights in little used corridors has never been a top priority."

Down three flights, boots noisy on the metal stair treads.

"How far down are we going?" William asked.

The bottom stair, then a swift left turn into the first chamber. "All the way," Radek said quietly.

The room was not large, and whatever its original use, now it contained nothing but a dozen or so military packing crates. The metal walls were bare, three sides of the room, while the fourth looked like a darkened mirror, like opaque glass.

"What is this stuff?" William said, almost running into Radek as he caught up, letting the beam of his own flashlight play over the crates.

"Emergency supplies of various sorts," Radek shrugged. "It is always wise to have a cache here and there in case of emergencies." He turned off his light and sat down on the nearest packing crate as William walked over to examine the fourth wall. "Turn your light off."

"It's a window," William said, his hand to the glass. "But it's night and…"

"Turn it off," Radek said quietly. "You will see."

"…we're underwater," William finished, wonder creeping into his tone. He turned his flashlight off. "Now what?" The window was completely dark. Nothing whatsoever could be seen beyond the glass.

"We wait," Radek said. He got up and went to stand by William at the window. "Wait."

It was a long moment before he saw anything, even with his eyes adjusting to the dark. One could believe one imagined it at first, a momentary pinkish glow. No, there it was more strongly. It was there. And then a tiny white light, a pinprick. Something very small, or something unimaginably large and very far away. It moved. It crossed the field of vision slowly.

And then another. Two lights, three. Four. Red and gold and white, moving separately and in unison. A train of pink lights evenly spaced, as though they were along a backbone, shifting together into one as whatever it was came toward the window.

"Bioluminescence," William breathed. "I've never seen anything like it."

"Nor will you, except in Earth's deepest seas," Radek said. "And they are just beginning."

A chain of blue lights, and then the darker pink, close and bright enough to cast a reflection through the glass, to illuminate the faint darker hooded shape tall as a man, long nimble tentacles. One brushed the outside of the window as though reaching for Radek's hand through the glass.

"It's some kind of…" William's voice was full of wonder.

"Squid, I believe," Radek said. "We have seen a number of them. This one — I almost feel that I am beginning to recognize him, and he me." He switched his flashlight back on, holding it low so that it would not glare off the glass. "Watch."

The long tentacle wavered, reaching toward the light and brushing against the window, tentacle tips uncoiling as though it thought to gently take it from Radek's hand. A moment, and then the tip lit itself, the same white light as the flashlight, passing against the window in three long passes.

Radek smiled. He raised the light in mirror, three long passes on the inside of the glass.

"It's trying to communicate," William said.

"Or perhaps I am," Radek replied. "Which of us is brainier, I do not know. But we can at least salute in passing." It coiled its tentacles again out in the frigid water, glowing softly, a pattern that must mean something complex, something beyond his wits. "If I am going to stay here forever, it is time to get to know the neighbors."

William turned his head. "Aren't you going home?"

"I am home," Radek said.

CHAPTER TWENTY-SIX

The Brotherhood

"SO," Dick Woolsey said, folding his hands in front of him on the conference table. He wished he had a file folder to open decisively. But he didn't. File folders were heavy and unnecessary, not worth shipping out on the *Daedalus* or *Hammond*. He could have acquired all the file folders he wanted when they were on Earth, but he'd had more important things on his mind then than office supplies.

Everyone was looking at him, waiting for him to continue, Sheppard, Teyla, McKay, Zelenka down one side of the table, Keller at the far end, then Carter, Lorne, and Ronon. Lorne had a tripodal cane with him, propped up against the table beside him. He was getting around, but it would be weeks yet before he was back to normal.

"So," Dick said again. "We have Todd arriving. He's agreed to come to Atlantis under our terms."

"Isn't that a little weird?" Lorne asked. "He's usually pretty careful unless he's got something up his sleeve."

"I think he's probably on the up and up," Dr. Keller said. It was unusual for her to speak up immediately in a meeting, and Woolsey felt his brows rise. "We have Alabaster and his grandson. I think this is a situation where he'd meet almost any terms we set."

There was a general sense of skepticism around the table. "Dr. Keller has worked with him extensively," Dick said. "Teyla? Do you have an opinion?"

"I think it is likely that he is eager to be reunited with Alabaster," Teyla said. She spread her hands. "But I cannot speak for the veracity of anything he says until we are in the same room. I do not think he can deceive me about his intentions face to face, but there is nothing I can ascertain from a transmission."

"We need to take every precaution," Sheppard said. He leaned forward in his chair, all taut lines. "We'll meet him at a rendez-vous point and bring him through blindfolded and under guard. Sam, can I borrow Cadman for that?"

"I'm here," Ronon said.

"And I need you here watching Alabaster," Sheppard said. "Two Wraith, two teams."

Ronon nodded.

"Yes, you can borrow Cadman again," Carter said. She looked amused. "But you can't keep her."

"I'd send Lorne, but…" Sheppard shrugged in Lorne's direction, who brandished his cane.

"I take it I'm with the crew here," Lorne said.

"Yes. You'll coordinate the security arrangements here." Sheppard looked at Dick. "Is there anything else I need to know about security wise?"

"Not that I'm aware of," Dick said. "There won't be any special arrangements for General O'Neill."

"O'Neill's coming?" Sheppard looked startled. "When did that happen?"

Carter was studiously examining her laptop.

"It hasn't yet," Dick said dryly. "I imagine I'll be informed about it this afternoon." Score.

John folded up his laptop and tucked it under his arm as people started filing out of the conference room. He hung back to let Lorne get ahead of him, still awkward untangling himself from table and chairs. Rodney hung back too, while Keller went ahead. So that was how it was.

Sam moved one of the other chairs out of Lorne's way. "Thank you, ma'am," Lorne said, stumping along.

"No problem."

Rodney hung back at Sam's shoulder. "So," he said. "Want to go over some calculations?"

Sam blinked. "Which calculations?"

Rodney stuffed his hands in his pockets, his old three sided smile on his face. "I'm sure we can find some calculations. I mean, it was awkward dealing with this thing between us when you were in charge here, but now you have the *Hammond* and I work for Woolsey... We could have dinner."

Sam blinked again. Her mouth opened and snapped shut. "Rodney," she said. "I'm not going out with you."

"Well, I mean, where's out?" Rodney said with a suave and insouciant smile. "It's just dinner in the mess with an old friend."

Sam turned and faced him, almost nose to nose as she was tall. "For the four hundred and forty seventh time, I am not going out with you. I am never going out with you. Not now, not next week, not next year. I am involved with someone else, and I am not interested. Got it?"

John winced.

"Got it," Rodney said.

"Good." Sam's pony tail flipped like a cat's tail lashing as she stalked out of the conference room.

"Good job, Rodney," John said, gritting his teeth. "Way to go."

Rodney looked after her and shrugged. "Is she really involved with somebody else, or is she trying to let me down easy?"

"She's really involved with someone else," John said. "Really, really involved. And Rodney, what the hell? You knew she'd say that."

"I figured it would be good for the old morale," Rodney said. "You know. A declaration of independence. If me and Jennifer are casual and not exclusive, there's no reason I can't see Sam."

"Except that Sam won't see you except on a platter with a sprig of parsley," John said. "Come on, Rodney. Can't you think of anybody to hit on besides Sam?"

"There's Teyla." Rodney stopped in the doorway as though the thought had just struck him. "She's hot."

"It took you almost six years to notice that?"

Rodney scratched his head, which was still white haired. "I

think it's the Wraith thing. Teyla was never my type, but now when I see her I just…"

"Want to kiss her feet?"

"Yeah, that."

John clapped him on the shoulder as he followed him out of the conference room. "I'll make sure you have a chaperone with Alabaster."

"Very funny."

John caught up with Teyla in the hall outside the transport chamber, where Lorne was just getting in. "I'm going to the lab level," Lorne said apologetically.

"We will wait," Teyla said, and let the doors close. She looked at John keenly. "You are troubled."

John blew out a breath. "Does it strike you that Rodney is acting strange? He just hit on Sam like a ton of bricks when he knew she'd shoot him down. What the hell was with that? That's not our normal Rodney."

Teyla tilted her chin. "No, it is not. Rodney is not normal. He has been a Wraith, and though he may like to think that he is as he was before, except for his hair, the Gift shows that he is not. He can still speak mind to mind, and it seems clear to me that there are other changes as well." She put one foot up against the wall beside the transport chamber. "You do not understand how a Wraith craves a queen's attention. He needs her mental touch. He needs her regard. We did not understand it then, but we saw this with Michael — how he fixed upon me as the only person who could give him what he needed. Sam is a queen to him, as she is perceived so by all the Wraith. Her attention, even her negative attention, is better than none. To pursue a queen and be refused is nothing. But one must try."

John frowned. "So Rodney has a predisposition to chase women who will kick him in the teeth?"

Teyla looked serious. "Moreover, he has been captured and held these many months. If you had just been recovered from months as a prisoner, would you not want me to rush to you with open arms?"

"Well, of course." John shifted from foot to foot. "But that doesn't happen sometimes. I mean, sometimes guys get back from deployment all messed up and their wives are in a totally different place. They want everything to be ok and to move on and to get on with life and have everything work and it just doesn't. There's just too much water under that bridge and too little common ground." He stopped. Or he tried to, but the words kept flowing. "Too many things you can't talk about and too many things you're ashamed of, too much blood on your hands. Or maybe there just wasn't enough that was right in the first place."

"John, he killed people. He led an assault on us where people were slain. He has put Major Lorne, who was his friend, through two surgeries and months of pain and discomfort. He cannot simply forget it as though it never happened, as though it were done by someone else. And he has fed on Jennifer, even though it was with her consent. These are things that change a man."

John put his arm on the wall and leaned his head against it. "You're right," he said quietly. "I don't know why I didn't see that."

"Perhaps because it is too close?" Teyla put a hand to his shoulder. "And because you are his friend and you wish that he did not have to go through what you have gone through?"

"Yeah." John closed his eyes. He could hardly remember coming home, and that in itself was strange. He should remember that. It was November, December. There were Christmas trees in BWI airport. He remembered that. But he couldn't remember who was there. Nancy, probably? Where had they gone? What had they done? It had been three weeks since Holland died, five weeks since Mitch and Dex. Had she brought the car or had they taken a cab? Gone on the train? He had no idea how they'd gotten to Crystal City. He didn't remember what she'd worn or what she looked like, if she'd had a little flag or a sign like soldier's wives sometimes did. Had she smiled or cried?

He wasn't sure if it was that day or another day that she'd put her arms around him and he had frozen, feeling only the weight of a cooling corpse against his breast. "What's wrong?" she had asked, words for which there was no answer.

"Ok," John said. "That's what Rodney's going through. And Jennifer…"

"Who shall Jennifer turn to? You? Me? Ronon?" Teyla shook her head. "Who are her friends besides Rodney? I can think of no one but Carson, and they are not close. She was shy when she first came here, overwhelmed by responsibility. And then Katie Brown's friends spurned her, seeing her as the reason Rodney broke up with Katie. The women who are her own age, like Laura, were all Katie's friends." Teyla leaned back against the wall beside him. "Jennifer is very much alone, and Rodney needed more than she could give. Jennifer is an honest person, and she will not give her lifelong vow to someone if she is not certain of it. How could she be certain now?"

"I'm not saying she should have married him out of pity," John said. "That wouldn't work. I just…" He straightened up, shrugging. "I just don't know what to do."

"I do not either, besides give him time to heal." Teyla shook her head ruefully. "He will always be Quicksilver, just as I am always Steelflower. I understand that. And you have known this bitter homecoming, as he has, and can be his friend. Perhaps it will be enough."

"And not expect him to be ok, even if he says he is," John said, nodding. "I get that. Four months in Antarctica with light duty."

"Did that help you?"

"I guess. It helped a lot more than four months in DC chewing my feet off." Antarctica had been so quiet. Restful.

"Then perhaps Rodney needs light duty that does not feel to him as though you are pushing him off in the corner?" Teyla suggested.

"Yeah. I'll have to talk to Woolsey. We can work something out. Some kind of project…" Rodney messed up was not a good thing, over and above it being Rodney. But of course he wasn't ok. It was just that John had wanted him to be ok, that Rodney wanted to be ok.

Teyla put her arm to his sleeve again. "John, he will be stronger in time. Just as you are."

"Yeah," he said, and he supposed it meant something that he almost believed it.

Lorne caught up with Cadman on the lab level, just where he'd expected her to be. She'd been in the armory, and she straightened up when she saw him. "Sir."

"Hey," he said. "I need to talk to you about something. I just got out of the briefing, and Carter said we could borrow you again."

Cadman looked pleased, as usual. She seemed to like being needed, though she was always careful not to make it look like she was gunning for his job, something he appreciated when he was running on three legs, so to speak. "With the Wraith?"

"Yeah. I'm in charge of security procedures. Todd's going to get here to meet with Woolsey and Alabaster, so we've got two parties of Wraith to guard. I want Ronon to handle Alabaster, and I'm going to send you to meet Todd on neutral ground."

Cadman nodded. "Should I pick somewhere we don't usually use out of the database?"

"That'll do," Lorne said. "Take a full squad of Marines with you. Whoever you think is best."

She looked thoughtful. "I'd rather have Sgt. Sandoval, if that's ok."

"You can have Sandoval," Lorne said. "I'll keep the newest guys here." He didn't need to add 'where Sheppard and I can keep an eye on them.' That went without saying. It also went without saying that he was making it very clear Cadman had moved up a notch, a leader with a certain amount of latitude for her own team. "I don't need to tell you to watch out, right?"

Cadman grinned. "Nope. I think I've got a pretty good idea that the Wraith can't be trusted."

"Even if you're Carter's niece or whatever," Lorne said.

"That's so weird."

He shrugged. "Matriarchal society. You take it like it comes."

"Whatever you say, Major." Cadman grinned again. "We'll take every precaution. I'll search Todd myself."

"Probably a good idea," Lorne said. "Can you send me Jones and Canifora in my office? I need to get my end of it straightened out before we regroup and report in…" He looked at his watch. "About two hours." He shook his head. "I don't know where days go."

"Same place they always do," Cadman said cheerfully. "I'll send the guys up." She turned to go and then stopped, her face suddenly serious. "Thank you, Major."

"No problem," Lorne said.

CHAPTER TWENTY-SEVEN

Reunion

THE SECOND briefing was shorter than the first, mostly logistics, and John was once again grateful that he had good people. Lorne was on the ball, and so was everybody else. The old timers had had five years to come together as a team, more or less, and the smoothness of the operations showed. Even Woolsey seemed pleased.

Afterwards, everyone was clustering around outside Woolsey's office talking, and John motioned Sam back in the conference room. "You know Todd's going to demand we turn the weapon over to them."

"I know." Sam pushed her bangs back. "Of course he's going to object to us keeping it when it's a knife at his throat. It can't do us any harm but it can kill all of them. It's a perfect weapon of mass destruction," she said grimly.

"Not really," John said, and she looked at him quickly. His throat was dry. "It'll kill Teyla and Torren and Rodney and about half the Athosians."

Sam met his eyes squarely. "We're going to destroy it."

"And what's General O'Neill going to say about that?" John asked. "Look, if the IOA gets wind of this, I have no idea what's going to happen. This is going to be like when the city was on Earth all over again and they wanted Todd for medical experiments."

"You can probably ask Jack yourself anytime now," Sam said. "It takes him longer to get from Washington to Colorado than it does from Colorado here, but you can bet he won't bring the IOA with him."

"Yeah." John frowned. "I have no idea how we got here. Wraith allies."

Sam grimaced. "You should have seen the Tok'ra when we first made contact. The idea of allying with a Goa'uld parasite… Let's just say it could have gone smoother."

Rodney's white hair stood out in the crowd. He was leaning over Alabaster now, explaining something very personally. Hoo boy.

"You know, Sam," John said, "when Rodney hit on you… He's not himself right now. He's kind of messed up. This being a prisoner of the Wraith thing has kind of messed with his head. He and Jennifer just broke up, and people don't always make a lot of sense when they first get back…"

"Tell me about it," Sam said, glancing toward the crowd around Woolsey's office door, Ronon standing back watchfully, keeping his fields of fire clear. Her voice was light but she didn't look at him. "I was captured by the Replicators for a while. Not a good scene. A pretty bad scene, actually. When I got back my boyfriend…" She took a deep breath. "He wanted to get married and it seemed like a good idea. You know. Get my life in order, stop flailing around wanting things I couldn't have, stop being alone… You make some pretty bad decisions when you're in that headspace."

"Yeah, I know." He hadn't thought — what? That Sam had been there too? She was strong, hard as nails. You could always count on Carter. She didn't have an ounce of sentimentality, didn't allow a moment of weakness. It was hard to imagine her blowing up her personal life, or anything else she didn't intend to incinerate.

But maybe she was different with real friends. He was. Maybe he was turning into her real friend, not just a guy she worked with that she liked. Maybe she was kind of lonely out here too, with nothing but email to connect her to home. It wasn't like she could pal around with her crew any more than he could pal around with Cadman or Hernandez or Salawi over there. But he had his team, and she didn't have hers.

Sam shrugged. "I'm not mad at Rodney," she said. "It's ok."

"I know it's messed up, but he's acting like you're his Wraith Queen."

She burst out laughing. "Oh, for real? Does that mean he'd actually do what I told him to for a change?"

"You could try it and see," John said, grinning. She'd been to that brink too and come back, worked through the messed up part like a torn muscle. Had other people? What if it wasn't just him, but a lot of other people too, on a secret journey that no one else knew about, with only hidden signposts to mark the way, Masonic handshakes to identify a fellow traveler?

"I might do that," Sam said. "And thanks for the word. I know you watch out for your team."

"Is that a bad thing?"

"No." Sam shook her head. "It's life."

The first symbols around the gate lit at the same moment that Airman Salawi spun around in her chair. "Unscheduled gate activation!" Hernandez hurried down the stairs to take up a firing position at the bottom as Merriman and Pulaski cranked the manual gate shield into place. The wormhole erupted blue behind it.

Salawi had her hand to her ear bud, listening for radio. "It's the SGC," she said, twisting around to tell Woolsey.

"About time," Carter said under her breath.

"Open the iris," Woolsey directed, straightening his tie.

Jack O'Neill stood at the window in Woolsey's office, looking out through the glass at the floor of the gateroom below, wishing he were somewhere else. He usually did when he was in this office.

Turning Atlantis back over to the surviving Ancients, telling Elizabeth Weir to pack up...

Trying to persuade those same Ancients that the Replicators bearing down on them weren't friendly, watching the first ones die... They didn't listen to him, even though he had their damned gene, even though he was their descendant. They were Ancients. But they died like humans. Just exactly like humans.

Taking over Atlantis on behalf of the Air Force, acting on a Presidential order that could always be disavowed, a cowboy getting ahead of his grade...

And now this.

Behind him, Woolsey lapsed at last into silence.

Down on the floor of the gateroom there was an authorized activation, a team heading out to one of their trade partners with a bunch of boxes to be exchanged for fresh foodstuffs. The last one on the team turned and waved cheerfully to someone before stepping through the event horizon, like it was no big deal at all.

Jack marshaled his thoughts. "You're telling me that you have a weapon that could kill all the Wraith and any human with Wraith DNA."

"I'm telling you that we have an Ancient device that was designed to do that, that the first Wraith believed would," Woolsey said. "Obviously we haven't tested it."

"So you don't know if it works, or if it does what they think it does," O'Neill said. The number of Ancient devices that worked the way they were intended to, with no side effects…

"That is correct," Woolsey said.

Jack nodded. "And where is it now?"

"I told Sheppard to hide it. No one else knows where it is. I don't know where it is."

"Good call," Jack said. Sheppard was the last person who would use it. It would be over his dead body, possibly literally. "And who else knows it exists?"

"You, me, Sheppard, Teyla, Colonel Carter, Dr. McKay and Major Lorne," Woolsey said.

"And the Wraith." There was that important point.

"Alabaster. Which means Todd — Guide — will know soon enough. And he'll want it."

Jack put his fingers to the bridge of his nose where a headache was building. You didn't get much more above grade level than this. "And you've got this new queen, Death, marauding all over the place, not to mention the regular Wraith cullings. A weapon that could save thousands upon thousands of lives."

"And completely destroy an entire sentient species," Woolsey said dryly. "Genocide on a scale the Goa'uld and the Ori never imagined."

"We can't give this thing to Todd," Jack said. He turned around. "You know we can't do that." Anger welled up in him, sharp and strong. How dare Woolsey make him play God? How dare he put it all on him, the millions of human lives lost to the Wraith balancing the destruction of an entire species? On him? "What the hell are you thinking?" he demanded. "You're handing me a doomsday weapon and telling me what? You want me to figure out what to do with it? What the hell gives you that right? Why not the President or the Joint Chiefs or the IOA? Why the hell are you dumping this on me?"

Woolsey squared his skinny shoulders. "Because you're the man who didn't nuke Abydos."

Jack took a long breath.

And that was where it all began. That was where the story started, the gate opening onto another world, the bomb that was supposed to close it forever. Five thousand people, five thousand ordinary villagers going about their lives, versus the safety of Earth from the Goa'uld. He could see it still, clearly enough to touch it, the blue sky of Abydos over golden sand, pyramid rising like a dream, like a mirage out of wild imaginings. Kids and goats, old men who needed dental work and women with wary eyes. The collateral damage was too high.

Jack turned back to the glass, closing his eyes. "The Abydonians all died anyway."

"Seven years later," Woolsey said. "And that was worth something." His dry voice ran on. "That's all we ever have, isn't it? That it's not today. That it's not on our watch."

Jack said nothing. Out in the control room one of the guards was flirting with the Airman on duty. He'd seen the bodies come back drained of life, withered to mummified husks. What do you tell their parents? What do you say happened? What do you do when their mom wants to open the casket? He could end that forever.

"We don't know what it would do," Woolsey said. "Besides kill the Wraith and every human with Wraith DNA. We don't know how large the collateral damage would be. Presumably you and some few others would be protected by the ATA gene. Obviously the Ancients would not have wanted this to work on themselves. But ordinary humans?"

"You're reaching for straws," Jack said.

Woolsey made some small noise behind him. "I am," he said. "But it's my job to think about the worst case scenario."

"And mine to think about casualties." The words came out sharper than he meant.

"We have the retrovirus," Woolsey said. "And we can inoculate all our personnel within a couple of weeks. We'll never have to send our people home that way again. The question is about the rest of the galaxy."

"We can't hold," Jack said. "We've got to use it or not. If we sit around holding it, we're just begging for something to go wrong. Nothing like this stays a secret. Not from our people, not from theirs."

"The first Wraith wanted to destroy it but couldn't figure out how," Woolsey said.

"They didn't have McKay and Carter." Jack turned around. "Ok. Let's get rid of this damned thing. If McKay and Carter can't figure out how to wreck it, I don't know who can. Drop it in a sun or down the event horizon of a black hole or something. They'll figure it out. They could probably destroy the universe if they tried hard enough. I'll give you Carter and you put in McKay. Let's see what awesomely dangerous plan they can come up with. And then…" Jack grinned ruefully. "We won't be anymore screwed than we already are."

Guide waited beside the Ring of the Ancestors, his breath a cloud in the damp air. The human soldiers left longer trails of mist: a faster metabolism, he wondered, or simply adrenaline raising body temperature? His own men waited with him, the drones nearly motionless, Bonewhite at his left hand ready for trouble. Guide didn't know if the humans would recognize or remember him, the man Sheppard had called Kenny,' but he wanted his second at his back. His fears for Alabaster had led him astray before now; he needed a man with enough authority to overrule him if things went wrong. It was an odd, unpleasant feeling, knowing he had made himself vulnerable, but he had felt naked — flayed, skinless — since the moment he'd seen Alabaster's face. He could not fully trust himself, and that had to be taken into account.

Bonewhite caught a flash of that thought, and took a step forward in spite of the watching Marines, his off hand extended to touch Guide's upper arm.

It may still be a trick. Send one of us — send me — instead.

And that would be the politic course, but Guide couldn't bear it, couldn't stand to wait, braced for the inevitable disappointment. He shook his head, the weight of his hair sliding against the leather of his coat. *No. Thank you, but this is mine.*

Bonewhite bowed, more deeply than was his habit. *We will attend your return.*

Thank you, Guide said, and broke the touch, looked to where Sheppard stood with Carter's kinswoman. He was pleased that she would be left here, guard and hostage — it was a fitting choice, and he knew Bonewhite also knew better than to trust her too completely.

"Very well, Sheppard," he said aloud. "I am ready."

"About time," Sheppard said. "Oh, just so you know, we're not going straight to Atlantis."

Bonewhite bared teeth at that, but Guide laughed. "I never expected it."

"Dial the gate," Sheppard ordered, and a moment later the Ring exploded with blue fire.

After the first passage, the humans blindfolded him. Guide submitted without complaint, amused that the young officer who performed the task had to stand on tiptoe to reach, and smelled of fear as he did it. He heard the Ring open, and then Sheppard said, "Ready?"

"I am ready."

"Three steps up," Sheppard said quietly. Guide could almost see him, see the faint, self-deprecating smile, his face turned half away so that no one else would guess that he spared a fellow Consort's dignity.

The stairs were there, and then the shock of the Ring. His boots rang on the stones of the City of the Ancients, and he reached for the blindfold before he thought better of it.

"Go ahead," Sheppard said.

Guide completed the gesture, loosened the strip of black fabric and let it fall to the floor. The gateroom was filled with a cool, pale light, the sky beyond the windows like the polished heart of a shell. The colored glass looked dull, dirtied, against the pure pale silver of the clouds. Woolsey stood at the top of the broad stairs, flanked by Carter and Teyla — Guide found a moment to pity him, caught between two such queens. There was also a grey-haired man Guide didn't know, his back straight and his eyes appraising. The tall Satedan stood beside him, his face a grim mask.

"Welcome to Atlantis," Woolsey said — a nice use of protocol, giving precedence to neither queen.

Guide bared teeth in what he knew was a disconcerting smile. "Thank you. It is — most interesting — to be here yet again."

"Under happier circumstances, I hope," Woolsey said, and Ronon stepped aside.

Until that moment, Guide had not entirely believed. There would prove to be some trickery, some reason for delay that would ultimately become an admission of deceit, or, at best, bones on some barren world. But she stood there, tall and fair in her long robe, her scarlet hair caught back by a band that spread like wings across her temples. Snow had looked thus once, when he had first seen her, young and strong and gallant, mistress of her hive. His breath caught, though he had thought himself prepared.

Alabaster.

Guide, she answered, and came down the steps toward him, holding out both hands.

He took them, silenced, and in her touch she whispered, *Father.*

Guide bowed his head over their joined hands, his hair falling to screen his face. Teyla might read his confusion, joy and wonder and fear that somehow this miracle might still be snatched away, but no other.

Child no more, he said at last, and felt his words break with their joy. He lowered his head further still, until his hair brushed their joined hands. This, perhaps, was what the Fair One had meant by music, their emotion joined and rejoined, delight and wonder feeding on itself. Alabaster caught the echo of his thought, and she smiled cool and proud.

But my father still.

Something moved then on the stairs. Guide straightened, startled, and the boy paused, looking warily at his mother. Alabaster smiled and beckoned, gathered him against her skirts to peer solemnly up at Guide.

My son, she said. *I call him Darling.*

Darling indeed, Guide said, and went to one knee. *Well met, Alabaster's son."

Well met, the boy answered, and his mother prompted him with a touch. *Snow's Consort.*

Guide smiled at the old-fashioned courtesy, at his grandson healthy and unharmed, and on the steps someone cleared his throat. Guide rose, drawing himself up to his full height, and Alabaster turned to face the Lanteans.

"I am in your debt," he said aloud. It was a cheap concession, they would have known it no matter what he said.

Behind Woolsey's shoulder, Sheppard smirked, his thought plain to read. Woolsey cleared his throat again. "Yes. That's — it's something we will certainly all bear in mind. In any case, we have much to discuss. But first, allow me to introduce you to another of our people's representatives."

He gestured to the gray-haired man who stood beside Carter. Guide made an appropriate response, his eyes flickering from one to another, assessing their response. Who was this stranger, and why was he here? Unless — yes, he thought, that had to be the answer. It explained why both Sheppard and Woolsey looked so wary: this was Carter's true Consort, come at last to support his queen.

"General Jack O'Neill," Woolsey said.

"A pleasure," Guide said, and meant it. Perhaps they could come to a better bargain after all.

CHAPTER TWENTY-EIGHT

Children of the Ancients

"WELL," Jack said, mostly under his breath. "This is different."

Carter gave him a look that he guessed meant 'not so much,' and Woolsey made a little movement like he'd started to tap his computer into better order. The Wraith formerly known as Todd showed his teeth in what was clearly meant to be an unnerving smile.

"There is much to talk about, I realize."

He was bigger than Jack had expected. Oh, he'd read the reports, scrolled through the photos — obsessively, during the weeks Atlantis was off the grid. He'd had time to get used to the idea that the Wraith looked a lot more alien than, say, a Goa'uld in its host, or the Ori, even the Priors, had time to try to get his brain around the idea that there really were aliens out there who ate people, and who looked a lot like people had always imagined vampires would look. He'd listened to Daniel theorize about that, the notion that vampire legends might be some twisted reflection of Ancient lore, a memory of the war that had driven them to take refuge on Earth, but it hadn't really prepared him for the reality of Todd — Guide — sitting at the far end of the conference table with his artfully disheveled hair and his tattooed face and, most of all, his presence. Jack hadn't thought much about immortality lately — the Goa'uld weren't, and the Asgard weren't, and that had pretty much seemed to cover it: naughty or nice, nobody lived forever — but looking at Guide, he was beginning to get a sense of what that long view might look like. He wasn't sure he liked it, and only then became aware that he was meeting Guide's eyes with more challenge than he'd meant. He matched the Wraith's smile tooth for tooth, and looked away. Carter gave him another quick glare, and he did his best to look innocent, as though he wasn't wishing he could kick somebody under the table. Carter rolled her eyes like she wished she could kick him back, and Woolsey cleared his throat again.

"Yes. Since you are here, there are several matters that we could profitably go over." He glanced at his computer. "The state of your alliance under, er, Queen Steelflower being primary among them. And Dr. Keller has made some significant advances with the retrovirus that she would like to discuss with you—"

"And there is also this weapon, is there not?" Guide said, with a mildness that deceived no one. "That should also be on the table, I believe."

Crap. Jack tried to look innocent and unconcerned, doubted he was any more successful than Sheppard, biting his lip next to Teyla. How the hell had Guide found out so quickly? Telepath, he answered himself. Alabaster knew; of course she'd told her father, probably in the middle of that touching greeting—

"We have recovered an artifact that Alabaster believes to be a weapon," Woolsey said, without a blink. "We have not confirmed that this is in fact what it is, or that it still functions. We know almost nothing about it at this point."

"It is a weapon," Alabaster said. Her voice was clearer, more musical than Guide's. Practice with her human flock, Jack wondered, or just natural timbre? "I have the memories of my foremother, Osprey, and I have seen and handled it. It is Hyperion's weapon, and it was made to destroy all Wraith, and any who share our blood." She nodded to Teyla. "This one can confirm what I say."

Teyla offered the smile Jack had seen her use on Earth, in the days of the IOA hearings. He wasn't really sure he liked seeing it again in this context. "I also believe that this is the weapon of Osprey's memory."

"We have no proof," Woolsey said, with emphasis.

"And I hope are seeking none," Guide said.

"We feel that, given the general unpredictability of Ancient devices, there is very little to be gained by pursuing the matter," Woolsey said.

"Until it seems advisable?" Guide asked. "Or expedient? You cannot seriously expect us to feel secure leaving this device in your hands."

"The Ancients believed it would work," Alabaster said. "No, they knew it would, even if they didn't care what its use might cost their children."

"Collateral damage," Jack said, under his breath. Guide glanced his way, and he realized that Wraith hearing might be better than he'd thought. Or maybe he hadn't been as discreet as he'd mostly meant to be. "Look, we have people — valuable people — who would be harmed by this thing, assuming it works, just as much as you would. We have some serious disincentives to using it ourselves."

"But you also have Dr. McKay," Guide said. "And the redoubtable Colonel Carter. I am sure that if they put their minds to the problem, they could find some work-around solution. And that returns us to the same problem. I say it again, you cannot expect us to leave this weapon with you."

"And you can't expect us to just hand it over to you," Sheppard said. "Come on, Todd, be reasonable."

"I am entirely reasonable," Guide answered, and Jack was sure that expression was a grin.

"We actually have more pressing problems to deal with," Woolsey said. "Specifically, Queen Death. Forgive me if I'm blunt, but if we don't work together to stop her, this putative weapon is going to become irrelevant to all of us."

Alabaster's gaze shifted, and Jack hid a grin of his own. Gotcha, he thought, and gave Guide his most limpid stare. Guide gave a thin smile, and dipped his head.

"As you say, Death is the more immediate problem. And I am willing to hold to my part of our agreement — for now." His eyes swept the table, settled on Carter. "But I say to you in all sincerity that it would be much better to resolve this issue before we go much further down this road."

"We'll continue to talk," Carter said, after a moment, and Woolsey nodded.

"Yes. There is still quite a bit to be discussed, and I'm sure we can come to some agreement regarding the device."

"Yes," Guide said. "I'm sure we can." He looked around the table again. "But, for the moment — perhaps it would be wise to pause and consider."

"And you will want time with Alabaster and your grandson," Woolsey said. "Of course. We can continue this later, perhaps after you've had a chance to talk to Dr. Keller."

Jack tuned out the rest of the courtesies — he could do that sort of thing in his sleep — and timed his departure so that he was at Carter's shoulder when they left the conference room. "Careful, Carter," he said in her ear. "I think the big green guy likes you."

She blinked, gave him a startled glance — what, Jack thought, she'd never noticed? He grinned, and slipped past her before she could say anything.

Corporal Hernandez stood at the top of the gateroom steps, his P90 at port arms. "Wraith in the conference room," he said to the pretty airman on duty at the control board for the Stargate. "Pretty outtahand."

Airman Salawi — Ayesha, she'd said her name was — gave him a sideways smile. "And Wraith in the control room," she said, gesturing with her head behind her to where the Wraith kid and Torren were playing quietly with a pile of Legos. Really quietly, especially for Torren.

"Outtahand," Hernandez said. But then pretty much everything about a deployment off planet was. On the other hand, it was awesomely cool.

The conference room doors opened, Woolsey trying to talk to the Wraith named Todd who was ignoring him and talking to Colonel Carter. Behind them, Colonel Sheppard was talking to the Wraith queen Alabaster as the others crowded out behind.

Teyla slipped around Carter and Todd and came over. "I hope that Torren is behaving?" she asked Dr. Zelenka, who had the duty officer's post.

"Oddly enough, yes," Zelenka replied, pushing his glasses up on his nose. "He has been very good."

Alabaster came up behind, Woolsey and Todd with her. "Darling, I hope you did not disrupt these men's work," she said.

The Wraith boy looked up from the Legos cheerfully, waving a complicated construction that might have been supposed to be a puddle jumper. "I was good," he said aloud, and then with more excitement, "I never met a human boy who could speak to my mind before!"

Teyla's mouth opened and shut as the Wraith named Todd guffawed.

"Well," Alabaster said gravely, "He is the son of a queen, and will be a blade of Atlantis."

Torren beamed up beatifically, Legos in hand.

CHAPTER TWENTY-NINE

In From the Cold

THE NIGHT was clear but freezing cold, and Jack O'Neill was glad he'd been forewarned to bring a heavy jacket. Carter was standing on the balcony, her elbows on the rail, her face tilted up to the sky where the aurora played in great sheets of light, red and blue and green chasing each other across the sky, laser bright and almost unreal looking. He'd seen the northern lights many times on Earth, but never anything like this. It was bright enough that the colors shifted slightly across her face like a light show at a concert, her mouth open slightly as though she could drink down light.

Jack came and stood at the rail beside her, shoulders not quite touching. "Penny for your thoughts, Carter?"

"I was thinking that the core composition of this planet must be fascinating for the world's magnetic field to interact this way with the solar radiation," she said, that same rapt expression on her face. "I'm wondering if there are exotic compounds in the core mix…" She broke off and glanced at him sideways. "Never mind," she said apologetically. "What were you thinking?"

"That it's pretty," Jack said. He leaned on the rail, cold enough to feel even through his jacket sleeves. "Is this the designated brooding balcony?"

She snorted. "Yep. One of them. This is the senior officers' brooding balcony, no one below Lorne allowed. The enlisted balcony is off the gateroom and the scientists prefer the one next to the mess."

Jack grinned. "And the junior officers?"

"Out on the south pier." Carter lifted her eyes to the lights again, pushing her bangs back from her forehead. "They get to fend for themselves."

"Builds character," Jack said.

She rested her elbows on the railing, looking out over the sea. "So."

"So?"

"The weapon?"

"Oh, that thing." Jack looked at her sideways. "A thorny Ancient conundrum for our pleasure."

"Jack."

He shook his head. "We don't know what it does."

"It kills Wraith," she said seriously.

"Carter, have we ever once, just once, encountered an Ancient device that did exactly what it was intended to do without bizarre and horrible side effects?" He frowned. "It probably kills Wraith and every other sentient creature in range, or else it doesn't kill Wraith and instead it kills sea turtles. Or it blows up every Stargate. Or it destroys all life in the galaxy, like that brilliant weapon on Dakara. There is absolutely no way that we're turning the damn thing on. Especially since it seems like it's an untested prototype built by a crazy guy who did genetic experiments on unwilling human subjects. No. Just no."

"When you put it that way..."

"You and McKay are going to get rid of it," he said. He looked at her sideways again, and she was smiling. "Which was what you wanted in the first place, right? Only you had to get me out here to put some authority behind it."

Carter shrugged. "I figured Woolsey might be reluctant to take the chance, especially since the IOA just roasted him."

"I think you underestimate him," Jack said seriously.

"I thought you hated him."

"Eh. He's ok." Jack shifted. The rail was cold under his forearms, even through a heavy jacket. "He's changed a lot. I expect he'd make the call the right way, but now if it ever comes up he can say that I pushed him."

"It may never come up if McKay and I can do it discreetly," Carter said thoughtfully.

He looked at her keenly. "Can you?"

"Of course we can." She tilted her head up, the playing lights making her look younger than forty one. "I haven't had a look at it yet, but Sheppard said it was a seamless naquadah casing, like a Stargate. Destroying it's a lot easier than taking it apart. We can always just drop it into a sun. That will destroy a gate."

"And you think that will satisfy our allies?" Jack made air quotes around allies.

"If Todd watches it go and monitors it with us, yes." Carter shrugged. "I can handle Todd. He's perfectly reasonable to work with. McKay and I can make it happen."

Jack nodded. "Ok. And what's the situation with McKay?"

"What you see. He still looks a little off, and he's got the residual telepathy. Beckett says that may never go, as that seems to be one of the most persistent things given its prevalence among the Athosians. But if it doesn't, then he's in the same boat as Teyla," Carter said. "We can all live with that, right?"

"The IOA won't have him on Earth, but besides that," Jack said. "You don't think he's compromised?"

She looked away, out over the wind-scoured ocean. "I can't answer that. There isn't anything to suggest he's not his old self. But I know Woolsey is reluctant to give him access to everything yet, and if it were my call I'd say the same. We don't know what happened in McKay's head. We can't be sure there's not something…" Her voice trailed off.

"You think there is," he said flatly. "Or you'd never bring it up."

Carter shook her head. "I don't know. There's something not quite right. It could just be the telepathy. Hell, it could just be trauma. I'd walk the same line Woolsey's doing — give him the benefit of the doubt, but not let him back in to every piece of code until it's been longer and I had more of a sense of it."

Jack nodded slowly. "Ok. That's fair. Time to make sure he's not a sleeper, running Death's hidden agenda."

"I'll keep an eye on him on this project," Carter promised. "Unless he double crosses and shoots me or something, we'll be fine."

And that was about as good as it got. "Anything else on your mind?"

"I've got a personnel situation," she said. She looked at him sideways. "Off the record?"

"Of course," he said.

"It's pretty thorny." Carter took a deep breath. "Franklin's a good guy, or at least I thought so. But apparently he has some kind of grudge against Sheppard from back in Afghanistan seven years ago, and he dug up all that old dirt on Sheppard's record and spit it around the weekly poker game. Which, you know, I'm not worried about from Sheppard's point of view, because his nose is clean and if Woolsey's not making waves then who cares about some charges he was cleared of seven years ago? I gave Franklin hell and he swore it would never happen again."

"So?" Jack said. "I think that's got it, right? If Sheppard's nose is clean, it's dead and buried."

"If that were the only thing." Carter shook her head. "Right now I've got *Daedalus'* 302 wing attached until Caldwell gets back, which means I've got Hocken. She's ok, no problems with her. But the way Franklin put it, it came out like he was the type to go making trouble for her. And the last thing I need is for my second in command to get Caldwell's 302 commander brought up on charges."

Jack was silent a moment, working through the chain of consequences. Caldwell was senior to Carter, and he'd hand picked Hocken for this command. He'd be pissed as hell, mostly at Carter that she hadn't managed her own guy enough to keep him from making trouble for Caldwell. He'd back Hocken up, and Carter ought to back Franklin up because he was hers, even if she'd privately like to swat him. If she did, Caldwell would flip, and if she didn't it would look bad for her, like maybe Franklin had a point and there was something behind it. Not that anybody would say that officially, but it was not what Carter needed. Competition for command of the battlecruisers was insane, and there had been some grumbles when Carter got the *Hammond*.

He'd heard them. Boy, had he. But there was one critical question. "Anything to it?"

"I don't know and I don't want to," Carter said, her eyes evading his.

Which meant yes, but Carter had managed to avoid being directly told by anyone officially in the chain of command. She wouldn't perjure herself. She was serious about her word of honor. Carter would twist and tie herself in knots to avoid being asked, but if she was asked under oath, she'd tell the truth. Jack sighed.

"I thought Franklin was an ok guy," she said. "Kind of a motor mouth, but a good guy. And I really need this team to come together. I need my second in command on the same page."

"You've got to talk to him," Jack said.

"How do I do that without telling him things that I don't know and that he sure as hell shouldn't know?"

"About the team," Jack said. "No, you can't say anything about Hocken. But that's a temporary problem, right? Caldwell will be back in a week and then she's his again. If Franklin's got an issue it's not going to come up when she's on another ship." He shoulder bumped her. "The problem here is whether or not you can trust Franklin, because yes, you've got to be able to trust him. The real damage here isn't about Sheppard or Hocken. It's about whether his CO can trust him not to run a personal agenda that's counter to morale and good judgment. Franklin's screwed himself, and he may not even know it."

Carter sighed. "I hate all these feelings," she said. "All these people feeling feelings that I'm supposed to do something about."

"It's part of the job, Carter."

"I know." She shoulder bumped him back. "It just sucks. I'll have to talk to him. With no nouns."

"Carter would like to buy a noun for $100," Jack said. "But she'll make do with an adjective."

"If it's a nice one," she said.

Jack looked up at the sheets of light across the sky. It was pretty. And also freezing. "Cold out here," he said.

"I've got to get back to the *Hammond*." She pursed her lips regretfully.

"In the next thirty minutes?"

"Well, no."

"Your papa will be pacing the floor?" Jack grinned.

Carter burst out laughing. "Should we sing *Baby It's Cold Outside*? Cause it sure is!"

"I can't remember all the words. Something about 'Baby you'll freeze out there'?"

She hummed along experimentally. "Maybe just half a drink more?"

"Only I don't have anything to drink."

"Neither do I," Carter said. "Sheppard has some beer, but somehow the *Hammond* doesn't have the captain's liquor cabinet."

"I don't suppose Woolsey stocked those VIP quarters," Jack said thoughtfully.

"He might have at that," she said. "It's the kind of thing he'd do."

"Baby, it's cold outside."

Inert, it still looked like something lethal. It gleamed dully with the cold sheen of naquadah, faintly mottled as though it were oily to the touch. There was no seam, no projector, nothing he could identify as a weapon.

Rodney turned Hyperion's weapon over and over in his hands. It had been easy to find. Sheppard had been thinking about it so hard trying not to think about it that he was practically shouting. Teyla's Gift might not work on humans, but Rodney's had been the real deal. He didn't have every nuance of course, not anymore, but with Sheppard standing next to him loudly not thinking about where he'd hidden the damned thing… It was like the old joke about not thinking about a hippo. The more you tried not to think about a hippo the more the only thing you could imagine was a great big purple one standing right in front of you. And that was dangerous with both Todd and Alabaster in the room. Like Sheppard would last ten seconds if Alabaster wanted to know where the weapon was!

Rodney tucked it into his jacket and strode off down the hall. There were a lot better hiding places in Atlantis than the one Sheppard had picked, ones that were a lot less obvious. Of course it was at the top of one of his favorite towers! But if Sheppard didn't know where it was, it wouldn't matter if things went sour.

He had no illusions he'd be able to hide it from Alabaster, but she wouldn't ask him. He was just a cleverman, not the Consort of Atlantis. For a moment he imagined how the touch of her mind on his would feel, not angry and prying, but alive with pleasure and admiration at his foresight and genius...

Rodney pushed the buttons for the transport chamber. He'd stow this somewhere safe, somewhere no one would ever find besides him. Yes, McKay would save the day again. That's what it would all come down to as usual. The door slid shut, and Rodney smiled.

The Old One woke from a dream of Athos, of the city of Emege and its proud towers, its streets strewn with petals in the wake of a spring dance, laughter and song ringing in his ears. He had last seen it beneath the Ancients' failing shield, had left with the fleet before the Culling began, and he sat for a moment, breathing hard, until his thoughts steadied again. This was what it meant to be old, to be eldest of an immortal people: the memories became endless, too, and there was no escaping them. Especially not in dream. Osprey had been of Athos, too, and her face was in his mind as he rose from his nest, summoned a young blade to comb and dress his hair. Highflight was neat-handed, effaced himself even as he worked, and the Old One nodded his approval.

You may go.

*Your pardon," Highflight said. *But — a message has just arrived.*

The Old One glanced toward the nearest screen, waved his hand to light it. Sure enough, a strand of data glimmered in the depths, and he nodded. *Very well.*

Highflight bowed again, and backed away, letting the chamber door close behind him, and the Old One frowned at the glowing characters. The message had come by roundabout methods, though he thought he could guess the source. He touched keys, entering codes to unlock the first layer of encryption, then entered the next combinations one after the other. At last the message blossomed, gold text on a dark screen, and he caught his breath as he read.

Hyperion's weapon. He closed his eyes, seeing again the ocean cliffs, the stone tower, the watery sheen of the naqadah as he turned it over and over in his hands. They had tried to destroy it, he had tried to destroy it, with increasing desperation, but nothing he had imagined had proved enough even to damage it. He had known when they sealed it away that it was not enough, that someday it would reappear to menace them. The Lanteans had it now, and eventually they would use it. Oh, they might hesitate for the moment, for the sake of those among them who shared some part of the Wraith DNA, but in the end, they were the Ancients' children. They could not help but use it, not just to save themselves, that was Guide's mistake, but because they were bound by their heritage as surely as were the Wraith themselves.

But at least that hesitation might save his people. He had not wanted to move so quickly, needed time to bring the wavering hives under Death's sway, but if the Lanteans had the weapon... They must attack now, before the humans decided to betray their alliance with Guide.

He glanced at his reflection in the sliver of mirror the ship obligingly provided. He had never been a beauty, but he had his pride, and Highflight had done well by him, brought his thin hair into decent order. The cut of his coat was good, gave an illusion of height and strength that he no longer fully possessed. It was possible, he supposed, that he would eventually age further — but none of them would live that long, if he did not act. He snarled at his reflection, and turned back to the console to summon the master of Death's household.

Tell the queen that I request an audience, on a matter of great urgency. With her alone.

Death admitted him at once, Mist shooing out a bevy of clevermen, and following them out without complaint when he was not invited to remain. The zenana was otherwise empty, just Death standing beside her throne, her back to the door, one hand resting on the high wing of bone that flanked her seat. In the moment, she looked as young as she was, barely out of her girlhood, bold and strong and desperately inexperienced. An older, wiser queen might have dissembled with her enemies, the Old One thought, might have drawn them in first, made sure she had them all, wrapped them up for the kill, but such a one could never have united so many disparate hives under her banner. Death was what she was, and there was no going back.

My queen, he said, and made his deepest bow.

Death turned, her head lifting, but he had seen the moment of exhaustion in her golden eyes. Still, her tone was light, almost caressing, and she relaxed gracefully into her throne. *My Old One. What is it that requires a private audience?*

No good news, I fear.

She was still for a moment, and then shook her head with a smile. *And when was it ever? Say on.*

And that was what he had loved in her from the moment he had met her, that willingness to face all dangers head on. *My queen,* he said again. *I asked to meet with you alone because this involves the history I have shared with you and no other, how we who are Wraith were made.*

It is well, then, to discuss this privately, Death said.

Before we escaped, the First Mothers and their men, the Ancients had already begun to fear us, the Old One said. *They had begun work on a weapon that would act against us and us alone, targeting those of us who carried the genetic markers they had used to change us. They had built a prototype, and that prototype — we stole it when we escaped.*

And did not destroy it, or you would not be here now, Death said. "Fool—*

We could not, the Old One said. *Believe me, I tried. I and all our clevermen, and nothing we did even scratched its surface. Nor could we open it, to destroy its works, and we did not dare abandon it, for fear the Ancients would find it again and turn it on us.*

They could not rebuild it? Death asked. Her anger had faded, he saw; she was listening with care.

We killed Hyperion who built it, the Old One answered. *And destroyed his records. There was no other who could duplicate his work.*

Death nodded. *Go on.*

The Old One took a breath. *My queen, the weapon has been found. It is in the hands of the Lanteans.*

Death snarled, showing all her teeth, her hands closing on the arms of her throne. *How has this been allowed to happen? Why did you not tell me of this, so we might recover it, protect it from the humans?*

I believed we were safest with it lost and unknown, the Old One answered. *What only one man knew to exist could not, I thought, be searched for.*

You were wrong, Death snapped. *And do you suggest we simply sit and await our destruction?*

No, my queen, the Old One said. *The Lanteans do not yet know how to use it, and I do not believe they will use it immediately. Thanks to — certain experiments in the past — there are humans who carry our DNA, and the Lanteans are tender of such. If nothing else, there is McKay to consider. They will wish to spare him if they can. It is my belief that if we act now, attack in strength and in concert, we can take them unaware, and destroy them before they have a chance to learn to use the weapon.*

Death leaned back in her throne again, her face like a mask of stone. *You said before we did not have the ships or the men for such a venture.*

I don't know if we do, the Old One said. *But, my queen, we cannot wait. Our hand is forced.*

She nodded slowly. *I cannot say I am entirely sorry. Better to put it to the trial than wait and maneuver. Very well. Summon my commanders and my hivemasters. We will attack Atlantis immediately and take them unaware.*

9 781905 586592